Confessions of a
WANNABE Vampire

By Joanna Ogan

ISBN-13: 978-1720571834
ISBN-10: 172057183X

For Claudia

CONFESSION 1
I want to be a vampire.

I creep through the shadows, keeping my gaze at a constant scan. I can't be captured. Not now. Not at this moment. Too much is at stake. I have one opportunity, just one, and I'm not going to fail.

A door opens further down the hallway, and I nearly leap from my skin. With my heart thundering against my ribcage, I shrink into the alcove beside me, flattening myself into the dark interior. I hold my breath and try to calm my heart rate, clenching my eyes shut.

The feet tromp past.

I release it at a slow trickle between pinched lips, and then count to one hundred. When I stick my head back into the hallway, the coast is clear. Not even a single dust particle appears disturbed.

In socked feet, I continue forward while maintaining my vigilance. I am so close. Almost there. Four more doors to go. Three…two…one…

As my hand closes around the door handle of the room I'm seeking, I stand up a little straighter, lift my chin, and firm my resolve.

It ends tonight.

I yank back the door with a flourish and step into the dim office, lit only by the leaping flames in the massive hearth.

My target's dark head lifts and silver eyes pierce me. One heartbeat…two. With a sigh, he returns his attention to the paperwork spread before him and summarily dismisses me.

"My Lord," I say, striding forward. "I haven't much time. Please."

He sets his pen down, rubs the area between his eyes, and observes my approach with weariness. "What is it this time, Danika?"

Was that exasperation in his voice? Yes, definitely exasperation. "I'm dying, My Lord." I bow my head. "It's serious."

"Mm-hmm," he mutters.

Now there's disbelief. I jerk my head up. "I'm serious this time, My Lord. I'm really dying, and I haven't much time left. You must help me. You *must*!"

"We've been over this a hundred times in the past year, my child. I will *not* turn you."

"But I'll die, My Lord." My gaze implores him. "What will you do then?"

"And what is it that you have?" He heaves another sigh, rubbing a finger in the space between his eyebrows with renewed vigor, as if hoping it'll make this conversation go away.

Ha! I'm not going anywhere, My Lord.

"It's called bovine spongiform encephalopathy." I slam my hands down on his desk and lean toward him. "The doctor says it's quite serious. Only a matter of days left."

"Danika," his eyebrows disappear into his hairline, "what you're referring to is commonly known as Mad Cow Disease. Tell me, child—how did you contract such a dreadful disease?"

"Uh—" I falter.

"Last week it was Andropause—"

"How was I supposed to know that that's male menopause?" I interrupt, disgust curling my lip. Now *that* had been an interesting conversation between the two of us.

"And the week before, it was Urticaria," he continues, ignoring me.

I shrug, straightening and looking away. "Anyone can break out in hives."

"Yes, but very few actually *die* from it."

The conversation isn't going as planned. Frustration sweeps through me and I bite my lip, frantically trying to find another way to convince him.

6

"There are hundreds—thousands—of people dying every day," he says sternly. "Pretending that you are one of them, *lying* that you are one of them, is wrong. You disrespect all those fighting for their lives. This needs to end." He waves a hand toward the door. "Now then, I am very busy. Go find Conrad, see if he'll give you an errand so you can leave the estate."

"My Lord," I begin, but he holds up the hand he's just been motioning toward the door with, silencing me.

"I will attend to you later, child."

And just like that, I've been dismissed. Heaving a sigh, I turn to the door, shoulders slumping, and walk toward it, literally dragging my feet across the thick carpet. *Scoosh scoosh scoosh.* Once there, I shoot him a forlorn look over my shoulder and find him watching me with exasperation, amusement, and a fierce love and adoration that he reserves only for me.

I hunch my shoulders further, heave another pitiful sigh, and leave, closing the door quietly behind me.

"Well that was a bust," I mumble to the empty corridor.

Except it isn't empty.

Conrad steps from the shadows of the alcove across the hallway, and I leap nearly ten feet. Slamming a hand over my chest, I suck in several deep breaths and attempt to get my heart under control.

"Geez!" I exclaim, licking my lips and shooting him a poisonous glare.

"Were you harassing Father again, Dani?" he asks, his warm, velvety voice like the fine whiskey I'd snuck from Lord Halifax's spirits cupboard a few weeks back.

"Of course I wasn't," I snap. "I was merely checking if there was anything he needed."

"And?"

"And *what?*"

"Did he need anything?" Conrad raises his eyebrows, much as our father had not five minutes before, disbelief evident in his matching silver eyes.

Instead of replying, I scoff, the sound defensive and extremely unladylike.

"I understand you're training to be a spy," he says wryly, "but your stealth needs some work." He nods toward the alcove down the hallway I'd sought cover in. "I sensed you were there the moment I left Father's study."

I follow his gaze. "Yeah…well…" Shrugging, I reach up and scratch my nose. "I knew it was you."

Except I totally didn't. Semantics…

Conrad is my adoptive brother. Well, sort of. It's a *really* long story.

Everyone knows the *Jungle Book*, with the young boy Mowgli, right? Abandoned by his human parents, he's raised in the wild jungle by a pack of wolves. Then embarks on a crazy adventure through said jungle to find a human settlement. It's one of my favorite stories, and my life isn't that much different than his.

Only, I was raised by vampires.

And not in a jungle, but in Phoenix, Arizona. Oh, and I have no intention of finding my birth family. I'm happy where I'm at, thank you very much.

I am what many call a "dumpster baby". Meaning, I was tossed in a dumpster to die when I was born. There, Lady Halifax came across my wrinkly, squalling body, rescued me from the trash heap, and well, the rest is history.

Or is it?

I am the only human living in the largest vampire coven in the Southwest United States. There are seven vampire Families who pretty much control the entire Northern Hemisphere, and lucky for me, I'm the adoptive daughter of one of those great families.

The Halifax Family.

Lord and Lady Halifax are around five hundred years old, give or take a century. Their son, Conrad, is a three hundred year old thorn in my side. He was chosen as their heir after a long, grueling decade of tests and an extensive selection process I know absolutely nothing about, so we'll move on with our story, and *possibly* revisit this later.

Rewind a bit to where I was talking to Lord Halifax. I'm sure you're intrigued by my intelligence and debate skills, right? I'm a master manipulator. At fifteen, I got it into my head that I wanted to be a vampire. However, the stubborn old coot—ha, *old*, see what I did there—refuses to change me. He's determined to have me live a stress free, peaceful, *human* life. Which, I might fervently add, I don't want. So I've decided I'm going to change his mind—one way or another.

I'm sure by now you've guessed how that's going for me. It's not. At all.

"Mother has been looking for you," Conrad says, and I raise an eyebrow, skeptical. "She mentioned something about dinner at Thomas'. Should I tell her you aren't interested?"

"Of course not," I bark, crossing my arms and sighing. I'm still frustrated by my lack of success with Father.

He frowns. "You don't seem to be in a good mood. Maybe I should tell her you're indisposed."

"Don't you dare!" I shoot him a glare. "Where is she?"

"Surveying the orchards, I'm guessing. She went out with Benice earlier in the golf cart."

"Thanks." I hurry past him.

The manor is beginning to stir as nightfall descends and the Family starts to wake. The estate is kept running around the clock; rain, snow, or sunshine. The day is reserved for those humans who are loyal to the Halifax Family, and the nights, for those who own it.

I skirt around a cluster of newbies, which usually refers to the ones who are less than twenty years old, and seek out the flaming red mane that distinguishes my mother. Not locating her anywhere between the east wing and the central hall, I spin and start toward the back terrace at a brisk walk.

A pair of mud boots awaits me at the door leading into the orchards, and after sliding my feet into the old Wellingtons, I step out into the warm night and scan the orchard that's lit up like a football stadium.

"Mother?" I call, leaping down the stairs onto the dirt path. She emerges from one of the lanes halfway across the orchard and lifts her hand to catch my attention. I wave back and start toward her.

In a blink, she's in front of me, clad in grubby pants, a button down shirt, and her own pair of Wellingtons. Her fiery hair is pulled back into an impeccable chignon, not a single strand out of place, and as always, her makeup is flawless.

"What is it, darling?" she coos.

9

"Con said you were looking for me."

She frowns, cocking her head thoughtfully. "Was I?"

Irritation flares, and snorting indelicately, I cross my arms and scowl. "I'm going to stake him. I swear I am."

She chuckles. "Relax, my love. What was his exact message?"

"That you were thinking about taking me to dinner at Thomas'."

Her eyes light up and she smiles. "Wonderful idea. Let me go change, and then we'll be off." She sweeps here gaze over me, lingering for a moment on my boots, and then meets my eye again, humor dancing in hers. "You might want to change as well."

"Nah," I shake my head. "I'll go like this."

I'm as argumentative and stubborn as I am a great debater and manipulator of all things Lord Halifax. She's learned that when I say I'm doing something, or in this case, *wearing* something, there is no point trying to convince me otherwise.

"Even with the Wellies?" she asks.

I glance down at the boots in question, pretending to consider my options, and then grin. "I'll change those."

It's not that my bright yellow and orange polka dotted mud boots aren't the most stylish, it's that going to Thomas' means I'll be scrutinized from head to toe by the hoity toity of the upper Scottsdale elite. I do have a reputation as a Halifax to uphold, mind you.

We enter the house together, but when she splits off for her room in the catacombs, I kick off the inappropriate shoes and race back toward the front of the manor where I'd discarded my Chucks this afternoon when I got home from school.

No sooner have I finished tying them up does Mother reappear, sporting a stylish, yet casual, knee-length emerald dress that makes her green eyes sparkle and her hair flare to life. She links her arm through mine, and together we step outside into the front circular drive, smiling at the newbie, Hayden, who'd retrieved my rather sensible Ford Fusion.

"Please let Lord Halifax know we've left for dinner," Lady Halifax instructs as I slide into the driver's seat and she takes the passenger's side. "We'll be home before ten."

A nod in acquiesce, and he shuts the door. I put the car into gear and away we go.

***

Thomas' is a five star steak house that boasts of an array of tantalizing wines, mouthwatering steaks, a vegetarian selection that'd make even the most particular of vegetable lovers weep with pleasure, and delectable desserts that make one's eyes roll into the back of their head.

The valet exchanges a number for my car keys, and Mother and I enter the restaurant to the scent of grilled meat and baking bread. It's heavenly, and my stomach gives a growl in anticipation.

Upon our entrance, the maître-d hurries forward with a wide smile, practically trembling with suppressed excitement.

"Lady Halifax," he hums. "A pleasure!"

She returns his smile. "Just me and Dani this evening, Anthony."

"Of course, of course." He motions toward a waiter. "Please show these two lovely ladies to a table."

The young man, bless his heart, hesitates. His face flushes, and he shoots a hasty look around the packed restaurant.

"We're full, sir," he mumbles softly.

"Of course we're not," comes the gritted response, uttered through clenched teeth and a false smile for Mother. "It'll be just a moment, My Lady." He grabs the terrified waiter by the arm and hauls him out of earshot. A few moments of hushed conversation, and the young man departs for the area behind an ivy covered divider.

"Well," Mother whispers, sighing, "those poor souls will be finishing their dinner elsewhere apparently."

"Should *we* go somewhere else?" I ask. I'm not a fan of preferential treatment simply because of who I am. For some reason, it makes me really uncomfortable.

She shakes her head. "Too late for that, my darling."

We only have to wait three minutes before a harried looking couple is rushed through the doors and we're escorted away from the maître-d's stand. We're seated in a secluded area,

11

away from prying eyes and overeager ears. My family is notorious. Very, very notorious.

There are many tales of vampires throughout the centuries. They're bloodsucking monsters who thrive on chaos and destruction. They turn into bats, control minds, feed on unsuspecting people; or they sparkle.

But I've never met one who did any of those things.

The vampires I know are kind, loving, considerate, and above all, abhor violence and murder. They only take from willing donors, and those men and women are compensated for their assistance.

In our neck of the woods, the Halifax Family is revered. They do much for the community, from charity to economic growth to city council. The branches of our family are wide spread and extend into parts of California, Colorado, and Nevada.

Orders placed and water glasses at our elbows, Mother flips out her napkin and lays it across her lap before turning her full, emerald gaze on me.

"How was school today?" she asks.

"Good, I guess." I throw a sliver of lemon into my water for flavor, and then take a sip. "I've got a math test next Friday."

She nods. "And your English test from last week? How'd that go?"

I mentally groan. It hadn't gone well. "I—uh—got a B."

Actually, a C-, but I'm not about to admit that to her. She'll flay me alive.

"Oh good for you." She beams proudly. "Are you ready for break? Doesn't it start next Friday?"

"Yeah," I say, and when she frowns, I amend, "Yes."

"There's a delegation coming from each of the Families next Saturday," she says, and I choke on a mouthful of water in surprise. She waits until I have my hacking fit under control before she continues, "They'll be here for two weeks, which is the duration of your break. Am I correct?" I nod. "Wonderful. You'll be able to learn the ropes of hosting prestigious company."

"Can't wait." My smile is more of a grimace, but she pretends not to see.

"Do you remember the names of the senior vampires in each Family?"

I can always lie and tell her I could recite them in my sleep, but then I'll be expected to do just that. So instead, I opt for the truth.

"I do not," I say, and though her lips thin in disapproval, she accepts my admission with a single nod.

Dinner arrives and conversation ceases as we dig in. While my steak is on the medium-well side, Mother's is still mooing in a most grotesque manner. Blood pools around the slab of meat, soaking her artistically arranged, perfectly seared asparagus stalks.

She finds me eyeing her plate with a slight curl to my lip, and laughter alights in her eyes.

"Care for a bite?" she asks, waving her fork at me with a piece of raw meat stabbed on the end.

"No," I say quickly, cracking a half smile, "I'm good. But aren't you going to get ill eating that?"

"It's not often I get to eat dinner with my daughter." She pops the bite into her mouth and chews.

I want to argue further, but I tuck into my plate instead. It's her digestive system…or rather, nonexistent one. The undead can't consume human sustenance, but Mother tries anyway. She's as stubborn as Father.

We enjoy our dinner with copious amounts of conversation, covering topics ranging from school to boyfriends—or my *lack* of one—to the latest orchard crop. When we finish, Mother pays, and we depart with our heads high and eyes straight ahead, ignoring the scrutinizing gazes of the high-class, uppity-muck-mucks.

The drive home is silent.

Already, I can see Mother is ill, her body rejecting the food. She rests her head back against the seat, eyes closed. Her pallor, which is normal for her undead state, has an almost green tint to it.

Finally, we drive through the gates of the orchard, and at her insistence, I stop to let her out. She waves me on with the instructions to go to bed, and with an uneasy smile, I pull away, and the darkness swallows her up.

13

CONFESSION 2

No offense...but horses make better company than humans.

You'd think that being a Halifax would endear me to my peers, maybe even make me popular. Unfortunately, it doesn't. It's probably my fault, though. When I was in seventh grade, several girls made friends with me. I had spent the first twelve years of my life being homeschooled by tutors at the orchard, and that year was my first time in private school. So when those girls befriended me, I was over the moon.

For a while.

It became apparent that all they wanted was the notoriety of being friends with the human Halifax. I was used as a go-go. Go here, go there. And when I would try and end the relationships, they'd pretend I was needed, a part of their little clique.

Conrad found out about it and he flew into a rage. Yes really. Literally *flew*. I'd never seen him so angry, and I haven't since. Anyway, I digress.

I decided then that it's better to be alone than to be surrounded by people who don't care, and never will. It doesn't bother me. I spend my lunch breaks alone, study in the library alone, and wander the hallways alone. And to be honest, I enjoy the solitude. The orchard is always packed with family. Unless the sun is at its apex, the house is boisterous and loud.

This next week is filled with midterms, and using studying as an excuse, I'm able to get out of everything associated with the arrival of the other Families, like interviewing nearly two hundred donors, cleaning the enormous conference room, and buffing the boardroom table—that easily sits a hundred—for *hours*.

Soon, the end of Friday rolls around and I hurry through the front door with one thought in my head: *Spring Break*. After handing off my backpack to a waiting vampire who'll be kind enough to take it to my room for me, I seek out Father, hoping he'll be up even though it's not quite sundown.

I've got my argument this time. For sure, for sure. I've done my research. A harmless disease that even Lord Halifax wouldn't be familiar with.

I find him in the conference room, overseeing the preparation of the computer and attached projector. I scowl. PowerPoints. Not my thing. The table is buffed to perfection, mirroring the overhead lights, and a young newbie, probably around ten-years-turned, is moving to each of the surrounding chairs, yanking off their dust covers and folding them up while another follows close behind, arms overflowing with the discarded cloth.

Father catches sight of me. "Good evening, Danika."

"Evening, My Lord," I say, rushing forward to press a kiss to his soft cheek. "Did you sleep well? You're up early."

"Much to do before they arrive," he returns, smiling warmly. "How was school? Did you do well on your math test?"

Of course I didn't. I was awful at remembering equations, and Geometry was the worst mathematical creation ever thought of by man. It is all about finding the area and dimensions of a rectangle that looks as if it's been drawn by Picasso. Who cares what the area is?

"I sure did." I beam. No point telling him I'm inept. He'll discover that for himself when he gets my report card.

"Good for you, child." But not really, is what his voice hints. His silver gaze can see right through me.

"I really need to talk with you, My Lord," I say, and he sighs heavily, turning the full force of an unimpressed glare on me.

"I don't have time for your arguments today, Danika," he states with a hard edge. "The delegates arrive in eight hours and

15

there's much to do." I open my mouth to argue, but he silences me with a firm shake of his head. "Not today."

Well then. So much for trying out my amazing debate skills.

He turns back to supervise the task at hand, and I slip out of the room. The house is as silent as a mausoleum, with no more than ten vampires having roused to assist in the preparations. Determined to not wake those who still slept, I slide on my Wellingtons and head outside into the orchard through the back door.

The stables are my favorite place on the entire farm. Housing just five horses, it's set off to the side as a separate entity with a corral and gate leading into open desert. It's not the largest building on the property, the manor and sorting barn dwarf it, but it's still well cared for and sufficiently stocked.

And it's my domain.

I don't handle the orchard's citrus. Mother forbids it, and Benice—the human property manager and overseer of all things orchard related—agrees. For some weird reason. They're like two peas in a pod.

I stride through the wide entrance to the sound of nickers, and five heads appear over stall doors. Dark eyes follow my progress as I sweep up the aisle, rubbing noses, giving pecks, and crooning greetings.

The large stallion in the end stall observes my approach with a steady regard I've become accustomed to. In the beginning, when he'd first arrived, a battered and abused animal, his trust issues ran as deep as the scars lining his flank. If anyone approached, human or undead, he'd scream and thrash and kick his massive legs out in hopes of connecting with an unsuspecting kneecap. Mother had warned me that healing him wouldn't be easy, but with patience and a gentle hand, I'd brought him around. Now, this magnificent, proud beast is named Chancelot. You know, like Lancelot from the Knights of the Round Table and second chances. Get it? No? Not good? Whatever.

"Hey handsome," I say softly. I reach a hand out, firm and sure, and he gives it a tentative sniff before bowing his head. I slide it from the tip of his nose up to his ears, press a kiss to the scar between his eyes, and rub his cheek with my other hand.

16

"Did you behave for Sophia today?" I ask, leaning my forehead against his, and continue to rub his cheek. He snorts and I chuckle. "Of course you did. You're such a sweet boy, aren't you? Did you have a good day? The weather was beautiful. Did you spend some time in the corral? I bet you had fun. Want to go for a ride? There's still an a couple hours before dark. We can make it to Devil's Ridge and back before then."

Mother doesn't like me out after dark, and she's adamant that the horses need to be secure in their stalls before sunset. Something about coyotes and rattle snakes. And I always aim to please Lady Halifax.

In the tack room, I replace the Wellies for riding boots, my sweater for a hoodie, and grab his bridle and thin saddle. Once fitted, I walk him out of the barn and across the corral. After unbolting the gate into the desert and throwing it open, I climb into the saddle, snag the reins, and click him forward with my tongue and a light tap of my heels.

Chancelot had been a race horse once upon a time. I'd done some research on him after he'd been rescued, and the medals he'd won were brag worthy. Unfortunately, as he got older, his victories became fewer and fewer and his significance became less and less.

With the desert stretched out in front of us, a cactus here and there, perhaps a rock if we're lucky, I give him freedom. His stride opens and he races across the packed earth with nary a care. Wind yanks my dishwater blonde hair from its tie, and his course mane whips stinging slaps against my cheeks and hands. His hooves eat up the ground, closing the distance to the cliffs up ahead, nearly three miles from the orchard. I can feel his muscles bunch and flex beneath my legs, and I grin madly with excitement and my own sense of freedom.

Out here, there are no inhibitions, no judgement, and no fakeness. Just open desert, the wind, the bright sunlight, and Chancelot's unbridled joy.

And herein lies the difficulty with retaining my desire to become a vampire. *This.* As a human Halifax, I have freedom where the vampires do not. I'm not governed by rules and regulations designed to keep my species safe. One wrong move by any vampire, one unwilling victim, one death, and the entire

17

world will turn on them. No redo's, no take back's. It's "go straight to jail, do not pass go".

Father said that two centuries ago, there was a vampire war that embroiled the humans. Hundreds of innocents died in that single year. According to Father, a new vampire Family, the Medicis, had sought a rise to power. They mercilessly crushed all who stood in their way, human or undead. The seven Families joined together, forming an alliance that is still honored today, and wiped out the Medici line. For many years after, they worked to repair the torn relations between human and vampire. Father described the peace efforts as tireless and said it took twenty-three years to reach an agreement between the two peoples.

As Chancelot continues his unwavering speed, an insane part of me revels in the knowledge that one wrong move, one hole, one stumble, and the mighty beast could throw me. Just like that, my life would be snuffed. To have that kind of ending is what makes me wholly human. Death. Anytime, anyplace. Vampires aren't as lucky. They can be killed, sure, but not with the same ease that humans can, and *are*.

The cliffs approach, and with a firm hand, I slow his pace to a trot and then down to a walk. His chest heaves, muscles quiver, and ears flick back and forth in rapid succession. He tosses his head, gnashing the bit, and I lean over and rub a hand along his sweaty neck.

"How was that, boy?" I pant, my own lungs straining. He doesn't answer, of course, and I throw back my head and let out a burst of laughter into the empty desert. "Ah, that was fun!"

At the base of Devil's Ridge, I slide from the saddle and lead him toward the small cow pond for a quick drink before we head back. This time of year, there's water, albeit murky and probably infested with parasites that'd shred my intestinal track, but in a month, the sun will have dried up every drop of it.

I loop his reins over the pommel and wander away while he drinks his fill as only a horse can. Picking up a rock, I cock back my arm and lob it out as far as I can toward the cliffs rising up in front of me. It collides with a small opening and the hollow resonation reaches my ears.

Some people love the forests, the green grasses, the abundant flora that thrives in moist environments. But me, I love the desert. I love the simplicity. The sunsets over the open desert dotted with saguaros. The sunrises that creep up and over the Superstition Mountains. The wildlife—minus the snakes and scorpions—that overcome drought, heat, and limited shade. Everything that makes the desert what it is, is what makes it *home*.

A head butt lets me know Chancelot's finished, and I look down at my watch to find that the hour is growing late. Though the days are longer with summer approaching, Mother will still be furious if I'm late.

"Let's walk for a bit, shall we?" I grab the reins and tug him forward. It'll be cutting it close, making it back at our current pace, but after the run I've given him, I'm not about to risk pushing him further.

I keep up a constant chatter. At first, it's pointless conversation about my exams, my fellow classmates, who are more focused on makeup, sports, and the opposite sex, and what I want to do when I graduate next year. He listens the entire way, never interrupting or laughing at the dreams I reveal, the secrets I've never told another soul. I'm soon baring my heart to him. The anxieties I carry deep inside, the fears that keep me awake at night when my human body should be sleeping.

I want to be a vampire, not because the thought of drinking blood fills me with delight—which it doesn't because that's just gross—but because the thought of being alone, of dying alone when the rest of my family continues living, fills me with terror. Can you imagine that loneliness? Knowing you're different. I feel myself running out of time, dying day by day. And I can't stop the clock. I can't *stop* it.

The gate to the corral comes into view, lit by one of the stadium lights that illuminate the entire orchard, and I sense him eyeing it with anticipation at the promise of fresh oats. Night is descending quickly, dusk hugging the day and beckoning shadows to come out and play.

Suddenly, Chancelot shifts, tensing, and before I can react, he bolts, yanking the reins from my hands. I make a desperate grab for them, but he's too far by the time I fully realize what's happening. He tears across the last quarter mile as if a coyote is nipping on his heels and thunders through the gate into the corral.

My stomach flips and I frown. Weird. I scan the desert to the left and then the right but find nothing. A sensation of being watched creeps up my spine, and as the hairs stand up along my arms and my scalp prickles in warning, I peek over my shoulder.

A body slams into me, and the scream I'm about to let loose dies a rather bloody death in my throat. The air is punched from my lungs upon impact. Eyes peer at me through the darkness, inches from my face.

A vampire. But not someone I recognize.

And then I hear it. Low growls. Guttural. Predatory. My heart skips a beat and I shrink against him, scanning the darkness blindly.

"Coyotes," he whispers, his breath a feather light touch against my neck.

I shiver. From fear. *Fear*. Sheesh.

Then they stalk out of the shadows of a nearby boulder, fur matted and eyes fixed entirely on me. The stranger shoves me behind him, but the beasts' gazes never leave me.

When faced with a life and death situation, most people would search for a way out, for some way to escape what's happening. For me, my first thought is "Mother's going to *kill* me" followed by "I'm going to skin them alive for getting me into trouble".

"Run!" he yells at the same moment they attack.

Instead of fleeing toward the corral and obvious safety, I lunge for a large rock, snag it, and pitch it at the coyote closest to him. It knocks the animal in the head, forcing it to stumble, and I waste no time in grabbing another and firing it toward a second.

Regardless of my assault, the beasts keep coming. The unfamiliar vampire keeps his body in their path and takes the first's impact with a grunt. Snarls fill the air. He throws off one, fends off a second, and cracks the neck of a third.

And I keep on throwing rocks. I'm good like that.

Under the deluge of coyotes, he's unable to do anything when one of the dogs peels away and starts toward me with careful, deliberate steps.

A four letter word my mother would frown at screams through my head, and I brace my feet apart in preparation of its attack. The inches shrink. Another growl erupts from the depths of its chest. Eyes pierce. Then it lunges. Grabbing a handful of course fur, I drop onto my back, plant my feet into its stomach, and launch it over my head. In an instant, I'm back on my feet and spinning toward it.

Even clenched for its attack, I'm still caught unaware when it shoots for my feet. I dance backward, but my heel catches something, a rock or a branch, and I tumble down. A cry rips from my throat as the beast wastes no time in lunging for me. Sharp teeth latch onto my forearm and blinding pain tears through it.

Suddenly, Chancelot is there. Snorting and stomping with his massive hooves. The coyote yelps, his teeth disappear, and then he too vanishes beneath the thundering onslaught of pissed off race horse.

Rolling away to avoid his crushing malice, I cradle my arm against my chest and swallow down the sob building in my throat. There is no pain. As long as I tell myself that, the agony screaming through my arm becomes nothing more than a dull ache. I have to stay strong. Father won't change me if I show any form of weakness. Especially pain.

But, man, it hurts!

I'm furious with myself when I finally manage to clamber to my feet and turn my attention to my companion to distract myself from the blood. Already, my vision is beginning to waver.

He stands alone, chest heaving and eyes fixed on the dark desert. His t-shirt hangs in shreds from his lean frame while his fashionably faded jeans are smudged with dirt, slobber, and blood.

His dark eyes swing to me. "Are you insane?"

I lower my injured arm to my side. "Probably. Why do you ask?"

"I told you to run." His gaze flicks to my arm where the blood runs in rivulets from the torn flesh. "You're human."

For some reason, his emotionless statement really irritates me. "Last time I checked."

He scowls. "You—"

A presence behind me forces him to pause. Assuming its Chancelot, I don't pay it any mind until a hand clamps onto my shoulder and jerks me back.

Conrad slides in front of me, his nails fully extended, and hisses. Primal. Dangerous. Territorial. "*Medici.*"

CONFESSION 3

I want to be a vampire, but I kind of have this aversion to blood. Nothing too serious. I just pass out...

Mother patches me up with gentle hands while I attempt to keep my afternoon snack from surfacing and my vision steady. Blood makes me...makes me...*really* shaky.

Her face is pinched and eyes are overly bright. She hasn't said a word since Conrad escorted me to the house, and dread curls in my gut at the chewing I'm going to receive once she's calmed down. Yvette, my former nanny, promised she would unsaddle Chancelot, brush him down, and put him up for the night for me while my wounds are being tended to. Lucky boy. He doesn't have to face Lady Halifax and her five hundred year old wrath.

Now clean, the damage isn't as severe as it'd first appeared, and I can breathe a little easier. She presses gauze to the wounds, where it sticks against the antiseptic ointment she's slathered liberally over each tooth mark. A newbie stands at her elbow, ready to hand items when requested. She holds out her hand, and another roll of gauze is passed over to wrap around my arm, followed by four pieces of industrial strength medical tape.

With a satisfied sniff, she lifts her gaze to mine. We stare at one another in silence for several beats, and then she waves her hand at the hovering vampires.

"Leave us," she commands, an edge to her voice.

They depart, taking the medical kit with them.

The moment they're gone, her expression morphs into fury. "Danika Jean Halifax! What were you thinking?"

Ah great... There she goes, using all three names. Nothing I say will be good enough at this point so I remain quiet and avert my eyes.

"You could have been *killed*," she seethes. "Coyotes and Medici spawn? Child! Have you lost your mind?"

Blood still coats my fingers and nails, and they suddenly become the most interesting thing in the world. "Sorry, Mother."

"I've been understanding and patient with you, young lady." Her eyes glow with disapproval. "I never should have allowed you to ride that horse, unchaperoned and unprotected, in the desert. I must have been crazy." She presses a hand to her forehead. "So help me, child, I will get rid of him if you *ever* put yourself in danger like that again. Do I make myself clear?"

"Crystal," I mumble.

She nods, sucking in a sharp breath through her nose. "Don't think this is over. Your father hasn't even *begun* with you." Her cool hand raises my chin until our eyes meet. "Did he hurt you?"

Surprised by the sudden shift, I stare at her for a moment without blinking. "What?"

"The Medici. Did he hurt you in any way?"

"N-no." I shake my head and return my attention to my bloody hand. "He saved me, actually."

She snorts indelicately, and I bite my lip to keep from smiling. "I find that hard to believe."

"But he did." I look up. "He took on four coyotes to protect me. Medici or not, I wouldn't be alive if it wasn't for him."

"We'll determine his fate once the Families arrive," she says. Climbing to her feet, she adjusts her skirt with a swish. "Until then, you are to stay away from him. Got it?" When I grunt in response and glance away, she grasps my chin again and raises it until she snags my gaze. "Danika. This is not a game. You *will* stay away from him."

"Yes, Mother."

She kisses my forehead and leaves.

Left alone, I slump back against the chair and close my eyes. Father's scolding will be a hundred, no a *thousand*, times worse than hers. I'll be lucky if I'm allowed out of the manor after tonight.

For Mother, the threat of taking Chancelot away will keep me from doing anything reckless, and she knows it. However, I can't deny that I have plenty of curiosity regarding my rescuer. Who is he? Where did he come from? Why did he save me? Since I've assured her I'll stay away from him, those questions will go unanswered. I can't risk angering her, especially in her current mental state. I think she'd really take the former race horse away from me.

With several hours left until the Families arrive, I head out to find Conrad. It was obvious he knew the Medici, and chances are, he'll be able to assuage some of my burning curiosity. If I play my cards right, I can wheedle some details from him about our unwelcome visitor.

I find him in the foyer, and I grab his attention moments before he steps out the door. "Brother Dearest, *where* are you going in such a hurry?"

He pauses. "Out."

"Yes, but *why*?" I stroll toward him. "Shouldn't you be watching the evil Medici in case he, I don't know, blinks?"

I'm not entirely sure where my protectiveness is coming from. Chalk it up to him saving my life. I'm now indebted to him.

"Aren't you a snarky one this evening," he says with a frown. "Does your arm hurt?"

If it did—which it doesn't because I'm determined to not feel it—I would never admit it. Not in a million years.

"Talk to me before you go?" Changing the subject will keep his mind, and mine, away from any possible pain.

He considers me for a moment, and I keep my expression mild in case he picks up on my inner turmoil.

"You can walk me out," he finally says.

"Right on." I try to appear nonchalant about it and fall in beside him. "So where ya headin'?"

He shoots me a sideways glance. "Is that what you wanted to discuss?"

"Of course not."

We wander toward a black SUV where several others linger around. I recognize them as the best of father's fighters, and I side eye Conrad but keep my questions about his security detail to myself.

"What do you know about that Medici?" I ask.

He grasps my uninjured arm and swings me around to face him, halting our progress. "Why do you want to know?"

I shrug. "Because I'm curious."

"Leave him alone, Dani. He isn't someone to make friends with."

I cock my head a little, narrowing my eyes. "Who is he, Con? He's not *just* of the extinct Family, is he?"

"Dani," he sighs, but I cut him off by yanking my arm back.

"He saved my life. Whether you or Father want to believe it, I would be dead if it wasn't for him."

I'd said the same thing to Mother. Hopefully, if I say it enough times, eventually someone will listen and believe me.

"Doesn't change who he is." Conrad tucks some loose hair behind my ear. "Leave him be, Danika. He's dangerous." His eyes flick toward the SUV. "I need to go. They're waiting." He spears me with a meaningful glare. "Stay away from him."

"Yeah, sure, whatever." I cross my arms and look away.

He climbs into the vehicle with the others, and it departs. I stay where I am until it disappears with the winking of brake lights in the darkness. Annoyed that I didn't get the answers I was seeking, I turn back to the front door and come up short.

Lord Halifax stands rigid in the opening, his expression a mask of stern disapproval.

Ducking my head, I approach with reluctant steps. The one and only vampire I fear in this world is my father. He earned the title Vampire Lord over four hundred years ago and has held it ever since. Not only is he one of the strongest of the vampire Heads, he's also intelligent and cunning. Nothing gets past him. Especially not his wayward daughter.

"Danika," he says, and I bow my head further and slump my shoulders at the reproach in my softly spoken name.

Another nifty thing about him? He never has to raise his voice. To anyone. For any reason. He commands enough respect and instills enough fear that his sound decimal remains consistent. Well, unless he's angry. And then he gets very, *very* quiet.

Like right now.

"My study. Now."

"Yes, My Lord."

I trail him through the manor, shuffling around vampires scurrying here and there to take care of last minute things before the Families arrive. One passes me with a vase of black roses, heading toward the conference room. Another zips by with an armload of clean sheets for a room in the underground catacombs where the delegates will sleep with everyone else.

Every decade, in the spring, one of the seven Families hosts the Heads and their retinues. It's an exuberant affair with meetings that last all night, every night, blood parties—which sound disgusting, by the way—and the reaffirmation of the alliance.

This year, it's our turn.

We make it to the study, and he closes the door behind me as soon as I enter. The fireplace isn't lit since this evening will be warm, but the room is illuminated by a hundred candles scattered upon every available surface.

I suppress my sigh of exasperation. The orchard *is* equipped with full electricity and running water, Father.

"Take a seat." He gestures to the two couches set before the dark hearth.

I do as bid and turn my attention to the blood still coating my fingers and nails. No matter how much I prepare myself for his scolding beforehand, even coming up with my own rebuttals, I'm still reduced to an ashamed, quivering mess in front of him.

"Are you well?" he asks, and I nod, aware he's questioning my injury. "Your mother says she's already spoken to you. Is that correct?"

"Yes, My Lord."

"Good. Now then, Danika." His voice softens further. "I would like for you to tell me what you did wrong."

27

I don't even hesitate, saying, "I took Chancelot into the desert too close to dusk."

"And?"

"I didn't sufficiently plan for any unforeseen accidents and was caught off guard by a pack of coyotes."

"And?"

I look up, puzzled. "That's it. No wait, it isn't. I let a coyote get the best of me, and I was injured as a result."

"And?"

"And what, My Lord?"

"What about your involvement with the Medici?"

I'm not following, and my frown deepens. "What about it? It's not like he and I are friends, or that we agreed to meet in the desert."

"Danika." His voice is reproving.

"Sorry, My Lord." I shrink into myself again.

"Now, your mother is saying that you claim he rescued you."

"Yes, My Lord."

"Elaborate please."

I clasp my hands in my lap to still the fidget, and recount the events, leaving nothing out. I tell of Chancelot fleeing, the Medici alerting me, and then the fight with the wild dogs. I explain how he took on multiple coyotes while I was faced with just the one.

By the time I finish, my hands are shaking and the fear I haven't let myself feel begins to take hold. I almost died. Holy shiitake mushrooms! I seriously almost died.

As much as I want to give all the credit to the vampire who saved me, it also belongs to my brave steed and his pounding hooves. I'll have to give him an extra carrot and sugar cube tomorrow as a thank you.

A knock at the door draws our attention, and I can sense him stiffen with annoyance. Heaven help the poor soul who's disturbed us.

"Enter," Lord Halifax calls, and a fifty-year-turned named Beatrice pushes open the door and steps one foot inside.

"I'm terribly sorry to interrupt, My Lord," she says, "but the Medici is demanding to speak with you."

"He can wait until the Families arrive," he states.

She nods, swallowing hard. "Yes, My Lord. I did tell him that. But he is adamant that he speaks with you immediately." She retreats back across the threshold and bows her head in deference when anger sparks in his eyes. "He has refused to entrust his message to me, claiming that it is for your ears alone."

"Very well. Bring him." He dismisses her with a wave, and as she closes the door, he meets my curious gaze. "You will make yourself scarce, Danika."

"My Lord, I really—"

"No."

He's already furious at our interruption, and it'd be wise to respect his command and disappear for the next hour. But I can't. I have to know the Medici will be all right, that Father won't hurt him before I've had a chance to repay my debt.

"Father," I begin, and his eyes narrow warily, "I hate to say this—"

"But you're going to anyway."

"Of course." I smile thinly. "I owe this vampire a debt."

He sighs, the anger expelling on a wave of resignation. "I gathered as much, child. A life debt, I'm to surmise?"

"Yes, My Lord."

"And that means that you've become his new champion."

"Yes, My Lord."

"Are you sure about this?"

"You taught me to always pay my debts. Just because he's dangerous doesn't mean I shouldn't do it. If I use this—him—as an excuse not to follow through, then what might I use the next time around?"

There is logic in my words, which he cannot discredit, and a tiny smile flicks up the corners of his mouth. "Duly noted, Danika."

"I know you don't like it," I continue, "and I know you're going to fight me alongside the Families, but you know I have to do what I can, right?"

He nods. "Very well. You may remain and see what you're dealing with. However," he holds up an index finger, "you will *not* make him aware of your debt. Understand?"

"Yes, My Lord."

29

"Now, until he gets here, tell me about school."

***

I recognize the man being led through the door in an instant, even though it'd been dark during the fight with the coyotes. His shredded shirt has been replaced with an old t-shirt, but he still wears the fashionably faded jeans covered in slobber, mud, and dried blood. Dark eyes sweep around the office before coming to a rest on me, and I feel the jolt all the way to my toes. If it wasn't socially unacceptable, I would probably start fanning myself and batting my eyelashes.

Father waves him forward, and flanked by four guards, the Medici crosses to stand in front of us. With a nod from the Halifax Head, he's nudged roughly onto his knees without a word, his hands bound behind him.

"You wished to speak with me?" Lord Halifax says.

Dark eyes drag away, breaking the spell gripping me, and focus on Father. "Yes, My Lord."

"Why? What makes you think I want to hear what you have to say?"

"Oh, you'll want to hear this."

Well, if that wasn't a smug response if ever I've heard one. I bite my lip to keep from smiling. He's got guts, I'll give him that.

"Do not test me, Medici." Father's expression darkens.

"Apologies, My Lord." He bows his head. "I mean no disrespect. I only want you to hear me out. Once we're done here, you can do with me as you see fit."

Lord Halifax grunts. "Your message?"

The Medici vampire looks up, meeting his silver glare. "In three days' time, there will be an attack. They seek to strike during the peak of the alliance negotiations, when the trust among the Families is at its weakest."

While my heart pounds, Father merely ponders the information. He rubs his chin, as if fiddling with an imaginary beard, and contemplates both the vampire and the bombshell he's just dropped.

Holy snickers! I struggle to bring my heart rate under control before the others in the room pick up on my fear, but as dark eyes settle on me again, I know I didn't manage it.

"Why should I believe you?" Lord Halifax finally asks. "You're a Medici; you're supposed to be extinct." He narrows his eyes. "Tell me, how did you survive, Alessandro?"

Surprise followed by unease curls in my gut. Father knows him. *How* does Father know him?

There seems to be a silent battle being waged between the two of them as the newly dubbed, Alessandro, refuses to answer and Lord Halifax waits patiently for his response. The tension in the room grows thick, suffocating.

"I should just kill you and be done with this." Father leans toward the Medici on his knees. "You are, after all, your Lord's chief commander. Am I right, Alessandro Hadrian Medici?"

I recognize that name. It strikes me like an electric shockwave zapping my brain into remembering. No. No, no, no. Not possible.

The vampire who holds my debt, who I will give my life to protect in order to fulfill that debt, is the right hand of Paulo Medici, the former Head of the Medici line who started the bloody war two centuries ago.

CONFESSION 4
Repaying debts and fulfilling duties is a b— Uh...you get the idea.

Have you ever had a moment when you realize you've made a terrible mistake? When you wish you could take back a promise or an action. Something that triggers another series of events.

Father can tell the instant I realize just that, and I slam a mask into place before anyone else can discern the chaos within me. Expletives I wish I could vocalize scream through my brain at the same time my face goes slack.

Knowing who he is changes everything and yet, nothing.

"How can I guarantee what you say is true?" Lord Halifax asks, returning his attention to the Medici. "What assurances do I have that you're not trying to disrupt the gathering of the Seven?"

"I saved your human's life," Alessandro says, nodding toward me. "That should count for something."

Father's brow lowers, a dangerous gleam making his eyes almost ethereal. "That *human* is my daughter."

"Apologies, My Lord." Alessandro lowers his head. "I meant no disrespect."

"Who is leading the attack?" Lord Halifax demands.

He clears his throat. "All who is left from the Medici line."

"All?"

"Yes, My Lord."

Lord Halifax cocks his head. "Even your Lord?"

"My Lord died during the rebellion," the Medici growls, "as you well know."

Father rubs his chin but says nothing. Instead, he looks over at me and raises his eyebrows. I stare back, waiting for what, I don't know.

Finally, he resumes his study of the shackled vampire. "To be honest, I don't know whether to believe you or rip you apart. Your Family are cheats, murderers, and liars. However, it is not my decision to make alone. As such, you will tell your story in front of the other Heads, and as the alliance dictates, we'll decide your fate as the Seven."

"Very solicitous of you, My Lord," the prisoner responds, nodding.

"Do not patronize me, Medici scum." Father's face darkens lethally.

Alessandro's eyes dart to me, and I meet his gaze straight on. As much as I don't want to have a life debt looming over my head, I can't, in good conscience, turn away from him. Not now. Not with the threat of dismemberment in his very near future.

By the look Father shoots my way, I know he's waiting for me to say something. To begin my job as the Medici's champion. But what am I supposed to say? That he's a changed man? He'll never be bad again? He's seen the error of his ways and will repent for his sins until the end of time? This isn't a parole board. I'll have to perfect my excellent debate skills before I go before the other Heads.

Is this a test? Do I start now? Must be since Father's staring at me expectantly.

"Well, you see, My Lord," I begin, but he cuts me off with a shake of his head.

"He's a devil's spawn, Danika," he says.

"Sure." I nod.

"He deserves death," Father states.

"Probably." I shrug. "He's killed his fair share too." I look over at Alessandro. "Right?"

"Uh..." he mumbles, unsure.

"Then we should kill him," Lord Halifax says firmly.

I think about that for a moment and then nod again. Father's definitely correct. He's a Medici, and they incited a war and killed innocent humans. He should hang…no, burn to death…no, drowning is good…no—

"Danika," Father sighs, "you're supposed to be arguing *for* the defendant. Not agreeing with the prosecution."

"Right." I tuck my hair behind my ears and adjust myself on the couch. "Let's try this again."

"Excuse me." Alessandro glances between the two of us. "What's going on?"

"This," Father motions toward me, "is your champion."

"My what?" He frowns.

"Your champion," I say.

"Why?" His dark eyes narrow in confusion.

"Because," I say patiently, as if speaking to a slow person, "you need an attorney."

"But you're human." He seems surprised. Very unwelcomingly. "And a teenager."

Annoyance flares and I lean toward him until I'm mere inches from his face. "And you, Medici, are about to go up against the angriest, most unsympathetic firing squad in the entire northern hemisphere. You ready for that? If my father's reaction to your presence is any indication, *you're not supposed to be alive.* Imagine how shocked everyone else will be, furious even, at discovering your existence."

"That's enough, child." Lord Halifax gestures at the four, silent guards standing around Alessandro. "Take him back to his quarters. We'll send for him when it's time."

They all bow, and then two step closer to the bound prisoner, drag him to his feet, and escort him away. Before he steps through the doorway, he glances back at me, cracks a half smile, and winks.

And my heart goes *pit pat.*

He winked at me! That flirtatious, Italian parasite. I mentally fan myself while physically pressing my hands to my cheeks to conceal the blush stealing up my face. If Father notices, he doesn't say anything. Bless his five hundred year old heart.

I stand with my family, to the left of Conrad, as the first of the Families arrive. Mother has forced me into a dress following a bath where Yvette, my former nanny, assisted for the first time in nearly ten years. I wear a soft blue, vintage skater dress with sparkly flats and an up-do that makes my head itch, and try extra hard not to fidget and tug at the hem of the soft material. What I wouldn't give for some jeans and my Wellingtons.

Conrad looks impeccable in his black, three piece suit while Mother and Father look, as always, sophisticated and in sync with everyone around them.

Lord Malcolm Broadhurst, Head of England's Broadhurst Family, strides in through the front doors, a wide grin on his face.

"Halifax!" he booms, grasping Father's hand and tugging him into a hug. "Good to see you again!" He receives a firm pat on the back in response, and once the two ancients release one another, he shifts to Mother. "And Lady Halifax, such a pleasure." He captures her hand and presses a kiss to the back of it. "You don't look a day over five hundred."

I roll my eyes, snorting softly, and receive a sharp elbow in the ribs from Con. What can I say? The Vampire Lord is one, cheesy dude.

"Conrad," Broadhurst continues, shaking my brother's hand, "how've you been?"

"I've been well, My Lord."

"Brilliant!" His azure gaze travels to me, widens, and he takes a step back. "Danika? Is that you?" I give him a stiff smile. "The last time I saw you, you were yay high." He gives an approximation of what my height would have been at seven. "I forgot how quickly humans grow."

I keep my smile fixed in place, but I groan internally. This guy, I swear.

Father motions toward a hovering group of Halifaxs, and one peels away and approaches the Broadhurst Head.

"My Lord," he says, "if you'll follow me, I'll show you to your Family's assigned quarters in the catacombs."

"Of course, of course!" Broadhurst turns and beckons his retinue closer. "Say your hellos quickly and we'll be off." They do as instructed and soon it's just Halifax in the foyer.

I look over at Conrad and mouth, *Really?*

With a crooked smile, he shrugs.

"Honestly, My Lord," Mother whispers to Father, shaking her head. "That man never changes, even after four hundred and thirty years."

The next to enter is the French vampire coven, the Duchamp Family. Lord and Lady Duchamp are thin, pale munchkins—though they're probably no less than five feet tall—who speed toward us with broad grins and outstretched hands that trembled excitedly.

"Monsieur Halifax," Lord Duchamp says, and the two men kiss on each cheek while Mother and Lady Duchamp greet in the same manner.

"How was your trip?" Father asks.

"Terrible," he shrugs, "but we are here now, so we can rest."

"Most definitely." Lord Halifax snaps his fingers and a newbie appears beside him. "Please show the Duchamps to their quarters."

"Yes, My Lord." She bows and then smiles at our guests. "If you'll follow me, please."

Once they've left, I glance at Conrad and sigh. "They didn't even say hello to us."

"Danika," Mother says in warning, "unless spoken to by one of the Heads, you are not to open your mouth."

"Fine," I grumble. I want to cross my arms like the petulant teenager I am, but I opt to clasp my hands behind my back and stare at the floor.

"There'll be time for their greetings later, daughter," Father says. "It was evident they were exhausted and didn't want to spend much time lingering."

"Yes, My Lord." At least he's given me an explanation. Mother's still annoyed with me for what happened earlier, and I'll face her wrath until she gets over it. Could take weeks. If I'm not careful, I won't find Chancelot in his stall tomorrow morning. Or is it today? A glance at the clock confirms it's

36

nearing two in the morning. I stifle a yawn. I need to remain until all the Families are welcomed into the Halifax manor. Sometimes, vampire rules and customs are a nuisance for a human such as myself.

Soon, the Italian coven arrives, all twenty of them. The Diavolo Family has seven children, and it appears that each of them, along with their lifemates, have chosen to attend the gathering. Lord and Lady Diavolo approach, smiling graciously, and another round of boisterous hugs and kisses ensues. To my horror, and immense embarrassment, my cheeks are pinched, which draws tears to my eyes.

They're escorted away just as the Japanese Nakamura Family wanders through the door. Instead of handshakes and kisses, we're greeted with bows.

As the Nakamura Head answers questions about their trip, my sweeping gaze comes to rest on a petite girl standing toward the back of the group. Her eyes remain downcast and hands clasped at her waist.

I can tell in an instant who she is. Or rather, *what*.

Human.

Nakamura must notice my attention because he walks her forward with a gentle hand on her back.

"This is Yui," he says, giving her a tender smile.

Father nods. "Welcome, Yui. Please make yourself at home. My daughter, Danika," he motions to me, "will be happy to keep you company for the duration of your stay."

I can't stop my eyes from widening. Would I now? I don't *do* friends, Father. Especially not humans.

Following that, they're removed to their quarters and we're left alone again. Unable to keep my frustration to myself, I spin toward Lord and Lady Halifax.

"Why must I keep her company during the alliance talks?" I demand.

Mother sighs. "We'll discuss this later, Danika."

"But, Mother—"

"Another Family is about to walk through those doors," she interrupts, her glare so frosty I can practically see my breath suspended in air. "We will discuss this later."

Sure enough, our East coast brethren, the Campbell Family, stride in, and another round of handshakes begins. Lord Campbell's austere countenance doesn't waver during the introductions and warm greetings, and his cold gaze flicks over everyone present with arrogance and disdain.

When they're escorted away, Mother shoots Father an indecipherable look. Something unspoken passes between them, and then she sighs and shakes her head.

Finally, the last Family arrives.

Thank the sweet potato pie I'd had for dinner. This is almost over, and then I can go to bed.

The Richter Family from Germany is my least favorite. They're loud, obnoxious, and very opinionated. However, they're also the best looking. Not that I notice, though.

Not with Alessandro Medici locked somewhere in the house.

Wait! Where did that thought come from? Nope. Definitely not. He's a total no go.

They, too, have a human in their midst. A boy not much older than me sporting an impressive head of gold and blue eyes that match my dress perfectly. When he smiles in my direction, dimples appear.

Sweet sassafras! That boy's dangerous.

Stilted conversation, interpreted by a Richter underling for his Lord, finishes up the welcoming phase of the gathering. They're taken off to their room to clean up and prepare for the night.

When just Halifax linger in the foyer, I sag and release a heavy sigh. The front doors are shut and bolted, and our Family begins to disperse into the manor to take care of "meal prep" and set up for tonight's first meeting.

"Can I go to bed?" Was that a whine in my voice? Yes, definitely a whine. I cringe and meet Mother's eye. "Sorry."

She purses her lips but nods toward the staircase to the above ground suites. After kissing each of my parents on the cheek and throwing Conrad a soft smile, I turn and take the steps two at a time.

I'm bone tired by the time I make it to my room, and I flop down onto the rose colored comforter on my stomach with my feet dangling over the edge of the bed. Slowly, I begin sliding the pins from my hair, moaning in the back of my throat with each release of a tightly coiled curl. When the last one is free, I drop the pain-inducing contraptions down on the nightstand, without budging much from my comfortable spot on the bed, and scrub my nails against my scalp.

My shoes slip off, hitting the soft carpet without a sound, and I close my eyes and exhale in relief. A few ticks of the bedside clock. I relax further, taking one giant leap toward blessed sleep.

Then a noise in the hall disturbs me. My eyes fly open, I push myself up onto my forearms, ignoring the protest my injury makes, and swing my attention toward the door.

It sounds again.

Frowning, I climb to my feet, stride forward, and yank the door open. Two girls stand on the other side, and one of them squeaks in alarm.

"Woah," I say, caught off guard. "Who are you? And what are you doing outside my door?"

I recognize the first girl as Yui, who'd come with the Nakamura Family. The other girl, a model-tall African American beauty with hazel eyes and a spring of curls framing her face, smiles shyly.

"Hi," she says. "I'm Laura. This is Yui."

An American, huh? With a hint of a drawl?

I nod toward the petite one. "Yeah, I met her." My smile is flat and very unwelcoming. "You, on the other hand, are new."

"Ah, yes, about that." She scratches her cheek. "Lord Campbell figured introductions could wait until everyone was settled and cleaned up."

"Nice to meet you," I say, and then motion toward the other doors down the hallway. "Feel free to pick a room and get comfortable. I'm going to bed."

"Oh but—"

I close the door in her face, cutting off whatever she's about to say. I'm exhausted. It's three in the morning, and I stood in the entrance foyer for hours, greeting every guest who came through the doors.

Introductions with the other humans can wait until the morning.

With that thought, I strip out of the dress, drop it on the floor, and pad back to the bed in my underwear. I should probably wash my face since it's coated in thirteen layers of makeup, but after a second of consideration, I slip beneath the covers, turn off the lamp, and roll onto my side.

There are many questions I have about the events of the past day, and I can't shut my brain down. Why is Alessandro Medici here? Why is he warning us of an imminent attack? Why did he save me? Can he really be trusted?

His face swims in my thoughts, and I snuggle into the covers, hiding a tiny smile within their lemon scented softness. I wish I could see him again—right now. He was *fascinating*!

A taste of the forbidden.

Slowly, the smile melts away.

Why, when I look at him, do I see pain in his dark eyes? What is he hiding? What hurt is he concealing behind that crooked grin? My heart aches for him, but I don't know why; I don't understand. I want to unravel his secrets, discover *who* he is.

CONFESSION 5

There are only two things I fear. My
father. And the heavy, oppressive darkness of the
catacombs.

Father's summons comes around six the next evening.
I'm to meet with the Medici, determine his purpose for coming
to the orchard, and relay the information to the Heads. They will
then decide his fate.

The corridor I wander down is a gradually, declining
ramp leading into the bowels of the catacombs. Since my family
is able to see in the dark, the passage is unlit, and the flashlight I
carry barely penetrates the heavy darkness. I'm flanked by two
Halifax newbs and trail behind a set of hundred-year-olds,
inundated with cool earth, the musty scent of dirt, and the
uncomfortable sensation that I'm walking into a trap.

What a fantastic start to my spring break...

Maybe I shouldn't have gotten up today. I probably
wouldn't be feeling like a lamb being led to slaughter. Ah, well.
Such is the existence of the Halifax human, aye? Am I in a bad
mood? Seems so. Can I think of a hundred—no, a *thousand*—
better things to do with my Saturday night than dealing with an
extinct Family's sudden reappearance? Most definitely. But alas,
there's this pesky little thing hanging over my head.

The debt.

I heave a sigh and hunker into my sorry excuse for a coat.
The chill in the air has seeped beneath the thin fabric of the
rather impractical, designer jacket that hugs my ribs. Since my

41

companions are impervious to the cold, I whisper jealous obscenities beneath my breath, fully aware they can hear me.

"Are you cold?" the newbie to my left asks, and raising an eyebrow, I shoot him a look that says, *Really?*

"I've forgotten what that feels like," he continues with an almost wistful tone. "Being hot. Cold. Hungry. I don't remember any of it."

"Do you regret becoming a vampire?" I ask.

He thinks about it for a moment. "No, not really. I was dying when Lord Halifax came to me at the Army hospital. He gave me a second chance."

Devon had been sired six years ago by Father. Wounded in Afghanistan, the former Special Forces soldier had been hanging on by a fine, silken thread. Death was imminent, his wounds too grave, and he'd been recruited by the Halifax Head for the Family's security detail.

That's what Father does. He finds those with skills, with ambitions and dreams, and gives them a new, immortal existence when their human life is snatched away. They're lawyers, doctors, teachers, those with business acumen, tech geniuses, and former soldiers.

The first three years, they're on lockdown within the orchard's catacombs. Sensitivity to sunlight and the bloodlust makes them unable to interact with humans. Finally, they're allowed out. They mingle with the orchard's workers, greet me as their Lord and Lady's daughter, and learn to cope with the constant hunger of being around the warm, fresh blood pumping through my veins.

Yes, you guessed it. I'm the guinea pig to test the newbs' self-control and willpower. Go me. I'm not bitter about it. I've been subjected to the ranks of newbies since I was five years old. And it's always done under heavy guard.

"What about you?" I ask my companion to the right. "Do you regret becoming a vampire?"

"Of course not, Miss," he responds.

Richard is another former Special Forces soldier who was injured in Afghanistan, and he's been with us for almost seventeen years. I've been guarded by him for every "inspection" of the newbies over the past ten years—ever since he passed

Father's assessment of his ability to protect me, and *not* go for my fresh blood—and he's my personal bodyguard.

I'm mildly surprised with myself that I've never thought to ask him if he regretted his decision to accept Lord Halifax's offer.

The air becomes colder and darker the further we descend, and my skin crawls with anxiety. I *hate* this type of suffocating darkness. It brings back horrible memories.

By now, we've passed the sleeping quarters and are approaching the final passage to where they're holding the Medici. Apprehension forms a knot in my gut.

"Be wary of him," Bronwyn, the hundred-year-old, cautions from in front. "He's been given enough blood to sustain, but not enough to satisfy. He'll be hungry, Miss Danika."

I nod. It's exactly as I'd assumed it'd be. He's weaker this way. Once he fully feeds, he'll be at strength, and as a—*at least*—three hundred year old vamp, his strength will be difficult to counter.

My paltry light hits the two guards who've been posted outside his door, and my heartrate picks up further, thundering against my ribs. We're so close now.

I'm three parts nervous and one part excited at seeing him again. Call me a rebel. This guy is one, dark dude I can't wait to talk to. I know he's dangerous, evil, a bad seed. He's the son of the most ruthless Vampire Lord to ever exist.

And he saved my life.

We cluster together before the door, but nobody makes a move to unbolt it and allow my entrance. Even in the faint illumination, I can see the hesitation in their eyes, written on their faces. They don't *want* to let me enter.

But they'll do it anyway.

Several minutes pass in strained silence, and then Richard shifts beside me, nodding once toward the final barrier between the Medici and me. Everyone tenses, the hundred-year-olds step closer, and the guards execute their orders.

The door is eased open.

From within the inky, dark interior, the clank of metal shackles and a silky laugh reaches my ears. "I was wondering when you'd come."

A chill races up my spine at the sound of his voice.

"You smell delicious," he hums, and I swallow hard, biting back the comment that he *sounds* delicious. "Ah, I can hear your blood pumping, your heart pounding. Are you frightened, little human?"

"Of you?" I scoff softly. "No."

"Hmm…you should be."

Richard hangs back at my side while my two, hundred-year-old escorts enter with an unlit lamp. One plops it down in the center of the table against the left wall and lights it. The flame dances across the stone room, revealing a mussed bed and a shirtless Alessandro Medici leaning back against the wall with his arms draped over his bent knees. His wrists are shackled and connected to a chain bolted into the rock wall.

"To what do I owe this pleasure?" he asks, meeting my eye where I hover in the doorway. "Have the Seven so graciously summoned me?"

Shoring up my resolve, I step across the threshold, moving further into the room, and smile. "Would that make you happy? If they have?"

He considers me for a moment, then glances at the four Halifaxs who've accompanied me on my indebted errand. Richard and Devon stand less than a foot behind me while Bronwyn and her brother, Philip, take up positions just inside the doorway. With a whispered command from Philip, the two guards outside close and re-bolt the door.

"I'm surprised Lord Halifax sent you down here," he says, returning his dark gaze to me. "I am, after all, a Medici. It'd be only too easy to rip your throat out and drain you of every drop of blood." He leans his head back against the wall, his eyes never leaving me. "You smell amazing."

His words are unnerving.

"Coconut lime verbena," I say, nodding. "It's my favorite."

He's silent for a moment, and then he chuckles softly, just the faintest whisper of amusement.

"The Seven *have* summoned you," I announce, getting down to business. "Tonight, they will decide your fate. Before that happens, however, I will be given the chance to argue your case."

"Why?" He cocks an eyebrow. "You want to be a lawyer when you grow up?"

"No." I can't tell him about the debt. Father's orders. "I'm practicing my debate skills."

He laughs. "A politician, then."

"Does it matter?" I raise an eyebrow of my own. "If I succeed, you won't be dismembered and left for the dawn's arrival."

"Sounds painful." His face relaxes and he closes his eyes. "I accepted my lot the moment I fled Italy for the Halifax estate, human. Whatever they decide, I'll comply. Such is my fate."

"I can change that for you." I clasp my hands at my waist and try not to fidget. "Tell me of the upcoming attack. Tell me *why* you ran away from Italy. Tell me why you're here." I swallow. "Tell me why you saved me."

His eyes open and focus on me. "Is that what this is about? You've become my champion because I saved your life? Is this some teenage fascination?"

Yeah...about that... Sort of? There's no way I'll admit to it, even under threat of pain or death.

I take a step forward, but Richard grasps my shoulder, halting me. "Don't approach him, Miss Danika."

"Ah," Alessandro breathes, "Danika. 'Morning Star'. Such a fitting name. You are, without a doubt, a morning star."

"And you, sir," I sigh, "are ridiculous."

"We're getting nowhere with this," Devon says, moving abreast of me.

I toss my arm out. "Be patient. His clock is running out and he knows it." My gaze is piercing when it meets the Medici's. "Right?"

"Your *father* has trained you well," he breathes, a smile kicking up one side of his mouth.

"Of course." I stand up straighter. "Now tell me why you've come here."

He closes his eyes again and exhales heavily. "To relay a message to the Seven."

"About an upcoming attack?"

"Yes."

"Why?" I frown. "Your Family is supposed to be extinct, killed off by the combined efforts of the Families two hundred years ago. Why would you try and help us? Save us?"

"Did you know that it was *your* father who killed Lord Medici?" He laughs, softly, humorlessly. I hadn't known that and I'm momentarily caught off guard. Sensing my disquiet, he continues, "Ripped him to shreds in the final hours before dawn and then cast his remains into the open fields of Carver's Meadow for the sun to torch."

Carver's Meadow. Where the Medici Family took their final stand. Hundreds of vampires, from every Family, perished there. When the night had ended and the new day began, nothing remained of that last battle.

Nothing but the memories.

"Why are you telling me this?" My hands tighten around each other, heart rate picking up.

"So you'll understand how much I don't care about your Family or any of the other covens." His eyes snap open, fierce and nearly black with rage. "And especially not about *you*."

In a flash, he's on his feet, two inches from my face, straining against the shackles and chain. The pain in his eyes goes deeper than what I'd first glimpsed. It's intangible. He's not just fighting the chains; he's fighting against the prejudices and stolen second chances, against the sins of a Lord and betrayal of a Family.

"You," he spits, "live a sheltered life, Danika Halifax. You've never had to fight for anything or anyone in your entire life. You wake up each day, never worried that it'll be your last." His voice drops. "You can laugh and smile with little care."

I can see the hurt in his eyes. Two hundred years' worth of it—sadness, anger, confusion. He's afraid right now. Terrified. He knows what the Heads will decide, has known from the moment he saved my life in the desert.

I don't fear him. I probably should. Father will scold me later for not putting space between us, but something is keeping me in this spot, mere inches from an ancient; one, who can end my life with a flick of his finger.

46

Swallowing hard, I close that scant distance. Though near enough his breath feathers across my cheek, I maintain a safe enough gap to avoid his hands. He sucks in a sharp breath, his fangs elongating at the scent of my blood beneath his nose.

"Do you want to kill me?" I ask, peering into his face. "Will that assuage your bitterness? Will that bring back your sire? Your coven? Your honor?"

"No," he rasps, dark eyes penetrating, "but it'll hurt Halifax in a way very few things can."

"If hurting my father is what you seek, then why are you warning us of an impending attack?"

"Miss Danika." Richard is right behind me, his suit brushing against my back.

"I'm fine." I keep my gaze glued to Alessandro, begging him to answer, encouraging honesty. I'm pretty sure I've lost my mind. There's no way he's going to be truthful. That's like asking a scorpion not to strike.

Neither of us moves for a beat—barely breathing. We're waiting for something we don't know, hoping for something we cannot fathom. Unable to concede, or maybe just *unwilling*.

"The attack will come tomorrow, starting in Tokyo." His voice is low, silky smooth. "It'll sweep across Europe, hitting Germany, France, Italy, and England." He straightens to his full height, towering over me. "The final assault will occur here, at your Family's orchard."

"Why?" I ask softly. "What do they hope to achieve?"

"Discord in the world," he responds simply. "Chaos."

"And if the Heads don't listen? If they don't believe you?"

He shrugs, taking a single step back. "Then that's on them. The blood of hundreds of innocents will be on *their* hands this time." His shoulders slump, as if weighed down by an invisible burden I cannot begin to understand. "I've done my duty; I've warned you. Now, please leave." He returns to the bed, lies down with his back to us, and releases a heavy sigh filled with unspoken regrets. "I'm tired."

I want to say more, to promise that I'll save him, that I'll relay his message and get them to believe him. But even *I* can't fully trust his words.

I suddenly doubt my debate skills. There's no way I'll be able to save this guy.

With that thought swirling in my head, I allow my four guards to escort me from the room. The moment the door slams shut behind me and the bolt is slid back into place, I drag in a shaky breath and meet the concerned gazes of my companions.

"What do you think?" I ask, uncertain. "Will they believe him?"

Bronwyn shakes her head, sighing. "I don't know, miss."

"Agreed," Philip responds when I look at him. "He's a Medici, Miss Danika."

The fire goes out of me like a candle snuffed. "If none of you believe what he's said, there's no way they will. He's doomed."

"He's a Medici," Philip says again.

"And you're a Halifax," I snap, annoyance flaring. "He had no more choice in a sire than you did."

"What will you do, miss?" Devon asks.

I sigh, running a hand through my hair. "No clue. Try to convince them, I guess. That's all I *can* do at this point."

"Do *you* believe him?"

Bronwyn's question makes me frown. Do I? Not just a little bit, but really, truly, wholeheartedly, unequivocally? Is there even an ounce of hesitation in trusting him?

To my surprise, I *do* trust him.

He has no reason to lie about an impending attack, and he'll accomplish nothing by disrupting the alliance discussions. No, he's telling the truth. Something's coming—something big, bad, and scary—and whatever it is, people are going to die.

CONFESSION 6
My awesome debate skills aren't so awesome.

I stand before the Heads, confident, with my argument concise and straightforward. I've told them exactly what Alessandro has said, leaving not a single detail out. And now they sit in their plushy chairs, around the massive table, and consider me with disbelief in their eyes and patronizing smiles.

"It's not that I doubt you," Lord Broadhurst booms, steepling his fingers together and pursing his lips, "it's that I doubt *him*."

"*Oui*." Lord Duchamp nods in agreement. "He is Medici scum."

"He has no reason to lie," I argue, scanning their faces. "He fled Italy to bring us this message, knowing full well that it was a death sentence."

"Forgive me," Lord Campbell interjects, his voice cold, "but I don't see how his running from Italy is of any consequence."

Of course you wouldn't, you old coot.

And Lord Campbell is indeed *old*. He's half a century older than Father, and has been a Vampire Lord almost from his inception.

Determined to remain respectful before the Seven, I bow in his direction, acquiescing.

"You are correct, My Lord." I grit my teeth, silently counting to five before straightening. "His running away isn't important. What *is* important is the message he carries."

49

"What do you propose we do?" the Halifax Head asks.

"Alert your Families to be prepared, to stay vigilant," I respond. "If something's coming, we need to be ready."

"And the Medici?" He cocks his head enquiringly. "What shall we do with him in the meantime?"

"Stay his execution," I say and immediately regret my hastiness.

"We shall not!" Lord Broadhurst sputters and receives nods of agreement from five others.

Father, however, just continues to watch me. "Why should we spare him?"

I think about that for a moment. Why should they? What do they get out of this? Sure, they'd have an inside into the Medici coven, and they'd be able to gain knowledge where it'd once been impossible, but I doubt they'd go for it. He's more valuable to them dead than alive.

The silence stretches as I flounder. Goodie gumdrops...my debate skills have abandoned me.

"That will be all, Danika. Thank you." Lord Halifax dismisses me with a thin smile.

I manage a soft, "Yes, My Lord", and then Richard escorts me from the room, his hand firm upon my uninjured arm. I don't even acknowledge the other Heads on my departure.

"That didn't go as planned," I state when we're in the hallway and the doors to the conference room are shut. "I had *so* much more I wanted to say." I heave a frustrated sigh and meet Devon's concerned gaze. "What?"

"Nothing, miss."

"No, you've got my attention. What is it?"

"It's really nothing."

I sigh. "Fine. On to Plan B."

My two bodyguards glance at one another, and then Richard says, "I hate to ask, Miss Danika, but *what* is Plan B?"

"No clue." I shrug. "Hadn't thought that far ahead."

Conrad appears beside me. "Mother wants you."

I jump and slam a hand over my pounding heart. "Geez, Con! One of these days, I swear, I'm going to haul off and stake you."

"Ha!" He strides away again before I can utter the furious words bottled inside of me.

The urge to call him back and demand to know why he isn't in the meeting with the Heads is strong. As the Halifax Heir, he should be present for their peace talks.

He's being lazy again, isn't he? Probably running his bodyguards ragged. Poor Patrick and Vincent. I mentally tap a fist to my chest and send out a silent, commiserating message to them. *I feel you. Hang in there.*

He disappears around the corner and the opportunity to chastise him escapes.

I find Mother in the office near the back door to the orchard, going over the account books. Her head is bent over the desk, and she's rubbing the butt end of a pencil up and down her cheek as she peruses the inventory list.

"You rang?" I sing, waltzing in and plopping down in the extra chair.

She doesn't even glance up. "You'll be taking the Heads' human members out tonight."

I sit up straight. "What?"

"Curfew is two."

"Mother." Annoyance flares.

"Show them the city, let them experience America. For some, this is their first time here."

"Mother!"

"You're dismissed."

My jaw drops open in outrage. "*Mother!*"

"Now, Danika!" Her head snaps up, and her expression is furious, almost desperate. "Please. Before the Medici is brought up from the catacombs, you will take our six guests and depart the orchard."

Ah. The fight leaves me. "Yes, Mother."

"Go. Get ready."

I stand and move to the door. Something makes me pause. "Mother," I turn back toward her, a lump in my throat, "do you think they'll execute him tonight?"

She sighs. "Most likely."

"But...he *saved* me."

"He's a Medici."

51

"Why does everyone keep *saying* that?" I snap. "He's being killed because of something his Lord did two hundred years ago? Where is the justice in that? How is that right?"

"Darling," her face softens, "there are rules we, as vampires, must live by. Rules that govern and protect us, which, in turn, protect the humans around us. Every decision the Head makes affects their Family."

"But he doesn't have a Family, Mother. Not anymore."

"The Medicis then, and the Medicis *now*, are still one and the same. They are evil, lawless. They do not follow the same rules we do."

I swallow, already dreading her answer. "So you think he should die?"

She considers me, her eyes sad, regretful. "I do."

***

I sit on the couch in my room, gazing at the television screen without really seeing the late night talk show that I'd turned on fifteen minutes before. My thoughts are elsewhere, a hundred miles away.

Or maybe just half a mile beneath the earth, within the confines of the catacombs.

I couldn't do it. I've failed as his champion. My awesome debate skills aren't so awesome, I guess. The Heads were unwavering. The moment we're away from the orchard, he's to be dragged before them, and by the time I return, Alessandro Medici will be no more.

Tears prick my eyes, and I blink quickly to dispel them before Richard, who's currently standing near the door, still as a statue, or Devon who stands beside the couch, notices and comments.

Why am I hurting so much for this man? I don't know him, know a thing about his past—other than his involvement in the war—and I definitely shouldn't be feeling this way. I don't understand. Teenage girls have such fickle hearts.

A stubborn drop escapes and trickles down my cheek, and I lift my eyes to the ceiling.

"Miss?"

I ignore Devon's question and Richard's inquiring gaze. There's fifteen minutes left until I'm to report to the front drive, and I need to bring myself back under control.

The two, former Special Forces soldiers glance at one another, a move I catch out of the corner of my eye. Something passes between them.

"You know we'd do anything for you, right, miss?" Devon asks, and I look over at him and then cast a look at Richard. "We'd follow any order you give." His expression is firm, resolute. "Any. Order."

Richard crosses the room to stand beside his comrade, and I scan both of their faces in disbelief. Did they...? My tears dry in an instant.

"No," I shake my head, "that's not an order I'll give." My face hardens and I meet their eyes pointedly. "Your loyalty is to my father, *first* and *foremost*. He'll kill you if you do this, and the Medici is not worth all that."

I have spent years garnering their devotion and respect, growing up beside them as my stalwart guards. I shouldn't be surprised by their show of deference to me, but I find that I am. And I shouldn't be warmed by it either.

"We served, Miss Danika, and fought," Richard says, "for injustice. If you feel that this man deserves a second chance, then we'll support you."

I rise and approach them. "No. You'll *not* override your Lord's direct order. If he deems the Medici should die, then we'll allow it to happen."

"Do you *want* to allow it?" Richard crosses his arms, his expression grim. "Will you be all right if he's executed later tonight?"

"Of course I won't be!" I shove a hand through my hair and disrupt the curls I'd so meticulously styled. "But I refuse to lose you," I jab a finger into their chests, "simply because I felt *something* for this strange man. You're too important to me." I flick a panicked look at Richard. "Besides, you're already in trouble with the Head because of my ride in the desert the other night, and even though I've told them it was my fault, you're still being blamed for my injury."

His eyes skim my bandaged arm but he says nothing.

I shake my head once, firmly. "The answer is no."

"Understood, miss." Devon straightens, nodding.

I reach up and pat their cheeks, giving them a strained smile. "I don't know what I'd do without you two."

They smile in response.

My feet take me over to the window, and I lean against the drapes and gaze out at the dark night. I can't allow them to see my face at the moment. Did two of my father's underlings just offer to break the rules and free Alessandro? I wasn't hearing things, right? As much as I want to save the Medici, I cannot go against Lord Halifax. There are many things he'll forgive where I'm concerned, but *this* is not one of them.

Dark eyes flash through my mind, haunted and weary, resigned to an inescapable fate. My heart twists. This isn't the first time I've wished to be stronger, to be more than just the Halifax human, but it's the first time I've physically ached to be someone other than who I am.

"It's time to go, miss," Richard says, dragging me from my thoughts.

Turning away from the window, I smooth a hand down my skinny jeans, adjust the sparkly shirt, and cast a critical eye over the hot pink heels I've donned for my night out. Hopefully Mother won't have anything to say about my outfit. At least I've put an effort into appearing as if I actually *want* to go clubbing with six, complete strangers.

Though I met two of them last evening—Yui and Laura—I have yet to meet the remaining four, and I have no desire to either. I have too much on my mind, and too much is at stake, to be going out and partying. Selfish, I know.

I follow Richard and Devon from the guest suites, to the foyer, and out into the drive where five black SUVs sit waiting, engines running. A smattering of suited vamps, from all seven Families, linger around the vehicles.

"Tell me again, *how* many bodyguards we're taking?" I mutter to Richard, scanning the unfamiliar faces with resignation.

"Each Family provided two bodyguards," he responds, "and your father has provided several Halifaxs as escort detail. Devon and I will accompany you as your personal protection."

Well…at least there's that.

I turn in time to see six people exit the doors, and I recognize Yui and Laura among them. The four girls are clad in mini dresses with heels, all long legs and eye-popping curves, and the two guys wear jeans and button down shirts. I'm speechless as I take them in. They are a walking, talking fashion magazine.

The group comes to stop beside me, and with nowhere to run without looking like a coward, I stay my ground.

"How are you?" Laura asks, showcasing a brilliant, white smile.

"I'm good." My attempt to return it falls flat.

She turns to the new faces. "Everyone, this is Danika Halifax." Back to me. "Danika, this is Simon Broadhurst, Natalia Diavolo, Peter Richter, and Stefani Duchamp." She gestures at each person in turn, and I greet them with a nod.

Simon is tall with brown hair, blue eyes, and a kind smile. I recognize Peter from the night before entirely by the dimple cratered in his cheek, and when he winks, I hastily avert my eyes toward Natalia. She and Stefani are like night and day. Where Stefani is fair skinned, blonde hair, blue eyes—lithe and graceful—Natalia is short and dark. Her eyes remind me of Alessandro, bottomless pools of obsidian, and I find myself unable to tear my gaze away from her and my mind away from the depths of the catacombs.

"Let's go!" Laura exclaims, flinging an arm toward the waiting convoy.

I blink a few times to bring the world back into focus. I drag my attention away from the Diavolo human and turn to Richard for direction. He ushers me to the SUV in the front, and I climb into the leather interior.

Doors slam up and down the line of vehicles, and then we're off.

I stare out of the window during the drive, desperately trying to pull my mind away from the orchard. Guilt rides me hard. Guilt and something else. Something I can't explain. An emotion that clenches my heart, tears at my very soul. It's as if I'm leaving a piece of myself behind. Weird.

For the hundredth time in the past two days, I find myself aching for dark eyes and secretive smiles. What has he done to me? Why is it, that after seventeen years, I'm finally drawn to someone, and he's an ancient undead from an extinct bloodline entirely responsible for the bloodiest vampire war in history? Why does the tortured look in his eyes get to me so much?

Ugh! I'm such a mess.

Finally, our destination comes into sight, and I clear my thoughts with a shake of my head. Time for mandatory fun, Danika…

Drip Drop is an under 18 club, one of the only in Phoenix. Nonalcoholic beverages along with munchies are made available, and the patrons are heavily supervised and policed. On Friday and Saturday nights, this place is crawling with teenagers testing their curfews. It's "hopping"—from what the girls at school say. Can you believe this is only the second time I've been here? *Can't imagine why…this place is great.*

We congregate on the sidewalk in front of the doors and wait while our Halifax escorts approach the bouncers to gain our admittance. I pretend to not notice the line that stretches the length of the block filled with skimpily clad girls and guys dressed to the nines.

With a nod, the two, burly men stationed at the entrance unclip the rope and motion for us to go in. I hang back until the others have moved through the doorway with their personal bodyguards in tow, and then I trail behind them, secure with Richard and Devon flanking me.

The beat reaches me first, a *thump thump thump* I feel reverberating through the depths of my core. The hallway ends and the dance floor—surrounded by full tables—greets us.

You know that scene in movies when the hot girls waltz in and everyone freezes and watches them? And then the handsome, popular guys who every girl drools over comes in behind them? That's *exactly* what happens next. I swear it. And having a bevy of bodyguards only adds to their allure.

Soon, my six companions are on the dance floor, shaking their groove thing, and I make a beeline for the empty table I'd glimpsed upon our entrance. There, I will stay for the rest of the time. I don't want to be here. Not really. Don't get me wrong, I enjoy going out to the occasional movie or for dinner, but this thing—clubbing—it's not my cup of tea. Never has been.

Devon gets me a soda from the bar, and I sip on it, watching the others dance. No one will approach me, just as no one will try and talk to them. We'll be observed from a distance with jealousy, awe, and even fear. Such is our existence.

My first time here, I was a freshman. Young, innocent, and unfamiliar with the way things work in certain, social circles. I didn't know that petty jealousies would override pragmatism, or that it'd make it impossible for them to realize they were stepping into dangerous territory.

And that *I* was the one at fault. At least, that's what Father said afterward.

I'm twirling the straw around my glass when my gaze lands on three familiar faces, and my hand stills. In a heartbeat, I'm searching for an escape route. Am I frightened of those girls? No. Very few things scare me. Especially not the three bimbos who ruined my first experience at *Drip Drop*. I just don't want a confrontation with them. Not now. Not at the moment, when my mind is filled with tortured eyes and a silky voice.

The moment they notice me, my heart skips a beat and I shoot an anxious look at Richard, whose gaze is darkening. He's noticed them as well.

They saunter toward us, fake smiles plastered to their overly, done-up faces. My first impressions of them had been that they were beautiful and fun. They were the embodiment of the femininity I desired.

That assessment changed when I was given a firsthand glimpse into their dark, manipulative hearts.

They won't get close enough to me. We both know it. But they'll still try. And for every foot they're unable to gain, their poisonous words will cross that distance unhindered.

The tension between us thickens, almost suffocating.

Laura plops down beside me, chest heaving. "Oh man, that was fun!"

I rip my gaze away from the three girls. "W-what?"

She frowns, flicking her eyes in their direction. "Friends of yours?"

57

"Definitely not." I snatch my drink up and give a hard suck on the straw, looking down at the table.

She motions the Campbell security team closer, and they tighten around us. One of our Halifax escorts hands her a glass of water, and she receives it with a smile.

"Being a human in a vampire coven has its problems, huh?" she muses, watching the three girls with sharp eyes. "You have to contend with other people's jealousies and prejudices, and forget about making friends." She takes a sip. "Everyone wants what you have, but only what they see on the surface: the money, the prestige, the hint of danger. They wouldn't want your *actual* life, though."

"I came here once, when I was a freshman," I say and nod toward the girls. "Conrad came with me then, and they were all over him, fawning and giggling." I give an exaggerated shudder. "Gross."

She laughs. "Oh I don't know. Your brother *is* pretty dreamy."

"Yeah," I scoff, "in a three-hundred-year-old, undead, walking corpse sense." She snorts and sips again. "Anyway," I clear my throat, "when he didn't pay them the attention they were desperately trying to get, they approached me. For Con, that's the last thing anyone should do."

"I'm guessing he didn't like it," she says.

I nod. "Of course. He's an overprotective, big brother."

"What did he do?"

"Sent them packing the nicest way possible." A smile forms at the memory. "Seriously, he's the world's worst playboy. But it was great. He wrapped them around his finger so tight, had them practically eating out of his hand, and then he told them that they were the last girls he'd ever be interested in."

"Ouch!" She leans closer. "And then what happened?"

"They blamed me, tried to toss their drinks on me." I fiddle with my straw, focusing on the plastic tube and dark, bubbly liquid in the glass. "They told anyone who'd listen that Con and I had something incestual going on, and people believed them. Father was forced to step in and clear everything up. It was awful."

"I'm sorry."

I shrug. "Don't be. It was a long time ago, and I've come to terms with the fact I'll never have friends of the 'warm blood' variety."

Suddenly, Richard is beside me, his expression urgent. "We need to go."

Confused, I shoot a frown at Laura, but her eyes are locked on the others in the middle of the dance floor. When I look over, I see bodyguards surrounding their charges.

"What's going on?" I ask.

"We can't talk about it here. Come on." Richard helps me up. "The vehicles are being retrieved."

Laura and I are hurried from the table. Instead of heading down the main hallway toward the front doors, we're directed to a back exit.

"What's going on?" I try again. Panic is beginning to unfurl in my gut.

"The Medici escaped," Devon says.

"*What?*" I choke. When Richard doesn't answer, I grab his arm and jerk him to a halt. "What does that mean? What happened?"

"I don't know, miss." His eyes dart left, right, up, and down. He motions the Campbell guards to tighten the circle, and I'm forced right up beside Laura. Her warm hand finds mine, and she clings onto it.

"Lord Campbell says he's sending ten more," one of her guard's relays, lowering a phone from his ear. "They just need seven minutes."

Richard nods. "We can do that. Let's go. We need to get them somewhere secure for the time being."

Laura's hand tightens on mine, and I give it a quick, reassuring squeeze.

"Is it true?" a Campbell demands as we reach the door with the bright "exit" sign lit above it.

"I'm not going to wait around and find out," Richard growls. "Our job is to keep them safe. Truth or not."

I'm beginning to feel the first tendrils of fear snaking through me. Something is wrong.

"Richard," I say, my voice hesitant. "Richard, what's going on?"

"The Medici had a final message for the Heads."

"What? What was it?"

He spears me with a lethal glare. "The Medici coven is coming for you. For *all* of you. Tonight."

CONFESSION 7
I probably could have paid more attention to self-defense class...

I don't have long to consider the news that Alessandro has escaped before the rest of his revelation hits me. I want to demand answers, find out *why* they're coming for us. What did we do? Why did the message only include the humans attached to each Family? What's going on?

Words lodge in my throat as Laura and I are shoved through the door and into a back alley.

She clings to me, hands trembling. Her anxiety is beginning to wind me up, and I silently run through different things I can say to allay her fears. Unfamiliar with comforting another person, I come up short on the best advice.

"Four minutes out," a Campbell guard says, and Richard nods in acknowledgment.

"Where are the others?" Devon asks, glancing toward the door we'd made our exit through.

"They're moving to a separate location," Richard responds. "It's safer not keeping them all in one place."

"Understood." Devon shifts closer to me. "Are you all right, miss?"

I nod. There's no point in admitting I'm scared. My pounding heart gives it away. A spurt of anger warms my core at the realization that Alessandro *knew* his coven was coming for us but didn't mention it to me during our conversation. All right...so...I know he didn't *have* to tell me, but it could have

61

saved everyone a lot of trouble, and I wouldn't have been forced to dress up and subject myself to a night out.

If I ever see him again, I'm going to stake him. Jerk.

"Halifax," a Campbell says softly, and the tone in his voice sends a chill up my spine. "We've got company."

"How many would you say?" Devon asks, pressing closer to me, and Richard cocks his heads, listening.

"Twenty, maybe more." He shoots me a look, something indecipherable shadowed in his eyes.

I can sense what he's leaving unspoken. The Medici have come, and in force. No fear. I can't allow myself to feel it. Conrad has been training me since I was small, and tonight, I regret my disinterest in the fine art of self-defense. I'll be lucky if I can keep Laura and me out of their hands.

Let's just hope I'm strong enough.

Richard pulls something from his inner, coat pocket and presses it into my hand. My fingers curl around the smooth wood. A stake. Our eyes meet.

This is the real deal, his gaze seems to say.

Having grown up with vampires, for me to take one of their lives would be just as difficult—if not *more*—than taking a human's. The thought of it makes me physically ill. My hand flexes around the weapon while my emotions are at war within me. I want to give it back, but I know he won't accept it. It's my best chance at surviving what's to come.

"Stay behind me," he orders, and I nod once, swallowing hard.

"If I'd known we'd be doing this," Laura mutters near my ear, "I wouldn't have worn heels."

A smile comes unbidden to my lips. "I know."

One of the Campbell bodyguards hands her a stake, and she receives it with a grimace. "I hate these nasty things."

All of our attention focuses toward the darkened portion of the alley. Nobody speaks, barely breathes, as we wait.

Out of the shadows they come, dressed in black, sporting leather jackets, silver chains, and multicolored hair. Tall, combat boots clomp across the broken concrete, dark eyes—so terrifyingly familiar—center on our tiny group with anticipation and excitement.

Holy shiitake mushrooms! There's *way* more than twenty! I clench my hand harder around the stake and Laura shifts next to me.

"We're going to die." Eyes wide with surprise and fear, Laura observes the numerous undead emerging from the dark.

And then everything and everyone pauses for a beat. Even the air itself holds its breath.

A chorus of hisses split the night, feral, menacing, and in a speed too quick for my human eyes to detect, the Families collide.

Laura and I find ourselves on opposite sides of the ensuing battle, torn apart by a furious tidal wave of vampires. I lose sight of her within the masses.

Richard yanks me to the left just as a Medici launches a kick into the area I'd been standing in. I don't have time to thank him before another three vamps are on us. I'm pressed back close to a wall, and I poise my hand with the stake in preparation for a counterattack. Dread and fear sit heavy within me. Should a Medici get through Richard's defenses, I'll be forced to use the weapon.

An undead comes too close, and bracing my leg, I kick out with the other one. It connects with his head, and he staggers back a step. His dark eyes focus on me, and with a crooked smile, he licks his lips.

"Gross." I shudder, my lip curling in revulsion. "You're disgusting, dude."

His expression wipes of humor, and that crooked smile turns menacing. "Give me ten minutes and I'll change your mind."

I consider him, tapping the tip of the stake against my chin. "Um…yeah…I could give you ten years and you'd *still* be gross."

He hisses and bares his teeth.

"Don't bait him, miss," Richard cautions, sliding in front of me.

Another three Medicis join their comrade, and we're forced backward into the wall. Richard holds a steady defense, blocking hits from all four while still keeping me behind him.

My courage is expiring and it's becoming clear we're outnumbered and overpowered.

Our little group is driven together once more, and Laura and I stand back to back. As one, we raise our stakes.

"Heels suck," she grumbles.

"Definitely," I agree. "Not the best shoes for kicking vampire butt."

"Seriously." She flinches as a Medici tumbles to the ground beside us. "I knew going out tonight was a bad idea."

Ha! A girl after my own heart.

"If we get out of this alive," she says, "I'm never going clubbing again."

"You sure? Looked like you were enjoying yourself on the dance floor."

"I can dance just as well in my own bedroom."

"Just curious," I say, my tone thoughtful, "are we really discussing dancing and heels in the middle of a fight?"

She doesn't immediately respond, but when she does, I can sense a smile in her voice. "It's either talk about random, inappropriate stuff or focus on the fact I'm scared senseless."

True. True. She has a good point, even if I can't fathom our line of conversation.

Suddenly, it's a different level of insanity. Screams rent the air, dismembered limbs rain down on us where we face opponents with the final shreds of our dignity. The masses shift.

"Danika!" Conrad's voice is like the sweetest sound, and my heart leaps with relief.

"Con!" I cry, frantically scanning the surrounding faces for his familiar visage.

"Hold tight!" he yells. "I'm coming to you!"

I'm trying. Oh how I'm trying.

I look over my shoulder, intending to tell Laura that help has come, and find her slung over the shoulder of a dark-eyed assailant and disappearing into the crowd. To my horror, our guards have been swallowed by the Medici, leaving us unprotected.

"No!" the scream bursts from my throat, and terror spikes through me.

I grip the stake harder, raise it higher, and glare down the enemy Family who is quickly swarming in. Taking a swipe at the vampire closest to me, I watch him dance backward with a laugh. Others join in, and another takes his place.

Like a game of cat and mouse, they tease me, egg me on. My movements become panicked, uncoordinated. Once again, I seem to have forgotten all of the training I've received from Con.

Rough hands seize me from behind. I shriek. Struggle. Claw and spit. Throw punches, launch kicks. But I'm hauled back, regardless of my fight.

I'm no match for a vampire. Not now, not ever.

The world upends as I'm tossed over his shoulder like a sack of potatoes. I pound on his back, screaming for everything I'm worth—shredding my throat in terrified desperation. I bite my tongue in my fight, and the tang of blood fills my mouth. A moan comes from the depths of my gut as my throat seizes.

For the first time in my life, I'm terrified.

We disappear into the crowd, following the same path Laura had, and I continue to thrash. His arms are a vise grip around my legs, keeping me clamped to him.

"You disgusting excuse for an undead!" I scream. "Lousy, no good, freak of nature. You should have been drowned when you were born."

He sighs.

"The Medici were slaughtered two hundred years ago because of scum like you," I continue. "Medici scum. Slimeball. Twatwaffle."

"Twatwaffle?"

"Shut up, you undead freak!"

He sighs again but falls silent.

I continue to berate him. Not sure what I hope to accomplish by deriding the guy, but it's definitely making *me* feel better. Sort of. The fear is giving way to anger.

To my surprise, we catch up with Laura and her abductor, and soon, the two guys are running side-by-side, allowing us to make eye contact.

"You all right?" I rasp, taking a break from ridiculing him long enough to check on her.

She nods. "You?"

"For the most part." Flattening my hand, I give a hard smack to his lower back. "But this undead freak is breaking my legs. I already can't feel my toes." I hit him again. "Schmuck."

Suddenly, the vamps come up short, and we're jarred against their backs. One hisses, and the other flexes his arm around my legs.

"Give me the girls."

My heart leaps. That voice! I'd recognize it anywhere. But why? Why here? Why now?

My captor chuckles. "Would you look at that? It's the runaway prince. I knew you'd flee to the Heads as soon as *he* let you go."

"Give me the girls," Alessandro says again, his voice taking on a menacing tone.

I meet Laura's confused gaze and try to keep the smile from my face. It wouldn't do to reveal how relieved and excited I am at being able to see him again—current situation aside—and I doubt she'd understand it either. Course, I don't fully understand it myself. I'm supposed to be angry with him.

"Who is he?" she mouths, and I give a quick shake of my head, my expression grim. Not now.

"What're you going to do about it?" Laura's captor oozes snide humor. "Run away again?"

Both kidnappers laugh.

Stupid, undead freaks. That wasn't even remotely funny.

"Hardly," comes the lethal response, and the warning tone in his voice has me craning for a glimpse.

He stands in shadow, his dark eyes reflecting the street lamp we've stopped beneath, and my heart does a funny, little flip flop at the sight of him.

No. I cannot and *will* not feel anything for him. Jerk. Everything tonight could have been avoided if he'd only warned me of this ahead of time.

All three men hiss. It's a warning, a threat, a promise.

Then the ground comes up to greet me. Or do I drop to greet the ground? Whichever it is, it hurts. I collide with the concrete with a bone crunching thud, and pain explodes throughout my body. I moan—deep and agony-filled.

"Danika!" Laura cries.

I blink my eyes open only to find my vision swimming and her face a blur. I scrunch them shut again, release another moan, and try again. I can hear a scuffle, a fight, but my disorientation keeps me from locating the source.

The Campbell human is thrown down beside me, and her breath is knocked from her upon impact. She rolls onto her back, her movements slow, gasping and coughing. As she struggles to draw air into her lungs, tears leak out from beneath her clenched lids and trail into her hairline.

I scoot closer, biting my lip against the pain shooting through me with each movement. My hands tremble as I clasp onto her left hand. I pull it to my chest, and then reach over and smooth her hair.

"Breathe," I whisper, wiping away one of her tears. "That's it. One inhale and one exhale at a time." I rest my head against the ground and blink a few times to keep her at least a little bit in focus.

She sucks in a breath, coughs, and releases it on a moan. Her eyes open, and she turns her head to meet my concerned gaze.

"Are you all right?" she chokes.

I consider lying and telling her I am, but figure honesty is best at this point. "No, I'm not. I can barely see you."

"We need to escape." She tightens her hand around mine, rolls onto her side, and begins climbing to her feet. "Come on, Danika."

I squint at her, trying to read her expression, but everything continues to swim before me. Her grip disappears for a moment, and then returns with renewed vigor. She tugs me up, and I weakly comply. All the adrenaline I'd felt earlier, during the fight, has fled, leaving me bone tired.

I manage to get to my knees before my strength abandons me, and I curl over and rest my forehead against the hard ground.

"Come on," she pleads softly, continuing to pull on me.

"I'm going to be sick." Nausea climbs further up my throat with every jostle.

"Please."

"I can't." Regret escapes on a breath, and tears prick my eyes.

"Yes you can." She squats down and wraps an arm around my back. "Come on, Danika. You can do this."

"Just…just give me a moment."

"We don't *have* a moment."

My vision wavers and weakness descends hard and quick. Closing my eyes, I sink closer to oblivion.

I don't know how much time passes before gentle hands lift me, bringing me back to awareness.

"I've got you," Alessandro whispers, adjusting me in his arms, and my head falls to his chest. "Are you all right? Can you walk?"

Laura shifts beside me. "Yes. We need to find the Halifaxs and Campbells."

"Do you have a phone on you?" he asks. A pause. "Good, then give someone a call; let them know where we are. She needs medical attention."

"I'm fine," I interject softly, my eyes opening. "Just a little headache. You can put me down."

Our eyes meet. "Are you sure?"

"Of course." I smile thinly. "My legs aren't broken."

"No," he cocks a brow, "but you've got a concussion."

My eyes widen in false surprise. "Is that concern I hear? This from the vamp who *could* have warned me ahead of time about his Family's intention to kidnap us."

"Yeah, sounds like you're all right." He sets me on my feet, but keeps an arm around me.

Laura connects with someone, glances around to determine our exact position, and then quickly fires off our location.

With a nod, she hangs up. "They're on their way. A few minutes." Her gaze spears me. "Conrad's with them."

That knowledge takes me one step closer to my breaking point. My throat seizes and tears threaten.

Hurry Con. I want to go home.

A thought strikes me, and I shoot Alessandro a look. He has saved my life a second time. Not just mine, however; he's saved Laura's as well. Now, the Heads will have a harder time justifying his death.

His actions don't make sense. Why hadn't he told me about all this? Why had he saved us? Why didn't he flee after escaping the orchard? He knows the Families want him dead simply for being the son of a traitor. He's walked right back into the Heads' hands.

In a blur, the Campbells and Halifaxs begin appearing. I can breathe a little easier now, and a quick glance at Laura reveals the same relief.

Conrad materializes in front of me, and without missing a beat, I fling myself into his arms, and they tighten around me.

Safe. Secure. Home.

CONFESSION 8
I don't know as much about the vampire world as I thought I did.

What a cunning man—seriously. He's too cunning for his own good.

It's been four days since the confrontation with the Medici Family, and we're currently in conference with the Heads. Laura's and my wounds have healed with no lasting effects, and in a fit of stubbornness, the shoes we wore that night have been disposed of in glorious, fiery fashion. The other five humans had managed to flee, unscathed, from the enemy's hands and spent those four days we'd been healing off traipsing around Phoenix. Though, to be fair, they only did it during the day. At night, they were locked down in the manor. Something or other about another attack by the Medicis.

The attack Alessandro had warned us about, the one that would bring discord and chaos to the world, didn't happen. None of us can say why. It just didn't. The members of the covens still back in their home countries had kept vigilant for any whisperings for three days, but in that time, nothing had so much as twitched in the twilight hours.

As a result, the Heads are disinclined to believe him. But I am happy to report, they aren't as gung-ho to dismember him as before.

Now, I stare at the Medici beside me with offended astonishment. He'd planned everything? Not the attack; that was all his Family. No, he'd planned to not reveal the details of our kidnapping until the last minute only to escape, find us, and save us. Why, you may wonder? So he'd be spared. So the Heads would see he was a "changed" vampire who could even be trusted to protect their precious humans. Very sly.

Father is astute, and he doesn't appear surprised by the revelation. Quite the opposite, in fact. It's almost as if he'd surmised as much.

I am, on the other hand, fuming. I am *not* a toy. My life is *not* a game.

But to immortals, maybe it is. They've forgotten what it means to be human, what it means to face their own mortality daily. To age, to hunger, to even die.

Beside Father, Lord Campbell shifts his chair and considers the Medici. "I assume many thanks are in order."

Well, *that* was quite a begrudging thank you. Maybe with a little more oomph next time, Lord Campbell.

Alessandro nods. "Yes, My Lord."

"Regardless," the Campbell Head continues, "none of this changes who you are."

"Of course, My Lord." The Medici inclines his head. "But I cannot change who my sire was." He looks up, meeting the eyes of the ancient. "Two hundred years have passed since the war. Now, I only seek a place to rest, to call home until Dormiam."

Dormiam? Huh. Is that Italian? Sounds Italian.

"What makes you think you'll receive that with any of the Families?" Lord Broadhurst demands.

"I know how the Medici Family operates, My Lords." He sweeps his dark gaze around the boardroom table. "I know of each planned attack, of every move they'll make to bring your Families down before Dormiam. I can help you." He shoots me a look. "I can protect your humans."

A few Heads snort in disbelief, and Broadhurst turns red and sputters. But it is Father who responds.

"As much as I appreciate your dedication, Medici, I cannot, in good conscience, agree. Your life will be spared, as the Heads have decided, but you will find your home, *and* your rest, elsewhere."

"Father," I say hesitantly, and he shifts his attention to me. "Forgive me, My Lord, but I still owe this man a debt." I lower my eyes to my wringing hands. "Laura owes him as well."

Lord Campbell narrows his eyes but doesn't respond, and Father's expression darkens.

"What is your point, Danika?" he asks, his voice dropping a decimal.

Well great...I pissed off the Halifax Head. Go me.

"His arguments are valid," I continue, swallowing hard. All eyes are on me now. "He has inside information and details that we could only dream of having. Why would you allow this opportunity to pass? Simply because you're prejudiced against him? Because he was born a Medici?" I'm getting warmed up now. "Because his Lord did something two hundred years ago? The sins of a sire do not make a child responsible. He is no more to blame for the war than *I* am."

"Danika." There is a threatening tone in Father's voice, and I shrink into myself. "You and I will speak in the hall."

He is out of his chair and striding to the door before I can swallow down my fear. I follow him into the corridor, clasping my hands tightly together at my waist. The moment we're far enough from the room to avoid eavesdroppers, he turns toward me with measured, calm movements. His silver eyes are bright, furious, and his fangs have elongated in response to his anger.

"What are you doing in there?" he hisses, voice low and soft.

"What you told me to do," I squeak around the terror. "You wanted me to argue for him."

He rests his hands on his hips, lifts his eyes to the ceiling, and heaves an enormous sigh. "That was earlier. When you were to argue for his *life*. This matter," he straightens and points toward the room up the hallway, "is entirely different."

"How so?"

"Danika."

I shrink into myself a little bit. I hate it when he says my name like that.

"You are insulting the Heads with your blatant disregard for tradition and established processes." His expression darkens.

"It is *our* decision if the Medici should remain. Not yours. Not the Campbell human's."

"Yes, My Lord."

"You cannot stand against them, daughter. Not in this."

"Forgive me, Father," I whisper, looking down and blinking away tears of shame.

He nods, sighing. "Very well."

"But…haven't you always taught me to stand up for those I felt were being unfairly treated?" I ask, meeting his eyes. "To stand up for what I believed in? How is this any different? How is *he* any different? I owe this vampire a life debt, and once a debt is established, it's to be seen through to the end. You taught me that."

"Do you know who Alessandro Medici *was* during the war?" The anger has left Father, but something else remains. An emotion I can't pinpoint. "Who he still *is*?"

I shake my head.

"A murderer, daughter."

I shiver as his words whisper over me.

"He slaughtered hundreds of vampires and dozens of humans. There was no hesitation, no prejudice in his killings. He did it for the pleasure, for the rush."

Man, what an evil dude. But still… People can change. Can't they?

"I understand that you wish us to give him a chance," Father sighs, "but at what risk, Danika? Your life, and the lives of the other humans we call family? The lives of every member within our covens?" He shakes his head slowly, sadly. "We cannot, and *will* not, take that chance." His hands are gentle as he cups my cheeks, tilting my face up until our eyes meet. "You, my beautiful child, are too precious."

"Yes, Father."

He presses a kiss to my forehead and then releases me. "Go and find Conrad. I'd like for you to do some training while the Heads and I decide what's best to do with the Medici."

And our conversation is over. I'll not argue with him.

"Yes, My Lord."

Dismissed, I move halfway up the hallway and then pause, turning back. Father stands in the same spot, his head bowed and shoulders slumped, as if carrying an unexplainable weight. He lifts his head, sighing, and glances my way. Seeing me watching him, he gives me a pained smile and waves me on.

***

I jog the perimeter trail of the orchard, maintaining a pace that's kicking my butt, all in order to keep my mind off Alessandro. Father's words continue to circulate, altering every opinion I've developed of the Medici.

Sweat stings my eyes and my chest heaves with each breath, but I push on.

I feel like crying and screaming at the same time, my emotions at war within me. What I feel for him is nothing more than fascination, I know that. He's a mystery I long to solve, a puzzle I am desperate to figure out.

I already knew he'd been involved in the war, and it was no secret that he has killed in the past. But can any vampire, including the Heads, say they've never spilled innocent blood? What about during their first three years, when the bloodlust is at its peak? Or after that? Relations between humans and vampires hasn't always been good. At one time, my family would have been hunted by those who feared and hated them.

I was aware beforehand that the arguments with the Heads wasn't going to be easy. Father had warned me as much. I guess I've put too much faith in my debate skills. The more I think about it, the more I realize that for some reason, I want to find the good in him. I want to help him find the good in *himself*. Call me an idealist, an immature child, an idiot.

The path curves, and I follow it around, my thoughts filled with questions. I don't notice the person standing in the middle of the trail until I nearly collide with him, and with a jolt, I skid to a stop.

Chest heaving, I raise an eyebrow at the vamp who's intruded on my solitude. "What do you want?"

"Only to see my fearless champion." Alessandro grins, though it doesn't quite reach his eyes. I consider him, unamused, and his smile gradually withers. "I wanted to thank you for everything you've done, Halifax. It took guts to stand up to the Heads."

"They didn't seem to think so." The memory of my father's displeasure is still fresh.

He shrugs. "They'll get over it."

"So has it been decided?" I press my cheek to my shoulder to soak up trickling sweat. "Are you leaving?"

He gives a sweeping bow. "Once the sun sets on the morrow."

"You have a weird way of talking," I say with a wry smile. "How old are you?"

"Why?" He raises his brows. "Not into older guys?"

"I prefer the human sort." What a crock that is, but I'm not about to admit to having a *thing* for him.

"I'm three hundred and ninety," he replies.

If I was drinking water at this moment, I'm positive I would have sprayed it all over his face. It isn't so much the fact he's that old—I'd expected as much—it's that he's older than Conrad.

"You're practically an ancient yourself." I grin. "Soon, you'll be doddering around your castle, reminiscing about the fifteenth century while sipping on your favorite A positive."

His eyes widen in mock outrage, and he gives a firm shake of his head. *"Never."*

I laugh.

It feels so good to do so. The last week has been like a blood-sucking leach, draining the pleasure out of everything

Then another thought strikes and my amusement dies. "So, you were around way before the war?"

His expression shifts, becoming guarded. "I was."

I'll probably regret this. Yes…definitely. Father's words begin circulating afresh, and I meet Alessandro's dark gaze straight on.

"Then, what exactly happened?" I ask.

"With what?" He narrows his eyes. "The war?"

"Yeah. Why didn't you stop your Lord?" I cross my arms over my chest. "Why did you kill people? Why didn't you just stop it all? Things wouldn't be so hard for you if you had."

"Wow." His voice is flat, emotionless. "What a series of questions."

"I'm serious." My hands flex over my biceps, pinching the soft muscle as I tamp down on the anger. "Why, Alessandro? Why didn't you stop any of it?"

"Fine. I'll bite." He leans toward me, snapping his teeth together to emphasize his statement, and then straightens, all humor vanishing. "Do you think it was as simple as just 'stopping' it? That I could tell my Lord he would never achieve his goals by starting a war?" A hard edge creeps into his voice. "That the other Families would welcome us with open arms if we just bowed before them?" He shakes his head and laughs, dry and humorless. "My sire would *never* bow, but there you go again, human, assuming you know everything. The world you live in today is *very* different from the world *I* grew up in. I survived, not by being a gentle, peace-loving vampire, but by fighting. That was the *only way* to endure."

I'm speechless and gaping like a fish.

He continues, "Just because my sire made wrong decisions, does that mean he was any less of a Lord? Does that mean I didn't love him? That he didn't *deserve* love, and I didn't *deserve* it reciprocated?" He closes the short distance between us and towers over me, his expression dark. "You made the mistake once before by assuming you knew me and what I've been through. But you cannot begin to fathom it. Not you. Not the human child loved and cherished by her vampire family."

I've been chastised numerous times by Father, Mother, and even Conrad, but this is the first time I've felt so utterly rebuked and defeated. I know there is pain within him. I'd glimpsed it in the catacombs. So then, why do I push? Why do I demand answers to questions he doesn't want to consider? Why do I remind him of a past he wants to forget? I can see a desperation within him, a desire to flee, to hide.

Who is this man? Why do I hurt with him, *for* him? Why do I wish I could change his past and give him a peaceful future?

Why does he affect me like this?

Silence stretches between us. His eyes never leave mine, as if he's expecting something. I don't know what. Forgiveness? Redemption? A second chance only *I* can give?

"This wasn't the conversation I was hoping to have." He sighs and steps back, and I feel his pulling away to the very depths of my soul. "I wanted to tell you thank you for attempting to argue my case, but I guess that was unnecessary." He gives me a tight smile. "See you around, Danika."

Ah, wait! I lift a hand, to grab onto him, to halt him, to give us just a few more minutes. Maybe even to apologize for hurting him. But I'm too late. The path is now empty in front of me.

I look around, an inch shy of frantic. Nothing but the trees greet my roving eyes. Not even Richard is present at the moment.

Now that I think about it, I haven't seen him since I started my run. Did he make himself scarce in order for Alessandro and me to have a moment? That's quite ballsy of him. If Father finds out, he'll be in trouble. He knows me too well, that bodyguard of mine.

I drop my hand to my side, heaving a sigh. Well great…

Voices reach me from within one of the rows of citrus trees, and I physically shake myself. It won't do to have my family see me so rattled by the Medici.

I start forward. Best finish my run.

"Barely a year left until Dormiam." A deep voice. Male.

I come up short at those words.

"Are you ready?" Same speaker.

"Of course. A five year sleep sounds wonderful." A woman this time. I recognize her voice as belonging to Candace, one of my former tutors.

But what is she doing working the produce? She's an intellectual, not one of Father's lower minions. The orchard tasks are usually reserved for the newbies.

"Do you think the Dilecta are ready?"

She snorts. "Probably not. You know how our Danika is. Still much growing to do."

Dilecta? Is that referring to me? To the other humans?

"They'll have to be. We go into the catacombs on the summer solstice whether they're ready or not."

"Lord Halifax will make sure she's ready, Hank," Candace says on a sigh.

77

Hank? Hank? Ah, the fifty-year-old lawyer who is one of the many Father designates to manage the Halifax estate. What are they doing out in the orchard?

"Have the human bodyguards and muscle been chosen?" she asks.

"We've narrowed the two hundred down to seventy-five," he answers. "After the delegations leave, we'll finish the interviews and begin training."

Though I'm totally lost, I still listen with bated breath. None of it makes sense. What is Dormiam? A long sleep? Like a hibernation of some kind? And Dilecta? They use both words as if they're names. And what language is it? Italian? Spanish? Portuguese? No...

I've heard it before. From Father. It's ancient, steeped in tradition, an elegant, dead language.

Latin.

CONFESSION 9
I guess some humans aren't so bad...

Conrad visits me just as I'm finishing preparing for bed. His black hair is slicked from the rain coming down outside, and his silver eyes take in my yoga pants and faded t-shirt with amusement.

"You know," he says, a smile turning up one side of his mouth, "Mother will buy you new clothes if you need them."

I survey my attire with exaggerated offense. "What's wrong with what I'm wearing?"

"Nothing." He laughs and shakes his head.

"Did you need something?" I resume brushing my hair. "I'm sure Father wants you to join the Heads soon for the feeding."

He presses a kiss to the top of my head on his way to the sitting area. "I've got a bit of time." He plops down onto the rose hued loveseat. "Wanted to check on you first."

"Don't get my couch wet." I meet his gaze in the vanity mirror. "And I'm fine, Con."

"*Are* you?"

I look away, but not before he sees the hesitation and pain in my eyes.

"Dani." He says my name with the gentlest of touches.

"I'm fine, Conrad," I sigh, but I'm not sure if it's said for his benefit or mine.

"You don't *look* fine."

My hand pauses and the hairbrush dips. I've got nothing to say to that. A certain someone has taken up residence in my thoughts, and I can think of little else other than obsidian eyes, a crooked grin, and the way his dark hair curls near his temples.

"The first week of the alliance meetings are nearly finished," he remarks, relaxing backward and draping his arms over the back of the couch. "Pretty soon, it'll be just us Halifaxs again."

I grunt noncommittally and begin sliding the brush through my hair once more.

"Your friend seems nice."

"What friend?" I ask, though I already know the answer to that.

"Oh come now," he snorts. "Are you really that stubborn?"

"Are you really just making random conversation?"

He eyes me. "What's the matter? You haven't been yourself for a few days now."

I just want to be left alone, to wallow in my misery and thoughts. There's too much on my mind to be having a pointless conversation.

I flash him a tight smile. "Seriously—I'm fine."

But I know he can see right through me. He's not just my brother; he's my best friend. He knows what I'm thinking long before I think it, and he can see through any lie.

His expression sags, and he runs a hand through his wet hair. "I'm sorry, Dani."

I toss the brush down and swivel to face him. "For what?"

"For everything." Regret flashes through his eyes. "For not protecting you from the Medici coven, for being absent from your meetings with the Heads. I know you needed me at those times, and I wasn't there."

"It's fine."

"But it's not." He sighs and leans forward. Bracing his elbows on his thighs, he scrubs his hands up and down his face. "It's really not." His hands drop and he meets my eyes. "You should be angry with me. This is how I know something's wrong. Is it the Medici? Has he done something to you?"

I wish I could be honest and tell him that Alessandro is totally innocent, but for some reason, I can't find the words. Instead, my gaze travels around the room, looking anywhere but at him. I can't admit that I'm a mess. Besides, he's so used to making women feel this way, I doubt he'd understand.

"He's no good." His voice is gentle, almost pleading. "He'll only hurt you."

Annoyance flares. But he isn't like that, I want to say. He saved me—twice. And he's funny, smart, and makes me laugh. Ugh! I *really* don't want to be having this conversation. Not right now. Probably not ever.

"Are we seriously discussing this?" I scowl. "I've been told by you and everyone else that he's a no good, rotten scoundrel. Stop reminding me."

"Dani—"

"Stop, Conrad!" I slap my hands down on my thighs. "I get it."

"No, I don't think you do. He isn't like one of those wounded birds you used to bring home when you were younger. Alessandro is not someone to play around with. He's a shrewd military strategist, Dani, and he'll use any weakness he can find to subjugate the Heads. He isn't worth this."

Something breaks in me and I hiss, "Worth what? Forgiveness? A second chance? A home?"

"He isn't worth your *affection*."

"And who are you to decide where my affections should wind up?" Anger blazes, hot and heavy. "Who are you to have dominance over my heart? I can care for whom I want. And if I fall in love, it's not your choice, it's mine." I jab a finger into my chest. "*Mine!*"

He raises his hands, almost placating. "I didn't come here to fight."

"Seems like it!"

He jerks forward on the couch, fangs elongating. "That's enough! I don't understand where this anger of yours is coming from, but you need to tone it down."

His words should give me pause, but they only fuel my ire. "You can't just come in here and tell me what to do. I'm not one of your newbies you can boss around, Conrad! Do not think

I will simply obey you because you're the heir to the Halifax coven."

"For f—" he cuts himself off, scrubbing a hand down his face. "When did I ever say you *had* to obey me? I just want you to be careful. That's all. Don't let your feelings get in the way of pragmatism."

"Oh ho! That's rich, coming from you!" I throw my head back and laugh, loud and humorless. "This from the world's worst playboy. What was her name yesterday? Pippa? Samantha? Isabelle? How about the girl last week? Jasmine?"

"That's enough, Danika."

"Vampires are just as helpless as humans to the emotions and feelings that control us," I continue, rising to my feet. "Just because you have the emotional maturity of a hamster, doesn't mean everyone else does."

His eyes darken, and he stands. "I think you've said enough. I'll say my goodnights."

I cross my arms and look away. How did it get like this? Even with everything going on in my head, I wasn't angry. Maybe a little hurt, confused, but definitely not angry.

"Yeah, I got it." I tighten my arms across my chest, and turn my head away from him.

"Sleep well, sister." And with barely the click of my door closing, he departs.

Once he's gone, I drop back down onto the vanity's stool, blinking rapidly against the burn of unwanted tears. My eyes land on the closed laptop still on the coffee table in front of the couch, and biting my lip, I look away again.

I can tell you exactly where these unwelcome and unstable emotions are stemming from. Confusion. Uncertainty. From the realization that my family is keeping secrets.

Dilecta—Beloved...Special...Chosen.

There are so many translations for that one word, but they mean the same thing. There is something about us—the human children among vampires. We're important to the undead. But the million dollar questions is why? What does it all mean? What is our significance, and why did Candace and her companion seem interested in our preparedness for Dormiam?

Curious. Very curious. Would Laura know? From what I've gathered over the years, Lord Campbell isn't the type to care for humans under false pretenses, and he's a shrewd and meticulous ancient one. My gaze returns to the laptop. If anyone were to know, it'd be Laura.

I grab my phone, punch out a quick text to her, and then pause, my finger hovering over the *send* button. I've never texted anyone outside of my family. Heck, I've never even had another human's number programmed in. This is a momentous occasion. I close my eyes and suck in a breath through my nose.

And…send.

My hand flexes around the phone as I sit and wait for her response. Will she text back? I haven't seen her much over the past few days. Maybe our bond hadn't really happened during the Medici attack. Maybe I was imagining that we'd connected over grotesque high heels and being slung over a vamps' shoulder like a sack of potatoes and hauled away. We'd had a good chuckle as we'd burned the shoes and exchanged numbers. Had I been inventing a friendship where there isn't one?

Heart plummeting, I activate the screen and stare at the message. *Delivered.* I will it to come back.

Then the word changes.

Read.

My leg starts moving, a nervous up-and-down. Then my fingers start drumming on my bent knee. I toss the phone onto the bed, wait for not even five seconds, and then lunge for it, activating the screen again.

Ten minutes pass. The jerking of my leg develops into a full blown pacing around the room, arms firmly crossed, phone gripped in my hand.

After twenty minutes, I set the phone down on the coffee table, beside the laptop, and turn away. I won't allow myself to be upset. Not again. But even saying that, I can't stop the disappointment that clenches my heart.

Humans are all the same.

***

Knocking drags me from sleep, and I sit up and look around groggily for the offending noise. After a moment, my brain clears enough, like a fog lifting and awareness resettling, and the door draws my attention. I turn on the side table lamp, throw back the covers, and after climbing from bed, pad across the cool carpet.

When I open the door, the person on the other side gives me pause.

"It's late, I know." Laura's smile is apologetic. "I've been in a meeting with Lord Campbell for the past two hours or I would have replied to your text."

"Ah...yeah." I rub the sleep from my eyes and step back. "Come in, please."

"I'm sorry for waking you," she says as she moves into the room.

With a shrug, I close the door behind her. "No worries. Everything all right?"

She seems distracted when she nods. "Hmm, yes."

"Want some water or something?" I ask, motioning toward the mini fridge and side table where I have an electric kettle and a selection of teas and instant coffees.

Because of the difference between mine and my family's sleep schedules, I've learned to care for myself. Mother has ensured there's a handful of staff on hand to assist and see to my needs during the day, but there's only so much a family of undead can do when their human gets hungry. So when I was twelve, I asked for a few essentials. I scored myself a mini fridge, and then proceeded to stuff it full of ice cream, bottles of water, and sodas. The table beside it holds an assortment of munchies ranging from a basket of granola bars to fresh fruits.

I grab her a bottle of water upon her request, and she takes it from me with a smile. Together, we sit down on the couch, and silence stretches between us. A very *awkward* silence.

I clear my throat, search for something to say, and when nothing comes readily to mind, I open the laptop and turn it on. As it powers up, she sips on her water and I stare at the computer screen.

Shyness clings to me. Surprising, since I'm never shy. I guess there's some hope buried within me that I'll actually make a friend. Won't Con be proud of me then...

"You didn't say much in your text," Laura says, breaking the silence. "You just mentioned Latin terms you didn't know." I nod. "What are they?"

The webpage finishes loading, and I gesture at Dilecta highlighted in the search bar. Her eyes sharpen in recognition.

"Ah," she breathes, leaning forward and scanning the page. "Beloved one." She shoots me a sideways look. "When did you say you heard it used?"

"Earlier this evening," I reply, "in relation to me."

"And me." She leans back. "And Yui, Simon, Natalia, Peter, and Stefani."

"What does it *mean*?"

She shrugs. "No clue. It's what Lord Campbell calls me, though. His Dilecta."

"It's got to be important somehow."

"Oh, no doubt." She nods and then glances at me. "I have to ask. What was with that text?" At my frown, she whips out her phone, pulls up my text, and reads, "'Laura, it's Danika. I have a question regarding two Latin words I heard recently'." The phone disappears back into her pocket. "That didn't really ask a question, did it? It was more a statement."

I keep my eyes on the computer screen, afraid that if I look and see the smile I can sense she's struggling to hide, I'll dissolve into a puddle of embarrassment.

"Well..." I trail off, my excuse fizzling out.

"Anyway," she shifts beside me, "tell me about the Medici." Her eyes are bright with interest when I turn, gaping. "What's his story?"

A niggle of jealousy. "There's—uh—nothing to tell."

"Oh come now," she scoffs. "I've seen the way you look at him."

My heart skips a beat. "W-what?"

"In the alley, after he saved us." She raises an eyebrow meaningfully.

Am I really that obvious? No wonder Conrad chastised me for my fascination with Alessandro. Chances are, even Father's noticed. Goodie gumdrops…

The conversation is veering away from the two Latin words that've joined my limited "foreign language" vocabulary, so I file everything away for later. I guess I'll have to bring it up at a more opportune time. Apparently, this is one of those "girl talks" that I've read about in the chick magazines I've snuck glances at in checkout lines. I'll never admit that I've partaken of their teen knowledge. Not in a million years; even under threat of pain or death. Gross.

"I don't really know much about him," I eventually say and shrug. "He's a mystery."

"One you're desperate to figure out, huh?" She nudges me with an elbow, her grin wide. "One wrapped up in gorgeous eyes, a killer smile, and a delicious accent. Does he make you all gooey and melty?"

"Does he *what*?"

Her smile broadens, all perfect, white teeth, and I hastily avert my attention back to the computer screen. She's entering dangerous territory with this conversation. One I'm not comfortable gushing over. Do I have some weird attraction to the Medici? Sure do. Is it forbidden? Oh definitely. Will I allow it to the point I get into trouble with the Halifax Head? Absolutely *not* with a capital N-O-P-E. If Father doesn't kill me, and Mother doesn't lock me in my room for the next ten years, Conrad will instill fear in me that'll haunt my dreams for the rest of my life.

My three hundred-year-old brother is a thing to be feared. I may argue and fight with him, but I'll never allow anyone, no matter who they may be, to come between us.

"So, is it true you've been with the Halifax coven since you were a baby?" Laura asks, breaking into my thoughts.

"Hmm-mm." I close the laptop. "I've heard that other abandoned children aren't so lucky."

She's silent.

"I guess I had a guardian angel looking out for me," I say with a faint smile, and turn to look at her.

"No, they're not." Her soft words hold a wealth of meaning within them, of broken dreams and lost hope, of a past

86

unforgotten. There's a flicker of something in her eyes. Pain. Loss. A grief so deep, it's bottomless.

Suddenly, she's not the same girl who knocked shyly on my door nearly a week ago, or the one who let herself go on the dance floor, discarding all her inhibitions, or the one who fought bravely by my side against an enemy coven.

My heart clenches and the need to protect, to save her, overwhelms me. She carries the same haunted, desperate look within her that I'd glimpsed in Alessandro.

"I—uh—should probably go," she says, rising. Her hands grip the water bottle tightly, knuckles white, plastic crinkling beneath the pressure.

I hurriedly stand, and she turns and strides to the door. Her long legs eat up the distance, and I'm left scrambling to catch up. The same strict upbringing keeps her from simply leaving without a parting comment, and for once, I'm grateful we're raised by the oldest of the old.

"Thank you for coming." I try a smile, but her eyes refuse to meet mine.

She nods once. "You're welcome. See you tomorrow."

It isn't much of a goodbye before she's disappearing through the door. I watch her go with concern wrinkling my brow.

How had her one question and my response turned into this? Our easy, fun conversation had become serious in the span of two seconds.

Another puzzle to unravel.

Another story to be told.

CONFESSION 10
Sometimes, in the face of fear, you've just got to fake it.

The year was 1812. Europe was in shambles, Napoleon Bonaparte blazed a fiery trail across half of the continent, and England was embroiled in a second war with the United States.

Vampires, determined to remain neutral during the conflict, chose to keep to themselves, govern their people, and avoid the war at all costs. In the midst of this tumultuous time, a new Family emerged, larger and stronger than the oldest of covens.

They established themselves as the Medici Family, led by Paulo Medici (born 1487 AD) and his coven brother Luca Medici (date of birth unknown).

In August 1812, a contingent of 300 Medici vampires attacked the city of Potenza, killing all but a select few of its inhabitants. The exact toll remains unconfirmed.

The Medicis were pushed back by the Diavolo Family, reestablishing itself as the dominant coven in southern Italy (formerly known as the Kingdom of Sicily). Several weeks passed with few sightings of the Medici coven.

On September 3, an army of over 1000 attacked Perugia in central Italy, decimating the city and slaughtering every citizen.

I pause my reading and look up when the door to Father's study opens. Simon hovers in the doorway, his eyes wide and frantic. Even from across the room, I can sense his anxiety. Something is amiss.

After a morning spent tending to Chancelot and checking on the new litter of kittens in the stable, I'd found myself ransacking Father's collection in search of the historical accounts of the war. If Lord Halifax was one thing, he was meticulous in his record keeping. Curled up on the couch next to the fire, I immersed myself in discovering any and all information I could about the war with the Medicis.

So far, I hadn't learned anything outside of what I already knew.

"What's wrong?" I ask, frowning.

"The—uh—I," he stammers, and then swallows hard and motions over his shoulder vaguely.

I slide the large book off my lap and onto the cushion beside me, and then climb to my feet. He backs out of the room as I cross it, continuing to gesture for me to follow. He leads me from one side of the house to the other, up the stairs, and into the common room on the second floor near the sleeping quarters.

The television is already on when we enter the room, and after a quick scan that confirms all the Dilecta are present, my gaze immediately snags on images flashing across the screen.

"There has reportedly been a vampire attack at the Christian Jones concert in Tokyo, Japan." An aerial view of the concert hall, illuminated by spotlights, and surrounded by the flashing lights of dozens of emergency vehicles. "According to reports, vampires entered the concert hall along with the humans. Shortly before the intermission, the attack began. Information is still flooding in as emergency crews take in the situation. So far, we're estimating nearly one hundred fatalities." Camera refocuses on the done up blonde behind the anchor station. "No word yet from the Nakamura Family—"

Laura shuts the television off and everyone sits frozen. I stare at the black screen sightlessly, desperately, frantically, trying to wrap my brain around what I'd just seen.

What? What was that? An attack? *The* attack? The Medicis' attack? My heart pounds and nausea climbs my throat.

Yui is pale and trembling, bordering on hysterical. "They don't answer when I call. I've already tried five times."

Five times? Holy shiitake mushrooms!

A glance around the room reveals that everyone is teetering on the knife's edge of hysteria. Eyes are wide, hands fidget, mouths are pinched. And all their attention is focused on me, as if *I* am the one with the answers.

"So…um…many of your Family remained behind, right?" I ask, a little uncertain. Yui nods, tears glistening in her eyes. "All right, someone should have answered by now. If it's dark enough that the other vampires can attack, yours should be awake." I meet her panicky gaze. "Try calling one more time."

She gives a short nod, and as she steps off to the side to call someone back home, I turn toward Laura.

"Anything from your Family?" I ask.

"Not yet." She shakes her head. "It's not sundown in Georgia for another couple hours."

My own panic is starting to rise. I clench my fists and give myself a quick shake, trying to relax my tense shoulders. This is bad, really bad. Alessandro had warned days ago of an attack. Why had we let our guard down? Why had the *Heads*?

Yui lowers the phone, her lip quivering. "Still no answer."

I nod, almost to myself. What in the seven continents is going on? What are we supposed to do? There's still *hours* left until the Heads wake up.

Don't panic. Don't panic. Don't panic.

"Turn the telly back on," Simon snaps. "We've got to know what's going on."

Laura hits the power button on the remote still gripped in her hand. The same anchor appears, and the headline claims multiple attacks.

"France, Germany, Japan, Italy," I read, and bile rises in my throat. In the short time we had the television off, the Medicis attacked the other countries. "They're taking out your homes." I turn and scan the terrified faces of the others. "What is going on? Have any of you been able to get in touch with your Families?"

Everyone shakes their heads, and for the first time, I notice the cell phones clutched in their hands.

On the television, there is chaos in the streets, humans demanding answers, calling for vampire blood—figuratively, of course—for retribution, for justice. The death count creeps higher as the details continue to roll in, and the ticker at the bottom of the screen proclaims close to four hundred innocents.

"They've started a war," I whisper with dawning horror. "That's what this was always about." The book I'd just read is still fresh in my mind, and the details are frighteningly similar to what I'm seeing now.

What do we do? We have at least four hours before we can justify waking the Heads. What would Father do in this situation? I think for a moment, my eyes never leaving the scene before me. He'd pacify the people. Yes. And he'd promise them we'd find out the truth and give them answers.

But none of us *know* the truth. The only one who does is currently asleep in the catacombs.

And then another voice joins the indecision. It's firm, almost chastising. And like a switch being flipped, or a lightbulb blipping on, an idea strikes.

We, the Dilecta, our coven's greatest asset, their link to the human world, will stand as a united front against the Medici coven. When the news stations come calling, and the journalists are banging on the front gates, we'll meet them head on.

"Guys. Hey!" I draw their attention. "We're the vampires' only line of defense." My gaze sweeps around the room, touching on each face. "We need to represent our Families. Out there. Stand firm, just as our Heads would."

Laura nods, albeit hesitantly. "You're right. You're totally right."

"We are children," Stefani argues, her accent heavier from emotion. "What can we do against an entire world? They are pissed off, no? We are facing an inquisition, Halifax. This will end very ugly."

"What do you suggest we do then?" Laura demands and jabs a finger toward the screen. "You want us to just sit by and watch them burn the world down?"

"Of course not," the Duchamp scoffs. "But we are insane to think that we can change the world's opinion. The Medici are doing a fine job destroying any credibility we have. This will be ugly, American. Trust me. This will not go as you have planned."

91

"Then we do nothing," Natalia tosses out. "We stay quiet until the Heads can be woken. Our interference in this will only make things worse."

I'm silent while Laura, Stefani, and Natalia debate back and forth. None of them are willing to concede, nor compromise, and their voices rise as the tension grows. Peter and Simon are focused entirely on their phones, their fingers flying across the keyboards as they send text after text. A sense of desperation can be glimpsed on their faces with each passing moment of silence and lack of response.

We're stuck. Like quick sand in a South American jungle. Or double-sided sticky tape.

The sun is at its zenith. We *cannot* wake the Heads. Not for any reason.

"Danika."

Laura's voice drags me from my thoughts, and I blink a few times, bringing her into focus.

"What do we do?" she asks, and with a quick glance at the other two girls, I shove a hand through my hair, facing her head on, steady, unyielding.

"I've already said my bit," I reply. "If we cower now, we'll always cower. And you know, I think it's exactly what they're expecting us to do." I raise my eyebrows. "We have nothing to hide; we're not involved in these attacks. We need to let the world know where we stand. We need to condemn the Medicis' actions."

"And you think we can accomplish that by talking to the press?" Simon asks, and I look over to find his gaze fixed solely on me, his phone tucked into his lap.

"I do. I really do."

"So...where do we start?" Natalia climbs to her feet, rotating her shoulders and rolling her head to loosen her neck.

I scan each of them critically. "First," I attempt a smile, "we change."

The six others depart the common area for their rooms to shower and change their clothes. In less than an hour, we'll be presenting ourselves to the local press on a silver platter.

I find myself in my room, stripped down to my skivvies, before reality comes crashing home with a terrifying jolt.

Outside my gilded cage—my perfect world of luxury and comfort—people are dying. *Hundreds!* Vampires are slaughtering them just as they did two hundred years before. And I'm frightened. More frightened than I've ever been. More than coyotes, dance clubs, and Medicis kidnapping me. More frightened than living the rest of my life alone, a fragile human. More than dying, more than being abandoned again.

But I guess this is a different fear, isn't it? It's not intangible, deep seated, buried within my delicate, human heart.

It's solid.

Real.

Very, *very* real.

Suddenly, the monster under the bed has a face, has a name. And it brings blood and chaos and violence. Death. The ending of life. The stealing of one's precious existence.

Tears rise, spill over, and trickle down my cheeks. My entire body has frozen. What do I say to the press? How do I convince them that the Families are innocent? That they still seek peace and an alliance?

Father. Mother. Help me.

Once, when I was younger, a gang of undead, not affiliated with one of the Seven, had attacked a family of humans in England. Justice was swiftly executed by Lord Broadhurst. Hours didn't stretch between the attack and his statement and actions. They were immediate.

I remember Father explaining that a Lord's duty was to protect his people, first and foremost, followed by the humans around him. By responding instantly to the attack, the Broadhurst Head had claimed responsibility for the undeads' actions while at the same time, assuring every one of his lack of involvement.

In essence, he had distanced himself from those rogue vampires.

I know that if Father, or any of the other Heads, were awake at this moment, they would do what we're preparing to do. They'd stand before the press in their Sunday best and promise justice.

A delicate pink, women's suit is spread across the bed with a white blouse and elegant, shimmery pink heels to match.

It's definitely not my style—more Mother's than anything—but it'll suffice.

I drag myself from my anxious stupor and dress quickly. The blazer is snug against my ribcage, forming to it like a chic, second skin. With trembling fingers, I fasten the buttons and then smooth my hands down the front. Next, the shoes.

I drop down onto the stool in front of the vanity, brush my hair with languid movements, and paw through the small box to the left of the mirror, containing a handful of bobby pins and hair ties.

Snagging out as many pins as I can, I set to work giving myself an approximation of the impeccable chignon Mother prefers. By the time I'm done, it's not nearly as perfect as hers, but it'll work for the interviews.

I stand, adjust my jacket with a jerk, snatch my phone, and hurry from the room to meet the others in the foyer.

Everyone else is gathered when I make it to the doors, and we appraise one another with admiring eyes. We look smart, sophisticated. Perfect representatives of the Families.

Benice appears, his face grim. "There are news vans near the gates."

I meet his concerned gaze. "Yes, thank you."

"Want me to send them away?"

I attempt a smile at his question, but it falls flat. Instead, I shake my head. "Please allow them entrance as far as the main drive. No further. Barricade it if you have to. They can be vultures when it comes to getting their story."

With a nod, he departs, shouting for several of the hovering, human bodyguards to follow him.

Left alone with the other Dilectas, I straighten my blazer—though it doesn't need fixing—and try and appear confident.

"So—um—once they come in and everything is staged, who's going to be the one to talk?" I ask. Surprise flits across their faces, and then eyes bounce around.

Laura is the first to speak. "I thought it was already decided that you'd do it."

"Me?" I stab a finger into my chest, nausea roiling. "Why me?"

94

"Is your house, no?" Stefani motions toward me, and Simon and Natalia nod in agreement. "And your idea."

"Yui?" Laura shoots the petite Nakamura a pointed look.

"Yes. You do it," comes the quiet response.

But I don't *want* to do it.

I keep that thought to myself. I doubt they'd appreciate me whining like a small child.

Silence descends, no one willing to volunteer to speak on the Families behalf, thus forcing me to be their spokesperson, and I swallow down the fear threatening to overwhelm me. Turning toward the front doors, I clasp my hands at my waist and await Benice's arrival with news that the metaphorical stage has been set.

As soon as he appears, my heart skips a beat and my hands grow clammy. Ten bodyguards are in tow, their faces grim in imitation of his, and they immediately surround us.

"Ready, Miss Danika?" he asks.

No. I'm not. Not at all.

"Yes," I manage.

We proceed through the doors, down the wide stairs, and up the asphalt drive toward where the early afternoon sun reflects off of dozens of news media vans. I can see the cameras are set, the men or women manning them already in place, fingers poised over the correct button.

It's the longest quarter mile I've ever experienced. Longer than the Tour de France, than the Boston Marathon. Longer, even, than the eight-hour flight to England I took when I was seven.

Our party reaches the collection of eager vultures, their beady eyes observing us with anticipation and a hunger that is only rivaled by the desert animals at the peak of summer.

Cameras flash, shutters *click*, and a fog descends over me. On autopilot and unaware of the words coming from my mouth, I stand firm before the salivating masses, the scavengers who seek to pick our bones clean. I stare down the anger, the prejudices, the malicious thirst for humanity's justice.

I do not cower.

I do not bow.

I am a Halifax.

CONFESSION 11
I wish I'd never heard the word Dilecta.

It's nearing ten in the evening, and the Heads have gone, taking with them their Dilecta and security teams. Angry is such an insignificant word to describe their reaction to the news of the Medici coven's assault on the world. Murderous might be more accurate. Or homicidal. I like that one much better.

And Alessandro? He vanished as soon as everyone emerged to find us waiting outside the catacombs' great doors. Not a word had passed his lips, and not a single emotion crossed his face. No twitch of an eye, no pursing lips. No anger to rival the Seven's. Nothing. He'd simply strode away, and later we'd heard that he'd disappeared into the desert.

Curious.

For Father, ever the astute, it hadn't gone unnoticed.

The Heads' insight into the workings of the Medici coven had vanished just as quickly as it'd appeared, and we were no wiser than we'd been prior to the attack. *I told you so* wouldn't go over easy with the ancient ones, so I kept my thoughts to myself.

I watch Lord Halifax while he watches the news. My short interview has been playing nonstop on every channel since this afternoon. Everyone is trying to dissect it and break it apart, to find any hidden messages buried within.

As if I'm trying to encourage more attacks. Or something ridiculous like that.

A clip of it begins again and I glance at the television. In it, I'm flanked by the other Dilecta, surrounded by an army of bodyguards, and I appear just as I'd intended in the pink suit—classy and businesslike. Tiny wisps of hair have escaped the chignon to frame my face, giving me a gentle look, and the smidgen of makeup I'd applied in a hurry accentuate my features just enough without overwhelming.

"Good afternoon," I greet, my voice clear and concise. "I am Danika Halifax. My companions and I," I motion to the six others behind me, "are here as representatives of the governing Seven." I clear my throat and sweep a firm, unwavering gaze around. "Earlier today, there were vampire attacks orchestrated in Japan, Germany, Italy, France, and England. I want to assure everyone that the governing Seven have nothing to do with these attacks, and we are doing everything within our power to find those responsible and carry out a swift and merciless justice. Our Families will work with local law enforcement agencies, Interpol, and all foreign governments to get to the bottom of this. Thank you."

I make to step away from the press, but a journalist in a smart suit and a comb over to rival my old sophomore Spanish teacher shoots forward, mike outstretched.

"Miss Halifax," his voice oozes false charisma. "Where are the vampire Lords right now? Why aren't they present?"

I give him my best *you're kidding* look. "They're sleeping, sir. The sun is still high."

Another steps forward. A woman in slacks and a polo shirt. "Why have they all gathered here at the Halifaxs' orchard?"

"For the alliance talks," I supply. "It's done every ten years to reaffirm the pact between the Families." I bow my head once, low and respectful. "Thank you for coming."

A cacophony of overlapping voices assaults our small group, and Benice steps forward with a raised hand.

"No more questions, please," he instructs, a thin smile stretching his dark face. "Any further information will be relayed once the Heads have awoken."

Father turns the television off before the scene of us being escorted back toward the manor. His silver eyes shift to mine and he sighs visibly.

"Oh my wonderful child," he breathes, wrapping an arm around me and pulling me in close. "I am so proud of you." A kiss to my forehead. "You did a marvelous job. I didn't get a chance to tell you. Thank you, daughter, for your quick action."

"I only did what you would have done." I can feel the tension clinging to Father, and I seek the only way I know how to diffuse it. With dumb humor. "Though I must tell you, My Lord. I'm dying, and the doctor says it's quite serious."

The same conversation. Same method of aggravating him. But also to bring a smile to his lips.

His laugh is short, soft, dry. "If the doctor says you're dying, it *must* be serious. What is it you have?"

"Anthropophobia."

"Ah." Another soft chuckle escapes. "A fear of people. Personally, I would say that all vampires have anthropophobia since it's more accurately, a fear of humans."

The tension has seeped from him, and I snuggle in closer. "Yes, Father."

After an entire evening in which I felt as if I were in the Inquisition, it is a blessed relief to finally have some peace. Who knew that my interview, brief as it was, would have brought down a storm of unprecedented proportions.

First was the conference call from the U.S. President with all Heads present. Then it was followed by a video call from the French Prime Minister, and Lord Duchamp and his cohorts had departed in a flurry of French profanity and kisses. The call from England's Prime Minister was a loud, boisterous affair, and the Broadhurst crowd departed.

Thus continued the phone calls and exits of the other six Heads until they had all departed for their prospective countries, damage control in full effect. None of the vamps who'd been left behind while their Lords were at the Alliance gathering had been heard from in the last day, and concern could be seen on everyone's faces.

As there are hundreds of coven members who hadn't accompanied their Heads, the silence is unnerving.

Something untoward had happened, and we all knew it.

The last to leave had been the Campbell Family. Laura promised to call when they made it home, so even now, I keep my phone clutched in my hand.

Before my eyes, Father begins to deflate, the tightly wound anxiety and anger bleeding from him. I snuggle in closer, providing what comfort I can.

"The world is furious," he says softly, rubbing his eyes with his free hand. "Two hundred years of peace destroyed in one day."

I don't know how to respond so I remain quiet.

"Conrad has been meeting with the Phoenix city council and the Mayor for several weeks in hopes of reaffirming our own peace agreements," he continues. "And now, all of that has been reduced to nothing. The trust we've established, the relationships we've built, *gone*."

A memory surfaces: Conrad departing late at night with a security team in tow.

So *that* had been where he was going. Makes sense now.

Lord Halifax falls silent, withdrawing into his thoughts. Left to my own, I gaze at his blood red tie with its Windsor knot level with my eyes and worry my bottom lip. Father is normally calm and collected in high-stress situations, so I'm unnerved at seeing him this rattled, this uncertain, this *lost*. He's worked tirelessly for two hundred years to maintain a peaceful coexistence between the two species—species? Is that the right word?—and now all of his hard work has vanished in the blink of an eye.

I don't know the right words to say to him. I doubt anyone does. The Heads may be frustrating and old fashioned, stuck on tradition and have a moral sense that irritates the best of us, but they're also loyal, honest, and fiercely protective of their Families.

Man, what a mess.

We sit in silence for what feels like hours, only broken by the occasional pop or hiss from the low fire in the hearth, but it isn't companionable, or easy. It is strained, filled with so many unspoken fears that it's nearly suffocating.

Finally, Father shifts, heaving a sigh. "I don't think it'd be wise to send you back to school at the start of the final term."

Surprised, I sit up. "Why?"

"You may not be a vampire, Danika," he says, his silver eyes sad, "but you're still a Halifax, and the humans are out for blood right now. They'll find any reason and opportunity to strike at me, at *all* of us." He shakes his head, almost to himself. "Definitely not safe."

"But what am I supposed to do in the meantime?" I can feel frustration rising. "What about school?"

"You'll meet with tutors here, at the orchard."

"Father—"

"Danika," he sighs, but I jerk to my feet. The stress of today and the uncertainty of tomorrow is finally weighing on me.

"Then why don't you just turn me?" I already know his answer, can feel it coming from a mile away.

"We're not discussing this." His voice is barely above a whisper. "Not right now."

It's the same, age-old argument. The one that leaves us furious and ignoring one another for days afterwards.

I know this isn't the right time. I *know* Father's in chaos, just like the rest of the world, but the fear and loneliness I feel daily is suddenly clawing upward, threatening to drown me. I don't want to be left alone during the day to face my fellow humans' ire. I don't want to be the one to stand firm while my family sleeps. I want to *be* with them. I want to fight *with* them.

I'm terrified.

And I can't do it on my own.

But Father doesn't see that. If he does, he's chosen to ignore it. In that moment, something becomes clear. Some*thing* clicks into place. And man is it painful. Heart-wrenchingly painful.

"What's a Dilecta?" I ask softly, swallowing hard. Surprise flickers through his eyes before it's quickly concealed behind his perpetual, stoic mask.

"Why do you ask?"

"I heard it recently in reference to me. And Laura Campbell says that Lord Campbell calls her that all the time."

"It's Latin."

His simple response hurts. I can't say why; it just does.

100

"Beloved," I say. "Loved. Cherished." I stand stiffly in front of him, meeting his piercing, unwavering stare head on. "What does it mean? Why do I feel that it's more of a title than an endearment?"

"Danika—"

"No, Father." I stamp my foot like a two-year-old. Yes, really. Not my best moment, I'll admit. "No more lies. No more evasive answers. Give me the reason why you won't change me because if there was ever a time to do it, it'd be now."

He leans forward, braces his elbows on his knees, and drops his head into his hands. "I was going to wait until you'd finished this school year."

I'm silent, holding my breath.

"Dilecta means Beloved," he begins, "and it's a term we've used for the past few Dormiam." He slouches back into the cushions and gives his tie a few jerks, loosening it. "Are you certain you want to know this?" When I don't respond, he sighs. "Very well. Every couple hundred years, the vampires have to go beneath ground, to essentially *hibernate*—Dormiam. During that time, a human, a chosen Dilecta, is tasked with overseeing and protecting the Family line—"

"For how long," I interrupt.

"Five years."

Five years? I feel like I've been punched. Or kicked in the gut. Whichever.

"Why?" My hands twist together at my waist. "Why do you need Dormiam?"

"It's physically necessary to our bodies." He crosses his arms, as if annoyed at needing to explain this to me. "We spend centuries weakening our bodies, exposing ourselves to sunlight and other harmful elements. This allow us to rebuild and cleanse. The earth acts as a kind of cocoon."

"How was I...how are your Dilectas chosen?" I can barely get the question out.

"They're brought in at birth—usually rescued from orphanages or the streets—and raised within the coven." He lifts his gaze to mine. "It's to garner the strongest loyalties."

I should tell him to stop, that I don't want to hear another word. But I can't. It's like watching a bad accident happen and being unable, or unwilling, to look away. You've just got to know how it ends.

"Every Dilecta goes through specialized training, which for you, is to begin this summer," he continues. "You'll be taught how to manage the estates, how to communicate effectively with the humans you'll be in contact with during Dormiam, and how to keep the Family secure in case of emergencies."

My life begins playing backward from this moment. Every physical training session with Conrad and my bodyguards. Every discussion with Mother about proper attire and presentation of oneself during social occasions. The instances when Father allowed me to join him in discussion with ambassadors and high-ranking government officials, including the Heads. His willingness to allow me to argue *for* Alessandro, to fight for him and protect him against the governing Seven. His agreement that I should fulfill my debt.

That's it. I don't want to hear any more. I'm done.

But I can't get the words past my lips. They're stuck, right there. So close.

"This is why I cannot change you, Danika." His eyes are trying to convey something, but I can't tell what. "You must be here to secure our line during Dormiam. It is too late to seek any other options."

Until this moment, I have never felt so alone, so abandoned. Betrayed. It hurts. So much I can barely breathe. It feels as if my heart is being ripped from my chest. My throat closes, my lip quivers, and with eyes swimming with tears, I look away from the silver gaze I'd loved above all else.

The man I've cherished, the father I've always loved, who'd rescued me and promised me the stars and the universes beyond, has dealt a devastating blow, sweeping my feet right out from beneath me.

I sense him rise, and when he reaches out for me, I take a step back, away from his comforting embrace. He says something, but I don't understand. As if in a trance, I turn my back and walk to the door. I don't spare him a backward glance, a parting comment, a reassuring smile.

I just leave.

102

My steps take me through the manor, up the stairs, and deposit me in my room before I realize where I've gone. If anyone has spoken to me on the way, I can't recall. I'm deaf and blind to everything but my own thoughts.

A Dilecta is an insurance policy the vampires have taken out. We're the assurance that their lines will be protected, their estates maintained and assets grown. Our lives are for one purpose only, and everything we've ever know—or thought we knew—the luxury, the love, the comfort and patience, it's all a lie.

We're slaves. Nothing more.

The side table lamp is on and the sheets are down, but the room that I'd once thought was the perfect escape is now a silk-wrapped prison. The luxuries I'd viewed as my parents giving in to my incessant nagging could now be seen as nothing more than pacification of their Dilecta.

Happy wife, happy life. But in my case…happy slave and all that.

I survey my surroundings and fight down the sour bile creeping up my throat, making my eyes water. Have the soft, rose hues, delicate cream furniture, and king-size bed always been so ostentatious? The perfume from the flowers in the vase on the coffee table is smothering, overly sweet. It's too much.

Dinner rises, and spinning on my heel, I hurtle myself toward the bathroom. I barely make it in time. Hunched over the toilet, gripping the porcelain, white knuckled, I sob and wretch.

I sob out the betrayal and heartache, wretch out the rich dinner of steak and shrimp. I sob out the loneliness and grief, wretch out the dessert of delectable macarons.

The minutes turn to hours.

My stomach has long quieted, but the tears continue to trickle down my cheeks. The pain of my family's lies has faded, and the longing—the desire I'd once carried close to my heart—to become a vampire, has withered. Anger now simmers beneath the surface. A determination.

They want a Dilecta. That's what they'll get. I'll give them the next six years of my life. I'll give them security. I'll give them hope. I'll protect them, fight for them, and keep their estates running.

103

However, I am a Halifax *no more*.

I should have known. Vampires don't do anything unless it benefits them.

"My dashing Sir Chancelot," I croon, rubbing a hand down his course hair, "you are looking mighty fine this beautiful Wednesday morning."

He nabs the proffered apple from my hand and doesn't respond.

"Did you sleep well? It was pretty cold last night, wasn't it?"

Again, silence.

"Another school day."

He finishes chomping the fruit and tosses his head.

"I'll be back to see you when I get home." I give him another pat. "Behave today and we'll go for a ride. I know it's been a while since our last one. I'm sorry. I've been on lockdown since the coyote incident. I promise we'll get out today."

With a parting kiss to his furry forehead, I leave the barn, skirt around the side of the house, and climb into the waiting SUV. As agreed, the only way I'm allowed to attend school is with a bevy of bodyguards to shadow my every movement. At first it was annoying, but after two weeks, I'm used to it.

So far, school hasn't been fun, and I almost—*almost*—regret returning. As of yesterday, I've had a total of one milkshake, two frozen lemon Icees, and a 44oz soda tossed in my face. It's only Hump Day in my second week back following Spring Break. My fellow classmates have been plenty busy.

I guess it's to be expected. I *am* the former daughter of a vampire coven (read the fine print).

Father has tried to explain, Mother has tried to pacify, and Conrad has tried to apologize, but I haven't spoken one word to any of them since that night. It's been three weeks. A very long three weeks at that.

What am I supposed to say? Something fun and witty? Something bitter and angry? Should I simply forgive them? Pretend that my entire life hasn't been a lie?

I've been raised with one purpose in mind, and I'm having a difficult time accepting that. My family, everyone here at the orchard, can no longer conceal the expectant gleam in their eyes. The air is almost saturated with their combined feelings of relief and anticipation now that I know. I guess they no longer need to pretend.

Desperate to flee the expectations of a Dilecta—which I was coming to understand were beyond my capacity at the moment—and monotonous routine of day-to-day orchard procedures, I'd returned to school at the end of Spring Break. Father argued, of course, as did Mother. But I remained firm. As a result, two human bodyguards accompany me to school each day, and it's never the same two. Today, is no exception. A man and woman, clad in black suits, sporting sunglasses and cold expressions, are the latest and greatest babysitters. Neither of them pays me any attention during the drive, and I turn my attention out of the window as we take the freeway on-ramp.

Mother and Father's betrayal hit hard. Conrad's…well, his was debilitating. For the longest time, he had been my best friend and confidant, more than a brother, more than a friend. He'd been the sun, the moon, and the stars. The strongest, bravest vampire I knew, who I desperately wanted to be like.

I have never seen him so torn, so broken, as when he'd come to me begging for forgiveness.

But I couldn't give it.

Because *I'd* been broken. Broken beyond repair. I feel isolated, alone. Swimming upstream, buffeted by rocks and a current that's ripping and shredding my body. How does one walk away from that? How do they pick up the pieces of their life after that kind of hurt?

"You'll always be my little sister," Conrad had said, and his words had twisted the knife deeper into my heart.

But I wasn't. Not really. I never had been. I was a tool, a method of survival.

The gates of the school come into view, putting an end to my musings. The SUV pulls into an empty spot near the back of the parking lot, and after snagging my backpack, I climb out.

The two bodyguards join me, and we begin the short trek to the back doors. Up ahead, several students cluster around the tail end of a few vehicles. I keep my head down, intending to edge around them, but unease clenches my gut when they all step into my path and force me to come up short. My companions shift in closer, their eyes alert beneath the black shades.

Smack! An egg smashes into my forehead. The slimy, raw white slips down my eyebrow, clings to my lashes, and continues a snail trail down my cheek. Another one hits, and I instinctively flinch. And then another. And another.

By the time they're done, I count two dozen eggs smeared on my face and clothing with shells embedded in my hair. A few areas sting from the impact. I'm positive that tiny cuts litter my cheeks.

The bell rings and the students race away, whooping and laughing. Animals.

Alone with just my companions, who also wear half a dozen eggs, I give them a scowl.

"You guys are useless," I mutter, reaching up and wiping a chunk of yolk and shell from my hair.

"We're sorry, miss," the woman, Remi, apologizes. "But it's not technically—"

"Yeah, yeah, yeah." I wave away her excuse. I know they can't draw their weapons on kids, even if they're throwing eggs. *Especially* if they're just throwing eggs. "They got inventive this time. Guess they got tired of cold drinks."

"Miss Danika." The man, Howard, steps forward.

"What?" I give him another thunderous look.

"Let's get you inside to clean up," he says and motions toward the doors.

I sigh. Luckily, I brought a change of clothes with me. I've taken to doing that since the whole drink-in-the-face thing started.

Did I mention that tensions between humans and vampires are at an all-time high? Society is demanding justice *and* answers, and the Heads are unable to give them. *Either* of them. No justice. No answers.

The Medici coven has all but vanished over the last two weeks.

The death count was staggering. Somewhere around a thousand. Nothing the Lords have done—the appeasement, the assurances, the investigations of their own—have managed to calm the masses and re-ascertain the relationship between the two peoples.

Peace is gone.

Not even the governing Seven were left untouched by the violence. Their covens were slaughtered during the attack—the reason no one was able to contact them during those first twenty-four hours—and not a single vampire was spared when the Medicis descended on their primary estates. Only those on the outskirts, the smaller manors and Family domains, were unscathed.

Laura, my one and only friend in this world of betrayal and chaos, says that things are much the same on her side of the country as well. Maybe worse. One of Campbell estates lucky enough to escape the Medicis' clutches had been burned to the ground while its inhabitants slept.

The world is crumbling.

We head for the gym and the locker room where I'll shower and change, and hope that I make it to my first class before the end bell.

***

W-what is this? Where am I? It's dark, cramped, and cold. I hurt everywhere. My head is pounding; my eyes won't open. Is that…is that *blood* I feel? Movement sends sharp pains through my ribs and right leg, and I whimper softly.

What's going on?

108

I frantically try to recall the events leading up to now. It's fuzzy, in and out of focus. I remember that the school day had ended; Howard, Remi, and I started back home. And then...

The rest is vague.

A truck slamming into my side of the vehicle. The sound of crunching metal, shattering glass, a scream, and then pain.

Oh the pain.

Followed by nothing.

I can feel the hum of an engine beneath me, the rhythmic *thump* of tires on an overpass, an occasional bump that jostles my sore body.

I'm in a trunk. I have a moment of disorientation, and then it's replaced by fear. *Why* am I in a trunk? Whose is it, and where are they taking me? What happened to Remi and Howard? Are they all right? The questions fly through my brain. But I'm no closer to answering them than I was when I awoke minutes—or has it been an hour?—ago.

I try not to think about the pain, but each breath is excruciating, every throb of my head drags me a little closer to oblivion. My throat constricts in fear. Tears burn beneath my lids.

Unconsciousness looms, a respite from the agony, terror, and confusion, and I welcome it with open arms.

When I next surface, the vehicle is slowing. My body hurts even worse, as if the muscles are weakening and the cold is settling in. Again, I can't open my eyes, and I'm mildly aware that my face is numb. I try to move my lips, to form any kind of a word, even a simple plea, but they're split and crusted in what I can only assume is more blood.

I drift off again, sucked back into nothingness.

***

If I ever were to make a list of the rudest awakenings known to man, having a bucket of icy water thrown in my face would have, at least, made the top five—perhaps even the top three.

I gasp at the shock of cold and then groan. My lids flicker up, and with bleary vision, I lift my head and look around. I don't recognize where I am. Not the smell of musty earth that tickles my nose. Not the bright spotlights that are focused on the chair I'm tied down to. Not the—Wait! I'm *tied* to a *chair*.

That realization sends my heart hammering against my ribs, and I give a feeble jerk against the bindings. My body screams in response, and biting my swollen lip—which I immediately regret after a sharp sting accompanies it—I allow my head to fall back against the hard wood of the chair.

Just beyond the bright lights, several people move and shift in the shadows. My attention snags on them and my heart skips a beat.

As they glide into the light, I shrink back into the chair, mewling as another jolt of fear shoots through me. These large, imposing men in black ski masks are far from innocent. They're dangerous. Sweet baby Jesus.

"Get the camera ready," one of them orders, and when two of the five men rush to comply, I realize *this* guy is in charge.

A tripod is positioned several feet away, and a handheld camera is clicked into place with its black, all-seeing eye focused on me.

I cower further, trying to disappear into my uniform blazer. I don't want to be on camera. I don't want my family to see me this way. I'm not dumb; I know how this is going to end. They'll record me saying some scripted piece, then they'll abuse me to send some kind of a message. If I'm lucky, they'll kill me afterward.

Darkness presses the outside of my vision, and the comforting embrace of unconsciousness looms, welcoming, companionable, offering solace and relief once more. But I blink against it, almost desperate to remain aware, to keep cognizant of the happenings around me.

It drags me under anyway.

"Hello, Halifax." A deep baritone.

My eyes fly open, and I find myself face-to-face with a black ski mask and blue eyes.

"It's so nice of you to join us." The man straightens, angling his body slightly toward the camera and the hovering men. "And welcome, viewers." He motions to me. "Let me

110

introduce Danika Halifax to those of you who don't know her—the Halifax Daywalker."

What? Daywalker?

He continues, unaware of my confusion. "Not long ago, we heard of a disturbing change to the vampires' abilities. Daywalking." He circles around me, keeping his focus on the camera. "Now, the night is no longer good enough for them, my friends. They are taking over *our* time."

I turn my head to track his progress, my eyes wide and words frozen in my throat. What is he doing? Where is he going with this?

"What we saw two weeks ago is only the beginning, people." His voice is grim, hard. "Now that they can walk among us, even during the day, we'll never be free. Our children will *never* be safe. We must eradicate them before they slaughter any more of us. They can never be allowed to create monsters," he flings an arm toward me, "such as *this*."

"Are you crazy?" I choke, the words finally coming to me. "I'm *human*."

He moves with lightning speed, yanking a stake from his pocket and pressing it to my throat. "Do you see? Do you see, my friends? How they manipulate? How they lie?"

"Look at my wounds!" I wheeze, trying to meet his eyes. "The blood? Vampires don't bleed. They don't injure."

His eyes are glacier blue, unyielding, when they finally flick to mine. "Evolution."

"You're insane." My throat constricts with fear. "Utterly insane."

He spins back toward the camera. "Vampires are great trackers—the very best—which is why I have to keep my face covered. They'll find me; they'll find my family. Once we take one of their own, they'll seek to repay *us*." He jabs a thumb into his chest. "That's what they do."

If I wasn't so close to another bout of unconsciousness, I might have laughed at his statement; he has *no* idea.

My head pounds, my ribs scream in agony at being roughed up by course rope, wrapping me to a chair, and my leg is going numb. Already, I can't feel my toes. All I want to do is sleep. Maybe just a quick nap? They won't notice while he rambles on, right? I'll be really fast, I promise.

When my eyes drift shut and my chin sags to my chest, a sharp tap on my uninjured cheek has me lifting my head with a jerk.

"Oh no you don't," the man declares. "We're *live*, Halifax abomination. You're not allowed to sleep."

Live? My eyes dart to the camera. That means the coven could be seeing this right now. And any of the other covens as well. This is bad. This is *really* bad. Reality is hitting me, the fog lifting, one second at a time. Clarity is even more painful than the injuries.

"You have to let me go," I whisper, my voice barely a breath.

"What was that?"

I attempt to repeat myself, but the words are lodged in my throat again, fear spiking through me. These men are declaring war. Medici aside, the governing Seven won't take kindly to one of their Dilecta being killed. Especially not on camera.

My mouth opens—

Suddenly, it's chaos. Glass shatters, dark shapes dart among the shadows, and the sound of men screaming echoes through the warehouse.

I can't track what's happening. Dizziness swamps me every time I try.

The man beside me races out of the spotlight and is swallowed by the surrounding darkness. At the same time, the camera is knocked over by one of his comrades. The device dislodges from the tripod and skitters across the concrete, coming to rest near a black combat boot.

I slowly raise my eyes from the boot, taking in the jeans, faded t-shirt, and finally the familiar face of a Medici vampire.

"You!" I breathe, shrinking back against the chair.

He bends down, picks up the camera, and then straightens, a smile twisting up one side of his mouth.

"Good to see you again, Danika." He steps forward, into the lights.

"I thought Alessandro killed you," I gasp. "You and your friend. When you tried to kidnap Laura and me."

112

He chuckles, his dark eyes taking in my appearance in one sweep. "You look…well."

"Screw you."

Probably not best to bait a vampire, but lucidity has returned with a vengeance, and the spike of adrenaline has caused much of my pain to fade.

He laughs outright. "I'm relieved to see your fire hasn't been extinguished since last we met. I do believe I still have bruises from my failed kidnapping attempt." As if to punctuate his remark, he rubs his lower back with his free hand.

And then, with a wink at me, he spins the camera around to face him.

"Hello, humans." He gives a ridiculous wave. "Mikey here, right hand of Lord Medici himself. I hope you've been enjoying the show. Sadly, this is where it ends." His dark eyes return to me, almost angry. But at what, I don't know. "Your message has been received, loud and clear." Eyes back to the camera. "Let the war commence."

As my heart leaps, he smashes the camera into the ground, obliterating it.

When he looks back up, his smile widens. "Ah, My Lord."

Nausea climbs my throat, as I turn my head to follow his gaze.

Alessandro Medici steps from the shadows.

CONFESSION 13

There are different heartbreaks, but nothing is as painful,
as gut-wrenching, as a family's betrayal.

The darkness has become my new best friend, my only solace in a world of betrayal and turmoil. There are no lies, no heartache. There's no pain and no confusion. No broken ribs or cracked femurs. My body is whole, undamaged; my heart doesn't bleed. Friends are true, and family is loyal and honest.

I welcome the darkness, the reprieve from a reality I cannot handle—one I don't want to face—where tears are my only companion and the inexperienced passion once blossoming within me has withered and died like a flower plucked from its meadow.

In it, my dreams are sweet, my longings attained.

Alessandro Medici. That's all I'd wanted. Him. Dark eyes and crooked, secretive smiles. A promise of adventure and excitement. I wanted to know him—his secrets and past. I ached for it like I'd never ached for anything before. To be part of his world.

Now, I just want to hide. To succumb to unconsciousness and block out the world around me.

The whispers above me hint at my brokenness. They hint at the damage done, at the scars that now mar my face, at the faded brilliance of my blue eyes.

This room has become a prison, this bed, a cage. Much like my bedroom at the orchard, I cannot look around the luxurious apartment without seeing appeasement, without feeling as if I *should* be grateful. The bed is overly large, the carpet too plush; the bathroom where my caregiver carries me for baths is all pearl and silver, tiled and opulent.

Not fitting for a prisoner of war.

Alessandro comes every now and then. To check on my progress, he says. To see if I'm healing all right. The undead who's been assigned to my care always imparts the same information: I'm well; I'm healing fine; I haven't eaten much, but still, enough. And though I've awoken each time he's come, I don't want to see him and keep my eyes shut and the blankets over my head.

Today is no different.

Mei, a petite, Japanese vampire with no ties to the Nakamura coven—she was quick to inform me—sits beside my bed in an ostentatious armchair, reading from her favorite collection of nineteenth century poetry. The chair is grotesque with bear claw feet, red velvet cushions, and an ornately designed wooden frame. It's also polished to a high gleam and reflects the firelight from the hearth like a mirror. Every now and then, her hazel eyes flick up from the page to see if I'm listening, and she reaches out to adjust the covers, even though they don't need tending.

Alessandro enters, as usual, and then halts next to the bed. I can sense his dark, silent gaze, probing beneath the covers. Assessing me. Weighing me.

Several minutes pass in tense silence.

Then he yanks the blankets off.

"Enough!" he snaps, flinging the heavy comforter to the far end of the enormous bed. "You've wallowed long enough. It's time to rise and shine, little human."

The surprise dissipates as his words sink in, and then I crack open my lids, sit up, and shove my mass of dirty blonde hair out of my face.

"Screw you," I spit, my voice rough from prolonged bouts of intermingled crying and sleeping.

"It's been almost a month." He crosses his arms, scowling. "Grow up."

"*You* grow up!"

"So eloquent."

115

"I don't have to listen to you." I scoot halfway down the bed—as far as my splinted leg and healing ribs allows—snatch the blankets, and pull them back up and over my head. "Leave me alone."

There's a rustle followed by the sound of the door closing, and through a slit in the covers, I see that Mei has left.

My heart twists painfully. I don't want to be alone with him.

"Danika." His voice is softer, gentler than normal. "You and I need to have a talk."

"I don't want to talk to you," I choke, tears rising. "You're a liar, a murderer. A *monster*."

He sighs and the bed dips. "Yes. Once upon a time. But not anymore."

"Liar," I breathe.

"Believe what you will, Halifax."

There's a weight behind his words, something left unspoken that has me sliding the comforter down enough to peek at him.

He sits with his back to me, shoulders slumped, head bowed, hands in his lap. I've never seen him so dejected before, not even when he was imprisoned in the Halifax catacombs. But any compassion I may have felt for him is overshadowed by anger and bitterness.

I allow my eyes to close, seeking that comforting embrace of unconsciousness once more, blocking out his presence. Movement to retrieve the blankets resulted in a twinge in my leg I wasn't quite ready for, reminding me with painful clarity of everything that transpired a month before.

"I didn't attack the humans," he says, breaking the silence. When I don't respond, he heaves another sigh. "I had hoped you'd be on my side, Danika. You were once my champion against the Heads."

"My one regret," I mutter softly, but his super sensitive hearing picks it up anyway.

"You owe me a debt."

My eyes pop open and the shock is electrifying. "What?"

His head turns and our gazes meet. "I saved your life."

116

Tears spring up and spill forth, trickling over the bridge of my nose to land on the pillow. I stare at him in abject horror, rendered speechless. Did he...? Had he just...?

"I am sorry," he scans my face, his hard expression softening, "but I need you. I need the help only *you* can give. I need the support of the covens. That's something only a Dilecta can do."

Hearing that word, coming from him, is my undoing. The heartbreak that had been leaking silently now escapes in a sob. But it isn't a cry of weary acceptance.

It's a battle cry.

It's fury and resentment, the desire to inflict bodily harm.

I launch my upper body at him, clawing and punching, frantic to hurt him, to make him ache as I do. I want him to feel the agony that keeps me wrapped up in darkness, suffocating on despair.

He takes my assault without a word. He doesn't flinch, doesn't fight against me, doesn't defend himself.

I slap him across the face. Hard. His head whips to the side. Straightens. The fight leaves me as quickly as it'd come, and I sag against him, weeping. My chest heaves and my throat burns. My sore ribs strain with each ragged sob.

He hesitates for only a moment before gathering me close.

I don't want this. I don't want him. But against my will, my body sinks into his embrace, reveling in it while hungering for more. As I nestle into his neck, bunching his shirt in my fist, he cradles my head against him, his hand surprisingly gentle where it cups my cheek.

I know the tears aren't only about that night a month ago. It's everything. It's the betrayal of my family, the unwanted future that's been thrust upon me, the violence spreading across the world, the truths that keep unraveling.

And beside the anger and all the heartache, there's homesickness. I want my mother and father; I want my brother's steady guidance and unwavering strength; I want Chancelot and the open desert; I want sunsets that light up the entire sky, and sunrises that proclaim in exuberant colors of a beautiful, new day.

Eventually, the tears dry, leaving me bone tired, and I pull away. I can't meet his eyes, suddenly uncomfortable with my behavior. Instead, I turn and lay down, pulling the blankets over my head.

He doesn't say anything.

For a brief moment, I'm grateful. The bed shifts and then resettles, and without a word, he leaves. I close my eyes, releasing my breath in a soft sigh, and allow sleep to claim me, a tiny smile on my lips.

***

The fire has long gone out when I awake, and a chill has settled in the air. Dull sunlight streams through the crack between the heavy curtains. Dust particles dance in the beams. Other than the thin strips of natural light, there is no other illumination, and the cold room is dark and shadowed.

I sit up, glancing at the clock on the bedside table, and note the time. It's nearing dusk. Mei should be arriving soon with a tray of food.

It's been a week since the break down in front of Alessandro. A week since he held me as I fell apart. Neither of us have mentioned it. I continue to ignore his existence, and he continues to visit me nightly, without fail, like clockwork. He's even taken to reading to me from old books I've never heard of in a voice that sends my heart into a pitter pat.

We've abandoned the discussion about the Medici attacks around the world, though the accusations still sit heavy between us. I haven't forgotten what he's done, what he's started. Soon, I tell myself. Soon I'll ask; soon I'll get answers; soon he'll face his crimes.

The minutes pass and I observe the sun's gradual disappearance through the slit in the curtains. My stomach growls in anticipation. The food is so good here, wherever it is they're keeping me, that I've become greedy.

The door opens, the domed tray appears first, and then it's followed by the dark-eyed Lord Medici, wearing his signature, crooked grin.

118

"You're awake," he says as soon as his eyes alight on me. "I was worried I'd have to toss your covers again."

I scowl, and then flop back down and jerk the blankets over my head. I'm not about to admit how pleased I am that it was he who'd entered with the food.

"I didn't bring my book with me tonight, Danika. It's time we talked."

Yes. Tonight.

I push back the covers and sit up again. "Go ahead."

His smile melts, and he lowers the tray onto my lap. "Eat first. We can talk afterwards."

"No."

"Suit yourself." He straightens, lifting the dome from the plate. "I didn't kill those humans. Whatever you think of me, I'm not like that anymore." I hadn't been expecting that, and his gaze captures mine, locking me in. "The Medici coven is governed by Luca. Any decision he makes, I am forced to comply. I, personally, haven't harmed another, human or vampire, since the war."

That name tickles my memories; Paulo Medici's brother.

"So you're saying that you're Lord Medici." At his questioning look, I raise an eyebrow. "You're the Heir to the Medici line. Why didn't you admit that when you went before the Heads? Why didn't you tell them about your Lord when you warned us of an impending attack?" Another memory surfaces. "And the stupid kidnapping! You'd planned all of that for some asinine reason. You had numerous opportunities to present your case to the Vampire Lords, but instead, you resorted to underhanded techniques."

"There you go again, Halifax. Thinking you know everything."

"Not even close," I retort, annoyance flaring. "You—Alessandro Medici—are the *Medici Heir*. I can't even wrap my brain around that. You spent days in my family's catacombs, a prisoner of your own silence. You pretended you'd been cast out by your coven, abandoned because of your sire, and I pitied you. I wanted to help you, to *save* you."

He remains quiet.

119

"You sought a place to call home until Dormiam," I continue, warming to my ire. "You stood in front of the governing Seven and requested sanctuary with them. Stood in the prison cell in the catacombs and made me feel as big as a cockroach simply because I wanted to help you. You're conniving—"

"So what?" he interrupts, his eyes flashing. "I manipulated the Heads and you to get what I wanted. Do you even know what that was? Or do you still prefer pretending that you know everything?"

His outburst silences me. Am I really pretending I know everything? In a way, maybe. I know he lied to me and played my father. But what I don't know is *why*.

I break eye contact, looking down at the plate laden with cheeses, crackers, and an assortment of fruit. I pick up a slice of white cheese and nibble on the corner, keeping my gaze glued to the plate.

"I wanted to test the Seven," he admits, dropping into the chair next to the bed. "I was hoping they'd changed, that they weren't the same stubborn, old men I'd fought against two centuries before." He laughs, low and derisive. "But they still were. Controlled by their prejudices and old-fashioned traditions. They'd forgotten what it meant to forgive, to forget."

"Too many died for them to forget," I counter, "and because they can't forget, they will never forgive."

"And knowing that I didn't do any of this by choice won't change their opinion, will it?"

"No," I disclose, meeting his eyes briefly. "Never. Your coven *slaughtered* their Families. There's no walking away from this."

He sighs and leans back, dropping his head onto the wood of the chair, and I avert my eyes back to the plate. We lapse into silence, and I focus on consuming the contents, one finger food at a time. Soon, the tiny blue flowers dotting the center of the china are visible, and I move the tray off my lap and to the side.

When the quiet continues to stretch between us, I fluff the covers, lay down, and turn my back to him. Several more minutes pass.

120

Finally he speaks, his voice quiet, weighted with something unrecognizable. "I don't want a war, Danika. Not again. I don't want more bloodshed and discord between humans and vampires. I just want to protect my Family, as any leader would. And I want them accepted, not hunted simply because they're Medici."

His words touch something within me. I remember Conrad's reaction to seeing Alessandro for the first time. *Medici scum* is what he'd called him. A murderer; a cheat.

"I want to give my people a place to call home. Somewhere they can rest their weary heads without fear, without prejudice. Somewhere safe, where they can be at ease to laugh, to just...*live*. I want them to be free."

"But at what cost, Alessandro?" I adjust the covers over my shoulder, tucking deeper into them.

"I'm not like my sire—never have been. I know you won't believe me, but he wasn't always evil and twisted. At one time, he was just and honorable."

I squash the snort of the disbelief before it can emerge. I doubt he'll appreciate any kind of deprecating remark about his Lord.

CONFESSION 14

I've never been obsessed with my personal appearance. My eyes are blue, my hair is blonde. Sure, I may have a nice smile. But the girl I see in the mirror now, her gaze haunted, her face marred by scars, makes me wish I could turn back the clock and truly care.

Trembling fingers trace the scars, still pink from freshly healed skin. They memorize every groove, every indent, every imperfection. Tears fill my eyes and spill over to trickle down my cheeks. They go unheeded as my gaze remains riveted to the physical proof of mankind's insanity.

Mei moves up behind me, her hazel eyes gentle in the vanity's mirror. "They will fade in time."

I nod silently, words lodged in my throat. Regret sits heavy within me. After having gone nearly two months without looking in a mirror, I wish I'd continued with my stubbornness. I wasn't ready for this.

"Come," she lays a hand on my shoulder, "let's get you cleaned up so you can take the tour Lord Medici's been planning since you arrived."

I tear my eyes away from the damage, hastily wiping the moisture from my cheeks. Pretending that her words don't send my heart fluttering, I shift toward the enormous shower. Steam swirls behind the glass door, a promise of a good scalding, and I allow her to slide the robe from my shoulders. Another set of scars; more proof of man's evil. My ribs are now visible, and though I've already committed to memory every thin, pink

122

crevice and every bump along the healed bones, I still choke on the sight.

My body is unrecognizable.

I step away from her, desperate to be in the hot water, hiding within the steam before I break down. She doesn't say anything when I yank open the glass door and disappear inside. I hear the bathroom door close with a soft click. Lifting my face into the scorching stream, I let the tears go.

There's been no word from the outside world in the eight weeks I've been with the Medici coven. If anything has changed in that time, Alessandro's been tight-lipped. But we don't hear much where we are, here in an old, renovated castle buried within the Carpathian Mountains in Romania.

I asked him if he knew how stereotypical it was for vampires to be living in a castle in Transylvania. His response? It was the first time I'd seen a real, genuine smile on his face. Like he *knew* how outrageous it was.

His request for my assistance has been accepted, albeit reluctantly. I'll help him as best as I can where Lord Halifax is concerned, but that's all I'm able to offer. My father is only *one* Head. Alessandro will have to deal with the others himself.

When no more tears fall, I scrub my hair and my body, rinse quickly, and shut off the water. Silence descends over the bathroom, disrupted only by the *drip, drip, drip* of the drain. A towel awaits me just on the other side of the glass door, but my mind is elsewhere.

Today is my eighteenth birthday, but instead of flowers and balloons, I receive scars; instead of happiness, I'm filled with regret.

Giving myself a shake, I shove open the door and snag the towel. It's warm and fluffy and smells of lavender and lemon. I wrap it around myself and step over the small lip onto the soft mat.

Without realizing it, I return to the mirror.

Just one more peek. That's all I need—just one more.

The pink jagged lines still dominate the right side of my face, though they've taken on a whitish hue from the hot shower. Once again, I trace the lines with my fingers, tracking their progress with my eyes.

My hand dips, halting its exploration. Something shifts within me, unfamiliar. Two parts determination, one part sorrow. I shake my head, clearing my mind, and—

Slap! Both hands connect with my cheeks, and I close my eyes. I soak in the sting, allowing it to wipe away that final trace of grief. These are battle scars, Danika. Battle scars. Chin up. You're the Halifax Dilecta.

***

I walk sedately beside Alessandro three hours later as he takes me on a tour of the castle. The passages all look the same, bearing a fascinating resemblance to a medieval castle I'd seen during my trip to England for the last Alliance discussion. Enormous tapestries are spaced evenly, and, in an ingenious twist, the light fixtures are designed to appear like torches fitted into wall sconces.

"Who renovated this?" I ask, awed by the sheer creativity of it. We've stopped beside one of them so I can inspect it.

"Luca," he replies and flashes me one of his signature crooked grins that, as usual, doesn't quite reach his eyes.

Surprised, I twist around to face him. "Do you live here with him?"

"The entire coven resides here, above and below ground."

How have they gone so long without detection? The Heads have a tight grasp on all vampires. There's no way they wouldn't have noticed a large gathering. And rebuilding a castle takes money and whatnot. How did they do this?

"You have questions." His voice breaks into my thoughts, and I jump a little.

"Ah." I nod, hesitant. "Yes."

At his insistence, I voice what I've been wondering. He doesn't respond, and I watch the different emotions flit across his face before he schools his features.

His silence is telling, and with the dawning of realization, something else occurs me, uncoiling in my gut like a snake.

"You've got a Dilecta," I say, but instead of responding, he turns and resumes walking. I fall in next to him. "Alessandro? You do, don't you?"

"Yes."

So the Medici coven has their own Dilecta. Interesting...

"He has been with our Family for nearly fifty years," he explains, his gaze focused straight ahead. "Before him, it was his father, and before him, *his* father. Their family owns the castle and the land surrounding it. With the help of his daughter, Marcus runs our numerous businesses."

I'm speechless. That's how they've managed to fly under the radar for so long? Because their Dilecta is in charge of their assets? Not just during Dormiam, but *all* the time. That's an insane amount of trust they've bestowed on this guy and his...did he say *daughter*?

"I'd—uh—like to meet them." I clear my throat, suddenly awkward.

"You're in luck," he flashes me a crooked grin, "that's where we're headed now."

The rest of the tour is a rather hasty affair, and before I know it, we're entering a dining room on the second floor. Alessandro promised me another tour at a later time, but I doubt that will happen.

Especially after I lay eyes on the disgustingly beautiful Bianca Demms.

She sits with poise and grace beside, whom I can only assume, is her father. A handsome man with salt and pepper hair, a trimmed beard, and striking hazel eyes that make me think of warm honey and green tea, Marcus Demms is the epitome of a wealthy businessman.

The moment she spies Alessandro, she squeals and leaps from her chair, all pretense of sophistication vanishing in sheer excitement. She flies across the room and launches herself into his arms, her face wreathed in the most breathtaking smile that even *I'm* in awe.

As he hugs her back, I avert my eyes and bite my lip. Hard. My hand rises, as if with a will of its own, and lightly touches the scars that sully my cheek. I turn my head to the side, away from their embrace, and meet Marcus' warm gaze. His eyes dart to the hand on my face and then soften further, a smile dancing across his lips. He rises from his chair.

"It's a pleasure, Miss Halifax," he greets, and his accent throws me for a loop.

British?

"Nice to meet you," I reply and take his proffered hand. "You have a lovely house—err castle."

"It is rather magnificent." He chuckles softly. "I'll have to give you a tour of the gardens tomorrow."

I smile for the first time in two months. "I'd like that. Thank you."

"Won't you join us for dinner?" He motions toward the table where I finally notice place settings for four people.

I nod gratefully and approach the chair opposite of where Bianca had been sitting when we'd entered.

"Why don't you sit here?" The chair next to him is pulled out further by a hovering vampire I've never met before.

I frown a little but move to Miss Demms' vacated seat while water glasses are rearranged.

"I'm sure they'll want to sit by each other," he whispers conspiratorially.

My heart clenches in response, but I manage another smile. "Of course."

How have I not known about his relationship with the Dilecta's daughter? Have I been so blinded by my own feelings that I never thought to ask if he had someone special? I'm such an idiot!

Alessandro is the first to step back, releasing her. He speaks low, too low for me to hear, but I'm still acutely aware of their close proximity to one another. Her delicate hand rests on his arm, her smile even more stunning.

When my glass is filled with water, I snag the crystal goblet and sip on it, staring at the pristine tablecloth as if it's the most fascinating thing I've ever seen. My mind puts up a brick wall, blocking any thoughts of the Medici Heir.

They eventually join us. He takes the seat across from me, and she claims the chair between her father and him. Plates are set before the three of us—a goblet of blood for Alessandro—and my gaze eagerly takes in the decent slab of prime rib and cluster of roasted asparagus stalks drizzled in garlic butter. My saliva glands respond instantly.

126

The next few minutes pass in companionable silence. I dig in, savoring each bite as it passes my lips. The meat is juicy, bursting with flavor, and I suppress the urge to moan. A quick glance at Lord Medici reveals him watching me, a wry twist to his lips, and I hastily return my attention to my plate.

"Alessandro tells me you ride."

Bianca's voice takes me off guard, and my head snaps up. "What?"

"You ride, don't you?" Her eyes twinkle with amusement.

"I—yes," I say.

"Wonderful!"

"Do you—uh," I clear my throat, "do you ride, Miss Demms?"

"Oh do I ever," she gushes, laughing. "I've been riding since I was seven. I do believe Father was at his wits end with me during my teen years." She throws a loving glance at the man in question. "I preferred the horses over people." Her voice drops. "I still do."

I like her.

I don't want to. She represents everything I'm not; everything I will never be. She's the embodiment of an idyllic life. Beautiful, accomplished, successful. Happy. She glows with happiness.

And me? I'm scarred. Angry. Bitter. I still feel the sting of betrayal, the suffocating loneliness. I ask myself daily—hourly—where do I belong? My broken body is a testament that I don't belong with my fellow humans. The fact I bleed is proof I don't belong with the vampires either.

My thoughts veer dangerously close to the smothering darkness I'd barely clawed my way out of. Already, the familiar arms beckon me, a promise of comfort, of oblivion.

As if subconsciously seeking Alessandro's dark gaze to pull me back to reality, my eyes flick upward. His fingers twirl the goblet, his focus on me, piercing and steady. By gradual degree, the tension drains and my body relaxes.

There are a hundred—a *thousand*—unspoken emotions swirling within those dark depths. Secrets I fear revealing, but long to know. The truth of his past, the hopes of his future. What makes the man tick; what keeps him awake when the sun is at its apex. The reason why he never smiles. Why, even now, he doesn't exhibit any pleasure or enjoyment sitting beside Bianca.

She lays a hand on his arm, to get his attention, and the spell is broken. I return my eyes to the food as he looks at her. I listen with only half an ear when she asks him about his trip to the States, and I completely tune out his response.

Soon, I've cleaned my plate, and with a full belly, exhaustion descends. I stifle a yawn behind my hand. What I wouldn't give for that comfortable, enormous bed right about now.

The door clicks softly, announcing someone's arrival, and relief washes over me the moment Mei crosses the threshold. She clasps her hands at her waist and inclines her head respectfully at the Demms.

"Sir, Miss," she greets. "I've come to escort Miss Danika back to her room."

"Oh!" Bianca's face falls, and she catches my eye. "Maybe tomorrow we can take a ride in the mountains?" I nod hesitantly. "Wonderful. We'll go after breakfast. Good night, then, Miss Halifax."

I rise, mumbling, "Night."

Alessandro stands, his glass now empty. "I'll escort you, Danika."

"Ah no." I hold up a hand to stop him. A quick peek at Bianca tells me she isn't quite ready to say good night to him. "Mei is just fine. Thanks, though."

My caregiver hurries forward, and I give her a grateful smile when she wraps an arm around me.

Without a backward glance, we leave the dining room.

I know that, in a way, I'm conceding defeat. But Alessandro isn't mine, has never *been* mine, and will never *be* mine. Yes, this is just another rusted nail in my coffin of isolation and pain. I have ten months until Dormiam, and then I'll return to my family and never see Alessandro or the Medici coven again.

Is it easy? Not by a long shot. Will I come to regret this in the months, and even years, to come? With every fiber of my being.

128

We meander through the corridors, our steps slow and measured. The arms supporting me are like bands of steel, and "appreciative" is an insignificant word to describe how I feel.

"Did you eat?" I ask, desperate to fill the silence.

"I did. A tasty O negative."

I try to repress the shudder. "That's…good."

She laughs. "How was your dinner?"

"Very tasty." I press a hand to my stomach where I can already feel the first stirrings of a stomach ache. "But very rich."

"I'll bring you some medicine," she says, noticing my discomfort, and I nod. "Would you like a bath? It might help."

I think about that for a moment and then shake my head.

We make it back to my room. I'm pleased to see the sheets are turned down and the lamp is on. She directs me to the bed where I sink onto the mattress and release an exhausted sigh. She continues toward the closet where my nightclothes are kept. My eyes snag on a small box with a large red bow, positioned beneath the warm light of the lamp.

"What is this?" I ask, reaching for it.

"That," she tosses over her shoulder, "is a gift from Alessandro."

I slide the small card free from its place beneath the ribbon and flip it open. The unfamiliar scrawl is slanted and elegant, a surprising contrast to the man himself, and a real smile tugs at my lips. The note is short, thanking me for agreeing to help him and urging me to "use it well". At the very bottom are words that cause my heart to swell.

Happy Birthday.

Curiosity piqued, I remove the ribbon and lift off the top of the box. Nestled within is a shiny new cell phone. Astonishment surges, and with trembling hands, I reach in and lift out the familiar weight. I nudge the power button with my finger and the screen lights up.

A laugh bursts from me. The background is a Chibi vampire. Dressed in a black suit and wearing a long, red cape, overly large eyes glare out of the screen menacingly.

It's the cutest thing I've ever seen.

Mei comes to stand beside me, holding my pajamas. "Alessandro said you're to call your parents and let them know you're all right."

***

Later that night, just like clockwork, Alessandro arrives, clutching an old tome of Shakespeare poetry and sonnets. Reclined against a smattering of plump pillows, I glance up from my perusal of the new cellphone.

He holds the book up, a mischievous gleam in his eye. "Thought you might enjoy a change in literature."

Shakespeare is *not* my thing. It takes a clever mind to understand his musings, and I am decidedly *not* clever. When I tell him as much, he drops down into Mei's plush armchair and opens it with a dramatic flourish.

"'Shall I compare thee to a summer's day?" His voice sends a shiver up my spine.

I shake my head. "No. You shall not."

"Come now." A crooked grin. "'Thou art more lovely and more temperate: Rough winds do shake the darling buds of May. And summer's lease—'"

"What does that even mean?" I interrupt, rolling my eyes.

"Fine." He flips forward a few more pages. "Since you don't enjoy love sonnets, how about this? 'My mistress' eyes are nothing like the sun; Coral is far more red than her lips' red.'"

"Seriously, Alessandro?"

He shrugs. His wicked grin sends my heart racing, and I scowl in an effort to mask how knee-weakening *aware* I am of him.

"Very well." The book is closed. "How about we talk instead?"

I cock my head. "What about?"

"You decide."

"Hmmm." I tap the side of the phone against my chin and consider him. "Tell me about your selection as Heir."

His body stiffens for a beat. "Why do you want to know about that?"

"Because."

130

Obsidian eyes study me, and a tense silence stretches between us. I hold his gaze, patient and relaxed. Finally, he sighs and runs a hand through his hair, causing the perfect waves to fluff up comically. I suppress a laugh.

"Watch yourself," his eyes narrow, "or I won't tell you."

I raise my hands, placating. "Sorry. Go ahead."

"So, Luca was named Lord after Paulo was killed," he begins, "which opened up the position of Heir. I didn't want the role. I didn't want to do anything other than heal." His lips thin. "But few of us survived the war, and deciding an Heir was crucial."

I nod.

"My selection wasn't as intense as what the Seven's Heirs undergo, that's for sure." He smiles flatly—more of a grimace. "I spent six months beneath ground, starved and isolated. Not a drop of blood was given to me during that time. When I emerged, warm bodies were presented before me."

"Did you...?"

He raises an eyebrow. "Did I what?"

"You know...?" I wave my hands near my neck vaguely.

"Did I rip out their throats and drain them of blood?"

I clear my throat, giving a jerky nod.

"I did not." His expression hardens. "That was part of my selection. I couldn't touch them. Not even a hair on their head."

Whoa.

"I came out of the catacombs in the clutches of bloodlust, and I had to sit in a room with twelve humans and *not* kill them." He gives me a meaningful look. "And that was only the beginning of Luca's tests."

He continues describing the numerous trials stretched before him, each task harder than the last. His selection took eight years from start to finish. During that time, Luca kept busy by siring hundreds more undead and replenishing their numbers.

As the hour approaches midnight, I repress a yawn. He must notice my exhaustion and finishes his story. Then, he gathers his book, rises, and bids me goodnight. I smile as he leaves, my heart lighter and my questions fewer.

131

CONFESSION 15

Moving on...nothing to see here...just another
crap day in Romanian paradise.

The next morning dawns with clear blue skies and a cool breeze ruffling through the trees. I'm groggy as I make my way to the stables, directed by a few of the castle's staff along the way.

Sleep had alluded me. After the discussion with Alessandro, I'd called Conrad's cell—the only number I'd actually memorized once upon a time—and left a message. Then I'd spent most of the night checking and rechecking to make sure the phone hadn't died. I'd managed to doze in between moments of panic, but they'd been so sporadically placed, I felt as if I hadn't slept a wink.

When I'd finally climbed from bed an hour after dawn, a set of riding clothes and boots lay at the end with a note from Alessandro encouraging me to enjoy myself. Another smile, similar to the one last night, had turned up my mouth and I'd dressed, feeling lighter than I had in a while.

The more I get to know the Medici vampire, the more enthralled I become.

Birds sing from the trees and sunshine warms my face. The scent of mountain air tickles my nose. I take the directed path around the side of the castle, sneaking a peek at the gardens Mr. Demms has promised me a tour of, and I smell my final destination long before I see it near the tree line.

132

The stables are a grand building, large and imposing. A vast corral opens to the left of the gigantic double doors, and a set of gates lead into the surrounding, wild forest. I can't help but marvel at the intricate stone and woodwork as I approach.

Bianca appears in the doorway, leading a gray mare with long legs, and the horse's muscles flex and bunch beneath her shiny coat as she ambles behind her rider. Under the light of day, Miss Demms is even more breathtaking than last night, and I find myself awed by both her and the beast.

She catches sight of me and a smile splits across her face. "Good morning!"

"Morning."

She stops and turns to face me, sweeping her emerald eyes up and down my body. "I knew they'd fit."

"What?" I frown.

"The clothes." She gestures to my outfit. "Alessandro asked if I might have something that would fit you. I'm so pleased to see they do."

My earlier delight at his thoughtfulness vanishes like a candle doused. "Oh...yeah. Thanks." To distract myself, I focus on her horse. "She's beautiful."

Her smile widens. "Her name is Storm." She shifts back toward the mare, rubbing a gentle hand down her nose. "She's a little hellfire to ride, which is how she got her name. The storms here in the mountains are insane."

"Back home, there's Chancelot," I say. An image of the former race horse pops into my mind, and with it, a wave of homesickness. "We rescued him about two years ago."

"What a clever name!" she exclaims. "Like second chances and Sir Lancelot from the Round Table."

She's the first person to ever get his name right off the bat, and I stare at her in surprise. "That's exactly it."

How can someone so beautiful be so nice? This is a fluke. She's only pretending to be nice to lead me into a false sense of security. Yes, that's it. Maybe she's already assured of Alessandro's feelings for her. No way would *I* be this nice to someone who could upset my place among his affections.

"Want to go for a ride?" she asks, breaking into my thoughts.

Realizing I'm practically glaring at her, I plaster on a smile and nod. She loops the reins over a bar and escorts me inside. The interior is shaded and cool, and the smell of horses, hay, and manure is strong. Several men hurry to-and-fro, carrying brushes, buckets, and an assortment of other horse-related items. When one goes rushing past, I glide out of the way and observe him halt near the largest stall where a stunning brown Arabian leans its head over the door, watching us with black eyes.

In less than ten minutes, a sleek gray, similar to Bianca's Storm, is saddled and ready to go. While one of the stable's staff tightens belts and adjusts the bridle, I pet the horse's nose and cheeks and croon gentle words. When I receive the nod from the stable hand, I swing up into the saddle. He shifts beneath me, adjusting to my weight, and I lean down and rub his neck.

Bianca disappears back out into the sunshine, and I nudge him forward, shooting off a quick thank you to the man.

We emerge into the corral to find both horse and rider already approaching the set of gates leading into the mountains. Excitement courses through me as I tap him forward, loosening my grip on the reins.

Eventually, the castle disappears behind us, swallowed up by the trees and our descent. Silence hangs between us, disrupted only by the *clop* of the horses' hooves and birdsong.

Our mounts amble down the uneven trail, curving periodically to the left. Here, the trees grow thicker, the forest denser. The birdsong has vanished somewhere along the way, but now the sound of rushing water creeps through the silence.

Finally, the path levels out into a small meadow beside a narrow river. Bianca dismounts, leaving the reins unsecured, and approaches the water. From atop Spartacus—yes, that's *really* his name—I watch her bend down at the shore, cup her hands, and scoop up water.

My lip curls in disgust. Even the act of drinking water is beautiful on her.

I shove down the jealousy gnawing my insides, dismount, and join her beside the water.

134

"This is my special place," she says, and this time, the smile she gives me lacks its usual pizzazz. "I come here when I want to be alone and think."

Something in the way she says that catches my attention.

"So tell me, Halifax—why are you here?"

I'm lost, uncertain how to answer. Why is she asking? Doesn't she know already? If not, then where do I start? Do I tell her about the attack, the kidnapping, and the subsequent rescue? Do I reveal the months of healing, both physically and mentally, I've endured? How about the ever-present darkness that hugs my subconscious like a warm, fuzzy blanket, always just a breath away?

As I stare at her and she stares at me, neither of us blinking, annoyance flares. No...she doesn't deserve the truth.

For the first time, I can understand Alessandro's words in the catacombs. The sheltered human child, the loved and cherished Dilecta, had no idea of the horrors of the world. Things could get worse, I knew that. The things he'd seen, he'd experienced and felt, probably didn't even come close to what I'd been through. Not by a long shot. But for me, everything had changed with the revelations from Father, and it'd been taken one step further with the attack by the humans.

"My father says there are changes coming, Danika. Big ones that'll shape the world between man and vampire." Her eyes are sad when they meet mine. "You're the Halifax Dilecta." It isn't a question.

"I am."

"Then your role in what's to come is by far the most important."

I can't think of what to say so I remain quiet. A part of me is confused, desperate to get answers to her cryptic message. Another part of me, though, is reeling from the change in the bubbly woman.

"Do you know what started the war two hundred years ago?" Her question takes me off guard. It's as if there's a wealth of hidden meaning behind it. Like she's testing me; hinting at something just out of reach, something I can't fully grasp.

"I'm not following." Unease is making me surly.

"What do you know of it?" she says simply.

135

"The Medici coven attacked, and the governing Seven were forced to join together and take them down."

Her expression hardens. "Wrong. *So* wrong."

The air between us grows thick with tension. Her gaze is firm, unwavering. Gone is the cheerful woman I'd met, and in her place was someone who made my hackles rise in self-defense.

"What do *you* know?" I snap.

"More than you, apparently." Anger laces her words.

"You don't even know me."

"And I don't *like* you, Halifax." All good nature is gone. "I don't trust you. This coven is my family. This is where my friends live, and the man I love protects it with everything in him. Though sometimes his views are skewed, maybe even wrong, he does his best." She takes a step toward me, her eyes flashing. "And I won't have someone from the outside, a Dilecta from one of our enemy covens, come in here and hurt anyone." She jabs a finger into my chest, forcing me back a step. "Especially not him." Jab, and another step. "I'll protect him." Jab. "You won't get him."

"I don't want him!" The words explode out of me. As soon as they're said, I want to take them back. I want him, so much it physically hurts, and saying those words feel as if I'm betraying my feelings for him.

"Remember what you just said," she warns, her eyes promising retribution.

With a final glare, she spins and strides to where Storm and Spartacus are grazing. I watch her mount up before I make my way to my horse and climb into the saddle.

Neither of us says a word the entire trip back to the castle.

***

I avoid people for the rest of the day, and when Mei arrives later in the evening to help me get ready for dinner, I feign sleep. She quietly lays out a fresh set of pajamas for me to change into should I "wake up" and departs with the softest click of the door.

My tears have long dried, weeks ago in fact, and so I lie there long after she's gone, staring at the cell phone on the nightstand, willing it to ring, begging it to light up with even just a text. I ache to hear my brother's familiar voice, his barking commands and wry humor.

In the dark, my fingers trace the lines on my face, mapping them out. I try to find the humor in it, though it's difficult and more painful than entertaining.

A tattoo. That'll be perfect. But what? Something that enhances the scars and makes me look fierce. I'll look like a biker or a thug or something. No one will want to mess with me then. Yes, I like that. Or…

I snicker.

A map. The ink can outline every imperfection, and I'll have towns dotted in. Conrad will get a kick out of that. Mother and Father, not so much.

And Alessandro— I cut my thoughts off, rolling onto my side and tossing the covers over my head. Nope. Not going there. Humor melts away, and my smile sinks from my face. These scars are not funny. *I'm* not funny.

Not anymore.

Suddenly, an unfamiliar jingle disrupts the quiet, causing me to jump. I throw off the blankets, sit up, and stare around the room, disoriented. My sweeping eyes snag on the phone, its screen illuminated, and I nearly tumble from the bed in my haste to grab it.

"Hello!" I exclaim, pressing it to my ear. The music continues. Frowning, I pull it back from my ear. I stare, wide eyed, at the screen. Conrad's number is visible along with the *Accept* or *Decline* button. With a short laugh, I hit *Accept*. "Hello! Con!"

"Danika!" His voice comes through, frantic. "Are you there? Can you hear me?"

"Yes, yes I can!" Blessed relief. "Oh, it's so good to hear your voice." I blink away the tears.

"Are you all right? Where are you? You're not hurt, are you?" Questions come in rapid succession. "Are you scared? Have they hurt you? Are you safe?"

"I'm fine; I'm good." I shove my hair back, resting the elbow on my bent knee to keep it pinned out of my face. "They're treating me well. I'm with the Medici coven right now."

"Medici?" he growls, and I suck in a sharp breath. His tone is lethal.

"H-he saved me, Con." For some reason, I feel the need to defend Alessandro from him.

"Ha! He probably planned all of it." A pause. "Where are you, Danika?"

The urge to tell him is strong, but something makes me hesitate. I'd promised Alessandro that I'd help him build relations with the governing Seven. This is part of my debt to him. Unease rises up and the excitement at hearing my brother's voice flees.

The lie rolls right off my tongue. "Europe somewhere, I think."

It's such a vague response, and he's quick to pick up on it.

He swears and then, "Where in Europe?" When I don't respond, he swears again. "I didn't call to fight. This is the first time I've heard your voice in two months, Danika. I need to know that you're all right."

"I've already said that I am." My heart twists, equal parts regret and homesickness. "They're taking care of me, Conrad. You saw the video, right?" He growls, low and menacing. "My wounds have healed, thanks to them."

"Where are you?"

"I've learned how to walk again," I continue, blinking against an onslaught of tears. "And I went for a ride today. Please," my voice cracks, "just let me be. Let me stay. I need to fulfill this debt, Conrad. You should understand."

"Forget the debt."

Despair rises. "Why does everyone keep telling me that? If it were anyone else I owed, you'd tell me to take care of it—no matter what."

"The world is divided, Dani. Now more than ever, we need our Dilecta."

138

I choke on the welling grief. "Dilecta? That's it?" I swallow hard against the lump in my throat. "What about *me*? What about Danika? Don't you need *me*, your sister?"

"Of course I do." His voice softens. "I didn't call to fight. Please. Just tell me where you are. Tell me so I can come get you."

"You're such a liar," I breathe. "Even from the beginning, that's all I ever was to you." The sense of betrayal sweeps through me anew, constricting my airways.

There's a voice in the background, and then Conrad's muffled response of, "Not now, Laura."

"Laura?" Shock spikes. "What are you doing with Laura?"

"Looking for *you*. Please, stop being stubborn and tell me where to come get you."

"No." I swipe away the tears.

"Danika Jean!"

"No, Conrad!"

"Where are you?" His growl deepens, taking on an unnatural edge that sends a chill up my spine. "Tell me where you are, Danika."

"Until this debt is paid, I won't go anywhere."

I hang up.

Chest heaving and eyes swimming with tears, I stare down at the phone, desperately trying to make heads or tails of our conversation. What just happened? How had I gone from being excited at hearing his voice to being filled with so much anger and disappointment? Where did I go wrong? Where did *he* go wrong?

And he's with Laura? Why? What does that mean?

So many questions, and not a hope in the world of answering them.

The jingle starts, Conrad calling, and I *Decline* the call and power down the phone. I bite my lip to keep the tears at bay and drop the device onto the nightstand, screen down. Nearly twenty-four hours I'd waited for that phone call, anxious, excited. Now, his voice is the last one I want to hear.

No more tears. I blink up at the ceiling. No more tears. I ball my hands into fists on my thighs. No. More. Tears. Each word is marked by a punch into the tender tissue. The newly healed bone smarts, but I drag in a deep breath, clench my jaw, and shove every ounce of heartache back behind the brick wall I've erected to protect myself.

CONFESSION 16

I am completely unequipped to navigate the rough seas of teen hormones and first crushes.

An hour later, I emerge from the bathroom, showered and dressed for bed. My lip stings where I've gnawed on it for the entire shower, struggling to keep the tears at bay and the hurt buried deep, and I flick my tongue over it lightly, wincing each time.

My weary gaze lands on Alessandro, sitting at the end of the bed, and I stumble to a halt, my heart accelerating. An emotion I'm terrified to acknowledge sweeps through me when he lifts his head, his dark eyes piercing.

"You skipped dinner." He points toward the small table in the sitting area where a domed tray sits. "When you healed and could walk again, I assumed bringing food to your room would end."

My eyes dart to it. "I didn't ask for a tray."

"You didn't have to. We're not going to let you starve."

I don't respond, but instead, look away. My emotions are a riot of contradiction. Relieved he's come to see me; annoyed that he won't really open up to me; thrilled at his thoughtfulness; frustrated that he's invaded my personal space; ecstatic that he's here, with me, instead of with Bianca.

Mainly, I'm disgusted at myself for feeling this way.

Today has been awful—one of those I just want to sleep the memories away kind of days—and he's the last person, but also the *only* person, I want to see. Another contradiction in itself.

"I spoke to Conrad," I find myself saying, and other than a slight stiffening of his shoulders, he exhibits no other emotion.

"And how is he?" There's an underlying *something* in his voice, but I can't place it.

"Pissed off and searching for me."

"Naturally."

I give him a questioning look. "You don't sound surprised."

He laughs softly, without humor. "Of course not."

"Laura Campbell was with him," I continue, looking down to where my hands twist together at my waist. "Father and Mother weren't, though."

"I wouldn't expect them to be either." He runs a hand through his hair. "Relations between vampires and humans are crumbling. They, and the other Heads, are busy doing damage control."

"You speak as if you know."

He gives me a look, and another soft laugh escapes. "It's chaos out there, Halifax. Luca's attack was ingenious as well as perfectly-timed."

The mention of his Lord isn't surprising, but the awe in his voice is what brings reality crashing home, much like being doused over the head by a bucket of icy water. My hands still. Why does he seem impressed? I thought he was on my side?

He doesn't seem to notice that he's rendered me speechless. "The covens are scrambling. Their numbers are diminished, and the world is turning on them. Much as it did us two hundred years ago."

I stare at him with dawning horror. What?

His gaze finally rises from the carpet and he takes in my wide eyes.

My heart plummets. How have I forgotten who he is? Trapped here, as I am, must have addled my brains. This is the *Medici* coven. It's not the Duchamps, or the Richters, or even the Broadhurts. This is home to the foulest, most corrupt Family of vampires in history.

And I've agreed to help them.

142

I need to leave. I have to find Con. My eyes flick to the phone on the nightstand. Will he come for me if I tell him where I am? Of course he will.

Alessandro must sense the change in me because his eyes narrow and then jump back and forth between the phone and me. Though confusion is written across his face, the acceleration of my heart rate is enough to alert him that something's shifted within me.

"What are you doing, Halifax?" he asks, his voice low, lethal. "What are you thinking right now?"

"I—uh—would like to—uh…" I inch toward the phone, swallowing awkwardly.

I'm within range of it when he moves, snatching it before I can, and I whirl to face him when he reappears behind me, holding my one lifeline up in the air, out of my reach.

"I told you to use the phone well," he says, cocking his head a little, "but why do I suddenly get the impression you're trying to do something incredibly stupid?"

Our eyes meet, and for the first time, I'm terrified of him. The threat promised in their obsidian depths is not one I should take lightly. I retreat a step, desperate to put space between us, and he closes the distance. Again, I move back, and he counters it.

"I just…"

"You just what?" he demands, his gaze so penetrating, I feel it unraveling all my secrets.

I shrug, words abandoning me.

Another step back, another advanced.

"I want to go home," I whisper.

"I thought you hated your family?"

"What? No. I *love* my family."

Our dance continues. Retreat; advance.

"But they lied to you."

"A minor inconvenience." I know I'm stalling, hedging my responses.

The closed door meets my back, and shock jolts through me. How have we crossed the room so quickly?

"Are you planning on going back on your word?" His face hardens and pupils dilate. "Truly, Halifax?"

When I don't deny it, his hand shoots out and grabs my throat. My head thumps against the wood, and he pins me to the door. While the hold isn't tight enough to cut off my air, it keeps me in place, sending an unspoken message. His nails elongate, and I feel them pinch the tender skin.

"Have you forgotten who I am?" He leans in close, and though fear claws upward, I meet him eye for eye. "Have you forgotten where you are?"

"How can I?" I choke. "You're just like the rest of them; only using humans as they benefit you. Spoiling them," my eyes dart to the phone in his other hand, "just to gain their favor and subjugation."

"I'm *nothing* like them," he snarls.

"You're *worse* than them." My anger rises. "You hide in your pretty castle, buried in your pretty mountains. You attack innocents who are too weak to stand against you; you slaughter hundreds of vampires without remorse. Even in two hundred years, you haven't changed."

He bares his teeth at me, fangs visible, and his breath feathers along the soft tissue of my throat where my pulse flutters. "Where was *their* remorse when they massacred my coven, Halifax? When your *father* ripped my Lord to shreds?"

My eyes close of their own accord, and I angle my head away.

But there's not just fear in me now.

There's something else, something I've never felt before. Desire, excitement, anticipation. A fierce ache gnaws at my insides. I want him to bite me; I want to feel the scrape of those razor-sharp canines. Just once.

"You are playing with fire, little human," he warns softly, his breath hot.

I turn my head back, prying my eyes open, and his gaze—nearly black with emotion— cuts right through me.

"I had no hand in those attacks, as you well know," he growls. "And I've done nothing but try to make you feel at home here."

"I'm still a prisoner," I counter, jutting my chin out stubbornly.

"I've made it possible for you to ride those beasts you love and admire so much."

"What do you want me to say? Thank you? You're the best?" The sarcasm rolls right off my tongue.

His surprise is palpable, and it's quickly followed by a rush of anger—if the tightening of his hand around my throat is any indication.

"I want *some* appreciation for going against Luca and treating you halfway decently." He leans in until our noses brush, anguish in his dark gaze. "I deserve that much, Danika."

My name on his lips is the sweetest sound, and my heart clenches. "And what do you want, Alessandro?"

Something flits across his face, some emotion I can't describe. Sadness? Remorse? Sorrow?

His answer comes on an exhalation, the barest breath. "Forgiveness."

"Why?" I search his eyes.

"Because," he chokes and clenches his jaw.

"Because why?" My breath holds, eager for his response.

"Because I need to protect my Family—I need to save them from Luca—and I can't do that without the aid of the Heads."

His family...of course.

Even though I'm expecting a reply similar to that, it's still like a knife to my heart. How can I be so stupid to think his desire for forgiveness may involve me? I want to laugh, a hysterical, half-insane cackle. Of course; how can I forget? I'm nothing but a tool, a means. And he has Bianca.

Performing a series of moves Conrad taught me that involves elbows and flying hands, I extricate myself from his grip and hastily flee to the other side of the room. He spins toward me, but I hold up my hands in supplication and back away.

"I won't go anywhere," I promise, biting my already sore lip against another onslaught of tears. "You can even take the phone with you. But please, just," I swallow hard, "go." Embarrassment floods my cheeks, and I keep my eyes averted.

Heartbreak constricts my airways, tighter than his grip, more aggressive, more unforgiving.

He looks down at the phone in his hand, looks back up at me, and with a sigh, turns and tosses it onto the bed where it bounces a few times before coming to rest next to my pillow.

"Keep it," he says. "I've got no use for another one."

I nod once.

"Eat your dinner."

"I'm not hungry." In truth, that desire vanished the moment I saw him sitting on the edge of the bed after my shower. "Take the tray with you."

"Don't test me, Halifax."

"Do you really think that's what I'm doing right now?" I cross my arms, tensing, and keep my eyes focused on the dark curtains.

"Isn't it?" A hint of something dangerous.

"I'm just finishing off a crap day the right way." My gaze sweeps back to his. "Thanks for your help."

His lip curls but he doesn't say anything, and I look away again. He crosses the room in four strides, yanks the tray off the table, causing the metal dome to rattle precariously, and moves to the door. There, he pauses and shifts back to me.

"Sleep well, Halifax."

I remain silent.

He leaves, the door slamming shut behind him, and hugging myself, I look up at the ceiling and blink away the rising tears.

Once again, I hate who I am. The Halifax Dilecta. A teenager with no concept of the world. A naïve little girl. The one Alessandro had once described. Bound to a Family through obedience, obligation, and unrequited loyalty. Scarred. Broken.

And suddenly, I want my mother, the woman who has all the answers.

I want my father, the man who approaches every situation objectively, intelligently.

I want the Arizona desert, and Chancelot, and sunsets. I want the smell of rain as it falls on the dry earth. I want Saguaro cacti as far as the eye can see, and Palo Verde stretched wide with their paltry offering of shade. I want wild flowers and seas of poppies that make the mountains come alive and look as if they're on fire. I want the uncertainty of the desert, the rough, unforgiving nature of it.

I want to go home.

Homesickness stabs me, and I suck in a ragged breath, squashing the sob building in my chest.

Where have I gone wrong? Where does this anger and bitterness come from? This hesitation and confusion? Why am I being forced to grow up? I don't want to. But why can't I turn back the clock?

Because you can't, my subconscious says. That's not how things work.

Father taught me to be strong and firm, to show respect where earned, and to earn respect where necessary. And yes, he taught me subservience, while at the same time, a steely resolve. Even from a young age, he was teaching me how to lead, how to rule in his stead.

How to be a Dilecta.

That realization staggers me, and I press the back of my hand to my mouth.

He never lied, he never prevaricated. When asked, he answered.

My eyes find the cellphone on the bed. One call, that's all it'll take. Do I want to go home? I look around the room, recalling every moment spent within it. Mei tending my injuries, Alessandro reading, the days I'd spent in lonely isolation.

Do I want to go home?

Yes.

I cross the room, snatch up the phone, and power it on. As the seconds pass, I flick my tongue over the teeth marks on my lip, again and again. Finally, the familiar Chibi vampire is visible, and with trembling fingers, I load up Conrad's number and open a message window.

And then I hesitate.

Can I forgive myself if I do this? Can I look myself in the mirror and justify what I'm about to do? Can I go back on this promise I've made?

I can't. I really can't.

A promise is a promise. A debt is *still* a debt, regardless who it's for.

I type out a quick message to my brother, and his response blinks in a half a second later, as if he's sitting with my number open, waiting for a text. Sighing, I set the device onto the nightstand and slide beneath the covers. I pull them up to my chin and flick a look at the illuminated screen. As it dims, eventually fading to black, I close my eyes and release a sigh, the words of the text the last thing I think about as sleep claims me.

I'm sorry.

C: *Where are you?*

CONFESSION 17
Sometimes, first impressions aren't always right.

The next morning, I make the mistake of journeying down to the dining room for breakfast. Not having dinner the night before spurred me out of bed, into a shower, through dressing, and out of the door, heading to the dining room on the second floor. A few of the castle's paid staff directed me when I became lost, but soon enough, I find myself walking through the large door in the familiar room.

The moment my eyes land on Marcus and Bianca, I want to flee back upstairs. But no—I stand up taller—I have decided to face everything head on. No more cowering in my room. I've been raised as the Halifax Dilecta, and that's exactly what I'll be.

"Good morning," I say, crossing the room and dropping down into an empty chair across from the golden beauty.

She sips her coffee, her emerald gaze considering me over the top of the delicate cup.

"Good morning, Miss Halifax," Marcus greets warmly. "I trust you slept well."

I nod. "Like a rock."

"Wonderful." He tears off a piece of scone and pops it into his mouth.

"How about you, Miss Demms?" I shoot her a wry look.

She raises an eyebrow, lowering her cup. "Quite well myself. Thank you."

The gentle, gracious woman was all façade. Her demeanor screams sophisticated businesswoman, and her lack of

149

patience with my arrival tells me I'm not wholly welcome, but not entirely *un*welcome either. Basically, she doesn't care whether I live or die.

Yeah…she's a peach.

Now that pleasantries are out of the way, I look down at the plate that's been set in front of me. Strawberries and cream crepes? My taste buds spring to attention.

"What do you have planned for today?" Marcus inquires once he's finished chewing, and I glance up from my reverential inspection of breakfast.

"I thought I'd visit the gardens."

At my response, he smiles. "May I join you?

"Sure." I pick up my fork and drop my eyes back to my plate. "I'd love that."

Without another word, I dig in. The first bite is magic, the second is absolute perfection, and the third is pure genius. I think that, by the fifth, my eyes have rolled into the back of my head. Soon, I'm scraping the last of the cream from the plate with the side of the fork, the scratch of metal on porcelain grating my nerves.

When I look up, both Marcus and Bianca are watching me with different expressions.

"Good?" he asks, amused, while she simply sighs and goes back to reading whatever is in the file spread next to her empty plate and half-drunk coffee.

I duck my head, a blush stealing up my face, and setting the fork down, laugh uncomfortably. "Very."

"Would you care to join us, love?" he asks his daughter.

She waves him away, not looking up from her task, and shakes her head. "With Luca returning later this week, I need to make sure the documents are completed for the blood bank in Adjud."

"Very well." He rises and presses a kiss to the top of her head. "Don't work too hard. You need to have time to prepare for his arrival."

"Of course, Father." She gives him a bland smile before returning her full attention to the file. "Have…*fun*."

The way she says that last word has me scowling at her while his focus is diverted, but the moment he turns, I school my expression, forcing a smile.

Nasty, little b—

"Shall we?" He gestures toward the door and I nod.

Together, we leave the dining room and head toward a wide, sweeping staircase made of stone. During the decent, Marcus begins a history lesson on the castle. By the time we make it to the bottom, I'm thoroughly immersed in his tales of fierce battles and damsels in distress.

"The castle was built somewhere around the turn of the fourteenth century," he explains, and motions toward a section of aged stone. "This is actually one of the original walls still standing when we purchased the land. Much of its ancient structure, however, had fallen to ruin. Our architects were able to reconstruct its original design, incorporating the old stonework in with the new."

We cross the foyer to a dim passage, lined with the familiar torch-like lamps, and my feet slow. The wall is covered in portraits, men and woman in different eras of dress.

"My ancestors," Marcus says, noticing my attention. "Every Medici Dilecta who has come before is represented on this wall."

Archibald Demms—I mentally snicker at the name— father to Marcus, is a dark, imposing figure of a man. While I can see where Marcus gets his looks from, there is a hardness in Archibald's eyes that is lacking in his son, and it sends an uncomfortable chill up my spine.

"Do any of them get turned once their duties are over and a new Dilecta is chosen?" I toss my companion a look over my shoulder.

He shakes his head, focusing on his father's portrait. "There are those who've asked, but the request is never granted. By the time a successor has come of age and stepped forward, we are too old and too weak to survive the change."

I've heard that before, from Richard. The alteration a human's body goes through is dangerous and excruciating, and there are those who are unable to survive the transformation. This is why, when a vampire chooses whom to bite and transmits the enzymes in their saliva necessary for vampirism, it is only done after serious consideration. The elderly and very young are automatically discounted. Most of the time, they are those in their prime, on the brink of death, with much to bring to the immortality bargain.

The next person in line is Francis Demms, a short, wiry man with a steely gaze. Beside him is Nigel Demms. Five men down—Rupert, Giles, Cyril, Reginald, and Hamilton—a woman pops up—Imogen Demms.

"Your family has a thing for weird names," I mutter, and he chuckles beside me.

"Sadly."

The corridor turns, this one well-lit and housing only two portraits. As we move down it, my attention snags on a stunning woman with green eyes and golden hair.

"Bianca?" I ask, frowning. But the name on the plaque is Rosalie Pemberton. And her high-waisted dress, pearls, elbow length gloves, and elaborate up-do are proof that she's not from this century.

"Not the first Dilecta," he says gravely, "but our most famous, by far."

"How so?" I scan her face, noting that the artist was able to perfectly capture the mischievous twinkle in her eyes, the slight quirk of her lips.

When he doesn't respond, I tear my gaze away and look over to find him scrutinizing me with something akin to disbelief.

"Have you no knowledge of the war?" He sounds surprised.

"Of course I do." I turn back to the painting. "Every Dilecta knows the history. But I don't remember any mention of a Rosalie Pemberton in my lessons."

"That is very unfortunate," he says softly, almost pained. "Her story is one that should never be forgotten."

The heaviness in his voice is confusing, and I find myself inspecting her portrait with renewed vigor, determined to discover her secrets, the story Mr. Demms has alluded to.

When nothing immediately jumps out, I shoot him another look. "Who was she?"

He sighs, turning sad eyes to the plaque beneath the gilded frame. "She was Paulo Medici's one love, the woman who stood beside him as a dilecta, and a *Dilecta*. Here," he motions to the next portrait, "is the man himself."

Eager to lay eyes on the one who'd started the bloodiest vampire war in history, I shift in front of it. But he is not what I'm expecting. When Father had told me the stories, I'd imagined a man larger-than-life, evil and chaos personified. This is the man who'd declared war on the world, killing hundreds of innocents, thousands of undead.

This man.

Soft brown eyes, like melted chocolate, a warm smile, a kind face. A hint of mischief, similar to Rosalie.

Shock and incredulity sweep through me. "Are you certain this is Paulo Medici?"

"Quite certain," Marcus replies, moving up beside me. "Not what you're expecting, huh? You see, he didn't govern his Family through fear and obedience, like so many Heads do. He did it with compassion, understanding, and intelligence. He was also extremely cunning, with a golden tongue."

His description fit the man in the portrait, but it went against everything I've ever believed. The man staring out at me looks like a brother, a father, an uncle. A best friend.

"T-that can't be right," I breathe, my eyes widening, and I spin toward him. "He attacked first; he killed first. He *started* the war." I don't know where the panic is coming from, the need to defend my beliefs, to defend everything I'd been taught. "He was merciless, unstoppable."

"He was angry, Miss Halifax." His eyes are no longer warm and friendly. "The Seven killed his Dilecta."

Horror seizes me, and I stagger back a step. "You lie. That's not possible."

"I assure you, it is *quite* possible."

Lies. All of it. My father wouldn't have killed a Dilecta; that, in itself, is a declaration of war. Something isn't right here. I know that history is often skewed, perceived differently, written to favor one side.

My eyes swing back to Alessandro's father, and I'm struck anew by his gentle smile, the small touch of laughter around his eyes.

I can feel myself fighting tooth and nail—clawing, punching, kicking—to disregard Mr. Demms' revelation. I don't want to believe it. I *can't*. To do so would go against everything my coven has taught me. The truth can be twisted; two sides to every story.

And now I'm stuck in the middle.

The desire to flee is suffocating, but I stomp it down. I cannot. I must approach this neutrally to find out the real answers.

A warm hand on my back drags me from my thoughts, and I look away from the portrait and into Marcus' steady gaze.

"Let's—uh—talk in the garden," I say, and for a brief moment, relief flits across his face.

He keeps his hand in place and escorts me the rest of the way down the corridor, around another corner, and through a set of double doors that lead out onto a veranda. Spread below us is the entrance to the gardens.

Within the tall hedges, the gravel path crunches beneath our feet. Marcus folds his hands behind his back while I hug myself in a futile attempt to keep from falling apart.

"The history of the Medici Dilecta is passed down to us," he begins, his eyes focused straight ahead, "to protect and remember. It is our duty to never forget what happened, and to always strive to ensure it never happens again."

"I don't think I understand," I admit, swallowing hard. "Why was she killed? A Dilecta is honored and cherished by *all* covens."

"Most of the time, yes." He nods. "But the covens were divided then, each desperate to rise above the other; to be the strongest, the most powerful. War among the humans had torn apart Europe, and the Heads vied to gain a stronghold in those war-torn regions."

"But where does Rosalie fall into all of that?" I frown, my hands tensing around my upper arms.

"Paulo Medici wanted the Heads to form an alliance, one that could assist the humans and rise above Napoleon."

154

What? His words take me by surprise. "But…"

"But what?" He gives me a sideways look. "You were told the Heads joined forces to fight the Medici coven."

"Well…yeah."

"He'd gone to them with a territory map, designating land to each of the Seven; land, Miss Halifax, they still claim today." He pauses beside a rose bush and fingers one of the blooms. "All of Japan for Nakamura, Italy for Diavolo, Germany for Richter. Does that sound familiar?" At my nod, he rotates toward the path again and resumes his trek. "When Lord Medici approached the Heads, he took with him, his precious Dilecta. Rosalie was grace and beauty, elegance and poise, and she was laughter and sunshine. As a result, she became coveted."

"Coveted?"

He inclines his head. "Coveted, Miss Halifax."

Enthralled with his story, I barely notice when the path opens up into a wide area. Marcus halts beside an enormous, bubbling fountain, and I finally take in my surroundings.

The different paths all end here, and I realize this is the center of the garden. A bench sits near the fountain, and an impressive, stone gazebo rests among the hedges, one of the gravel trails ending at the base of its stairs.

"One of the Seven's heirs took notice of her," he says, drawing my gaze back to him. "But she was tied to Paulo in more than just name. She was the other half of him, and he, of her. Only death could separate them."

"And death did," I whisper, awareness settling over me. "The Heir killed her, didn't he?"

"It broke Lord Medici." He moves to the bench and sits down. "In retaliation, Paulo killed him, declaring war on his coven." Leaning forward, he braces his forearms on his knees. "But they still didn't act."

"So he attacked innocents?"

"In an effort to draw them out, to spur them into action."

"But still…*innocents*, Mr. Demms."

"Yes, Miss Halifax." There is something in his voice that causes me to drop the subject.

"So the war was all about revenge?" I bite my lip. "Why don't the history books say that?"

"Because the Seven do not like to be reminded of their sins," he replies.

At one point in time, I'd said the same thing. Do they think they're that righteous, that blameless of crimes against humanity?

There is sorrow in his eyes when they meet mine. "A Dilecta and a vampire are not to be together. Sadly, it has become taboo. Paulo and Rosalie are proof that once death claims their mortal, a vampire will lose the final traces of their humanity."

"But what about—"

"Yes," he interrupts. "Though their hearts are bound, they are forever apart."

I lower myself down beside him and consider the fountain. Little droplets land on the stone side periodically, accumulating small puddles and discoloring the gray to a darker shade. It's almost like a jailbreak, where every drop seeks to gain freedom from the ever constant flow.

Birdsong echoes from the trees in the surrounding forest, from the bushes and flowerbeds, like a discordant orchestra, and a butterfly glides gracefully through an opening in the hedges, its muted colors almost completely faded beside the bright hues of the flora.

"There have to be exceptions," I finally say. I don't mention the hope within my chest crumbling.

"None," he counters, shaking his head. "A Dilecta's one duty is to his or her Family. They are the bridge between the two worlds, a protector and guardian. With an approaching Dormiam, there is no room for anything else."

"How was Rosalie any different from the rest of us?" I ask, turning my head to meet his eyes.

"As I've already said, she was more than just his Dilecta. She was his equal in both intelligence and cunning, and much of the alliance agreement was *her* idea."

I recall the woman in the portrait, the similarities between her and Paulo. They were the perfect match, the perfect balance to one another.

"What about Alessandro?" My eyes snag on a butterfly, and I watch its slow progress.

"What about him?"

"He stood beside his sire and fought. He killed innocent humans and slaughtered his fellow undead."

He grunts. "Any questions you have about him, you'd best ask him yourself."

I give him a look, and his smile returns.

We both relax back against the bench, allowing the serenity of the garden's center to seep in, and a companionable silence stretches between the two of us—enemy Dilectas, on different sides of a long-standing war.

CONFESSION 18

I'm no genius at poetry, but I think it was Sir Walter Scott who said, "Oh, what a tangled web we weave when first we practice to deceive." Seems <u>someone</u> missed the memo...

Twilight falls, bathing the gardens and surrounding forest in a soft glow. The ever-present chill of spring has finally faded, and the warm, welcoming embrace of summer now beckons. Freshly turned soil, the honeyed scent of lavender and vanilla, and the musky hint of fir, ash, and pine intermingle with the temperate air, announcing the official start to the Summer Solstice.

There is now one year until Dormiam, and it's reflected everywhere I look. The anticipation dances in the eyes of every Medici vampire, in the wide smiles that stretch across their pale faces, in their laughter.

But for me, it's like a ticking clock, a countdown to the next five years as a Dilecta.

Three days have passed since the walk with Mr. Demms, and the garden has become my new refuge. Bianca seldom ventures within the green hedges, choosing the stables instead, and Alessandro has been avoiding me, just as I have him, following our argument. Here, I am free from the suffocating responsibilities and expectations, from the inquisitive stares of the Medici vampires.

I'm not the Halifax Dilecta among the shrubs and flowers, within the silence and solitude, and I'm not expected to

158

reach out to the Heads and repair two hundred years' worth of animosity and hate.

The details of the war are still not fully known to me, but I've come to realize that mistakes were made on both sides. A Dilecta was murdered, a Family sought justice and revenge, and when it wasn't given, sucked innocent lives into their mess.

Now, neither is willing to admit their fault; neither is willing to step forward and fix what they've done. Instead, they're doing it again—involving humans in their supernatural war.

Smells waft through the open, dining room door, the mouthwatering aroma of grilled steak and garlic roasted vegetables. My taste buds are once again at rapt attention, anticipating the delectable fare being provided.

I tug at the hem of my summer dress, and then run my hands over the bright yellow and orange flowers that cover it, smoothing out imaginary wrinkles. I know he's going to be in there. Man, I haven't been this nervous since I started real school. Will he notice the dress? The sandals and my pretty, pink toenails that Mei painted? My hair? I touch a hand lightly to the upswept curls she'd styled for me.

Let's do this, Danika!

I step through the doorway.

Marcus is in deep discussion with a tall gentleman I don't recognize. While his dangerous presence dwarfs the Medici Dilecta, his air of deference says he works for Mr. Demms. Neither man acknowledges my entrance.

Drawn of their own will, my eyes seek Alessandro, eager to see him after so many days—though I'll never willingly admit that—and my heart plummets when I find him standing beside Bianca. I take in her hand on his arm, her face turned up toward his. Jealousy flairs hot within me. Tamping down on it, I allow a brittle smile to stretch across my lips and head toward the table.

"Ah, Miss Halifax," Marcus calls, and I pause next to the vacant chair I was about to claim. "Come here for a moment please."

I join him and his companion, still retaining my flat smile. "Good evening, Mr. Demms."

"Lovely evening, my dear," he responds, and then motions toward the man beside him. "Allow me to introduce my associate, Hector Abrahms. Hector, this is Danika Halifax." He smiles. "Hector, here, was instrumental in your rescue. It was his men who located you and alerted Alessandro to your whereabouts."

We shake hands, and he considers me with crisp blue eyes. "A pleasure, Miss Halifax."

I nod, retrieving my hand from his warm grip, and clear my throat.

"Miss Halifax has been staying with us since then," Marcus continues, taking a sip of whatever amber liquid is in the glass he clutches.

"I am pleased to see you have healed well following your ordeal," Hector says, his gaze focusing on the scars blemishing my right cheek. "I am sure I'm not the only person horrified by what you went through."

"Ah, yes." I reach up and subconsciously rub my cheekbone. "It was pretty scary."

"Any word on the men who did it?" His question is directed at Marcus. "The video cut out after Mikey delivered his rather, colorful message."

Mikey? The name is familiar, and I find myself frowning, trying to recall who he is. And then it hits me. My kidnapper the night at the club. The one who'd emerged from the shadows in the warehouse and declared war on the humans. I haven't seen him since that night! What happened to him?

"Ah yes, Mikey." Mr. Demms smiles, and as if reading my mind, says, "He's with Luca at the moment. After delivering the Halifax Dilecta and Alessandro here, he took his place beside the Head." Just then, someone appears and gives him a nod. "Splendid! It appears that dinner is ready." He motions to the table. "Shall we?"

He's with Luca Medici? But he'd been there, at the club, because of *Alessandro*, and he'd been at the warehouse because of *Alessandro*. Right? Unless the two of them are staging a coup? No. That's impossible. I've seen no evidence of it since I've been here. Then that would mean...

I'm in a daze as I join everyone at the table, and the next five minutes pass in silence as we all drape napkins, reposition silverware, and settle into our plush chairs for dinner. The squat wine glasses are filled with ice water, and plates of rolls are set between us.

Marcus and Mr. Abrahms pick up another conversation, this time, leaving me out of it, and their voices drone on as I stare at my plate and try not to notice the two people across from me.

"How have you been, Danika?" Alessandro's voice sends a shiver up my spine.

I shrug, snagging my glass and putting it to my lips. I look off toward the kitchen entrance and take tiny sips to keep from answering.

"Apparently, she's been spending her time in the gardens," Bianca supplies, quirking an eyebrow. "She's abandoned the stables and her love of riding."

Only because of you, you nasty witch.

"Really?" He sounds surprised. "Why?"

I maintain my silence and water intake. When my gaze catches on the rolls, I grab one and replace the water with a bite of bread.

There has to be more to the story than I'm hearing. No way have I been that blind, allowing him to play me.

"How is Conrad?" His next question takes me unaware, and I nearly choke on the half-chewed bread.

I finish chewing, swallow, and take a quick sip of water before replying. "He's—uh—well." I don't admit that just yesterday, I'd sent him a text with my location. After many days of deliberation, I'd decided that I needed to return home in order to find out the rest of the answers to the war. I wasn't going to find those here, among the Medici. Besides, I'd best serve my promise to Alessandro by speaking directly to Father.

Several vampires stride through the doorway with plates held aloft, and as my stomach growls in excitement, they begin depositing them in front of us.

"Garlic butter steak with roasted vegetables," Bianca hums. "My favorite."

A goblet of blood is placed before Alessandro, and with a sly grin and a wink, he takes a sip. "AB Negative. My favorite."

161

She scrunches her face and shudders. "You're so disgusting."

"What?" His eyes widen innocently, and she giggles. *Giggles*, people! Gross.

My appetite, already wavering on the precipice, vanishes, and I gaze down at the plate morbidly, wishing to be anywhere but here, sitting across from the world's most grotesque couple. Another spurt of jealousy, one I stomp into powder. Even for all of her faults, Bianca can bring out a playful side of him I'm rarely allowed to see.

Does that make me sound possessive?

Now, I wish to disappear; the gardens, the stables, my room. Anyplace is preferable to here. Jealousy and anger aren't a good combination for me. I need to make sense of this new development and figure where Alessandro factors in to all of it.

Dinner progresses. Marcus and his guest keep up a steady conversation, and Alessandro and Bianca seem to vanish into a world comprised of only one another. I sit, my eyes glued to my plate, and sip on water. As the minutes pass with no change, I push back my chair and rise. Immediately, conversations cease and four sets of eyes focus on me.

I hesitate. "I—uh—don't feel well. I'm going to lie down."

It's the oldest excuse in the book, and everyone present knows it. None contradict me, and with a small bow of my head, I hurry from the dining room. Once in the corridor, I cut to the right.

The hallways and stairs are empty, which in itself isn't surprising, but the hundreds—possibly thousands—of lit candles that illuminate the enormous foyer, stairs, and passageways are definitely out of the ordinary. I ponder the abnormality of it during the descent of the grand staircase. When I reach the portrait gallery, candles are absent, and the torches along the walls are turned down low, sending warm light up and down the hallway and casting shadows over the ancestral faces.

The gardens beckon, and I'm through the double doors, down the veranda's steps, and crunching up the pathway toward the center in a matter of moments. My right thigh muscles protest the hurried pace, but I merely grit my teeth and push on.

Iridescent lights line the trails, frosting the green hedges, flowers, and shrubs in bluish-white and making them appear ethereal, and the full moon overhead adds an extra layer of illumination to my route.

I follow the twisting path, enter the central part of the garden, and skirt around the bubbling fountain, making a beeline for the dark gazebo. I enter its obscure interior, allowing the gloom to settle over me, and breathe a sigh of relief.

"This isn't your room."

I leap at the voice and whirl around. "What? Did you follow me?"

"Why not?" Alessandro leans against the column to my left, concealed within shadows. "Your sorry excuse for a lie wasn't believable. I had to find out why."

"I came out here to be alone."

"Why?" He cocks his head, inquisitive.

A shiver of awareness tickles up my spine. Even from the opposite side of the gazebo, I can smell his faint cologne.

"You're angry with me for some reason." Moonlight flashes in his eyes for a split second. "What have I done?"

"Nothing." I hug myself. My thoughts are a cluster of epic proportions, and I can't make heads or tails of them. How is he involved? Why do I feel as if he's been lying to me the entire time?

"Oh, I doubt that," he breathes. "Your heart rate says otherwise."

Stupid betraying emotions. "Fine." I meet his eyes dead on. "Tell me about Mikey."

"What about him?" A hint of suspicion.

I raise my chin a notch. "The club? The warehouse?"

"I told you I had nothing to do with any of that," he interrupts.

"Yeah...I don't think that's true." Betrayal slices through me. "Is it, Alessandro?"

"Where's this coming from?" He straightens, wary.

"You were all part of Luca's master plan, weren't you? Being captured by the Heads, warning us of an impending attack, the Dilecta being kidnapped and you escaping to 'rescue' us?

Everything was preplanned." I frown, hugging myself tighter. "Except...*you* planned it. Not Luca, not Mikey. *You*."

He pushes away from the column and steps into a beam of moonlight. His eyes are nearly black, his face taut with suppressed emotion.

"You were Paulo's greatest weapon, his ultimate commander," I continue, retreating a step. The words are harder to get out now. "You knew the perfect way to get to the Heads—through their Dilecta. After all, isn't that the reason your Lord started the war?"

Something shifts in him, his face becoming a cold, indifferent mask. "So you figured it out, huh? Bravo, Halifax. What do you want me to say?" Fury makes his voice soft. "Yeah, I planned everything. Right down to the minute detail, including the exact moment I was to escape."

"Why did you lie to me?" I choke, betrayal constricting my airways. "Going so far as to tell me that you have to do everything Luca tells you to? Pretending that you have had no hand in the attacks on the humans?"

"I was the distraction," he says simply. "The Heads never saw the attacks coming because their focus was on me."

I press a hand to my forehead, words abandoning me.

"Luca isn't like Paulo; he isn't kind, he isn't forgiving. He rules with fear and violence. You can't begin to fathom what we've been through in the last two hundred years trying to rebuild our Family."

"You'll gain no sympathy here," I state, dropping my hand. "I don't care."

"I had thought—no...I'd *hoped*—that over the last two months, you'd have changed your outlook on a few things."

"You thought wrong!" My voice rises in anger. "You should have just taken me back to my coven instead of dragging me off to your castle in Romania." I brush past him, and when he reaches out to me, I sidestep around his hand. "Don't *touch* me—never again. I'll not champion you to the Heads, Medici. You are exactly as my father said you were."

"Well then," a husky voice, low, lethal, dangerous, "it would appear, Dilecta, that your use is expired."

"Luca," Alessandro moves up beside me in a blink, "when did you get back?"

The man who steps from the shadows and into the lights of the garden sucks the breath from my lungs. He isn't tall, nor short; he isn't broad, nor skinny. He is average in every way possible. Only his three-piece suit, perfectly tailored to his body, screams of his wealth and status.

Something deadly simmers beneath the surface. He is the embodiment of evil, of darkness and death, the very air around him reeking of blood.

Against my will, I shrink back, closer to Alessandro. Fear ignites in my gut, sending tremors through my limbs.

This man terrifies me. More than my father. More than oppressive darkness. More than loneliness.

Luca gives his Heir a pointed look. "Mikey!"

The vampire in question melts from the shadows. "Yes, My Lord."

"Please kindly show the Halifax Dilecta the extent of our hospitality." Lord Medici refocuses his dark eyes on me. "And keep her somewhere her coven can't detect her. I can already smell their approach."

Alessandro tenses beside me. "What did you do, Danika?"

I tear my eyes away from Luca and meet his angry gaze. "I-I sent Conrad my location. He should be arriving tonight."

He moves away from me, hurt flashing across his face, and his uncle redraws my attention.

"Mikey," he commands and flicks his hand in my direction.

I stumble backward as Luca's second-in-command descends on me with a crooked grin. Terror bubbles up, similar to the water's dance in the fountain, and as I'm tossed over Mikey's shoulder like a sack of potatoes, a scream lodges in my throat.

"One moment." Lord Medici appears beside me and lifts my chin until our eyes meet. "Those humans you are so quick to defend, Halifax, are not so innocent. They're killing vampires by the dozens, and have for hundreds of years. The Seven you put so much faith in have buried the truth, just as they did the history

165

of the war, in favor of their hastily constructed peace. They ignore the annihilation of minor covens because as long as none of the governing Families are touched, all is fine."

As his words sink in, nausea climbs my throat. More lies. They wouldn't do that. But at the same time, I realize the truth in what he's said. How similar it sounds to the facts behind the war.

"Three days ago, a small coven was completely destroyed," he continues, and I close my eyes to block out his penetrating gaze. "Do you think your beloved Heads did anything? Do you think they avenged their brethren?" I can feel his breath on my face as he leans closer. "They did *nothing*. Not even when you, one of their precious Dilecta, was attacked. They stood before the masses, with their empty words."

Tears burn beneath my lids, and my nose itches. Pressure builds in my chest.

"Your life has become just as meaningless as the rest of ours." His voice drops a hair. "Just a warning, Halifax. If so much as *one* of my vampires is harmed by your brother, I will personally rip your throat out and feed you to the dogs."

A shiver races up my spine at the whispered promise.

CONFESSION 19

Sometimes, embracing the darkness within ourselves takes us one step closer to redemption.

I'm in a daze, my mind reeling from Luca's appearance and Alessandro's betrayal, and with little fight, Mikey carries me through the ground floor of the castle, down a candlelit corridor, across a wide landing with towering archways, and into a darkened hallway lined with wooden doors. At the end of it, a Medici newbie steps forward and yanks open the door on the left. A dusty, dim staircase is visible on the other side, and the knot of fear in my gut tightens further.

Another newbie joins Mikey, and the two underlings disappear as the stairs curve to the right. The sound of their feet clunking down can still be heard, softening the further they descend. Mikey adjusts me over his shoulder and proceeds them.

The minutes tick by as we move down in silence, and the air grows colder the deeper we travel. As the temperature drops, my thoughts clear and confusion quickly takes over.

Where are we going? I scan the shadowy stairwell, shifting to glance under his arm. Nothing but a curving, concrete wall and wooden stairs are visible through the gap.

I know I should be fighting, but something keeps me immobile. Fear? Uncertainty? Resignation? Grief? Another below-the-belt hit of betrayal.

I barely notice when the downward trek levels off and the lead vamps start up a long tunnel. No outside light penetrates the darkness spread before us, and the small lamp one of them carries gives off paltry illumination, barely cutting through the surrounding gloom.

We enter into a large, cavernous room, and I twist to take in my surroundings, ignoring the bite of Mikey's grip on my thighs. The moment I realize what the cages are, my stomach flips and panic overtakes me. I spin and jerk against his hold, desperate to escape.

"No!" I shriek, wriggling and writhing. "No! No!" I pound a fist on his back. "Let me go! Let me go!"

He chuckles gruffly. "And there's the fire, Halifax. Thought you were just going to let me throw you in a cell without so much as a peep. Here I was, thinking 'where's the fun in that?'."

My screams echo off the walls and around the chamber, a continuous plea for them to release me. He laughs as he carries me to an empty cell and tosses me inside. I land with bone jarring contact on the packed earth. Before I can get my bearings, he steps back out and slams the door shut with a loud *clang*.

My chest heaves and my body shakes as I crawl toward the bars on my hands and knees. Don't leave me down here. Tears clog my throat and prick my eyes, distorting my vision. The nightmares will come. It's too dark. Please.

The words I want to say, the pleas I'm so desperate to make, are lodged in my throat, and all I can do is gasp like a fish.

Something akin to pity flashes through his eyes, but then it's gone just as quickly. His face hardens, matching those of his companions. With cold, indifferent expressions, the three turn and make their way back across the dirt floor to the wooden staircase, leaving me at the mercy of the creeping shadows.

I pound on the bars, rasping thin breaths in and out. "Don't take the light. Please don't take the light."

The faint illumination recedes with their departure and I'm sunk into darkness. Memories assault, unforgiving, unprejudiced. A seven year old me, exploring the catacombs with a toy flashlight. The beam dying halfway into the caverns. Becoming lost. No one had heard my soft cries, and I'd spent the entire night, trapped beneath ground, in the stifling, overwhelming gloom.

And now, I feel just as trapped, just as terrified, as I did then.

The minutes turn to hours. My pleas fade and I sit in shock, leaning limply against the cool metal. I close my eyes, trying to block out the dank, suffocating darkness. The chill in the air has long since settled into my bones, calming the violent shivers, but now, a perpetual sting resides behind my lids. No matter how hard I try to cry, or how many times I blink, the effort is in vain. No tears fall, and the burning remains.

This is a fear I've never overcome.

I pull my knees up to my chest and wrap my arms around them, pressing back into the stone as far as I can. The course rocks bite into my shoulder blades and along parts of my spine, but I welcome the pain it causes. Embrace it. I release a shaky breath and swallow hard, keeping my gaze glued to the impenetrable, shifting black outside the bars of my cage.

Father used to say that to despair is to realize your limitations, and that to overcome those limitations, one must embrace their despair. I can't say why his words spring to mind at this moment, but they rise within me.

There have been many moments over the last two months when I've teetered on the edge of utter hopelessness, a breath away from tumbling into the calm, motionless void. But I'd always been pulled from the brink, talked back from the edge with compassion and laughter.

Now I plunge, unaided, downward, hitting the surface without causing so much as a ripple. *Embrace the despair. Realize your limitations.* Father's voice echoes through the chasm, encouraging me deeper beneath. *Realize them, my child. Overcome them.*

I close my eyes, release all of my pent up anger, bitterness, and grief on a sigh, and allow myself to sink.

Can I change what happened two hundred years ago? Alter the injustice and pain both sides have suffered? Is it possible to bring back Rosalie and Paulo or the Head's Heir who was murdered? Can I change the fact that vampires view death and chaos differently, the fact they lie and cheat, that their perceptions are often twisted and skewed? Can I change Alessandro's lies? Luca's desire for vengeance? The Heads'

169

misguided sense of honor? *Their* lies and *their* deceit? Does this anger have to define me? Hold me back? Control me?

The oppressive despair pulses around me—once, twice, thrice—sending ripples across the surface of the watery depths.

Can I take back the fact that I trust Alessandro, that even with his lies, I've come to respect the Medici vampire with dark eyes and secretive smiles? Can I change the gratitude I feel, the relief that he's rescued me from more than just mankind's prejudiced aggression? Can I stop the feelings building within me, the words I'm not confident to utter?

More ripples.

Can I change *who* I am, my purpose, my future? Can I change the responsibilities weighing on me, the expectations put forth, the constant feeling of failure that hangs over my head like a death sentence?

The ripples grow, coming quicker, stronger, closer together. They spiral out and away, disappearing into the darkness that surrounds me. Everything begins to shift.

I *am* the Halifax Dilecta. I'm not perfect; I'm human. Just as vampires have made mistakes, as have I. I may not be able to change *anything* about the situation, about the Medicis and the governing Seven, but I can be what my father trained me to be. I can be the bridge, the protector and guardian, between humans and vampires.

I squash the terror of the darkness. It's time to rise, time to take my place as the Halifax Dilecta.

I dig the cellphone from the pocket of my summer dress, sending up a silent thanks that Mikey didn't search me and Luca was too distracted to notice I carried it, and power it on. The screen lights up, causing me to cringe from its brightness. Blinking away the moisture, I twist the phone back around to find the screen cracked from Mikey's less-than-gentle drop.

I bite my lip. Will there be reception this far underground? Does the crack mean the phone is broken? Will this work?

I'm holding my breath when the first text from Conrad buzzes in, and I release it with an excited squeak. Five more alerts. Three messages from yesterday, one from earlier this morning sent by Laura, the final one sent an hour ago.

He's here. He's found me.

My heart leaps in relief, and I quickly fire off a response to his most recent text. But when the status registers as *sending* for a few seconds too long, I stare at the reception bar, watching it waver between one and zero.

"Please," I whisper, lifting the phone high above my head and moving it around in an effort to find the best signal. "Please."

Message not sent.

I retry, wait a minute, and then release a curse that would make Mother blush and scold me senseless.

Using the light of the cracked screen, I stand and survey my surroundings. Maybe if I move to another spot, I'll have a better chance. The next ten minutes consist of message rejections, resends, and a constant walk around the small cell with the phone held aloft.

Suddenly, a sliver of noise disrupts the silence beyond the bars, and I freeze, my heart picking up a frantic pace. My hand, still grasping the phone, lowers and presses the bright screen against my flower clad stomach, immediately sinking me into darkness.

"I thought you'd be languishing away down here." Alessandro's amusement cuts through the gloom. "Instead, you're sending messages."

"W-what are you doing here?" My voice quivers. "Come to poke fun at the girl in the cage?"

"Hardly."

"Then go away."

"Can't do that. I've come to talk."

I squint into the darkness. "Oh yeah? What if I don't want to listen?"

"Tough. You're stuck in a cage." A foot scuffs to the left. "You've got no choice but to listen."

"Piss off, Medici." I straighten and lift my chin a notch.

"Oh, I'm plenty pissed off."

I grit my teeth at his quip. "That's not what I meant."

He laughs, low and derisive, and the sound emerges from my right. I spin toward it, searching.

"Is this some game to you?" I snap, and he chuckles again, softer, deadlier.

"Like a game of cat and mouse," he responds. "How does it feel being the one entrapped? The one at the mercy of another?"

I recall his stint in my family's catacombs. "I'm having the time of my life. Didn't you?"

An intoxicating combination of emotions swirl within me, but I can't isolate a single one. Humor, anger, excitement, anticipation, resentment, and delight.

"I don't appreciate people lying to me," he growls.

"You don't say?" I blindly reach for the bars and, once I find them, press my face between two slats. "Sucks, doesn't it?"

"You promised you'd help us."

"And you promised you were nothing like Luca."

I can sense him move, closing the distance to the cell. His breath is warm against my cheek, alerting me to his arrival, but I don't budge, even though my heart thunders against my ribs. It takes everything in me not to reach through the bars and touch him.

"Humans have been slaughtering vampires for hundreds of years," he says softly, his words a feather light touch. "Luca has only done what is necessary to protect our Family. Just as your Head has done, Halifax."

"Maybe."

"You're blind."

"And *you're* blind, Alessandro. Tit-for-tat doesn't make murder acceptable."

"We're never going to agree."

"Probably."

"What about the men who attacked you? Did they deserve to live after what they did?"

My heart skips a beat. "Maybe. Maybe not. That's not for *you* to decide."

He falls silent.

I have a moment of uncertainty, squinting into the darkness, but the soft brush of his breath across my cheek lets me know he's still there, just a finger length away. He's so close; all

172

I need to do is reach out. An inch, nothing more. But doing that means I accept my feelings for him. No…I'm not ready.

I push myself back from the bars. "Go away, Alessandro. I'm done *listening*."

"Luca plans to kill your brother tonight. The moment he crosses into our boundary, Danika, he's free game. Along with the Campbell Dilecta who travels with him."

I freeze, bile climbing my throat, and turn my head to peer at him blindly. "Another lie."

"You can save him."

"Lies."

"Promise to help us."

Tears constrict my airways and I choke on a cry. "*Never.*"

"I'm to lead the attack," he states. "You know I'll do it; I'll kill him."

Embrace the despair. Rise above it.

The situation is out of my hands; I can sense it. Whether I want to help the Medici coven, whether I agree with anything they've done, I've been sucked into this. This right here, the feud between our two Families, is part of that gap I, as a Dilecta, must bridge.

"Fine." Shoulders slumped and head bowed, my acquiescence comes on a sigh, heavy with pain and resignation. "I'll do it." Slowly, I raise my head and stare at the place I know he stands. "But tell me something, Alessandro. Why me? Of all the Dilecta, why *me*?"

"Because," a fingertip down my cheek, the barest of touches, "you're mine."

My breath stutters and stomach flips. "What did you say?"

Silence.

"Alessandro?"

More silence. Not even the air shifts.

I activate the screen. Luminescent light fills the cage and touches on the area outside the bars. I sweep the light around and find scuffed dirt and boot prints.

He's gone.

CONFESSION 20
The only downside of returning betrayal with betrayal is the guilt.

Minutes pass; another hour. The silence is smothering. Even my yells for Alessandro are swallowed by the thick darkness that not even my phone's screen can penetrate. I'm left with nothing but my thoughts and a lingering hope I don't dare entertain.

His parting words don't make any sense—not with Bianca in the picture. Bitter annoyance ignites, colliding with the jealousy that's been at a constant simmer. I ball my hands into fists and give my head a firm shake.

Nope. I won't let him play me again.

Voices interrupt my musings, and my head snaps to the right. A faint light grows brighter as the new arrivals draw closer. At first, I can't understand what they're saying, but as they approach, I realize they're speaking in rapid Italian.

A lantern comes into view followed by two Medicis clad in tall combat boots, black jeans, and long trench coats that reach mid-calf. Their eyes glitter like black diamonds as they zero in on me pressed against the bars, watching their approach with apprehension. Their discussion ceases immediately.

"Dilecta," the one holding the lantern greets in a warm voice, and bows his head in a respectfulness that surprises me.

I step back from the bars warily. "Where's Alessandro?"

"Lord Medici is overseeing the assault," the lantern-bearer replies, and nods at his companion who then approaches

174

with a set of keys. "He has asked that you join him on the ramparts."

"Where is my brother?" I brace my feet apart and lift my arms, prepping to defend myself should the "key man" attempt more than unlocking the door. "And my coven?"

The Medici with the light stays silent.

The key is inserted. With the sound of grinding metal, the door swings open, and he returns to the lantern-bearer's side.

My exit is hesitant, contemplative; like a rabbit testing the air outside its den. I peek out first, focusing on the two vamps several feet away, and then one foot follows. When neither of them move, the other foot and my torso join the rest of me.

With a satisfied nod, the lantern-bearer spins and begins striding across the cavern toward the tunnel and stairs to the surface, taking the light with him. My heart jolts, and I hurry after them, not wanting to be left alone in the dark again.

The climb is long and tedious. My body, already fatigued, begins a gradual decline toward pass-out-at-any-moment exhausted. The tender bone and weakened muscle strain beneath the repetitious bunch and flex of the uneven ascent. My breathing becomes labored. Since Mikey had carried me all the way down, I hadn't put much thought into what all would go into actually climbing back out again.

Definitely not the highlight of my day…or week.

After what feels like hours, we emerge from the cool stairway into the familiar corridor lined with wooden doors.

The first thing I notice is the sound—shattering glass, crumbling brick, guttural bellows and hisses. It's the convergence of feuding Families.

There are two hundred years' worth of emotion in their cries; two hundred years' worth of hate and prejudice. There's an unspoken history, a hint of betrayal and vengeance.

"The Halifax Heir did not arrive with just Halifax," the lantern-bearer says, leading the way down the hallway. "Members from each of the governing Families fight beside him."

His words are a punch to the gut.

We turn the corner, and through the great glass windows that line the new hallway, I can see chaos just on the other side.

175

Medici, dressed similar to my escorts, collide with those from other covens, all fangs and nails. Deep hisses, filled with a rage and self-preservation, saturate the air.

I tear my wide eyes away from the scene and start toward my companions, a shiver of dread racing up my spine. I've taken three steps when the glass in front of me explodes, and I stumble backward, lifting my arms in a futile attempt to protect my face from the flying shards. I feel the sting on my cheeks and along my arms, and I grit my teeth against the pain, swallowing down a cry.

Three vampires tumble through the opening, into the hallway. As two of them turn to face my escorts, the third spins toward me with a grin.

"Miss Halifax."

"Richard!" I immediately recognize my Halifax bodyguard and fly into him, tears of relief filling my eyes.

He shoots a look over his shoulder, wrapping a protective arm around me. "We need to go. Your brother is waiting."

"Wait!" I shake my head. "I can't. I have to go to Alessandro."

"No can do, Miss Halifax. I've got my orders."

"Richard, no!"

His lips thin, and with an apologetic look, he lifts me and tosses me over his shoulder.

I smack his back with my fist. "Put me down, Richard. That's an order."

These guys have a thing for carrying me over their shoulders, don't they? Princess style must be *so* overrated…

"Sorry, miss." He leaps through the shattered window, jostling me when he lands, and takes off through a mass of gyrating, hissing, grunting vampires. None of them pay him any attention.

Fear accelerates through me, and I pound on his back frantically. "Take me back to them. He'll kill Conrad if I don't go to him." I begin thrashing, ignoring the tightness in my ribs and my stinging arms and cheek. "Take me back! Please!"

I recognize the area of the grounds he's racing across, and I twist to face the battlements where Alessandro stands. I need to go to him. I promised I would. Can he see me? Can he tell that I'm being dragged off against my will?

Across the distance, our eyes meet. My stomach jolts in shock at the anger glimpsed there, and I shrink into myself in sudden fear.

No. No, please.

His gaze snaps to somewhere in front of us, in the direction Richard is heading. With a sinking feeling, I realize he's found Conrad. My heart skips a terrified beat, and I resume pounding on my bodyguard's back and pleading for him to return me.

When I glance back to Alessandro, it's to find he's vanished.

And now, I can't get to my brother quick enough. "Hurry, Richard! Hurry!"

If he's confused by my sudden request change, he doesn't show it, and thankfully, puts on a burst of speed. We skirt around another mass of brawling undead and cross an expanse of lawn littered with moaning wounded.

Soon, he's skidding to a halt, and rough hands drag me from his shoulder. I'm spun around and pulled into a tight embrace that sends my ribs screaming in agony. But I recognize these arms, and this strength, and this comfort.

Conrad.

No sooner does he release me then I'm pulled into another hug. This one is warm and soft, and I sink into it with a sigh of relief, forgetting, for just a moment, the anxiety unfurling in my gut.

"You're safe," Laura murmurs, and I bite my lip against the rise of tears. "We've finally found you."

Reality comes crashing home and I pull back. "No, you can't. I-I can't. I have to go to him."

"Who?" Conrad demands, his eyes spitting fire. "Medici?"

"What happened to your face?" Laura gasps, horrified. She reaches out and gently pulls out a shard of glass embedded in my cheek. And then another, and another. One by one, she drops them into the grass, her face a mask of dismay.

"They don't hurt," I say hurriedly. Adrenaline is a killer beast during moments of high-stress.

I step back from her and come up against a solid chest, and a glance over my shoulder confirms it's Con.

"You're not going anywhere," he growls. "I've finally got you back."

"No, you—" My eyes snag on Alessandro approaching behind him.

An undead from one of the seven covens rushes him. Alessandro plants his hand in the center of the vampire's face and shoves, launching him back twenty feet in the air. A Halifax sweeps in from his left, and after blocking an uncoordinated swing, Alessandro nestles his fist into the undead's gut with enough force, my brother's minion disappears into a cluster of hissing, spitting fighters battling it out several feet away.

His dark gaze never leaves mine.

It's both terrifying and incredibly attractive.

Richard grabs me and shoves me behind him at the same moment Conrad shifts protectively in front of Laura. I don't have time to consider the confusing nature of it before the Medici Heir is upon us.

"Halifax." His greeting is deadly soft.

"Medici scum," Conrad spits.

"She is mine." Dark eyes flick to me. "Give her to me."

"She is the Halifax Dilecta." Con stares him down. "She's going nowhere but home."

Alessandro raises an eyebrow. "Danika?"

"You dare call her—"

I step around Richard and cross the short distance to Alessandro, interrupting my brother. It's hard to ignore the surprise and shock on their faces the instant they understand the implications of what I've done.

I've chosen the Medicis over my coven.

I meet Conrad's eyes, my own swimming with tears. "I'm sorry, Con. I tried to tell you."

"What are you *doing*, Danika?" he chokes, hurt crossing his face.

"I made him a promise." I swallow hard against the lump of despair. There's no going back now. Embrace it.

178

"Whatever it was, it's not worth this."

The image of him, dead and awaiting the rising sun, flashes through my head. "Yes. It is."

Grief rises swiftly, and I gasp on a sob, turning my head away from him. A soft, feather light touch on my bleeding cheek has me locking eyes with Alessandro. His hand hovers, uncertain, and his eyes take in the wounds on my face and arms.

Suddenly, an iron grip closes around my upper arm, and I'm jerked back from him and into a set of familiar arms. Richard entraps me, holding me firm against his chest.

In a flash, Conrad lunges at Alessandro, and Halifax and Campbell security teams close in around Laura and me. All I can do is watch them fight, a scream building in my throat.

It's an even back-and-forth. Con lands a hit; Alessandro counters it. Their speed becomes nothing more than a blur, and I struggle against my bodyguard's hold, panic clutching me.

Conrad appears, his body flying through the air, and collides with a large tree. On the next breath, Alessandro materializes, yanks him up again, and they disappear into a flurry of flying fists, feet, and gnashing fangs.

Minutes pass.

And then the two Heirs freeze. As if time itself has stopped.

The growing hysteria reaches a climax and explodes from me in a gut wrenching scream, mingling with Laura's own cry of anguish.

Alessandro grips Conrad by the throat, elongated nails piercing into his windpipe. He holds my brother aloft, a breath away from ending it, from ending the Halifax heir.

My thrash becomes more frantic, desperation clawing upward and threatening to suffocate me. I don't know why Richard's arms loosen—surprise at Conrad's defeat, fear at losing the Heir—but I take advantage of it and wriggle my way from his hold. The second my feet hit the ground, I shove through the surrounding guards. I'm sprinting across the lawn before the Halifaxs and Campbells realize I've broken free.

"Let him go!" I shriek. "Alessandro!" The distance between us is as vast as an ocean. Fear chokes me, desperation propels me. "Let him go! I beg of you!"

179

Dark eyes meet mine, and I jerk my head in some approximation of a *no*.

If you do this, my eyes scream, I'll never forgive you. *Never!*

He turns his head, transferring his attention back to Conrad. "Your life is spared, Halifax, because of a promise I made to your Dilecta. Remember that. She is mine until Dormiam. Stay away from her."

Just before I reach them, he releases him with a snap, and my brother crumbles to the ground. I collapse at his side and with trembling hands, gather him close. His arms encircle me, like a vise.

"I'm sorry," I wheeze, burying my face in his neck. "I'm so sorry." Tears burn but I blink them away. "I'm sorry, Conrad."

"What have you done?" he whispers. "Dani, what have you *done?*"

"He promised me he wouldn't kill you. He promised."

"I cannot save you now."

"I know." My voice wavers. "Please forgive me. I had to protect you."

He pulls back and cups my face, his expression the gentlest I've ever seen it. "I know, sister. And I understand." His gaze flicks to Alessandro, pauses for a moment, and then returns to me. "You need to go, Dani. I promise I'll find you again, and *nothing* and *no one* will stand in my way of taking you home."

I don't want to let go; doing so means I'm accepting the terms of my agreement with Alessandro. It means I'm abandoning my coven, abandoning my role as Halifax Dilecta. But I have to. I have to stand up.

I detach myself from him and rise on shaky legs. Laura immediately takes my place, and for the second time, I note their bizarre intimacy. Something must have happened between them during the last two months.

Alessandro's touch is tentative, as if he isn't sure of himself or me

I shift away from him, my body stiffening. "Don't."

His hand drops away.

The crowd parts and Luca emerges, striding across the lawn with Mikey, Bianca, Marcus, and Mr. Abrahms trailing behind. A twisted smile adorns his pale face, and his dark eyes take in the scene with bitter pleasure.

"*Bravo*, Alessandro." His grin widens and he slaps his Heir on the back. "*Molto bene.*"

Alessandro doesn't respond, but his body moves subtly closer to mine, as if to protect, to guard.

"Now then, Halifax." Luca sweeps his gaze over all those assembled. "Duchamp. Broadhurst. Diavolo. Nakamura. Richter. Campbell." He growls the last coven. "It's a pleasure to see everyone again after so long. I hope you've been enjoying our hospitality." His voice oozes with merciless hate, a quietly suppressed rage.

He approaches me, and once again, I find myself shrinking beneath his lethal glare. Though he looks sharp in his black suit with a blood red tie, his clothing does little to conceal the cruelness simmering beneath the surface. Vampires from the seven covens cower away from him in a surprising show of submissiveness and even fear.

I'm frozen in place, terror keeping me immobile. I don't even so much as flinch when he reaches out and trails a finger over where my pulse flutters erratically in my throat. I swallow hard and his eyes watch the obvious movement.

He cocks his head, moving his attention to Conrad and Laura. "Hmm…another Dilecta. And who might you belong to? No, don't tell me." His smile dips, turning into a sneer. "Campbell."

One minute he's in front of me, and the next, he's jerking Laura to her feet and wrapping his hand around her throat. Conrad struggles to his feet beside her, something close to fear flitting across his face.

Luca shoots him a sideways look, as if gauging his response, and then looks back over his shoulder at me. Con's eyes dart to mine, and his muscles tighten, coiling.

A slow smile contorts the sneer, and he releases the Campbell Dilecta with a jolt.

"The most beautiful revenge," he says, beginning a slow saunter toward me, "would be to take the Campbell's Dilecta, just as they did to us." He reaches me and I stumble back a step. "But I don't think so."

Alessandro tenses.

Luca yanks me to him and whirls to face Conrad, who already has his arms around Laura. "An eye for an eye, Halifax." He bares his fangs. "A sibling for a sibling."

His fangs pierce my skin, and my surprised scream dies in my throat. His lips are eerily cold, a contrast to the warm blood I feel trickling down my neck. My eyes roll into my head, and I sag against his arm.

Before the black embrace of unconsciousness grabs me, I'm mildly aware of Alessandro straining against multiple vampires, his face a mask of outrage and fear. I'm mildly aware of my brother frozen in place, eyes wide with astonishment.

And I'm mildly aware of a long, soul searing scream.

But who's, I don't know.

CONFESSION 21

Am I a vampire? This should make me happy, right?
Only...I'm not sure it does.

I recognize the classroom, the whiteboard, the windows overlooking the bus lane. The tall trees outside are bursting with leaves that sway from a slight breeze. There are the desks covered in lame graffiti, written in freshmen hands, and Mr. Jones, the graying, rotund history teacher whose heavy breathing fills the silence. The walls behind him are covered in posters from World War I and World War II, depicting women urging people to purchase bonds, to support the war effort and the soldiers fighting overseas. There are announcements of new weaponry and breakdowns of the uniforms for each war.

"Miss Halifax." Mr. Jones' voice cuts through the stillness, and I snap my attention to him, nervous. "Can you answer the question?"

A quick scan shows that he and I are the only two present, and my unease grows.

"Could you—uh—repeat it, sir?"

He sighs. "Who was Viktor Carnigov?"

The name rings a bell, and my face scrunches in thought. "He was..."

"Yes, Miss Halifax?" Impatience creeps into his voice.

"The father of...vampires, sir?"

He nods. "Very good. Yes, he was the father of vampires, the first of his kind. All others came after him." He leans back in his chair and crosses his arms. "And do you remember what happened to him?"

"He disappeared, sir." I mimic his posture, though my chair is not as comfortable as his appears. "Around the 14th century, wasn't it?"

"Yes, Miss Halifax, but how? And why?"

Conrad had said it was because he was obsolete, viewing the changing world with scorn and distaste, and that he'd gone beneath ground to spend the rest of his days in slumber to escape it.

Father, and many of the Heads, however, believe he was slayed.

"I'm not sure what happened to him, sir," I admit.

"Then let me ask you this: do you believe he's still alive?"

My eyes widen at the question. "I don't honestly know, sir."

"Fair enough." He cocks his head, thoughtful. "Let's say that he's still alive, hiding somewhere, biding his time." I nod. "What do you think he would do in today's world? How would he react to the relations between vampires and humans?"

I think about that for a moment. Viktor is old vampire, ancient, traditional. He isn't from this time, and he wouldn't see things as my father does. Humans are a food source, a method of reproducing and spreading.

"He'd be lost," I say eventually. "Uncertain. Possibly even angry with what he sees."

"Why do you say that?"

"Because," I gnaw on my lip, "he reigned during an age when slayers were prevalent, people lived in fear of vampires, and tales of the undead were whispered around hearths at night."

"And what about the vampire war two hundred years ago?"

His question takes me off guard. "What about it?"

"How do you think he'd react to it?"

"Umm," I shrug, "I'm not sure."

"Think, Miss Halifax. Use your brain." Something creeps into his voice, something that sets my teeth on edge. "Would he have taken a side?"

"I don't see how that's relevant, Mr. Jones." I frown, confused, my surroundings starting to sink in. "Why exactly am I here? What is this? After school detention?"

"Just answer the question."

"I don't want to." The unease is back. "What's going on? I don't understand why I'm here."

The images around me begin to shift and whirl, the colors colliding like a swirling mixture of paints. I can't rise from the desk. Something is keeping me in place, immobile. A glance down sends my heart hammering against my ribs. I'm strapped to the chair. A scream builds in my throat.

The masked men appear, their dark eyes, startlingly familiar, the only thing visible upon their covered faces.

I struggle against the bindings, opening my mouth to release the scream, but no sound emerges, just silence and air. The ropes hold me fast, unbreakable, without the slightest give. A soft sob escapes, desperation and fear gripping me.

"We'll make you regret your devotion to the vampires," they chorus in deep voices that drip with malevolence. "Daywalker. The blood of thousands of innocents bathe your hands."

I shake my head, gasping on denial. I ache to tell them that I'm human, desperate for them to understand; I need them to hear me, to believe me.

"We'll make you pay for what you've done," they continue, and their combined voices echo eerily in the dark warehouse. "Blood for blood."

Suddenly, warm liquid tickles my toes. I glance down and a swift wave of nausea hits me. Horrified, my eyes take in the blood pooled beneath my chair and smeared over my digits. The longer I stare, the higher it rises, completely smothering my feet and climbing up my ankles. I wriggle harder against the ropes, my breath escaping in an explosion of terror. Something catches my attention, and I snap my head up as another jolt of shock punches me.

185

An entire lake of thick crimson surrounds me, covers me. Warm and sticky.

"The blood of thousands bathes you, Daywalker." The men's voices echo in the silence.

No! That's not true! I didn't kill them! I strain against the bindings, trying to lift my body from the blood quickly climbing my torso. Please!

Then I see him, striding toward me across the smooth surface, leaving barely a ripple in his wake.

Luca.

His eyes are black; a dangerous gleam that sends a chill up my spine. There are a hundred promises, a million threats. A smile of unspoken horrors to beget; a twist of his lips, a glint of sharp teeth.

I find my voice and scream.

"Danika." My name is a whisper on those cruel lips. "Wake up."

I thrash against the ropes, my gaze glued to his.

"Wake up, Halifax."

I continue to scream.

A hard slap across my face, and my eyes snap open, wide and panicked. I scramble backward in the covers, frantic to get the red, silk sheets off my legs. Each breath is agony in my burning lungs, and I can feel hysteria climbing, sealing my airways.

Another stinging slap.

I freeze.

Bianca hovers near me, her face a mask of annoyance. "Enough, Halifax!"

Anxiety trickles out as confusion rises up. I look around the room, taking in the familiar surroundings.

"What—" I lick my dry lips. "What's going on? What happened?" The last vestiges of the nightmare begin to fade. "I don't—I can't—" Frowning, I scan the room again.

"You've been asleep for a couple days," she says, straightening away from me. "Give yourself time to adjust. Here," she hands me a glass of water, "drink." When I down half of it and come up coughing, she sighs. "Slowly, Halifax. It's not going anywhere."

Bit by bit, the fight between the covens comes back to me. Conrad and Laura; the altercation between the two Heirs; Richard holding me back, and—

My hand goes to my throat and the thick bandage. "Am I..."

"What?" She cocks an eyebrow. "A vampire?"

I gaze at her in frightened anticipation.

After an inordinate amount of time in which my anxiety level increases tenfold, a hint of a smile kicks up on side of her mouth.

"Sadly, no." She rises, crosses the room, and throws back the thick curtains. Gray sunlight pours through the glass, and her eyes flick toward my hands clutching the glass in my lap. "That'd probably hurt, if so."

I look down to find a beam warming my pale knuckles. The expelling relief is far from silent, and I choke on the emotions bubbling up within me.

I'm still human.

"Why?" I ask, lifting my gaze back to hers. "He bit me. Why didn't I change?"

She shrugs. "No clue. I guess my understanding of vampirism causes are limited like yours."

"How long was I asleep for?"

"Couple days. You lost quite a bit of blood."

I snort. "Ha!"

"We're leaving tonight," she says, and my sarcastic smile melts from my face. "The covens will return for you, and they'll bring more with them. Father and Lord Medici think it's best that we move you somewhere they won't be able to find you."

"Like?" My heart pounds. They're moving me?

A smirk. "You'll see."

Uneasy, I finish the water and replace the glass on the nightstand. Silence settles over the room, and for the first time, I hear the soft patter of rain. My eyes lower back to my hands, littered in tiny cuts, and I trace one of them lightly with a fingertip.

"Your coven cleared out of here pretty quickly once Luca bit you."

I glance up at the weariness in her voice, and she turns from her survey of the gardens outside the window.

"I didn't *ask* him to bite me, Bianca," I say defensively.

"No," she sighs, "I don't suppose you did. Lord Medici is a complicated man." She smiles thinly and shifts back to the window.

As I watch, she seems to curl into herself. Her eyes glaze over, and some emotion—pain, heartache, grief—flits across her face. It's minute, the faintest pinching around her mouth and flutter of her lashes.

But it's enough.

"You're in love with Luca Medici." My mouth sags open in astonishment.

She tenses. "Yes."

"But…"

"What?" She turns her head and pierces me with an emerald glare, as if daring me to judge her. "You think he's too dangerous? Volatile? A murderer? You assume he doesn't deserve someone's love because he's a Medici?"

"No!" My eyes widen. "I thought you were in love with Alessandro." Though I will admit I'm horrified and shocked to learn of her affections toward the evil man.

The fight leaves her in a whoosh, confusion alighting in her features. "Alessandro? Why would I be in love with Alessandro?"

"Well…you know…" I gesture widely, but her confusion only grows.

"No," she shakes her head, "I *don't* know."

"Because of…the—uh—dinner," I squeak the last word, and she stares at me in silence. "And the—uh—ride to the—uh," I clear my throat, finishing lamely, "lake."

"You think I'm in love with Alessandro because I threatened you at the lake, and I have some form of relationship with him?" She crosses her arms.

Well when she says it *that* way…

"Listen, Halifax." She rubs the space between her eyebrows, frustrated. "He and I are like siblings, nothing more

188

than best friends. He's known me since I was a baby. And besides, the conversation at the lake," she purses her lips, "I didn't specify *which* Lord Medici I was in love with. Did I?"

"Ah...no."

"Not that it makes any difference." She hugs herself and turns her attention back to the rain soaked gardens.

Silence descends over us once more, and I find myself considering her with new eyes.

What if her attitude is derived from a broken heart? What if she's concealing her emotions behind a mask of perfection in order to not reveal them? If a Dilecta, even one in training, is not supposed to love a vampire, then she's drowning in the forbidden.

"Well," she says, breaking the silence, "I'd better go inform Father that you're awake." She pushes away from the window and strides to the door. There, she pauses and turns back to me. "What you've figured out, Halifax, don't tell anyone. I'll smother you in your sleep if you do."

***

Nightfall finds us seated around the table in the dining room. Alessandro and Luca sit across from Bianca and me, and Mr. Demms takes the head while the ever-present Mikey takes up position just behind Luca.

The Medici Head twirls a crystal goblet with long, elegant fingers, his dark eyes focused on the dip and sway of its bloody contents. His mouth, normally twisted in a cruel sneer or spewing venomous words, is relaxed and blessedly silent.

Fear pumps through me with every heartbeat, clenching my gut and clawing its way up my throat. I swallow it down, stomp it into submission. As if of its own will, my hand covers the bandage on my throat. I keep my eyes averted. The last thing I need is to draw his attention.

A man I don't recognize stands beside Marcus, a file open in his broad hands. He removes a sheaf of paper, sets it in front of Mr. Demms, and retrieves six tickets from the folder.

"The plane leaves Henri Coandă International tomorrow evening," he explains, and Marcus nods. "It'll arrive at Kavala, and from there, a car will take you to Keramoti where the *Rosalie* is anchored in anticipation of your arrival."

"Very good." Mr. Demms nods again.

"I have secured passage for Mr. Michael—"

"Mikey," the vampire interrupts. "I haven't been Michael in two hundred years."

"Apologies, sir." The gentleman inclines his head.

Over the top of Luca's head, I make eye contact with Mikey. He gives me a crooked grin and a wink, and I avert my attention back to the itinerary.

"Mikey will ride with us," Marcus says, tapping at something on the paper in front of him. "It's less than a twenty minute drive from the airport to where the yacht will be anchored."

"Very good, sir."

"We'll have him below deck before the sun rises." He says this for Luca's benefit because the Vampire Lord nods in acknowledgment.

"Lord Medici and Mr. Medici will join you three days later," the gentleman continues, and my gaze flicks to Alessandro for a brief moment.

He isn't coming with us? Why?

"Is the security team standing by?" Marcus asks, flipping to the next page in the stack.

"Yes, sir. There is a team to escort you to Henri Coandă, and another one on standby in Kavala to escort you to the yacht. From there, the boat's team will take over."

"Well done, Victor." Mr. Demms gives the gentleman a pleased smile.

The name sends a chill up my spine, reminding me of the nightmare Bianca had awaken me from.

Viktor Carnigov; the father of vampires. First of his kind.

Why had I dreamed about him? Why now? That portion of the dream, with Mr. Jones, had been more of a memory than anything else, and I can remember the discussion I'd had with him freshman year. Even at that time, I'd been confused by his questions; almost as if he were trying to convey an unspoken message. It hadn't made much sense, and I'd pushed it to the back of my mind as I'd done many things at that age that hadn't pertained to my drive to become a vampire.

And that included dead ancients.

I can feel Alessandro's eyes on me, but I keep mine stubbornly fixed on the Medici Dilecta and his young assistant. Even though the relief at finding out Bianca isn't in love with Alessandro was staggering, I can still feel the betrayal and hurt circulating through me. I've abandoned my coven because of him, turned my back on my family to protect my brother. At one time, I believed the Medici vamp to be something other than the manipulative jerk he is. I'd been burned, my feelings had been burned.

"Well, if we're done here," Bianca rises, "I think us humans should get to bed." She throws me a look and I follow her out of my chair. "Good night."

With a dip of her head in parting, she loops her arm through mine and tugs me toward the door. I'm momentarily taken aback by her touch, and I give her an incredulous look as we turn our back on the table and the men.

Once in the hallway, she releases me and starts toward the stairs leading to the upper level rooms.

I stand frozen to the spot, uncertain and just a little bit confused, my mind frantically trying to unravel her motive. But she doesn't turn back, she doesn't pause and beckon me to follow.

She's disappeared by the time I shake myself from my stupor and start after her. I've made it up ten of the twenty-two steps when the sound of my name causes me to pause. I turn back to find Alessandro at the base of the staircase, his hand resting on the stone balustrade.

"What do you want?" I demand, arching a brow. "Come to tell more lies? Or are you coming to gloat about me choosing your murderous coven over my own?"

I know I'm entering dangerous territory by insulting his Family, and by the slight hardening around his mouth, the slur hasn't gone unnoticed. What can I say? I thrive living on the edge.

"I wanted to see how you were faring." He clenches his jaw, annoyed.

191

"How I'm *faring*?" I cross my arms. "I'm *faring* just fine, no thanks to your uncle." I scowl. "And no thanks to you."

"I didn't bite you, Halifax," he snaps defensively, running a hand through his already mussed hair. "And I *saved* you from being turned. Luca," he gestures toward the dining room where the men are still gathered, "was ready to flood your veins with his venom. You know what happens after that."

Apparently, I really didn't know because I'd woken up earlier fully expecting to be a vampire. Well…technically, I didn't expect to wake up at all. But who's complaining, right?

"He had every intention to turn you, Danika," he continues. "I could smell the venom in the air. Your brother and I, together, were the only thing that kept him from releasing it into your bloodstream."

My brother? What did Conrad do?

As if reading my mind, Alessandro replies, "He promised to leave, to take the covens from the Medici land and not return here."

"And you? What did *you* promise?"

He hesitates.

I snort and shake my head. "Figures."

CONFESSION 22

The world is darker and scarier than I knew, and I really was a sheltered, spoiled child.

Henri Coandă International Airport isn't the largest airport I've been to, but it definitely ranks up there as one of the busiest. From what Mr. Demms said, it's one of two hubs in Bucharest and sees the most travel in Romania. Everywhere we look, there are lines. Lines for ticketing, lines for baggage, lines for security. Even with our protection detail and VVIP passes, courtesy of Mr. Demms' business associates, we still find ourselves following the herds.

I'm not a stranger to drawing attention; as the only human in the Halifax coven, I've been the focus for much of my life. However, our little group hauls in too much. Frankly, it borders on ridiculous. Eyes follow us. Whispers chase our heels. Suspicion and fear shadow every gaze. Children are tucked close to mothers, husbands shift protectively toward their wives, large men flex their muscles in a show of defiance and intimidation, though unease can be glimpsed behind their courageous facades.

Bianca carries herself with confidence, ignoring the stares. Her blonde hair is upswept in a messy bun that appears more stylish than actually "messy", and with her skinny jeans, ankle boots, flowy blouse, and bombshell figure, she looks as if she's stepped right out of a fashion magazine.

I'm not jealous. Nope. Not at all.

She and I are sandwiched between Mikey and another vampire I've never met before, and Mr. Demms strides near the front of the group with his assistant, Victor, and Mr. Abrahms. While the three men in the lead discuss the itinerary and our next step, the four of us in the back, along with the three human bodyguards who follow in our wake, are silent and watchful.

A gift shop to my left beckons, and I wonder fleetingly if they'd mind too much if I stopped and bought a souvenir of my time in Romania—just something small like a shot glass or even a postcard—but those in the lead show no signs of stopping, and I continue on with a small tinge of regret.

We reach our gate, and a representative for the airline is waiting for us at a large door. Marcus greets him, they exchange a few words, and then we're ushered through the door and into the jet way. Outside the small windows, the airport lights are overly bright, appearing almost smeared. A light drizzle forms thin rivulets on the glass, distorting our view of the happenings on the tarmac.

Silence hangs heavily in the air; tension so thick, it can be cut with a knife. Something has everyone on edge.

I shoot Bianca a look, but her eyes remain fixed straight ahead, her mouth a grim line. A glance at the two Medici escorts reveal the same wariness. Questions gnaw at me, but I keep quiet.

We curve with the jet way, and the door to the airplane comes into view. Several people in flight attendant uniforms hover in the doorway, but their smiles are far from pleasant— more brittle, strained. They observe our approach apprehensively, their eyes anxious.

The airline representative halts at the door, whispers something to the gentleman attendant, and then our group enters the plane, one at a time.

When I pass the cluster of flight attendants, I hear "Daywalker" hissed at me. My gaze snaps toward them, and a petite woman pales and cowers back.

My eyes widen in surprise. They're afraid of me? Why? I scan each of them, noting the slight tremble of their hands. No, not just me. *All* of us.

After being directed to a seat across the aisle from Bianca, I sink into the plush leather and turn my attention to the tarmac below.

Though the interactions with the airplane's crew had been fleeting, it was long enough to open my eyes to what I'd been detached from at the Medicis' castle. All of the details following Luca's attack on the world, mankind's reaction to it, the tenuous relations between humans and vampires, I'm seeing it now—fear, hate, and prejudice.

The peace is dead.

A spurt of anger warms my core. Does Luca realize what he's done? Alessandro? Do they even care?

"Father bought out all of First Class." Bianca's voice breaks into my thoughts, and I look over to find her examining a fashion magazine. "You won't have to worry about the stares until we get to Greece."

I'm not sure if I should be grateful or concerned by Mr. Demms' actions. Settling on gratitude seems better for my mental health, so I give her a thin smile.

"That sounds good," I mumble.

She turns the page and dismisses me.

Mikey plops down in the vacant seat beside me, grinning. "M'lady."

Horrified, I stare at him.

"We've got almost six hours to get to know each other," he says, and his smile widens as my horrified expressions grows more—well—*horrified*.

***

Two hours into the flight, and I'm ready to throw open the airplane door and leap out into the dark unknown. Screw stabilized cabin pressure and the 35,000 foot drop. Mikey is an incessant talker. And by incessant, I mean he *never* shuts up. He bounces from one subject to the next, barely allowing me a chance to comment. I'm half convinced the guy doesn't breathe. As for me getting sleep? Well...sleep is overrated and *so* last week.

When Bianca rises from her seat and moves to another several rows from us, a stab of longing pierces me. Can I move without appearing rude? One glance at Mikey's animated expression squashes that question, and I sink back into the leather, releasing a frustrated sigh.

If he notices my annoyance, he gives no indication, and continues his relentless chatter about his life in France over two centuries ago when there were no rules, no regulations; when vampires drank from the vein without fear, and humans bowed in fear before them.

Several times, I've wanted to ask if he realizes what he's saying, but proper etiquette keeps me from interrupting and broadcasting my annoyance. Instead, I listen with half an ear.

The flight attendants assigned to First Class serve us with trembling hands and wary eyes. Though Bianca, her father, and Mr. Abrahms are treated with the barest of respect, the rest of us are observed with guarded expressions.

Especially me—much to my surprise.

After another two hours of Mikey reliving the past, he's summoned to the front where Mr. Demms and Mr. Abrahms sit.

I breathe out a massive sigh of relief, lean my head against the plastic visor covering the window, and close my eyes.

A rough jerk snaps me awake, and my eyes pop open in surprise. Bianca hovers over me, reminding me of when I awoke following Luca's bite, and her fatigue-lined face is pinched in impatience.

"We've landed in Kavala," she says, straightening, and carries her leather backpack in her hands.

I scrub my eyes to clear away the dryness and lingering sleep, and glance around the cabin. Other than Mikey and his companion guard, who I finally learned is named Seth, we're the only two left.

Sensing my confusion, she motions toward the curtain. "Father is seeing to the security team waiting in the jet way. Hurry up."

My body protests in exhaustion when I climb to my feet, and I stifle a yawn behind my hand, blinking a few times to clear away the resulting moisture. I fall in beside her, and she sails through the curtain with her head held high. The two Medicis cover our rear as we step into the doorway.

The moment the other passengers catch sight of Mikey and Seth, they freeze, and some even scramble backward.

196

"Ignore them," Bianca whispers, shooting me a firm look. "They do not exist, and their fear cannot touch you."

But among the terror and restlessness gripping my fellow humans, I also sense something else, something deeper, darker, deadlier. Whispers hang in the air, foreign and unrecognizable. I can't understand what's being said, but when Mikey and Seth stiffen behind us, my stomach flips.

The tide shifts, changing course.

Mikey lets out a warning hiss, his teeth exploding from his gums, moments before the first human launches himself at us. Bianca latches onto my arm with an iron grip and yanks me out of the way.

I have a fleeting moment in which I marvel at the passengers' ability to fight in such close quarters before I'm thrust out of the door and into the jet way. I spin back just as she struggles through and joins me.

Together, we watch in horror as Seth is set upon by a ravenous group of men with wild eyes. He's all teeth and nails, throwing one off just as another leaps on. His screams of rage fill the air, punctuated by hisses and growls. His dark eyes, so similar to Alessandro's, flicker toward us momentarily before he vanishes beneath a pile of bodies.

I swallow down a cry.

Mikey appears, his expression fierce and his clothes torn. He scans both of us quickly before shoving me up the jet way. Bianca turns and rushes away, her eyes already seeking her father.

"Don't watch," he says softly, continuing to push me toward the cluster of bodyguards standing protectively around Mr. Demms and Mr. Abrahms.

"But...Seth..." I choke on the swelling revulsion and misery.

"Just go." He gives me another push.

A set of strong hands grab me, and then I find myself in the middle of the guarded circle, huddled close to Mr. Demms. He gives me a once-over. Satisfied that I'm still in one piece, he nods to the bodyguards.

They make quick work escorting us from the gate, through the small airport, and out into a parking lot where four cars await us. Nobody speaks the entire way.

I'm thrust inside the third vehicle, Mikey slides in beside me, and in a flash, we're pulling out of the parking garage into an empty side street. My heart continues to pound, and I press my hands to my cheeks, sucking in gulps of air.

"What just happened?" I gasp, turning wide, terrified eyes on my Medici guard. "What happened to Seth?"

He gives me a patient look, sadness in his eyes. "That's what's been happening all over the world, to every vampire caught alone in public."

"*Everywhere?*" I feel the prick of tears.

"Everywhere, Miss Halifax."

Grief and fear overflows. "This is your fault. Yours and Luca's, and Alessandro's. You started this; you destroyed the peace."

"Is that what you keep telling yourself?" He drops his head back against the headrest and sighs. "You've been living with your head in the sand then. Either that, or your family neglected to tell you that there never *was* peace between the two species, just a tenuous relationship." His eyes pierce mine, resolved, unflinching. "Wake up, Halifax. You're not in Kansas anymore."

I open my mouth to deny it, but something gives me pause. Uncertainty? Comprehension? What if it's the truth? What if I've been hidden from the horrors of the world, wrapped in bubble wrap and down pillows? What if every attack, every atrocity, every vampire slayed, is concealed by the Seven?

"These old bones are tired." Mikey's soft exhalation is overly loud in the tense silence.

***

The *Rosalie* isn't a yacht. It's a cruise ship.

Everything is polished and gleaming; the rooms are luxury size; the beds and towels smell like lavender; closets are stuffed with dresses and drawers are bursting with undergarments and active wear. There's a fitness center, a training room filled with punching bags and rubber mats, a swimming pool, hot tub, a theater, a game room. The list goes on.

It's a little overwhelming, I must admit.

The day is half over by the time I emerge from my assigned room, clad in the swimsuit and bright pink cover-up I found in one of the dresser drawers. As much as I don't want to swim, it's better than pretending to sleep a moment longer. Already, boredom is eating away at me.

I pad silently through the carpeted hallway toward the stairs to the upper deck, scanning for any unfamiliar faces. Where is everyone? Without seeing even so much as a maid, I climb to the pool deck and step out into the sunshine.

All around me is blue. Shimmering topaz and sapphire; glittering diamonds. The Mediterranean Sea is crisp and exotic, cool and breathtaking. Its famous sandy beaches are nowhere in sight; just blue as far as the eye can see.

Bianca is reading, reclining on a lounge chair beside the pool with overly large sunglasses and a floppy hat that casts shade over much of her upper half. Her long, tan legs are stretched out and a small diamond winks in her belly button.

I raise a hand in greeting, and she acknowledges my arrival with a slight raising of the book and a page turn.

Well then…

After snagging a vacant lounger, I drop my towel onto the soft plastic, peel off the wrap, and slip my feet from the sandals. I sneak a look at her; she turns the page. I glance at the water, and back at her.

A mischievous grin kicks up one side of my mouth.

If I land this *just* right…

I take a running leap and…*splash*!

I resurface to Bianca screeching like a banshee and flicking water off her legs. She grips the book between her thumb and forefinger and shakes it several times, and I watch with increasing glee as it drips.

"You!" she shrieks, stabbing a finger toward me.

A laugh explodes from me, and I dive backward in the water, putting distance between us.

"Get out!" She launches to her feet, tossing the book down. "Get out right this minute!"

I guffaw like I haven't in ages. And swim further away.

"You ruined my book, you Neanderthal!"

I laugh harder.

CONFESSION 23

I always wanted to see the world. I just didn't think I'd be forced to do it against my will.

"You need to block," Bianca snaps, sliding beneath my hit. She straightens long enough to jab an elbow into my gut, and I grunt as the air bursts from my lungs. "Come on! Block me!"

Another swing; another hit.

"I need a break," I gasp, shakily blocking her next attack. "We've been training since six this morning. I'm tired, Bianca."

She twists and kicks, connecting with the forearm I barely raise in time. "No excuses! You don't get to complain about being tired when you're in a real fight. Those people out there," she gestures vaguely, "are driven by fear, and they will do everything they can to destroy you."

Her next onslaught comes before I can draw in a breath in preparation. A rapid succession of fists, elbows, and feet that cause me to stumble back even as I defend myself from each hit.

"What you can do now, especially when you're this exhausted, is what'll make the difference between life and death." She lands an elbow to my cheek, and I stagger back a few steps. "Come on, Danika. Block me!"

"This is the third day of constant training," I snap, spitting out a gob of red-tinged saliva onto the mat. "My ribs hurt, and my leg," I smack the femur in question, "isn't strong enough yet."

"If you're going to get off the boat in Syracuse," she straightens and crosses her arms, "then you're going to know how to defend yourself. Your face, as ugly as it is, is well known because of that video."

My mouth drops open. "Did you just call me ugly?"

"Are you hard of hearing as well?"

"I know you're trying to bait me. It's not going to work."

"No?" She buries a fist in my stomach before I can blink. "No wonder Alessandro keeps playing with you. You're so naive."

I double over, coughing and gasping for air. Her words hurt, like a knife being buried in my heart.

But they do the trick.

I uncurl myself and meet her cocky grin with a glare.

"*That's* what I'm talking about." She beckons me. "Let's do this, Halifax."

Receiving my third wind—or is it my fourth?—is like a blessing in disguise. I launch myself at her, fists flying, and she counters gracefully. Striking low, I connect with her upper thigh, and before she can accommodate the dip in her leg, I'm dropping down and taking a swipe at her feet.

With a laugh, she dances backward. "Come on, Dani!"

I don't let her see how the use of my nickname surprises me. The only other person to call me that is Conrad.

Ten minutes passes.

We collide and I wrestle her to the mat. She clocks me in the chin, and while I'm distracted with the stars dancing in my vision, she plants her feet and shoves. I fly over her head and land a few feet away on my back, jarring me senseless.

I suck in enormous lungfuls of air. Exhaustion ripples through every muscle, strains every tendon. I'm ready to quit, and she knows it.

"Get up," she instructs, rolling to her feet. "Let's finish this."

I lick my dry lips, intending to tell her I'm done, but something flashes in her eyes and I pause.

She extends her hand. "Get up, Dani."

"Why?"

"Because you're not weak, and you don't give up."

"Ha!"

"Work until your body breaks." Sweat drips down her temples. "Fight until there isn't an ounce left in you. Persevere, even when you want to quit. *That's* how you'll survive." She keeps her hand outstretched, unwavering.

I stare at it as her words sink in. How many times over the past few days have I teetered on the edge of cowardice and fear? How many times have I considered, quite literally, jumping ship? Giving myself to the humans and accepting my fate? Abandoning everything just so I can finally sleep again?

But no matter how much I want to admit defeat, I cannot. I was raised to be strong and resolved, to not give up, no matter how hard life gets, and my body and my mind have been trained from a young age to be resilient.

When I was twelve, my training was kicked up a notch. I struggled for days to acclimate, to memorize and overcome the new regimen, but my body continued to weaken and deteriorate. It was then that Conrad said, "The only person who can break you is yourself, Dani."

I meet her steady regard with my own determination and reach out for her hand. She clasps it firmly with a sweaty grip, yanks me up, and then grins.

"Ready?" Her eyes glitter with anticipation.

My slight smile grows. "Bring it."

***

"Castello Maniace." Mr. Demms leans against the railing beside me. "The citadel of Syracuse. It was built in the mid-13th century by Emperor Fredrick II." He points toward the left. "And do you see the walls? There used to be a moat there, and the only way into the fortress was over *that* bridge right there." He flashes me a smile. "From the 14th to the 16th centuries, it was used as a place of residence by the queens of Sicily."

"You know a lot about it," I say, squinting against the midday sun and surveying the aged structure the *Rosalie* is curving around.

He nods. "I have an affinity for history. I've been to it several times over the years. It has a remarkable past. Take, for instance, that in the 15th century, it was a prison." He shoots me a look. "Can you imagine the prisoners' stories, their crimes?" He shakes his head, fascinated. "Then in the 16th century, it was used as part of the fortification for the city and the harbor. Its purpose has changed throughout generations of rulers."

"Are you boring her with history lessons?" Bianca joins us at the railing and smiles warmly at her father.

He leans over and gives her a quick peck on the cheek. "Of course not, love. We're just admiring the Castello Maniace. How are you? Did you get lunch?"

"I did."

"Good. We should be going ashore in," he glances at his watch, "thirty minutes. Captain James projected we'd be into port by two."

She considers the ancient castle, nodding. "That should give us a bit of freedom before we meet up with Luca and Alessandro."

My heart skips a beat at the mention of the Medici Lords, but for two, entirely different reasons.

"A team will be assigned to you," Marcus says, meeting my eye, and I nod. "You will go in disguise, and I would advise that you don't take it off for any reason."

If *not* being myself gets me off the boat, I'll turn into anyone they want.

"Are we in Syracuse?" I ask, turning my attention back to the land mass we're maneuvering around.

"Not yet." Bianca points toward a larger portion with numerous buildings and hordes of people. "*That* is Syracuse. *This*," she gestures at the city beside us, "is the island of Ortygia."

"Also known as Città Vecchia, which is ancient Greek for 'Quail'," Marcus adds.

She throws him an exasperated look, but continues, "And it is home to many of Syracuse's famous landmarks. I recommend visiting it while we're here."

The *Rosalie* moves away from the island and toward the harbor. Marcus excuses himself to confer with Mr. Abrahms and our security teams, and the two of us fall into a companionable silence.

Unease trickles through me. Do I *really* want to leave the yacht? I've never been frightened or anxious about living my life and doing everything there is to do—I took Chancelot into the desert close to dusk, faced down coyotes, and fought off the Medici coven when they came for me—but suddenly, I find myself hesitating.

Because now, I'm no longer human.

At least, not in the eyes of the world, thanks to that viral video—which, I might add, I *still* haven't watched.

As we pull into port, the unease intensifies until my stomach is full of knots. I conceal my trembling hands in the pockets of my maxi skirt and dart a quick glance at Bianca to see if she's noticed my disquiet. When she doesn't so much as blink, I look back at the busy docks.

Other than appreciative nods, the people don't pay much attention to us, and we're dismissed just as soon as we're noticed.

"Miss Demms. Miss Halifax."

We both turn at the sound of our names.

A suited man inclines his head. "I'm Nathan. I'll be in charge of your security detail."

"Well now." A slow smile forms on Bianca's face, and her eyes dance. "Aren't you gorgeous."

She isn't wrong there. He *is* gorgeous. Dark hair, green eyes, a chiseled jaw, and oh my, that body.

He clears his throat, suddenly uncomfortable, and I can't help the giggle that bursts from me.

"Are you married?" she asks. "Oh I certainly hope not. You're too beautiful to be taken."

He fidgets.

"Do you have any brothers?"

"No, miss. I'm an only child."

"Pity."

She continues to appraise him, taking her compliments a bit too far. I shudder to think what Mother would say if she heard half the things coming out of Bianca's mouth.

Finally, he snaps. "Miss, please. I appreciate your compliment, but I…"

"You what?" She raises a brow. "You're flattered? You should be, you gorgeous thing. Now, go get my father and relieve yourself of command."

An awkward silence descends the moment he disappears through the door, and she shifts back to the railing, all humor gone from her face.

"What—" I clear my throat, "what was that about?"

"He's incompetent," she states. "If he became rattled simply because I was complimenting him, then he has no business being in charge of my security." She flashes me a dark look. "And you shouldn't allow someone that useless to protect you either."

Words escape me.

"Besides," she adds, "it got *you* to laugh."

***

One team leader change later, and I'm climbing into a rented, compact SUV with four bodyguards. I'm squished between the two largest as we leave the docks behind and start across the city toward the historical district.

In the reflection of the rear-view mirror, I catch sight of my disguise, and my nose wrinkles. Ugh.

It can only have been contrived by Bianca because it's just plain ridiculous. The khakis, bright yellow polo, and socks with sandals is bad enough—no, really, it's bad enough—but my hair has been pinned back, and I'm sporting an auburn bobbed wig smooshed down with a visor, and a pair of oversized sunglasses that remind me more of bug eyes than a fashion accessory. I look like a "How to Look like a Tourist" fashion pamphlet vomited on me.

She'd smiled triumphantly when I'd emerged from my room, and I almost wanted to smack her. One minute she's nice, and the next, I'm reminded how much of a witch she is. Mr. Demms only made it worse when he'd tried to conceal his laughter behind his hand, and Mr. Abrahms had laughed out right. Shoot me now.

To make matters worse, my escorts are dressed in a similar fashion, except they all wear Hawaiian shirts with bright flowers all over them.

We look absurd.

Our first stop is the Piscina Romana, the remains of an ancient Roman amphitheater and cistern. While we meander through the crumbled structure and take in what once was, I notice that we are given no more than a passing glance.

A brief flash of gratitude for Bianca—that's all I allow myself.

The self-guided tour eats up barely thirty minutes, so we head off on foot to the Catacomba di San Giovanni with the flow of tourists. We arrive just as a group is heading below ground for the tour. One of the bodyguards disappears into the crowds to secure us tickets for the next tour, leaving the rest of us to wander through the remains of the ancient church.

As before, we blend in with the other tourists and receive minimal attention, and I move freely among the collapsed interior. Soon, we're summoned for our tour, and we join the others congregating around the petite tour guide.

For forty minutes, we're walked through the twisting tunnels of the ancient Roman and Christian burial tombs. The catacombs are extensive, and I am sucked into the history of how death was viewed and bodies were treated in that age. The tour guide jumps back and forth between Italian and English, and I soak up every second of that musical language.

When we reemerge into the sunlight, I'm hungry, thirsty, and ready to visit more sites.

Our small party returns to the Piscina Romana, clambers into the vehicle, and starts toward Ortygia. The going is slow with traffic at its peak, but I sink into the leather seat and enjoy the cool AC and the passing scenery.

I've learned the names of my escorts during the tour of the catacombs. There's Nico, the guy with the beard; Harris, the largest of the bunch; Zed, the green-eyed hunk, and Dan the Man (at least, that's what his comrades call him). They're a silent, overbearing bunch, and I'm pretty sure they terrified half our tour group.

One wrong turn, and we find ourselves lost in a series of windy backstreets. Here, the traffic congestion is nonexistent, and we're surrounded by quaint homes and picturesque cafés.

Zed pulls off into a narrow alley and parks. "Let's eat."

My stomach growls in response, and I nod, grinning.

There are many cafés to choose from, and Nico glares from behind his dark sunglasses, scrutinizing each one. After a bit, he decides on a small one surrounded by thick bushes that overflow with fragrant flowers. He orders for everyone since none of us can read the menu, and soon we're seated and waiting for the food.

Silence stretches, none willing to break it, and the tension level rises. I don't know what to say, and it's obvious they aren't too comfortable with me either, regardless that we've spent the entire afternoon together.

It isn't until our dinner is served that we all breathe a collective sigh of relief.

I grab my sandwich and lick my lips.

Suddenly, an uneasy sensation in the pit of my stomach makes me pause. My scalp tingles and the hair along my arms stands on end. With my mouth open and poised to bite down, I slowly look up to discover four sets of eyes fixed on me.

And it hits me then.

This is a test.

CONFESSION 24
Despite everything, I think I am falling for Alessandro.

My heart shrivels and dies a little.

What have I done to make the world think I'm anything other than what I am? Where did I go wrong? I *am* the *human* Halifax, always have been. It's never been questioned, never disbelieved. People have never looked at me with fear or uncertainty. Sure, there's been dislike, even jealousy, but never fear.

The four sets of eyes are unblinking, unwavering. They penetrate to the deepest parts of my soul, weighing, judging, awaiting something.

And I know what they want to see; what they *expect* to see.

Without averting my eyes, I take a big bite.

I'm sure the food is supposed to be flavorful with the bread toasted to perfection, slathered in basil pesto, and piled high with tomatoes, spinach, and an assortment of other vegetables. But all I taste is prejudice, each mouthful like sawdust.

Bite.
Chew.
Swallow.
Bite.
Chew.
Swallow.

I keep going until the sandwich is gone, and I wipe my hands on the napkin, never looking away from the four bodyguards and the judgement in their eyes. Their food goes untouched, their glasses of water remain full. I don't wait to see if they'll eat, nor do I stop to wait for them. I push back the chair and rise, tossing the napkin onto the plate.

"I'll be in the car." I turn and stride from the café, chin up, eyes straight ahead. I refuse to let them see how broken I am; I refuse to let them see my pain.

I return to the rental car, and a few minutes later, they join me.

"Where to, miss?" Zed asks once we're situated.

"The docks."

Tension fills the silence for the duration of the drive back to the *Rosalie*.

I keep myself together by sheer stubbornness. I ignore the tears clogging my throat, the thin breaths through a constricted airway, the pain twisting my heart and gutting my insides. I ignore the shame, the anger, and the confusion. I ignore Zed's flicked glances in the rear-view mirror and Harris' and Nico's cold air beside me.

We reach the yacht, Zed parks, and I follow Harris as soon as he opens his door and climbs out. My feet take me up the platform and onto the boat, and I don't even spare them a backward glance.

Refuge beckons within the confines of my room, and I seek it as if being chased by the hounds of Hell. Once the door is closed behind me, I lower myself onto the bed and gaze sightlessly at the oil painting of a dancing ballerina.

It'll be hours still before everyone returns and we depart for open water again. Hours in which to dwell on my thoughts, on the pain and the anger. Hours to descend into despair and allow my circumstances to consume me.

Or not.

I can shake this off. Go for a swim. Run through Bianca's training routine. I can sweat out everything, forget everything; become stronger.

I can't change how people see me, but I can change how I see myself.

I throw on some shorts and a tank top, slide on my shoes, snag a bottle of water from the mini fridge and a towel from the freshly laundered pile on the bathroom counter, and then slip through the door into the carpeted hallway. As usual, it's empty, and I waste no time in making it to the training room.

Once inside, I flip on the light, set my belongings on the floor beside the door, and then wander across the blue mat to the far side where the iPod and docking station are located. I browse through the playlists until one catches my fancy.

To *Eye of the Tiger*, I get down to business.

Is the music cheesy? Totally. Do I really care? Nope. It builds a fire within me that cannot be dampened. Flames dance through my core, ignite in my blood. The punching bag in front of me becomes every weakness, every prejudice, every grief and sorrow I've kept bottled within me. It's the lies and betrayal I've struggled to forgive; the rejection I've felt my entire life from my fellow humans; the loneliness I've endured surrounded by the undead. Never belonging; never truly accepted.

I don't cry.

I fight, and I sweat, until my knuckles are bloody and my muscles quiver, on the point of collapse. Until exhaustion has chased away the despair. Only then do I stop; only then do I take a step back and drag in a breath.

And then I feel *him*. A whisper of his presence. Tender. Contemplative. Protective.

"How long have you been there?" I ask softly, not lifting my head from where it rests against the course plastic of the punching bag.

"Long enough."

I don't want to admit it. Not to anyone. Not to him, and definitely not to myself. But the truth is staring me in the face. It's in every flutter of my heart, every somersault of my stomach. It's in the anticipation warming me from within. It's in the stuttered breaths, the shy lift of my eyes, the tremble of my hands.

I've missed Alessandro—terribly, achingly.

The hours spent with Bianca haven't been solely for the purpose of becoming a stronger fighter; it's been to forget him.

To forget how he makes me feel when I'm with him. To forget how I yearn when he's gone.

"Have you been well?" His voice is low, gentle.

My heart clenches and I meet his dark, penetrating gaze across the distance. How can you disarm me so easily, I want to ask. How is it that your simple question can summon forth every emotion I've been suppressing for days? Why? You're irritating, stubborn, hold your secrets too close, and lie too easily. You frustrate me at every turn. So then, why?

I already know the answer. Beneath his hard exterior, he's kind and warm and fiercely loyal. He pulled me from the depths of hopelessness when I was drowning, resuscitating me with courage and lighting my way out of the darkness. He's been a shoulder to cry on and a support when I've needed it the most.

Though his words are filled with deception, his actions speak much louder.

Alessandro shifts beside the door, a fresh bottle of water clasped in his hands. I ignore the way my heart flips over itself when he starts across the mats toward me. I ignore how my nerves fritz in excitement at seeing his face again.

He stops next to me and holds out the water. With no more than a dip of my head in thanks, I release my grip on the punching bag and accept it. I'm unable to tear my eyes away from his. Unable to do anything other than drink in his face while the bottle of water goes untouched.

"You look as if you've been training hard," he remarks, and a tiny smile dances along his lips.

"Ah…yeah." I blink a few times, taken aback by his amusement. "Figured it couldn't hurt to get in an evening session before dinner."

His eyes drop to my knuckles. "Feel better?"

I follow his gaze and consider the cracked skin and congealed blood. Do I? Honestly and truly? I release one hand from the plastic bottle and flex my fingers, and then my eyes return to his.

He moves a step closer, and I tilt my head back, eyes still captured. His finger brushes across my cheekbone, over the scars, and trails down my jaw, his touch soft. My breathing stutters and my heart skips a beat.

212

"Have you been well?" he asks quietly. "You look exhausted."

I should smack his hand away and tell him not to touch me. He manipulated me into turning my back on Conrad, into putting my debt and my promise to him above the Halifax coven, above the Family who's raised me. I should shrug him off, leave the room and him behind. I should inflict the same kind of pain on him that he's done to me. I should run. I should escape into Syracuse and locate Diavolo.

I should do all these things.

But I can't.

I can't tear myself away from him; I can't step back; I can't stop sinking into his obsidian eyes. I'm lost right now, drowning in confusion and uncertainty, terrified for my life, dreading tomorrow. I need someone. I need *him*.

Words escape before I can squash them, passing my lips on the barest breath. "I missed you."

His eyes search mine. "What happened?" When I don't respond, he reaches up and cups my face. "I can see it even when you try to hide it. Talk to me, Danika."

He's undoing me. Completely and irrevocably. His simple touch and gentle compassion are unleashing everything I've kept concealed. Grief rises and I swallow against the tears in my throat. Complaining that the world hates me sounds pathetic considering everything he's endured for two hundred years. So then, how do I tell him what's wrong? How do I put into words the chaos within me? How do I explain that I'm broken?

For the first time, I can understand his darkness. I can see the judgement that crouches upon his shoulders like a vengeful ghost. I can see the centuries of desolation he's masked behind a visage of indifference. I can see my own pain reflected in his eyes.

"How do you stand it?" I ask, my voice barely above a whisper.

"Stand what?" He raises his other hand and tucks the hair that'd come undone during my workout back behind my ear.

"The hate."

Alessandro stills, his fingers lingering on my jaw.

213

"How do you ignore their fear of you?" I bite my lip— hard. The pain helps keep the tears at bay, but it does little to erase the distressed expression twisting my face. "How do you pretend they don't see you as a monster?"

"Because I'm *not* a monster." He withdraws his hands and looks away.

Panic ignites in me. Panic that he'll pull into himself, and that whatever this is, between us, will end; panic that he'll walk away, that what I feel will consume me like a ravenous fire, and I'll never escape.

Fueled by some unnamed emotion, and with a boldness that surprises even me, I grab his wrist and return his hand to my cheek.

"What are you doing?" he demands softly, and our gazes snag once more.

"The world thinks *I'm* a monster," I choke, closing my eyes and leaning into his hand. "They think I'll hurt them and their children. They shy away from me as if I'm going to attack at any moment." I release a shaky breath. "Just the thought of hurting babies makes my insides twist."

He doesn't say anything, just stares at me in rigid attention.

"They don't understand I'm human." I shake my head, my hand clenching around his wrist. "How can you stand it?" I'm fighting tears now. "How do you stay strong when everyone is telling you you're nothing, you're evil, you're a fiend? How, Alessandro? How do you not scream and rant and rave?"

"Because it doesn't work." He slides his hand into my collapsing pony tail and rubs his thumb over my scars. "I bellowed at the top of my lungs. I ranted and raved. I pleaded and begged. Nobody listened. Nobody cared. Everyone—human and vampire alike—turned their backs on what was left of the Medici coven." He rests his forehead against mine, closing his eyes, and his voice drops to a whisper, heavy with suppressed sadness. "Eventually, you stop noticing the fear and the hate, Danika. You won't see the way they cower away from you. You become oblivious to the whispers."

But no matter how much you pretend you don't notice, you're still hurting. I can see it; I can feel it. Stop denying your

214

pain. I desperately want to say that. I want to break down his walls, crawl beneath his façade of endurance, wrap him in compassion and understanding.

My eyes become glued to his mouth, the temptation a hairsbreadth away. I want to. I *need* to. Sweet baby Jesus, I've lost my mind.

Keeping my grip on Alessandro's wrist, I tilt my head and brush my lips against his. Feather light. Just a taste. They tingle from the brief contact, already aching for more.

His eyes pop open, and his breath catches.

Our gazes lock.

One heartbeat. Two.

"You—" He cuts himself off and jerks away with a hissed expletive. Running a hand through his hair, his gaze flicks to mine before he turns and strides to the door.

I watch him with a pounding heart, shock keeping me immobile.

At the door, he stops abruptly, lowers his head, and stares at the knob gripped beneath his hand. "Forgive me, Halifax, if my words or actions have been misconstrued in any way." He shoots me a look over his shoulder, and something much like regret flashes through his eyes. "It was never my intention."

My heart plummets, confusion swirling in me. "I thought—what about—you…"

"Again, my apologies." He nods his head contritely.

Anger rises, crushing the confusion and astonishment at his rejection. "No. You don't get to do that." I clench my jaw and ball my hands into fists. "You don't get to string me along, call me 'yours', make me feel this way, and then turn around and rebuff me. How dare you?" Eyes narrow. "How. Dare. You?"

"When the time comes, you'll be grateful I did this."

My mouth drops open in disbelief. "What?"

"I'm almost four hundred years old," he says brusquely. "It's always about the chase, the suspense of the game. The catch isn't as satisfying."

Pain lances my heart. "You're lying."

He looks away, his shoulders stiffening, and that's the only proof I need. My anger evaporates, and I'm left reeling with bewilderment once more.

"You're *lying*," I repeat. "Why?"

There are a hundred unspoken emotions within his dark eyes when he glances back at me. I take a step toward him before I can stop myself. I'm desperate to find the words to halt whatever is happening. But he's already withdrawing into himself.

"I'm sorry." With a final dip of his head, he flings open the door, steps through, and closes it behind him.

Too many feelings well up, suffocating, overwhelming. My hand, still poised in a frantic attempt to grab him, slowly closes into a fist, and I drop it to my side.

It's over. The heartbreak is staggering, and the anger that weaves its way through it is explosive. I turn and throw the bottle of half-drank water at the wall. The plastic crunches upon impact and water splashes around the inside, but it remains intact.

A scream bubbles up in my throat, and balling my hands into fists, I spin and strike. My bloodied knuckles connect with the punching bag, splitting anew, and a smear of fresh blood remains behind on the stiff plastic. Adrenaline infuses my exhausted muscles, and I expel everything in a rush of rapid punches and kicks at the innocent training equipment.

I release an anguished sob at the same moment my fist meets the bag, and disgust twists my face. Why am I crying? Stop crying! Become stronger instead. No one can hurt you then. This won't break you. Come on, Danika.

Unable to fight it any longer, I grit my teeth and give in to the rising, bubbling chaos I've repressed since stepping onto the airplane in Romania. As it bursts from me with every punch and every kick, one, ragged sob at a time, I'm unaware of the presence on the other side of the door. I'm unaware of the hand pressed to the wood, of the bowed head, of dark, tormented eyes concealed behind clenched lids.

I'm unaware that at this moment, I'm not the only one breaking.

Gradually, the tears dry, the anger seeps away, and exhaustion returns. Silence hangs heavy in the air, disrupted only by my heaving breaths. Blood drips from my clenched fists onto the mat, a splash of red against royal blue.

The door opens behind me.

I don't turn. It's not Alessandro.

A low whistle. "You sure did a number on yourself."

I bow my head, glancing down at the self-inflicted wounds. "What do you want, Mikey?"

He's beside me in less than a blink, and from the corner of my eye, I see he holds a first aid kit in his hands.

"I don't need help." I turn to brush past him, and his hand snaps out and grabs my arm.

"You're human, Halifax. You can't go wandering around the *Rosalie* with blood pouring from open wounds."

I look down at his hand and then back up into his face. "The world doesn't believe I'm human; why should I?"

His expression darkens, all humor vanishing. "What are you, a petulant child?" He drags me across the room to the table with the iPod and docking station, drops the medical kit onto it, and then swings me around to face him. "Regardless what the world believes you to be, you are *still* human."

A thought strikes, and when I snort softly, he looks up from his inspection of my knuckles. "What?"

"I was just thinking how this is probably the first time you haven't thrown me over your shoulder like a caveman and carted me off."

He grins mischievously. "I can still do it if you want."

I hold up my free hand, shaking my head. "I'm good, thanks."

With a wink, he returns to the task at hand—ha, see what I did there?—and resumes his examination. After a moment, he nods and breathes out a small sigh of relief. "Nothing appears broken. Just split skin."

We lapse into silence as he begins cleaning and treating the wounds. The peroxide he pours over them clears away some of the blood, but its quickly replaced by white foam and an excruciating sting that brings tears to my eyes. He pats them down with a wad of gauze, smears antiseptic ointment, and then begins wrapping them with soft, fluffy bandages.

"I'm over two hundred years old," he says, eyes focused on his work. "Before I became a vampire, I was the son of a French earl. Rich, spoiled, and selfish." He pauses, unwraps a portion, adjusts the gauze, and begins again. "One day, I came

217

across a beautiful woman washing her clothes beside the stream that ran through my father's property. I immediately wanted her for myself." He secures one hand and starts work on the other. "She was breathtaking and kind. But, it was the spring of 1789."

My sophomore year, for English lit class, I had to read *A Tale of Two Cities*. 1789 was the year the French Revolution began.

"War tore us apart, just as it tore France apart." His voice is low with a hint of sadness. "It didn't discriminate, didn't pick sides. It destroyed everything and everyone in its path. It was merciless, unforgiving."

There is so much weight behind those words, so many unspoken emotions. Years and years of heartache and grief.

He begins wrapping my other hand. "Can you withstand what's coming? Can your feelings remain unchanged through everything? Can you forgive the decisions he'll be forced to make in the coming weeks?"

"I wasn't even given a chance," I reply softly. "I was rejected before anything could begin."

"Danika, you are the Halifax *Dilecta*, not some average human."

"I know."

"Your duty to your family trumps anything else." Mikey secures the gauze and looks up. "Can you really say you have time for love and relationships? War with the humans, war with the vampires—this insanity is ripping the world to pieces." He sighs, leaning back against the table. "Look, I get it. I do. But you two are on opposite sides of a centuries-old conflict, and the animosity between the covens is only growing stronger." He gives me a flat smile, very unlike his usual wide grin. "I'm sorry to say this, but Alessandro turning you down is probably the nicest thing he could have done for you."

CONFESSION 25

The knife of betrayal swings like a pendulum, severing fragments of my soul with every pass.

The next day dawns with annoyingly sunny skies and crisp aquamarine as far as the eye can see. A faint breeze lifts the tiny tendrils of hair along my temples as I lean against the railing, sipping on a cup of coffee. My eyes scan the horizon, searching for any sign of land.

Nothing but blue.

Last night, I'd taken leave of my senses. There is no other way to explain why I did what I did. No reason. Mikey was right. There is too much at stake right now. The war with the humans; the war with the vampires. Love and relationships, first crushes and first kisses—none of that matters right now. My loyalties lie with the Halifax coven; his, with the Medici. This is a line neither of us should cross.

I take another sip of the dark, liquid gold and blink my eyes hard, trying to ease the stiffness of my lids. This morning found me angry, exasperated, and disappointed. Not in him—in myself. For not knowing better, for not taking a step back and opening my eyes.

Does it hurt? Am I heartbroken? Did I spend the night wallowing in self-pity? Yes. I drag in a deep breath, filling my lungs with salty sea air. But today is a new day. I've got things to do, a bridge to build, relations to restore. The ache in my chest that'd formed last night has faded to a scarcely noticeable throb.

A shadow falls over me, and I turn my head just as Bianca steps up to the railing at my side, clutching her own coffee cup. She's clad in tight leggings, a black sports bra, and running shoes, and her hair is pulled up into a high pony tail.

I mentally groan.

She casts me a sideways look, her emerald gaze sparkling beneath the bright sun. When I glance over, an eyebrow cocked, she leisurely looks away again. She lifts her cup, keeping her eyes on the horizon, and takes a sip.

Awkward silence stretches between us, broken only by the lap of water against the hull. Sighing, I finish my drink and turn to leave.

Her voice gives me pause. "I was fifteen when I realized I was in love with Luca." She laughs softly beneath her breath. "So young. At first, it was this teenage angsty-type. Hearts on notebooks, writing Mrs. Luca Medici on everything, daydreaming of an eternal life spent with him." She leans forward, bracing her arms on the gold chrome railing. "As I grew older, it became stronger, fiercer, more passionate. It consumed me. And I couldn't escape it.

"When it reached the point that I would either do something foolish, or I'd wind up completely and utterly destroyed by Luca, Father told me that love between a vampire and a Dilecta was taboo." She turns her head and our eyes meet. "He wasn't being mean or selfish or trying to hurt me; he was protecting me," she smiles thinly, "from myself."

Horror sweeps through, widening my eyes. "D-does *everyone* know about last night?" I'm mortified that my feelings have become fodder for gossip. "Is it necessary for you to tell me your life's story?"

"It doesn't hurt any less knowing it never would have worked out." Her eyes scan my face, noting and subsequently dismissing the glower twisting my expression. "And it doesn't mean that it won't continue to hurt in the future."

I laugh, soft and humorless, and lift my eyes to the sky. "Seriously? What is this?"

She shakes her head, turning back to the ocean view. "An intervention of sorts. I've been there, done that." She slaps a hand against her chest, over her heart. "Got the badge to prove it."

What the heck? I tighten my hand around the coffee mug, ignoring how my knuckles protest at the action. Mikey was bad enough. Now Bianca? Who's next? Luca? I shudder at the idea of the Medici Head trying to encourage me against feelings for his Heir. He'll probably just rip out my throat and be done with it.

"This is ridiculous," I mutter.

"I wish," she turns her head and spears me with a dark look, "that I'd had people to talk sense into me when I was salivating after Luca like a love-struck fool."

"I'm not—"

"What?" she snaps. "Salivating? No, you're worse. You're like a kicked puppy." She straightens and tosses the remnants of her coffee over the railing. "No man wants a woman who cries at the slightest provocation. Grow strong and *stay* strong. Let it guide you."

"Yes, *sensei*. Teach me more, *sensei*."

She scowls—and even that looks pretty on her. Gross.

"I don't appreciate your sarcasm," she retorts, whirling toward me. Her eyes flash dangerously. "If you want to act like a spoiled crybaby, then so be it." After throwing me a nasty look, she brushes past me and disappears into the dining room.

The moment the sliding door slams into its frame, signaling an end to our unwelcome discussion, shame descends over me. I know she was only trying to help, just as Mikey had last night. Her words, though unkind, were not entirely untrue. I *was* acting like a kicked puppy, and wallowing in self-pity wasn't going to do anything toward winning Alessandro's affections. If anything, it'll just show him how young and immature I really am.

Determined to apologize, I head inside to track her down. I deposit the used mug onto a small table as I pass and hurry into the deserted hallway. I check the training room first, but the lights are off and there's no sign of her. I frown and worry my bottom lip, debating where to search next.

I'm outside her bedroom door before I make a conscious decision to look there. After three attempts and no answer, I find myself wandering the corridors and different levels of the yacht with no destination in mind.

Within the bowels, near the sleeping quarters of the vampires, voices begin tickling my senses. At first, they're indistinguishable, nothing more than a rise and fall of garbled noise. As I draw nearer, their words begin to take form.

"...are meeting in Paris in five days."

A familiar voice. Mr. Abrahms?

"Every world leader?"

Mr. Demms?

"Yes, sir." Mr. Abrahms again. "The governing Seven will be joining them for extensive peace talks."

"Are the teams in place?"

Luca? What is this? What's going on? I inch closer, interest piqued and unease forming in my gut.

"Yes, My Lord. They're awaiting your orders," Mr. Abrahms says.

"Very good." There is pride in Luca's voice, along with something else. Is that...excitement?

Dread crawls along my arms and prickles my scalp.

"Venue?" Luca asks.

"The Hôtel de Ville," Mr. Demms responds. A rustle of paper. A pause. "Here. Security will be tight. It's where they house the administration of Paris." Another pause. "We'll need to be inside before they lock it down for the conference."

I slump against the wall and struggle to rein in my galloping heart. What is this? Are they...? No. Impossible!

"Once we're in, we'll have one chance to do this." A new voice. One that sends ice rushing through my veins. "We'll have to hit them fast, and we'll have to hit them hard. From the moment we strike, there'll be no more than a few minutes before their security responds."

Fresh betrayal slices through me. *Alessandro.*

I can't listen to any more of this. I don't *want* to. But I'm unable to walk away. Frozen in place by shock, horror, and a fear so deep spots dance in my vision. I slap a trembling hand over my mouth before the emotions bubbling up my throat can burst out and alert them to my presence.

I have to hear this.

"Will the Heads suspect an attack?" Mr. Demms asks, his voice thoughtful.

"I wouldn't put it past them," Alessandro says. "They're a suspicious bunch. Have been for centuries. They'll take precautions and will have their own security measures in place."

"How do we counter them?" Mr. Abrahms. Silence greets his question. And then, "The Halifax Dilecta."

"No." Alessandro snaps immediately. "She's not a pawn."

"Alessandro." Warning oozes from Luca. "She's a means. Do not forget that. You made me a promise."

"And it's one I'll fulfill, My Lord. But she is a child. And a Dilecta."

A child? The stake in my heart is driven deeper.

"What does her status have to do with this?" Mr. Abrahms demands. "She is our perfect way in. The Halifax Head will do anything to have her returned to him."

"We *value* our Dilectas," Alessandro growls, and even from the hallway, I can sense his anger. "She should not be used this way, My Lord."

"I agree." Mr. Demms says.

"Why don't we ask her?" A pause. "Come in, Halifax." The Medici Head calling my name cuts through the numbness trapping me in place. I start. "Join us."

The door whips open and Alessandro is framed in the doorway. His dark eyes take me in, huddled against the wall with wide eyes, and a muscle flexes in his jaw as he sweeps his gaze over me, lingering slightly on my bandaged knuckles.

"Bring her in," Luca orders.

I'm a pawn, always have been. From the moment I was rescued from the warehouse outside of Phoenix, my purpose has only ever been as a pawn in their twisted chess game. And now my time has come; my stage is set.

Alessandro reaches a hand toward me. Anger surges, crushing the fear, and I slap it away. Our eyes meet. His are empty, detached. Mine—I'm sure they're filled with the rage and disgust crashing through me. I do nothing to conceal my emotions.

"You're despicable," I spit.

223

"I told you you'd thank me, Danika." He steps to the side so I can enter.

I sweep past him into the room with as much dignity and grace as I can muster. I'm sure my mother will have been proud of me. My chin is lifted, my expression is cold, my shoulders are squared.

In this moment, I'm the Halifax Dilecta.

***

"You will seek asylum at the U.S. Embassy," Luca instructs, his ageless face impassive. "Once word reaches your coven that you've been recovered, they'll be quick to respond."

"What's keeping me from simply exposing your plans to my father?" I lift my chin a notch higher and glare with as much hatred as I can. "Once I'm within the safe circle of the seven covens, I'll be protected."

It's been three hours since I've entered the room. I'll not waver before evil. I cannot.

He raises an eyebrow, his eyes flashing. "Do you plan on betraying me?"

"Oh you betcha." I nod emphatically. "First chance I get."

"Alessandro." Luca flicks his eyes toward his Heir.

"Your debt," Alessandro says quietly.

I stiffen. "And you'd use that against me?" I keep my eyes on the Medici Head. "What if I decide to abandon that and return to my family anyway?"

"Mr. Abrahms." Luca stares back.

"Your person will be affixed with an explosive device," the security expert responds. "Should we feel, at any time, that you are going against the plan, we will detonate. Be it at the embassy, Hôtel de Ville, or in a crowded marketplace."

My skin crawls and the fire within me dims a little. "An...explosive device?"

"While we are aware that it will do little against the Heads," Luca says, "it will still wipe out everything within a two-mile radius." He cocks his head, thoughtful. "Are you willing to risk hundreds—possibly thousands—of lives?"

224

At my silence, a smile turns up one side of his mouth. He knows he's got me.

"So, like what, I'm supposed to just enter the peace talks with an explosive vest?" I slap a hand to my chest. "Right here? All of this?" I circle my hands around my chest. "Isn't it going to be a little obvious that I've got *bombs* strapped to me?" My voice has risen, bordering on hysterical outrage.

"Your outfit will be specially designed to accommodate it," Mr. Abrahms says.

"And the Embassy isn't going to search me?" I sweep my hands down my body. "They're going to send me through a security scanner the moment I enter. What are you guys, amateurs?"

"Come now, Miss Halifax." Luca leans back in his chair and swirls the remaining blood in his crystal goblet, his long, elegant fingers gently pinching the stem. "What do you take me for? I've been around long enough to figure out ways to work around those pesky scanners." He shoots me a wry grin. "But I don't see the need to explain myself to you. Why is it necessary for you to know and understand the components of the explosive device? Hm?"

Taken aback, I can only stare at him in silence.

"Regardless," he sighs, "all you need to do is show up outside the Embassy. We'll take care of the rest."

But I need more details! I have to know everything so I can tell Father!

I school my features lest I betray my desperate thoughts, and those gathered around the large table consider me with ranging emotions.

When I'd entered three hours earlier, I'd expected something other than what greeted me. Mikey was present, along with Mr. Demms, Mr. Abrahms, three vampires I wasn't familiar with, Luca, and Alessandro. To my relief, Bianca was nowhere in sight. I don't know what I would have done had I seen her among those plotting to take down the Heads and the human, world leaders. All of them sat around a polished, oak table, sipping on tea from dainty china cups, or goblets of blood, with maps and blueprints spread out before them.

"You know that this plan will destroy the world, right?" I finally meet Alessandro's dark gaze. "The peace talks are a chance for humans and vampires to restore relations and move forward after what you did. You're going to ruin that."

"Humanity is a small price to pay to destroy the Seven," Luca states. "Do you think they're innocent of crimes against my coven? Do you think they haven't killed their fair share of vampires?"

I tear my eyes away from Alessandro and return them to the Medici Head. "Who are you? Judge, jury, and executioner? You have no right to determine their fate."

"And they had no right to kill my Family!" He explodes from his chair, fangs and nails elongated in rage. "They hunted us like animals, slaughtered us in our beds. Slayer organizations were formed for the sole purpose of wiping out the Medici line. They *deserve* retribution."

Slayer organizations? I've never heard of those.

"My Lord." Alessandro shifts closer. For whom, I don't know.

"And you've killed thousands of them!" I should be cowering. Why am I not? Why am I yelling back at him? Have I gone crazy?

A bellow unlike anything I've ever heard before explodes from Luca, and with a giant swing of his arm, he swipes the table to the side. It splinters against the wall, shattering the delicate tea service and crystal goblets. In a blink, he's towering over me.

Now, I feel fear. Now, I cower.

He seethes with fury. "Mikey."

"My Lord."

"Escort Miss Halifax back to her room."

"Yes, My Lord."

Mikey grasps my upper arm and pulls me up from where I shrink into myself, trembling. I avoid eye contact with the Medici Head and allow his right-hand-man to drag me from the room.

Silence follows us as I trail him through luxurious corridors, up staircases, down hallways lined with doors. My surroundings don't register through the fog of fear. When he opens my door and thrusts me through, I snap out of it in time to whirl on him.

"Mikey!" I exclaim, and he pauses. "This is madness. What he's planning is madness."

His expression goes cold. "No, Danika. What he's planning is retaliation. Two hundred years in the making."

CONFESSION 26

I can scream until my throat is raw, and I can fight until my strength gives out, but my chance for escape has been swallowed by a violent sea.

I pace, for hours, up and down the prison cell disguised as a guest room. My brain is a cluster of epic proportions, a million thoughts swirling within. I can't distinguish between any of it.

My entire life, I've loved and admired vampires. I've wanted to be one, have ached for it with every part of me. Their flawless skin, fighting abilities, immortality, grace and beauty. They encompassed every one of my fantasies and secret dreams.

But now, it's changed. I don't want it. I don't want this life, to be a Dilecta, to watch as my family is slaughtered, to watch a vampire coven, the very people I've respected for so long, tear the world to pieces. I feel as if I'm drowning in uncertainty, suffocating on confusion and questions I cannot hope to answer.

There is so much hatred wrapped up in those Medicis, so much anger and vengeance. I've glimpsed it many times before in Alessandro's dark eyes. And earlier, I witnessed it in Luca.

Mikey's parting words continue to circulate, driving a knife deeper and deeper into my heart. *"We watched our entire coven being slaughtered. They crushed us, Danika. Drove us into hiding for two centuries. They covered up their lies, rewrote history, and convinced the world that the Medicis were evil incarnate. It's time to take back our fate."*

It was only after he'd left that I'd found the words to say. Whether they are the right ones, I don't know, but with so much revenge, when will it end? When will we learn to forgive? When will we turn our backs on our own follies and realize that everyone is struggling, that everyone is hurting? When will we accept that we cannot change what happened in the past? We'll continue to kill each other until nothing remains of either side. And then where will we be?

I nibble on my thumb nail, my gaze riveted to the colored diamond pattern disappearing beneath my feet as I tread across the plush carpet.

Two options lay before me. I can meekly accept Luca's directive and assist them in destroying my family and killing innocent humans. By not fighting against him, I can, potentially, survive another day.

Or I can find a way to escape before we reach Paris. If I can make it to one of the branches of the Seven, I should be able to request asylum from them. Until Mr. Abrahms fits me with the explosive vest, I can still escape.

But I can also be killed in the process.

I snort softly. Even embracing the fear, there's no contest. My father didn't raise a timid child. He raised a Dilecta. And I've got three days to figure something out.

I shoot a glance toward the port window where sunlight streams through. Should I escape right now? No, we're still too far from land. I'm not a strong enough swimmer to make it before I drown. My gaze travels to the clock on the nightstand. I need to keep busy. The time to escape will come later.

With determination sweeping through me, and a renewed fire blazing through my veins, I change into workout clothes, lace up my shoes, and head for the door. The moment I open it, an enormous body blocks the opening.

I meet Zed's firm stare with an unwavering one of my own. "Move."

"My apologies, Miss Halifax, but you are not to leave your room. Mr. Demms' orders."

"I'm going to train," I snap, crossing my arms.

"I'm sorry—"

"Don't apologize," I interrupt, scowling. "Just move out of my way. We're in the middle of the Mediterranean Sea. How am I supposed to escape?"

He hesitates, and I use that as my chance to slip past him. Out in the corridor, I stride toward the stairway leading to the second level that houses the training room. A hand closes around my upper arm, and I'm yanked back before I can place my foot on the first step.

"Let go of me, Zed."

"I have my orders, Miss Halifax."

I jerk my arm, trying to dislodge his hold, but it doesn't budge. "I said to let me go."

He pulls me around to face him. "I have my orders."

Something sinister trickles through me, and I cease my struggle. Lifting my eyes to his, I allow a slow smile to curl up one side of my mouth. When his eyes focus on my morphing facial expression, I lick my lips hungrily—Mother, forgive me...your daughter is naughty—and take a step toward him.

"You smell good," I purr, and lifting a hand, I trail a finger down his cheek and along his jaw. His pulse jumps in his throat, and my eyes drop to it, my smile widening further. Lightly, I scrape my nail over his pulse and his body stiffens.

"You're not a vampire," he rasps, and his throat bobs in a hard swallow.

"No?" I raise an eyebrow, allowing the other side of my mouth to stretch up. "Care to find out?" He swallows hard again and delight shoots through me. "Did I just find your weakness, Zed? Are you, dare I say it, scared of vampires?"

His hand releases my arm abruptly, and a soft laugh escapes me before I can stop it.

"You play a dangerous game, Daywalker," he breathes, and his eyes promise a thousand deaths.

"Just stay out of my way," I narrow my eyes and lift my chin, "and I'll keep your secret." He takes a step back, and I resume climbing the stairs. After a few, I pause and turn back. "Oh, by the way," I grin, "this boat is *crawling* with vampires. You're currently providing security for the Medici Head."

I can't begin to describe the glee that ignites at his reaction. Who knew a grown man could go stiff with fear? His

230

face leeches of all color, and his eyes bug. I guess this cold, unfeeling bodyguard isn't as tough as he pretends.

"You really didn't know?" I'm mildly surprised. "You contracted with Mr. Demms without knowing the full details of your assignment?"

"We don't ask questions of our clients; we just provide our services."

"Sucks to be you." I shrug, toss him a wink, and continue my climb. "Should probably rethink that clause in your contract." The words are thrown over my shoulder as I disappear onto the second floor.

The training room is empty when I arrive, and I flip on the lights and do a quick scan. The blood is gone from the mat and the punching bag, and a fresh pile of towels and unopened bottles of water sit beside the iPod and docking station.

I press a hand over my pounding heart and flick a hasty glance over my shoulder to see if anyone has followed me. What the heck was that? Did I just...? A half-hysterical laugh bubbles up, and I slap a hand over my mouth just as it bursts out.

Shaking my head and chuckling beneath my breath, I wander across the room, snatch up the iPod, and find a good playlist. With Green Day blasting through the speakers, I get down to business, blocking out everything but my burning muscles.

An hour later, I'm sweating and feeling pretty accomplished. I down a bottle of water, grab another one for the trek back to my room, and leave, hitting the lights as I go. The hallways are deserted as I descend to the guest quarters. Not even a bodyguard hovers around. I make it to my room undisturbed and lock the door behind me.

After downing the second water, I toss the bottle into the trash, strip off my sweaty clothes, and commence with a piping hot shower. Half an hour later, I emerge from the bathroom and crawl onto the bed.

With not much else to do other than nap, I curl onto my side and hug a pillow to my chest. Sleep will give me a reprieve from my thoughts. It has to.

As I sink into unconsciousness, I shove everything from my mind. I clear away the fear of what tomorrow will bring, the anger at Alessandro's final betrayal, and the anxiety that I cannot change what's coming. I embrace oblivion, tipping headlong into its loving arms.

But the dreams don't stay away.

They come—ruthlessly, unchecked. Screams fill the air; blood paints the ground and walls. Dark eyes fill my vision. Fangs and angry hisses. Anguish builds in my chest, suffocating me. No! No no no! I struggle to form the words, to give voice to the swelling grief. But no sound emerges. Desperation claws upward.

My eyes pop open and I lunge up, chest heaving, breaths ragged. I scan my surroundings in frightened bewilderment. Dusk has settled outside the small port window, sinking my room into darkness. The disorientation clears by gradual degree as my eyes adjust to the gloom.

Mouth dry, I lick my lips, sucking in another uneven breath. Sweat clings in all the annoying places—my hairline, the back of my neck, my kneepits—and I tug up the sheet and bury my face in it, using it to dab up the proof of the nightmare. The final vestiges have faded, but I'm still left reeling from the sheer reality of it.

Several minutes pass while I pull myself together, and then I shove back the covers and slide from the bed. My eyes land on the porthole, and I move over to it and stare out at the growing night.

Darkness means vampires. Vampires means no chance of escape.

I shoot a look at the door behind me, gnawing on my bottom lip. Perhaps they're in planning with Mr. Demms and his associates? This might be my one chance.

Resolve firmed, hair pulled back into a ponytail, and sandals in place, I cross the room to the door. Turning the handle with an aching slowness, I pull it open just enough to peek through. The hallway is empty.

My heart skips a beat, and I creep the door open wide enough for me to squeeze through, and then I slide it closed behind me with the slightest *click*. Aware that if I waste time, I'll be discovered, I turn and sprint the length of the corridor, take the stairs two at a time to reach the first deck. I shove through the door and out into the open air.

Choppy waves and brutal wind greet me, whipping my hair from the tie and sending it smacking against my cheeks. I rush to the railing and stare down at the roiling water, all determination extinguishing like a snuffed candle.

"No," I gasp, and the words are torn away by a gust of wind. "No!" I pound a fist against the cool metal beneath my hands. "Why? Why can't anything go my way?" Expletives burst out only to be swallowed by the storm.

Suddenly, a hand grabs me, and I'm jerked around and away from the railing.

"What are you doing? Are you insane?" Anger dominates the question. Anger and shock. And even...*fear*?

Face to face with the oh-so-familiar dark eyes, I stumble back a step, wrenching my limb from Alessandro. He holds fast, tightening his grip to bruising pain.

"What are you doing out here, Danika?"

"You're hurting me." I look out at the churning Mediterranean Sea, and silently add *in more ways than one*.

"I'm not letting you go until you tell me what you were thinking," he growls. "Do you really believe throwing yourself overboard is going to change Luca's plan? Do you think he's going to *care* that you've drowned?"

"I don't care!" I yell, my eyes snapping to his. No way am I going to admit my plans to escape. Let him believe I'm considering something more drastic.

"Have you lost your mind?" He grabs my other arm and gives me a rough shake. "We're half a day from land. What do you hope to accomplish?"

I shove my hands into his chest, twisting my arms for release. "Let go of me!"

"This isn't the way."

"I don't need you to tell me that!"

"Then why? Why would you do something like this?"

Anger boils over, and instead of trying to extricate myself, I lean forward, tilting my face toward his, and narrow my eyes. "Why would *you*?"

I allow him to see every emotion swirling within me—all the hurt, grief, and disappointment. Every moment of betrayal, every knife slash to my heart. Every ounce of anger consuming me—anger and disgust.

He clenches his jaw but doesn't respond, and I look away again. Furious tears prick my eyes, but I blink to clear them away before he can see. I won't give him the satisfaction of knowing he's broken me. I won't let him see how utterly he's destroyed me.

His grip loosens, and he releases one of my arms. "Come on. Let's get you back to your room before Luca discovers you've ventured out."

"Yeah, sure," I mutter. "Wouldn't want your precious Lord ripping out my throat before he can blow me to smithereens in the peace talks."

"Sarcasm is unbecoming." He escorts me through the door and down the stairs to the hallway housing the guest suites.

"Shut up."

Silence shadows us the rest of the way to my room. At the door, I yank my arm from him, turn my back, and glide through the door without a backward glance, slamming it in his face behind me.

***

It's no surprise when, several hours later, Luca pushes open the door and enters my room. I don't look up from the floor, nor do I rise from where I slouch sullenly in the posh armchair. Mr. Abrahms follows on his heels, a briefcase clutched in his right hand.

Though I pretend to ignore what he carries, I'm acutely aware of it. My heart rate increases and dread unfurls in my gut.

He sets it down on the table at my elbow, brandishes a key from his breast pocket, and unlocks the case.

Against my better judgement, I sneak a peek at it. Call me a sucker for pain, or even a glutton for punishment. I should have known what was in there—I *did*—but I just *had* to glance, *had* to see for myself that Luca's depravity was truly that deep.

234

The explosive vest is simple in design, sleek and form fitting. Tiny wires trail from numerous, individual pockets which house, I can only assume, the bombs themselves, and the right shoulder and side are secured with plastic clasps.

I'm unable to tear my gaze away from it, even when Lord Medici wanders over from the door.

"We will arrive in Marseille in about five hours." Luca lowers himself into the chair opposite me. "From there, Mr. Demms has secured us private passage to Orly in Paris."

"Orly?" I find myself asking.

"An airport."

I nod, swallowing against the lump of fear lodged in my throat.

"Come in, Bianca," he orders, and the door opens and the blonde beauty enters.

Her eyes immediately find me and then move to the vest Mr. Abrahms is fiddling with. She pales. Luca waves her over, and she walks toward us with hesitant steps.

All right...so I can rule out Bianca being part of their plan.

"Show her how it works, Hector."

"Yes, My Lord." Mr. Abrahms begins breaking down the vest's components to the unsuspecting Bianca. He instructs on how to fit it to my body, how to activate it, and how to secure it in case I should attempt to free myself from it.

"Wait a minute!" I gasp, shrinking back in the chair as realization dawns. "You expect me to put that thing on *now*?"

"We should give you time to adjust to it," Luca responds nonchalantly. "After all, we can't have you attempting to escape before we're in Paris."

His words are like ice water through my veins. He knows about earlier. Holy shiitake mushrooms.

With a smile that's more of a sneer, Luca rises from the chair. "Come, Hector. Leave Miss Demms to see to it."

The two men depart, and she whirls on me, holding the vest gingerly, fearfully, in her hands.

"What the heck is going on?" she demands. My eyes fasten on the explosive device—my ultimate demise—and I swallow down a moan. "Dani! What is this about?"

"I'm going to die," I choke. "They're going to kill me." I tear my gaze away from it and meet her emerald one. "I am bait to lure in the governing Seven at the peace talks in less than three days. They're using me to kill the world leaders in the conference."

"What?" Her words escape on a breath, eyes widened in shock. "But my father—"

"Is involved. Don't put your faith in him."

We both return our attention to the vest. A few minutes pass in silence, and then she shifts and looks over at me.

In this moment, we're thinking the same thing. There's no way around this, no escape. If I don't put on the vest now, I risk not only my own safety, but also Bianca's.

I rise from the chair as she steps closer to me, and I pull the shirt over my head, toss it on the bed, and face her. Neither of us speaks as she unclasps the latches, slides it into place, and then clicks them shut again.

It's weighted, but not uncomfortably so, and it hugs my curves like a body glove. None of the pockets containing the explosives stick out, and the material is cool against my overheated, adrenaline-infused skin.

Our eyes meet.

It's too late.

CONFESSION 27
Sometimes, the scariest monsters aren't hiding in the dark.
Sometimes, they're human...

I'm frozen in place. Hands touch me, rough and impersonal. My arms are physically lifted, I'm spun this way and that. And the hands continue to brush my skin.

More wires are being added to my body—wires connected to tiny microphones—tiny microphones connected to a listening device—a listening device connected to Luca. Whatever passes through my lips, he'll know, and whatever passes through others', he'll know. Escape is impossible now. From the moment the explosive vest was fitted to me, every hope I'd harbored vanished, one-by-one.

I keep my eyes downcast, aware that if I so much as glance in Mr. Abrahms' or Mr. Demms' direction, the tightly wound fear coiling in my stomach will explode and I'll collapse in a trembling heap. I must remain strong. Giving in to the suffocating emotions won't do me any good.

I ignore the conversation around the hotel room. It doesn't pertain to me anyway. Final plans are being made, timelines reconfirmed. The Medici coven's six, highly trained security teams are positioned, awaiting the signal. The rendezvous point is established.

All their chess pieces are in place.

The final pawn is preparing to move.

I never imagined my life reaching this point. Who would, right? From the moment I'd encountered Alessandro in the desert outside the Orchard, this has always been the end result. I never thought I'd be the downfall of the governing Seven, that it'd be *me* who destroyed them. They are ornery, often misguided, and terribly old fashioned, but they are my family, my friends.

Grief rises up, pinching my throat.

Tonight is the peace conference. Tonight, I'll walk through the doors of Hôtel de Ville, a human sacrifice. I'll sit among the world's leaders, secure beside my father and brother, and I'll nod and agree with them, all the while biding my time— or rather, *Luca's.*

Will they forgive me? Will they understand that I had no choice? Will they realize that circumstances were beyond my control? I hope so.

The microphones are finally attached, and the wires are taped into place. My shirt is tossed at me, and I barely catch it in time. I hug the soft cotton to my chest. The wiry man tending to the equipment covering my body casts a critical eye over his work, and then with a satisfied nod, turns and hurries to Mr. Demms.

Alone, I lift my eyes from the carpet, bite down hard on my lip, and glance at the corner where Bianca sits, observing the various activities around the room with barely veiled contempt. As if aware that my gaze has sought hers, she looks over at me and our eyes lock. Something passes between the two of us, a comradery of some sort.

I avert my eyes, pulling my shirt on, and swallow down another wave of fear just as Mr. Demms' voice cuts through the noise.

"The Halifax Dilecta is ready," he calls, and the room quiets. "In five minutes, she'll depart for the Embassy." He gestures to a cluster of men by the window. "Stand by to follow her." They nod, and he points to another group. "You'll be joining me at the Hôtel de Ville."

Those gathered begin to disperse, heading for the door with briefcases and stacks of paper. My assigned team departs as well, throwing me a parting promise that they'll await me in the lobby of the hotel.

In a few short minutes, only Mr. Demms, Mr. Abrahms, Bianca, and I remain in the suite.

Marcus drops into a vacant armchair with a sigh, scrubbing a hand over his face.

"Father?" Bianca rises from her chair and crosses to his side. "Can we talk for a moment?"

He looks at her, a tired smile turning up his mouth. "What is it, my darling?"

She darts a look at me before dropping down beside him and resting her hands on his knee. "Why are you doing this?"

He glances in my direction, his eyes unreadable, and then he heaves another sigh and looks down at her with sad fondness.

"Why, Father?" she presses. "Why *this* plan? Why now?"

"Bianca, love, must we go into this *again*?" Exasperation creeps into his voice.

"These humans are innocent," she argues, shaking her head. "They are involved with the governing Seven for no more than a simple desire for peace. I implore you, please rethink this. What do you hope to gain by killing hundreds?"

Mr. Demms reaches out and rests his hand against her cheek. "Hundreds who have turned a blind eye to every atrocity perpetrated against the Medici coven. They have ignored our plight," sadness flashes through his eyes, "have disregarded our pleas. They no more deserve to live than the governing Seven and their Heirs." He pulls his hand back, leans his head against the chair, and closes his eyes. "They, too, must pay for their crimes."

"Father—"

"Enough, Bianca," he snaps with another tired sigh. "Finish preparing Miss Halifax and escort her to the lobby where her security team waits."

Silently, she climbs to her feet and crosses to my side. With gentle hands, she adjusts my shirt. When she lifts her hands to smooth my hair down, I raise my eyes to hers and let down my barriers, allowing her a brief glimpse of the terror clutching me. She blinks a few times in rapid succession and looks away.

Mr. Abrahms appears at her side. "I'll take her. Why don't you stay here with your father?"

She spears him with a disgusted glare. "Thank you for your thoughtfulness, but I can handle this."

239

"Really, Miss Demms, I insist." His voice brooks no argument.

They stare at one another, waiting for what, I don't know. Eventually, she nods, once, firmly.

With a flat smile, she pulls me into a hug, and I find myself clinging to her with desperation. Don't let go of me. Please don't let go. But I know she will. Because she has to.

"I'm sorry," she breathes in my ear just before she releases me and steps back. Inclining her head at both of us, she spins and returns to her chair in the corner.

"Come, Miss Halifax." Mr. Abrahms motions me to the door, and on wooden legs, I follow.

***

If I'd known ahead of time just what they had planned, I would have prepared myself in some way. How, exactly, I'm not sure, but I would have managed. I wouldn't have gone into this blind and trusting.

A block from the Embassy, the SUV pulls into an alley, and the security team climbs out, dragging me, bruised and bleeding, with them. No sooner have I gotten my bearings then I'm sent on my way with the instructions to walk to the gates of the Embassy.

I step out into the waning sunlight and begin the short trek to the checkpoint, ignoring the concerned glances from passersby. I keep my chin up and eyes straight ahead, fully aware that my face is horrific.

Mr. Abrahms didn't pull his punches when he was making my story more "realistic", as he described the reason for his abuse. The swollen cheekbone, bruising, and split lip were a testament to the first step of the Medicis' plan.

Anger and fear course through me, buffeting against my tattered psyche. But I can't afford any distractions, and that includes my own feelings. The lives of hundreds rests on my shoulders—quite literally—and there isn't time to wallow. I can do that later when this is all over.

The Embassy's gates come into view.

When this is over and I'm back at the Orchard, I'll give myself time to mourn. I'll mourn for my youth, for young love and first crushes, for humanity, for broken dreams and trampled hopes. Right now, I'll stay strong. I'll be the Dilecta my father trained me to be. I'll face this head on, and I won't back down.

By now, the posted guards have noticed my approach, and they emerge from the shack to stand near the gates.

I have to play along. Flicking a fearful glance over my shoulder, I hurry closer to the promise of protection and safety. I raise my hands and scan their faces, and they take in my bloodied appearance with a variety of reactions.

"Help me," I choke, real tears forming in my eyes. The relief is genuine. "I'm an American, and I seek asylum."

"Stop!" one of them orders, and I come up short, darting another look over my shoulder.

"Please help me." Panic enters my voice. "Please. My name is Danika Halifax, and I'm the human daughter of the Halifax coven. They're here in Paris for the peace negotiations." I lift my hands higher, supplicating. "Ask your boss; ask anyone in there," I point at the building behind them," but please, just help me."

The shortest of the guards hurries to the shack while the other four keep their attention trained on me, their hands poised on their holstered weapons. We have a tense stare down during the short minutes their companion is conferring with those inside. Soon, he's back and motioning me forward.

Time blends together once I step within the sanctuary of the U.S. Embassy. People appear, men and women in suits, armed soldiers, and a medical team. I'm taken down a maze of hallways and deposited in an office with a plush couch and bright, warm flowers.

Mr. Avery Preston, the American ambassador, appears. I only recognize him because of past dealings my father has had with the gentleman. He takes in my dirt and blood stained attire, and I can see the astonishment flash through his warm, brown eyes.

"Miss Halifax," he says, rushing toward me, and the doctor tending to the wounds on my face shifts just enough I can make eye contact with him. "What's happened to you? I never thought I'd hear that you'd appeared at my Embassy's gates."

"I never thought it myself," I admit, my eyes swimming with renewed tears.

"What happened?" He lowers himself onto the couch beside me. "Where have you been for the past three months?"

An idea strikes, and I drag in a deep breath. I won't be some meek sacrifice, Luca.

"I'm so happy to have escaped that nightmare," I say, for the benefit of those listening through the microphones. "It wasn't easy," I gesture at my bruised face, "as you can see." I suck in a breath through my teeth as the doctor presses too hard on the tender cheekbone, and he whispers a quick apology.

"Anyway," I continue, "you wouldn't believe me if I told you." I grab the pen peeking from his breast pocket. "It's been one nightmare after another. I've been to Syracuse, Romania," I quickly scrawl *paper* onto the palm of my hand, "and the Mediterranean Sea. It's so beautiful! Have you been?" He narrows his eyes at the word, and I raise an eyebrow meaningfully. "Oh, I can't forget Greece." I lean toward him, lowering my voice conspiratorially. "Does Father know how bad vampire/human relations have gotten? I had the worst experience on my flight from Romania to Greece."

By now, he realizes I'm rambling and motions to one of his hovering aides. A notepad is produced from nowhere, and I receive it with almost greedy anticipation.

I set to work.

Keep talking. Tell me about the conflict.

He nods. "I do believe Lord Halifax is aware, though I can't say for certain how he hopes to handle it. The peace negotiations tonight are supposed to be a step in restoring those relations."

As he talks, and the doctor continues his ministrations, I begin to write.

Don't react. Not a sound. I'm wired, and they'll hear everything.

He scrunches his face in thought and continues his own ramble. He explains what they've been doing in Paris; how he's

242

been in communication with both the Halifax coven and the Duchamps; how they've spent weeks in discussion.

And while he describes the things they've been attempting, I proceed with my frantic explanation.

I've been a prisoner of the Medici coven for the past three months, and I'm here as part of a plan. Tonight, they intend to infiltrate the peace discussions and murder everyone present, vampire and human alike. They have six teams ready for the command, and the human support for the coven is currently securing positions within Hôtel de Ville.

"How is Father?" I ask, pausing my writing. The next thing I reveal will send him, and everyone present, into a panic. I need to get the conversation going. "And Conrad? I haven't seen Father in months, and the confrontation at the Medicis' castle didn't turn out well."

"I believe they're doing all right," he replies, and I set the pen back to paper. "The Duchamps assisted them in the search for you when you'd initially gone missing." I write *I've got a bomb strapped to me*, and he freezes, his words faltering. "Uhh…"

"I was in Romania the entire time," I say, and quickly write *Keep talking. You cannot stop talking.* "Do you know when I'll be able to see my family again?"

"Uhh…" he swallows hard, "soon, if that's what you want."

Thank you. "I'd love that. I've missed them so much. Can I go to the meeting tonight? Do you think Father will let me?" I look up from the paper and his eyes, stricken with fear, meet mine.

He grabs the pen. *What do we do?*

Get me out of Paris.

"Are you hungry? Thirsty?" he asks. *The bomb?*

"Thirsty, actually." *Won't detonate unless I do something to sabotage the plan.* "I'd love a bottle of water." *But you need to get me out of Paris just in case.*

Can we remove it?

I shake my head. *It's tamper proof.*

By now, word has spread quietly around the room of what I carry on me. Armed soldiers begin filing into the room,

243

and the civilians evacuate. Everyone remains silent as the act between Ambassador Preston and I continues.

"Thanks for the water." I receive it with a grateful smile and make a point of opening the lid with as much noise as I can. "So what time do the negotiations start?"

"At eight, Miss Halifax," the aide at his side responds.

"Will I be able to go?" I hand the notebook to the Ambassador. "I want to see my father and brother."

He clears his throat, passing our written conversation off to an armed soldier. "I'll see what I can arrange. Would you like to get yourself cleaned up first? Your face…"

I cringe. "Y-yes. That'd be good."

The soldier looks up from the scribbles, his expression darkening, and I meet his eye. Silently, I convey my apologies that I'm unable to provide more details about the attack. Though I am privy to about eighty percent of their plans, there isn't enough time or paper to explain it all. They can only take what I've given and prepare from that.

He nods once and gives it to another soldier at his side. With a wave of his hand, the room clears just as silently as it filled, and I'm left alone with the doctor and Ambassador Preston.

He lays a hand on my shoulder and smiles sadly. "I'm glad that you came to me. We'll get you taken care of and delivered back to your family."

"Thank you." I motion to the door, and he climbs to his feet and pats me on the head

"Take care of her, Doctor Aimes," he instructs.

A soft laugh escapes from the handsome man currently rubbing antiseptic ointment on my cheekbone. "Of course, sir."

With a final nod, the Ambassador departs.

I look at the doctor. "Thank you for patching me up."

"Of course, Miss Halifax." He slowly begins removing the latex gloves. "But I must say, you are quite the little actress."

I squeak in terrified horror. "W-what?"

He pulls a vibrating phone from his pocket. "Hello…yes, Mr. Demms. Yes of course." A pause. "Her wounds are patched." Another pause. "Well, there's been a change of plans. She's tipped them off to the original plans… No, sir. The

244

soldiers are responding to her information…Yes, sir…They are planning to take her out of Paris…Understood, sir." He hangs up and heaves a sigh.

My eyes are glued to him. He's a mole. Luca stationed someone *inside* the Embassy. It'd be funny if it wasn't so terrifying. He knew I'd try something, and he didn't trust that I'd keep my mouth shut.

"Mr. Abrahms is giving you another chance," Dr. Aimes says, slipping the phone back into his inner pocket. "He won't detonate the vest since it's too early yet. In exchange, you will find a way to enter the peace talks and get Ambassador Preston to take you to Hôtel de Ville."

"No," I whisper, and for some twisted reason, courage emboldens me. I sit up straighter. "No. I won't."

"I would suggest, Miss Halifax," his voice oozes lethal promise, "that you rethink your stubbornness. He is still listening. Unless you want to die right here, you'll do as you've been told."

"You're not my father." I lift my chin a notch. Stupid stupid stupid. What is *wrong* with you?

He stands, chuckling. "I'm the man who'll determine whether you live or die. Don't forget that."

CONFESSION 28

Hope is toxic. It only leads to heartache and disappointment.

Why didn't I see this coming? Hm? Why didn't I realize that Mr. Demms, Mr. Abrahms, and Luca Medici are three of the most intelligent men I've ever met? Why did I think I could get something by them? They knew I wasn't to be trusted. They knew I'd turn on them as soon as I could. I flat out admitted to the Medici Lord that I'd do just that.

Doctor Joseph Aimes, Luca's minion and spy extraordinaire, has secured me transport to Hôtel de Ville. Ambassador Preston did well in hiding his surprise when I *miraculously* changed my plans from leaving Paris to seeking my family at the peace talks, and I knew he'd realized the situation without me having to write it down. A car had been summoned, and with the doctor-turned-traitor as my escort, we left the Embassy just as the sun began sinking below the horizon.

The drive across the city takes an inordinate amount of time, thanks to peak traffic. I keep my focus on the passing scenery and ignore every attempt at conversation my unwelcome companion makes. Eventually, he gives up and we fall into a tense silence.

Like I want to talk about the weather, numbnuts.

Darkness falls upon the city, and one-by-one, lights pop on—headlights, streetlights, porch lights, restaurant signs—and cut through the encroaching gloom with determination, unaware that soon, a different type of light will join their ranks.

The dark glow of destruction and chaos.

A chill sweeps up my spine, and I suppress the answering shudder. Whatever happens, I have to remain strong. No weakness. My hand rises as if by its own accord and presses against the pocket housing an explosive charge situated over my heart. The fear that had once gripped me has now faded to a state of resignation.

The car finally pulls to a stop at the security checkpoint in front of a breathtaking, architectural masterpiece. The driver confers with the guard while another conducts a rapid check of the vehicle for explosives or weapons, and I almost want to bare my chest to him and admit that *I* am a walking bomb.

Our credentials are confirmed, and then we're ushered through.

When the car comes to a stop near a set of heavy, wooden doors, Dr. Aimes opens his door and climbs out. He stands to the side and holds it for me, and with slow, deliberate movements intended to irritate him, I creep across the seat. Annoyance flares in his eyes, and I allow a calculative smile to turn up one side of my mouth. He can't yank me from the car without passersby noticing, and we both know it. With my father and brother inside, he doesn't dare risk getting his throat ripped out—as he surely would should he touch me.

Malicious delight warms my core, and taking a page from Bianca's book on sophistication, I climb gracefully from the seat, sticking one leg out and then the other. I'm fully aware that I look ridiculous. I'm wearing Chucks, tattered jeans, and a short-sleeve, plaid button down someone in the Embassy had been gracious enough to find for me. But I don't let my attire dim my pleasure at exasperating the good doctor.

Am I playing with fire? Will I regret this later? Yes, to both. Do I care at the moment? Not by a hair.

On the cobbled walkway, I flatten the smile and cast him a bland look. When he stares back, I raise my eyebrows and jerk my chin toward the doors.

"You're an infuriating child," he hisses, and I can't help the smug grin that springs up. He grabs my arm, hard, and urges me forward.

I hide my painful grimace—that's going to leave a mark—by turning my head and looking up at the hundreds of windows spread along the side of the building. I've seen many impressive sights over the past few months, but this is probably the most awe-inspiring.

"And don't even think about alerting anyone to your 'situation'," he says, leaning in close. "All efforts to sabotage the plan will be futile. Everything you could possibly do has already been accounted for."

I wipe my face of all emotion before looking back at him. "Ambassador Preston? Everyone in the Embassy? I'm sure by now they've moved into place to intercept any insanity Luca has planned."

His attempt at a charming smile is anything but. "Lord Medici has planned for *every* eventuality."

I scoff and roll my eyes in the perfect imitation of an annoyed teenager, masking the spark of fear and anger that ignites at his words. Do you think I'm laying it on thick? I can't decide if I need to step it up a notch.

A muscle ticks in his jaw.

Yep. Totally need to step it up.

No sooner has that thought formed than he's dragging me toward the doors flanked by multiple security guards. He releases me and pulls out the documents from the Embassy, confirming our credentials.

One guard receives them and peruses their contents, and then with a nod, hands them back and opens the door for us.

I'm surprised. No really, I am. Do they not intend to search me? What if I'm carrying some type of weapon, or—you know—a *bomb* of some kind? They're just going to let us through the doors? Have they no care for the officials, world leaders, and vampire Heads present here tonight?

We're ushered inside, and a new form of astonishment swoops in. All thoughts flee.

This is Hôtel de Ville? This? It's a level of breathtaking I've never experienced before. My eyes can't take in everything quick enough. Towering archways, gilt designs, painted ceilings, draping chandeliers.

Dr. Aimes starts forward, dragging me with him, and I'm forced to tear my gaze away from the stunning neo-Renaissance designs. More people force us to stop and we're subjected to another questioning and presentation of credentials. It's all rather tedious, but I'm finding enjoyment in the doctor's rising frustration.

Score one for France.

Finally, we pass through a doorway into a large room.

And then Father and Conrad are in front of me, and Dr. Aimes releases me as if he's been burned.

Lord Halifax pulls me into a rough hug and I stiffen. I haven't known compassion over the last three months. The hands that've touched have hurt, have bruised and drawn blood. What is this?

Slowly, it sinks in.

I know these arms. I know this comfort and security, this strength and assurance. How many times have these arms held me? How many times have they shielded me?

"Daddy." The word escapes on a breath, and his arms tighten a fraction. I haven't called him that since I was a little girl, since I needed him to chase away the monsters under my bed and kiss my boo-boos. And right now, I'm living in a nightmare I can't wake from, held captive by the monsters that won't be chased away.

Conrad's arms join Father's, and together, they encircle me with a feeling of safety. I sink into them, fighting the rise of tears. I can't let myself cry, to do so would show weakness.

Lord Halifax disentangles himself from us, and Conrad doesn't waste any time pulling me fully into his arms and tucking me in beside him.

"You're human," he says beneath his breath, relieved, and I nod against his shoulder. "I was worried that Medici would turn you anyway, regardless of my promise to leave Romania."

Father turns to Dr. Aimes who observes our exchange with open interest. "Thank you for delivering my daughter to me."

The good doctor bows—like the idiot he is. "Of course, My Lord. I am *always* at the service of the great, governing Seven."

Con snorts softly, and I bite my lip to keep the smile from forming. What a brownnoser.

"Now that your duty is done," Father motions toward the door, "please let yourself out."

He opens his mouth, probably to object, but the glare he receives from the Halifax Head has him snapping it shut again. He inclines his head graciously, turns on his heel, and departs.

"What a tool," Conrad mutters.

"Can't say I'm sad to see him go," I agree.

"What has happened to you?" Father's attention returns to me, and his silver gaze takes in the cuts and bruises. "Where have you been? Conrad has been tearing apart half of Europe to find you after you disappeared from Romania. And the bite. Tell me about the bite." He grasps my chin and tilts my head to the side to view the nearly-healed puncture wound. "Interesting." A soft touch to the scars on my neck. "Luca Medici isn't one to forego a 'turning'."

"Is this really the time, Father?" Conrad says, scanning the room.

Father nods. "Yes, you're right, son. Come, let's get her settled in the back room."

Over their shoulders, I can see the other Heads as well as a handful of men and women in business suits, and their smiles don't quite reach their eyes. Instead, they watch me with a sort of wariness that sends my heart slamming against my ribs.

Did they get my message? Is that why there is so much distrust in their eyes?

My three hundred year old brother brushes a feather light touch over the bruising on my cheek, and the darkening of his expression has me fearing—is *fearing* the right word? I don't *technically* "fear" for them—for Mr. Abrahms' life. If Conrad gets his hands on the Medici security expert, the human will rue the day he struck me.

Under his protective hold, I'm escorted from the room, and trail Lord Halifax through a series of corridors and arched doorways. Finally, we descend a set of stairs into, what appears to be, the basement.

A large door awaits at the end of the bright hallway lit by iridescent lights. Its flanked by five men in business suits, sporting firm, resolute expressions.

"My Lord! Excuse me, My Lord!"

I recognize the voice immediately, and I can't contain the sigh that burst from me. Is this guy my watch dog or something?

We pause and turn back to the advancing Dr. Aimes, and unbeknownst to the reckless doctor, Father's body stiffens and coils, prepped to attack.

In a flash, the Halifax Head has him within his grasp and slams him against the wall. Fangs elongate and nails extend as rage sweeps through the ancient vampire. He leans into the human's face.

"Listen, *pest.*" Father's voice is disturbingly soft. "I don't know who you are, or who you *think* you are to my daughter, but I haven't seen her in three months," his hand flexes around Dr. Aimes' throat, "and we're going to have our reunion *without* interference by annoying parasites. Do you understand?"

The good doctor swallows hard and gives a jerky nod.

"Disappear," Father breathes, leaning into his face, "or I'll *make* you."

The moment his grip lets up, Dr. Aimes bursts out, "I'm her tending physician. I need to see to her care."

I've seen Lord Halifax angry on several occasions, usually when I do something stupid—like take a ride in the desert close to dusk—but I've never seen his eyes turn red. Mother says that expresses a desire for destruction, for death, for murder. It's rare to see it in the ancients, if ever. A human can go their entire lifespan and never see a red-eyed vampire.

My heart skips a terrified beat.

Father's eyes glitter the brightest red, and he hisses deep from within. "Conrad."

Con tenses. "Yes, My Lord."

"Take Danika inside."

"Yes, My Lord."

I open my mouth to object, but his arm tightens, and I close it again. Shooting Father and Dr. Aimes a parting look, I allow my brother to physically guide me to the steel door. The five guards go through a series of security checks—fingerprint, voice, retinal—and finally, the bolts within slide back in authorization.

"Don't look back," Con urges as we step through the doorway.

As soon as we're inside, the steel door is slammed shut and the bolts reengage. I scan our surroundings with interest.

The room is far from empty. In fact, it's pretty darn crowded.

A team of doctors? And armed soldiers? Who are those in the suits? My gaze snags on a large device in the center of the room, blinking and emitting a low hum.

"That's a jammer," Con answers, noticing my attention. "It'll block all transmissions within the room, incoming or outgoing."

My eyes widen and my breathing stutters. Does that mean? Is it possible? Do I dare hope? Is it okay for me to do so? Tears spring up, unbidden, and I turn my head into his chest and suck in a shaky breath.

"You're safe, Dani."

A sob escapes, and I press in closer to him, balling his shirt in my fist.

"Come on." He moves me further toward the middle, away from the door. "Let's get that vest off you."

At the Halifax Heir's nod, a handful of people descend on us, and I'm whisked from his arms.

The next thirty minutes pass in a blur. I'm inspected by a cluster of doctors who tend to my injuries, re-clean and re-administer antiseptic, and scrutinize the visible scars left from the humans' attack three months before. After my femur is tested, I'm handed off to another group of people who move me to another section of the room. The doctors depart quickly, along with a collection of armed soldiers, and I'm left alone with only a handful of others, Conrad, and the bomb technicians.

My shirt is removed, and I stand in front of the onlookers with wires sprouting from every crease and crevice. They make quick work of the microphone and all loose wires associated with it. Finally, I'm down to just the vest. The fabric covering the different chambers is cut away to expose the explosives and connecting wires.

And then everyone pauses.

It isn't a calm pause, or a relieved pause, or even a contemplative pause.

It's tense, uneasy. Afraid.

I know without them having to say it. The weight settling in my stomach at the looks they cast one another is evidence enough.

They cannot diffuse it.

By now, Mr. Abrahms and Mr. Demms are aware that my reception is blocked. As long as I'm in here, and as long as the jammer is active, I'm safe, but the moment I step from this room, I'm done.

I'm going to die.

One of the men gives Conrad a slight shake of his head. "I'm sorry."

"No." Con jabs a finger toward me. "Remove this. Now."

"We can't." He returns his eyes to the explosive vest. "There are too many fail-safes. Should we attempt to interfere with it, the vest will detonate manually."

"I don't understand." Conrad snaps, grabbing the man by the front of his shirt and yanking him toward him. "You said you could remove it." The human chokes and gasps against his tight grip. "Save her! You promised you could save her!"

All he receives in response is a choked grunt.

"Brother," I lay a hand on his forearm, the muscle tensed with anger and panic, "let him go." His eyes swing to mine, and I blink against the tears distorting my vision. "Let him go, Conrad. He's an innocent. You have to release him." I can see my own despair reflected in his eyes. "You have to. Please."

"Dani."

"Let him go, Con."

One by one, his nails retract, and he pulls his hand back, his gaze never wavering from mine. The bomb technician coughs and staggers away, and he's gathered close by his comrades.

The Halifax Heir bows his head. "Leave us."

At his directive, the rest of the humans rush to the door. The bolts are withdrawn, and the heavy metal swings open to reveal an empty hallway. As the technicians scurry through the opening, one of the guards appears and waves Conrad forward.

They speak in low tones. A few glances are shot in my direction, but otherwise, neither approaches where I stand near the jammer. But even from here, I can tell what's being said.

My heart sinks. The Medici attack has begun.

CONFESSION 29

I'm in love with Alessandro Medici. Isn't love supposed to make you happy?

Conrad disappears after that, leaving me alone with blinking computer screens, the humming jammer, and instructions to not leave the room.

Like I'm going to go wandering. I'm a walking bomb, and I don't have a death wish. Sheesh!

I pace the length of the room, straining my ears to detect the slightest noise beyond my steel, protective cage. I don't know how long passes—minutes, hours. It's endless, the humming and blinking, the nervous silence that fills the air. I hate being left alone with just my thoughts. Then I starting thinking…*things.*

Bad things, dangerous things, things that can get me killed.

The whirring of the bolts retracting splits the quiet, and I spin toward the door, my heart in my throat. It can't possibly be Conrad…

The air leaves my lungs in a *whoosh.*

Alessandro.

How? Why? Impossible! He can't be here! He's supposed to be on the main floor, fighting with everyone else. What is he doing here?

He steps over the prone bodies of four of the guards, gripping the fifth by his throat.

I stumble back as he advances into the room, his dark gaze sharp like a knife when it finds me. It takes in the uncovered explosives, the bruises on my face, and the alarm in my eyes.

He releases the guard, and the man's body slumps to the floor in a heap.

"W-w-what are you d-doing here?" I stammer, fear snatching my words.

His eyes turn a fiery red.

I have a moment to prepare myself before he closes the distance and drives me backward into the wall. With nails extended and fangs elongated, he grabs onto the vest and yanks. When it doesn't budge, he yanks again. The straining fabric cuts into my shoulders, and I bite back a cry.

"What are you doing?" I exclaim, raising my hands to shove him away.

He yanks again on the vest, desperation bleeding through his actions, and the panic lining his face gives me pause. Instead of pushing him, I press my hands to his chest.

"Stop, Alessandro."

"*No.*" He yanks it again.

"Just stop. It won't come off."

And before my eyes, he crumbles to his knees. Burying his face in my explosive covered stomach and wrapping his arms tightly around my waist, he growls from the depths of his chest.

"I'm sorry. I'm so sorry."

The knife in my heart twists deeper, and I lean my head back against the wall. "You don't get to apologize. I don't accept it."

"I know. But I never meant for this to happen."

The emotions swell further. "Liar," I choke. "What did you think would happen when Luca planned to use me? That he'd send me in with a bouquet of roses for the Heads?"

"I didn't agree to this."

"I don't care."

He buries himself deeper. "I'm sorry, Danika."

"You are *such* a jerk." I blink against the rising tears. "You made me fall for you, and then, not only did you reject me, but you strapped me into an explosive vest and sent me here as a sacrifice."

"Danika—"

"No!" A sob escapes. "You don't get to do this." Anger fuses with the heartbreak and fear. "You abandoned me." I punch his shoulder. "You left me to Luca and Mr. Abrahms." Another punch. "You let them beat me. Look at my face." I hit him once more. "Look at it!"

He lifts his head and sweeps red eyes over the injuries.

"You did this. *You.*"

"Danika—"

"No." I blink hard against the tears. "You have done nothing but lie and hurt me." The lump grows in my throat. "You aren't allowed to be here. You can't save me now and pretend that nothing's happened." I give his shoulder a shove. "I hate you. Do you hear me? I. Hate. You."

He returns his face to my stomach, and I release the sob building in my chest.

"*I love you.*" His words escape on a breath.

I moan, denial sweeping through me, and knock my head back against the wall, hard enough it hurts. "Lies. I'm not fool enough to believe you."

The nearly four-hundred-year-old ancient has said the words I have so longed to hear. But they do nothing but sear my heart.

His arms tighten around my waist.

"If you loved me, you wouldn't have threatened to kill my brother," I weep softly. "You wouldn't have blackmailed me to stay with you. Everything that you've done to hurt me, you wouldn't have—if you loved me."

He rises to his feet and reaches up to cup my face. I flinch away from his touch, but with gentle hands, he smooths over the bruises and split lip.

"I love you. Halifax Dilecta or average human, I *love* you."

"Shut up. I hate you."

His thumb brushes away a tear trickling down my cheek. "I know."

"Go away and let me die." I jerk my face out of his hands. "You've always wanted me dead because of my father. So just leave."

"Never," he breathes, and reaching out, cups my face once more. "You've always fascinated me. From the moment you armed yourself with a rock and refused to run, I've been captured."

"Just stop it."

"Let me turn you."

"*What*?" My breath stutters. What the heck?

"If you turn, this bomb can't kill you." His eyes are fierce. "Please." I shove him away, and he has the grace to take a few steps back. "Please, Danika."

"No!" I cry, nudging past him into the open room. "Man, you are so selfish!" I whirl back around. "What about the hundreds of humans in the building? What about the hundreds surrounding it? Are you that insane?"

"I can't lose you." His eyes have returned to their dark state, but now they're tormented, pleading. "At the end of the night, you're going…"

"I'm going to what? What, Alessandro? Leave you? Abandon you as you've done to me?"

He clenches his jaw. "I'll not lose you."

"So you'd *tie* me to you?" Anger returns. "I will decide my own future, thank you very much. I won't become a vampire. Especially not with *you* as my sire."

Hurt crosses his face. "Ouch. But I deserve that."

I hug myself and look away. "I don't want your apologies and empty words. Just leave me alone."

"I made a promise to Luca, and if I go back on it, he'll kill you."

"He's going to kill me anyway."

He prowls toward me, and I back away until I'm pressed against the table with the jammer. His eyes never stray from mine.

"You leave me no choice then." The words are so soft, I almost don't catch them. Looping an arm around my waist, he pulls me to him. "I *am* sorry. Just know that everything I've done, every lie I've told, has been to protect you."

His eyes flick to the jammer, and my heart plummets.

"What are you doing?" I demand, turning my head to see behind me. "Alessandro?"

The humming dies.

My eyes snap back to his, horrified.

"Forgive me," he breathes, and then presses his lips to mine in a soul stealing kiss.

It's everything I've ever wanted, and everything I can never have. It's happiness and content, grief and loneliness. It's the promise of *forever*, but the reality of *never*. It's every hope harnessed and every dream lost.

It's goodbye.

My knees buckle, and his arm tightens around me, holding me up. He buries his hand in my hair and deepens the kiss. Stars dance beneath my lids; oxygen is snatched from my lungs.

I want to push him away, to put distance between us. But I can't. I can't end this. I can't let go of him. Not when I *know* this is his farewell. We'll never have this moment again. This chance.

All too soon, he lifts his head. The urge to protest is overwhelming, and my eyes flutter open to find him gazing at me with a softness I've never seen before. He brushes a finger lightly down my cheek, and then he leans forward and presses a soft kiss to the bruise inflicted by Mr. Abrahms.

The sensation of his lips against my cheek has me closing my eyes again, and I find myself leaning into him.

So shameless, Danika Jean. What would your mother say? Nevermind...I don't care.

"I must leave you," he says, his voice gruff in the silence. "Promise me that tomorrow, you won't hate me too much."

My eyes pop open just as he releases me, and with a sad smile in parting, he turns and disappears through the doorway. I watch him go in frozen astonishment, my mind reeling. What does that mean? Why would I hate him? Well...more than I already do, of course.

Several minutes pass.

Finally, I head for the door. Dread sits heavy in my stomach. I carefully step over the motionless bodies, pausing long enough to check for a pulse. The relief I feel at each flutter in the five men is staggering, and I lean against the wall in the bright corridor, breathing deeply.

Thank you, Alessandro.

Noise above has me lifting my head to the ceiling and eyeing the thick concrete with wariness. Up there is the battle; up there, people are dying. I can't stay in the safe room any longer, not with the jammer disconnected. My signal has already been reestablished by Mr. Abrahms. I have to face what's coming. If they still wanted me dead, I would have been disposed of as soon as Alessandro had turned the device off.

I clench my trembling hands, dragging in a steadying breath, and take off at a sprint down the hallway. The stairs come into view, and I take them two at a time to the door at the top. There, I pause with my hand on the knob. I lick my lips, clench my eyes shut, reopen them, and suck in another breath.

I twist the knob and shove the door open.

The lights in the hallway I step into flicker ominously, reminding me of a scene in one of those horror movies Conrad likes. Bodies litter the floor, blood pooled beneath them. I try not to look as I pick my way forward, treading cautiously around them. Most lay on their sides or stomachs, but a few have fallen on their backs. Their eyes are wide in horror, their mouths open in a silent scream; throats are shredded, ripped apart by sharp canines and merciless violence.

I gag and cover my mouth with the back of my hand. I lean against the wall at the intersection of hallways, and bowing my head, close my eyes to block out the site of more slaughtered in front of me.

Anger and disgust. The only two things I can feel at the moment. The only two things I'll *allow* myself to feel. I can't become bogged down by fear and desperation, or even grief. I have to keep going. I have to put a stop to this.

It takes what feels like forever to make it down all the corridors leading back to the meeting room where I'd met up with Father and Conrad. It was the last place I'd seen the Heads; it's where I'll start my search.

It's chaos. Destruction. More bodies; more blood. Vampires, security for the Seven, mingle with the fallen humans. I can't bear to look, but I do anyway, seeking a familiar face among the dead.

No Conrad, and no Father. I breathe a small sigh of relief and quickly leave again.

The scene outside the room is like something from a movie. Or a nightmare. None are alive here.

I follow the trail of death down multiple corridors until I make it to a set of heavy wooden doors, thrown open to the outside. I dread what I'll see beyond them, the sight that'll greet me. I know it'll be forever ingrained in me, an image I'll carry to my grave. Whether that's today or in fifty years.

Let's do this, Danika! Straightening my shoulders, I enter the fray.

Never in a million years could I have prepared myself for this. Gunfire rips through the night, screams of dying innocents serenade Paris. Vampires clash, nails and fangs.

And more bodies. More than I can count; more than I can bare to consider.

My attention is snagged by something in the distance, and a scream builds in my throat as I dash forward, half running, half stumbling. Please make it in time. Please make it in time.

Nearly there!

Rough hands grab me and yank me back, and the building scream explodes from me in fury. No! No!

"Let go!" I twist against the hands. "Let go of me!"

The grip tightens, biting into my skin, and I spin enough to see who holds me. My blood runs cold.

"You're one sneaky, little brat," Mr. Abrahms growls. Blood covers his left arm and the right side of his face, and I can see that he's favoring his left leg. "You're going to watch, Halifax. You're going to see Luca exact his revenge for the death of his brother."

I fight against his hold, but even wounded, he's stronger than me. Any elbow or fist I throw, he easily dodges. My desperation grows as I'm forced to witness the scene unfolding in front of me.

Alessandro circles Father who's pinned in Luca's arms. The Halifax Head is wounded and missing an arm, and he watches the Medici Heir with red eyes that spit venom.

"On the hill overlooking Carver's Meadow," Alessandro's voice cuts through the chaos, and everything goes eerily quiet—even the battle seems to hold its breath in anticipation, "you took my Lord's life. And then you left him to the morning sun." His eyes flick toward mine, widen, and then harden. Clenching his jaw, he returns his attention to Lord Halifax. "You and the other Heads betrayed my coven, my family. You turned the world against us and sent us into hiding for two hundred years."

I know what's coming. I can feel it through every part of me. My heart rebels at the idea; my soul cries in ultimate betrayal.

"Please," I whimper. "Please don't. Alessandro, no."

He ignores me.

"Tonight, Lord Halifax, you stand for your crimes." Alessandro looks over at me, and for a split second, I can see the regret in his eyes. "Tonight, you shall pay for what you've done."

My heart stops. *No.*

The stake is driven in first, and Father—ever the stoic—doesn't utter a sound. He meets my eyes, bares his teeth, and takes it with the grace of a five hundred year old vampire.

Inside, I'm screaming; inside, I'm shattering to pieces. Outside, though, I'm frozen, unable to tear my gaze away from Father's final moments. Pride swells at his obstinacy, even at the end.

I can hear Conrad's bellow from somewhere in the mass of undead surrounding the three ancients, but I keep my eyes glued to Lord Halifax's. From this distance, I can see the resignation within their silver depths. Resignation and love. And the encouragement to stay strong, to not give up, to keep going.

He flashes me a quick smile, and I can almost hear his thoughts. *Live.*

I love you, I mouth.

He nods once.

I clench my eyes shut as Alessandro's hand shoots out and slices through Father's neck.

CONFESSION 30

I never got to apologize to Father, or make amends for my stubbornness. A regret I'll carry to my dying day.

I'm now good and royally screwed. And I should care. I *should.* I should fight Mr. Abrahms; I should try to escape, try to break free, return to Conrad.

But I can't.

I can't tear my eyes away from Alessandro. I can't stop seeing him drive the stake into Father. I can't stop hearing the sound of Father's body hitting the ground. I can't block out the soft *thump* of his head.

And I can't breathe.

What is this? Why does it hurt so much? It's like someone drove a stake into *my* heart. Why can't I look at Alessandro and hate him? Why do I want to hold him? Why do I want him to hold me? He just killed my father, the Head of our coven, and one of the governing Seven. So then, *why?*

Because he didn't have a choice. I know it. I can see it in the haunted gaze he turns my way. He begged my forgiveness; he knew I'd hate him afterward. In place of the hate I cannot feel, there's anger, but also regret. There's a sense of finality to our volatile relationship that has always been doomed to fail.

We are truly on opposite sides now.

Mr. Abrahms drags me backward, away from my Father's fallen body, just as the vampires converge on one another again. My eyes, riveted to Alessandro, widen with anxiety. When he takes a step toward me, Luca slaps a hand to the center of his chest to halt him.

What? What is this? Reality hits, and the desperation I haven't allowed myself to feel rises with a vengeance. This is the finale! Me! I'm being moved into position for the vest to be detonated.

I begin my struggle anew, throwing punches and elbows, kicking my feet back toward his injured leg. I writhe and twist.

"Let go!" I cry. "I won't do this!" I seek my brother in the crowd, and my voice rises to a shriek. "Conrad! Conrad, help!" I know the Heads are out here fighting. If I can just—

Mr. Abrahms slams a bruising hand over my mouth, forcing my teeth to bite into my injured lip. Tears spring to my eyes at the pain.

"Shut your mouth," he hisses.

Blood tickles across my tongue, and I scream a muffled curse against his dirty hand.

We're back in the building, moving down corridors littered with bodies. I don't know where he's taking me, and I can't afford to wonder. I have to stop him.

I go limp.

When his injured leg bows under the new weight, his arms slacken enough and I twist myself free. He is quick to catch himself before he collapses, and his eyes lift to mine.

I allow a slow smile to spread across my face a split second before I plant my feet, twist, and execute a roundhouse kick. My foot connects with his injured arm with solid impact, and he stumbles back a few steps, a nasty name exploding on a breath.

I tsk him. "You kiss your mother with that mouth?"

His expression turns murderous. "My mother's dead."

"Really?" I balance on the balls of my feet, anticipating his counterattack. "That's a relief. She doesn't have to see your ugly face anymore. Not sure she'd condone your rather *nefarious* activities."

Was that totally below the belt? Not even close. Dude's a bad guy, people.

For being injured, he moves quickly, catching me off guard. His punch connects with my already damaged cheek, and

I crash to the floor on top of one of the fallen. Stars dance in my vision and pain, mixed with numbness, spreads from the wound. Fresh blood begins a thick track down my face and drips onto the exposed charges.

He fists his hand into my hair, and I can do little but clutch my scalp as he drags me down the hallway. I'm forced to scramble over dead bodies as he sidesteps them, and soon, multiple DNAs mingle with my own.

Focused on keeping him from ripping my hair out, I don't notice we've entered a room until he flings me to the floor and releases his hold. Pain is everywhere, and I can't immediately lift my head from where it rests on the tile.

Just give me a minute. I just need a moment. That's it.

"What did you do to her?" A familiar voice filters through the haze settling over my brain. Mr. Demms?

"Most of it's not hers. Don't worry," comes Mr. Abrahms grumbled response. He grabs me beneath the arm and hauls me up. "Come on, Halifax. Let's get you situated." He tows me across the room and tosses me roughly against the wall. "Stay here, and keep out of trouble."

I slump where I've landed, tasting the blood pooling in my mouth. I have no words, even the ability to form sound has abandoned me. Agony infuses my jaw, clings to my teeth, throbs through my skull. Most likely, he's shattered my cheekbone, maybe even my jaw. Ugh! Guess I've got scars to match the other side of my face now.

Through bleary eyes, I watch as Mr. Demms and Mr. Abrahms begin conferring with one another about something involving setting more charges, all rigged to my vest. I will be the primary detonator. Whatever that means. Doesn't sound good.

My lids fall shut, and I sink into unconsciousness.

***

The sound of my name comes from far away, through layers upon layers of peaceful oblivion. I recognize the voice, but disorientation keeps me from latching on to its owner. I don't want to wake up. Waking means I have to face the unbearable truth that my father is dead; I have to face the pain stabbing my heart, the torment of my broken body. It's like three months ago all over again. Only this time, Alessandro isn't here to put me back together.

A sob builds in my chest until it releases on a gut-wrenching moan.

Arms lift me gently and soothing words are uttered in soft tones. I curl into the comfort and manage to crack open my eyes enough to see who this is.

Conrad. Sweet relief.

I don't have enough energy to consider the fact that he holds me, the whys or the hows. I just snuggle in closer. My brother. Home.

"What are you doing, Bianca?" Mr. Demms voice hammers into my throbbing skull, and my eyes pop open again at the incredulity in his question.

"What are *you* doing, Father?" she counters.

For the first time, I see the guns in her hands—two of them—pointed at her father and Mr. Abrahms.

"My duty," he snaps, shock widening his eyes. "As should you be."

"You didn't think that Luca's plan was insanity?" Her face is red with anger, emerald eyes glittering dangerously. "You didn't question that this is *murder*? You just went along with it?"

"Drop the guns, Bianca." He raises a placating hand. "You don't want to do this."

"Look at her!" She shoots me a glance. "What made you think it was okay to hurt her? She's a child, Father!"

"She's the enemy!" he bellows. "She is the Halifax Dilecta!" A flash of anger crosses his handsome face, and with deliberate movements, he withdraws a remote from his pocket. "Stop and think about what you're doing, daughter. What this will mean."

Her eyes flick to the detonator and her fingers flex on the triggers. "Don't."

Mr. Abrahms shifts beside him. "Remember your place, Miss Demms. You are the Medici Dilecta-in-training. Your loyalty lies with this coven."

"Shut your trap, Hector," she retorts. "It's *your* hands that are coated in her blood." Her gaze never wavers from Marcus'. "Don't do this, Father. I'm begging you."

"Miss Demms." Mr. Abrahms takes a step forward.

The explosion from the gun echoes around the room, and I clench my eyes shut and grit my teeth as a ringing begins immediately in my ears. When I open them again, Mr. Abrahms is on the floor, clutching a bleeding leg.

"I told you to shut your trap." Bianca keeps the gun trained on him. "One more time, and I'll hit something more vital."

"What is wrong with you?" her father yells, turning wide, horrified eyes to his friend. "You could have killed him!"

"He deserved it. I've never liked him. Now, put the remote down." She flexes her hand around the grip on the pistol aimed at Marcus. "Don't make me pull this trigger on you."

"You wouldn't dare."

"Try me."

"I'm your father."

Her voice softens. "I know. I don't *want* to, believe me. But I will."

"No you won't, baby." He smiles soothingly. "I'm your only family. You won't hurt me."

"Put the remote down, Father."

Instead of obeying, he flips a switch, and multiple lights flicker on. "We're all going to die right here, baby. All of us together. We won't have to be alone. This is for us, for everyone, for Luca and Alessandro."

She's starting to waver in her determination. I can see it in the way her arm dips and the gun drops a fraction. "Don't make me do this. Please."

The glitter in her eyes is no longer anger, but rather, sadness and grief. Maybe even a hint of regret.

"This was always the end result, Bianca." Mr. Demms lowers his eyes to the detonator. "Everything we've done has been for this moment. The moment when the world remembers the Medicis and all they're capable of. It's when we rise from the shadows and reclaim our place."

"We've never *had* a place," she says softly. "You know this. Why are you pretending you don't? You're the history buff. They have always been a minor coven. You and Luca just pretend otherwise. You pretend you've been brought so low, but you've never risen *that* high."

"Hold your tongue, child!"

"Listen to me, Father." Tears spill over and trickle down her cheeks. "This is madness. Blowing up Paris, slaughtering hundreds of innocent humans, murdering the Heads. This won't bring peace; it'll divide us further."

"They'll immortalize us!"

I can't look away from Mr. Demms and his thumb hovering over the button I can only assume is for detonation. I am holding my breath before I realize it, bracing for the inevitable.

Bianca is breaking from the inside with tiny cracks forming and splitting outward. Tears flow unheeded, and anguish twists her beautiful face. But even as she shatters, her hand remains steady, the gun unwavering.

"Please, daddy," she chokes, shaking her head. "Don't make me do this."

"It was you, wasn't it?" His voice is hard, bitter. "Tonight. Warning them. Forcing us to change our plans."

"I had to."

"They knew we were coming!" He clenches his jaw. "Why? Why would you do that to us?"

"Because this is wrong!" she cries. "How many have already died? Lord Halifax? Lord Duchamp? Are they not enough?"

The Duchamp Head? No!

Conrad must sense the change in my emotions because his arms tighten a fraction. "End this, Miss Demms. Now."

Marcus shoots him a poisonous glare. "You don't order my daughter around, Halifax trash."

No. Not Halifax trash. Conrad is Lord Halifax, the coven Head. Ah, what a bittersweet thought.

"You're threatening my sister's life, Medici scum," Conrad seethes. "Don't test me because I'll rip your throat out before you can press that button."

"Try it!"

"Both of you stop!" Bianca exclaims.

Conrad's chest rumbles beneath my ear, but he doesn't argue.

Mr. Demms, however, stands up straighter and scowls at her. "Why are you listening to him?"

"Because he's not the one preparing to kill a couple hundred people. Now put it down."

"No."

She closes her eyes, drags in a deep breath, and reopens them. "Please."

"I taught you how to use those guns. Do you remember? We've spent hours at the shooting range. And now you dare point them at me?"

"Then stop this madness!"

"I should have left you in that orphanage, you ungrateful child. Your loyalty is only skin deep."

The words slice through her shaky composure, and as her body hunches forward, a gut wrenching scream erupts from the depths of her soul. Once released, she quickly straightens, refocuses the gun, and meets his eyes dead on.

"I love you, but I'm sorry, daddy," she whispers. And she squeezes the trigger.

Another loud report echoes through the room, and Mr. Demms crumbles to the floor as red blossoms across his chest. While the rest of us are frozen in astonishment, Mr. Abrahms doesn't waste any time in launching himself across the short distance and reaching for the detonator.

Conrad moves in a flash, kicking out quickly, and the remote skitters across the floor, away from his reach. "Nice try. But now," his voice drops dangerously low and Mr. Abrahms blanches, "you're mine."

Richard appears beside my brother. I blink a few times, bringing his familiar face into focus, and confusion rises. Where has he been hiding this entire time? Why haven't I seen him until now?

I don't have too long to deliberate before I'm passed off to my bodyguard, and then he turns and begins making his way across the room to Bianca. She hugs herself, sobbing silently, and the guns lay discarded on the table at her side.

How much courage did it take to stand up to her father? How much strength must she possess to be able to do what is right and pull the trigger? It has to hurt on a level I cannot even fathom. My heart twists in sorrow at her grief.

"Miss Demms," Richard says, and she peers up at him through her tears. "Can you please take the vest off of her now?"

Leave it to him to not show any compassion in her time of misery. The guy must be made of stone.

She nods and hastily wipes her cheeks. "Yes, of course."

He places me on my feet, and I clutch his arm for support, my vision wavering.

Time seems to slow as she begins deactivating the vest, unlatching the clasps, and unlooping wires. It isn't until she slides the black material over my shoulders that I release the breath I'd been holding. Gingerly, she sets it down on the table beside her pistols and heaves a relieved sigh.

Richard shrugs out of his suit jacket, throws it over my shoulders, and then buttons it up. It does little to conceal my sports bra, but it's better than nothing, and I give him the barest nod in appreciation.

"Well then," she turns back to me, "you look like crap."

In any normal situation, I would be offended. But I have to agree with her. I manage a small nod.

She turns my head with gentle hands and examines my swollen cheek and bruising to my jaw. Her mouth is pinched with unease, and her emerald gaze glistens with fresh tears.

"This is awful, Dani," she whispers, her brows furrowing. "You need medical attention right now."

I shake my head and throw a hand out to her. Not yet. Please. I try to convey my desperation with my eyes. I have to know that this fight has ended. Luca needs to be stopped.

Conrad joins us and gives Richard a hard look. "Get her out of her." He glances over his shoulder at a cowering Mr. Abrahms. "I've got some business to take care of."

He doesn't need to say anything else. Richard knows; Bianca knows; *I* know. And remorse is the last thing I'm feeling. Even as a big advocate for humans, I can't bring myself to feel anything other than sick pleasure at the fact that this despicable excuse for a man is going to witness vampire retribution.

Is it wrong to feel this way? Should I try and spare his life? It was his hand that stole my ability to speak, his hand that made me choke on my own blood. I'm silenced because of *him*.

Conrad looks at me, as if waiting for my permission to dispense justice, and I twitch my head in some approximation of approval. The last thing I see before Richard sweeps me through the door is my brother's eyes flickering to bright red, and the last thing I hear as the door slams shut behind us is Mr. Abrahms' bloodcurdling scream.

FINAL CONFESSION
I don't want to be a vampire.

Bianca manages to stitch her composure back together, probably with copious amounts of super glue, duct tape, and spit. Her tears have dried, and she surveys the body-strewn hallway with renewed focus—and with a coldness I've never seen before.

We start forward with slow, careful steps.

"I came here immediately after you left the hotel to relay the details of Luca's assault," she says quietly. She shakes her head and then laughs beneath her breath. "What an adventure *that* turned out to be."

I watch her warily, in case her fragile self-control cracks, and listen as she begins describing the events leading up to my arrival here. According to her, everyone had been skeptical, even suspicious, as she'd explained first about the expertly designed and crafted explosive vest I'd been fitted into, how I'd be smuggled into the peace talks, and Luca's ultimate aim with me being present. When she started to break down the security teams in place, revealing the positions of Medici coven contractors staged throughout both the Embassy and Hôtel de Ville, they began to sit up straighter and take notice.

As soon as the Heads and their Heirs arrived, she was forced to explain it all again. By then, however, the Paris officials and their security had already started making plans to counter what was coming.

"Your brother," she shoots me a wry look, "is terrifying, but not nearly as much as your father."

272

Pain lances my heart, and I swallow hard against the swelling grief. I won't allow myself to wallow—not yet. First, we need to end this.

Her shoulders sag for a brief moment, and then she lifts her head, straightens herself, and gazes straight ahead.

And in that short span of weakness, I'm reminded of *her* sorrow.

Later, I'll hold her and let her break. I nearly laugh at that thought. She'd rather play chicken with a viper than let me comfort her.

"Your brother and Lord Halifax didn't believe me," she continues. "They wanted to kill me and be done with it. For some reason, they held off." She smiles lightly. "Can you believe they hooked me up to a lie detector and had me tell the details all over again?"

If my jaw wasn't broken and my face numb, I probably would laugh. I *totally* believe it. Father is old school—no wait…*was*. Father *was* old school. And the only one who could curb Con's impulsiveness. Not even Mother can wrangle him in.

"Anyway," she sighs, "I had to tell them everything *five* times. I couldn't miss a single element of the assault. When I was done, I pulled your brother aside and assured him that you were all right, still human, and desperate to return to your coven."

Ah…yes. I'd turned my back on the Halifaxs during the fight at the castle.

She loops her arm through mine when I stumble over someone's discarded shoe and shakes her head at Richard who'd snapped into motion to assist. "I told him why you'd stayed with us, even though you didn't want to. He seemed interested when we discussed the training you'd done on the *Rosalie*. He's impressive." A wistful tone has entered her voice, and when I side-eye her, she squeezes my arm and winks.

I let the horror infuse my expression, or what's visible of it through all the swelling and bruising. Who is this and what has she done with Bianca? A wink? Laughing? Smiling? She and I are frenemies. We don't get along even at the best of times. Plus, we're in the middle of a war. I get that she's seen Luca for the monster he is, but Conrad? Gross!

"I'm kidding," she whispers, eyes turning sad. "I'm taking a sabbatical from men for a while. They're too complicated. Anyway," she heaves a sigh, "your brother doesn't fully trust me. I promised him I'd save you and get you out of the vest, and he promised that if I failed, he'd kill me." She shrugs. "Guess things worked out."

I turn my head slowly, my face slack with disbelief. Did she just crack a joke? What is this madness? But I already know the answer to that. She's holding herself together by sheer force of will. She's laughing and joking so she won't break. I want to pull her into my arms and let her fall apart, but I hold myself back. She's my greatest chance in finding Luca, and I can't risk her collapsing before then. Is it selfish? You bet. Do I regret it? With every ounce of me.

"When the assault started," she says, "they hid me away in some secret room to wait. That was where Conrad came for me after Mr. Abrahms pulled you back into the building."

Did they all know what was going to happen? Did they plan for me to be taken to a room and left to die? Whatever the case, I'm not ashamed to admit how relieved I am at their timing.

We've finally reached the doors to the outside where the battle rages. My steps falter as unease settles over me. Bianca hesitates as well, and we cast each other troubled glances.

As if reading my thoughts, she murmurs, "This is it. Once I step through those doors with you, Luca will know I've turned against him. I didn't realize how hard this was going to be."

Of course, I want to say. You've loved him for nearly half your life. This will officially end any chance. It's all right to waver.

While we linger at the threshold, Conrad joins us and hovers behind me, his body coiled. He doesn't say anything to break the silence, and it continues to stretch between us until it's as taut as a bow string.

"So...," Richard's voice cuts through the tension, "should we go?"

Three, incredulous faces turning toward him would be comical—I mean, come on! This is *Richard*—if it wasn't for the fact that he's right. We should go. We *need* to go. So then why are we hesitating? Why are all *three* of us hesitating? I can understand me, and maybe Bianca, but Conrad?

His silver eyes meet mine, and I see the indecision and anxiety within them. My heart twists in painful realization. It isn't that he doesn't want to take down Luca and end the battle. It's that he's now Lord Halifax, and he isn't ready for that title. Once he steps through these doors, he'll become the Halifax Head for real.

I let go of Bianca and reach out to him, and he closes the distance almost eagerly. I lay my palms against his cheeks, framing his face, and convey every ounce of loyalty, devotion, and love I possess through my eyes.

And then I slap both hands against his cheeks.

Bianca gasps.

Richard stiffens.

Conrad's eyes widen.

I firm my expression, sending encouragement with a hard glare. No weakness. Stand strong and fight. This is Father's legacy. Protect it.

A slow smile spreads across his face, and he reaches up and covers my hands with his own. "Message received, sister."

I pull my hands away, but not before giving him a gentle pat.

Without wasting another moment, the new Head of the Halifax coven bursts through the doors, and we follow close behind him. And then come up short.

The battle is silent, vampires and humans frozen.

Dark shapes vanish into the shadows of the surrounding streets. They disappear over rooftops and melt into alleys. The Medici coven is escaping.

I scan the fleeing for any sign of Alessandro or Luca, and my heart skips a beat when I find them on the outskirts of a path between two buildings. They both pause and shift back, and over the distance, my eyes meet Alessandro's.

Goodbye, he seems to say.

Bianca tenses beside me and her face hardens. She's been snagged by Luca's dark glare. They gaze at one another for several heartbeats, her breath frozen in her lungs.

Then he spins, breaking the spell holding her captive, and the two vampire Lords join their comrades.

She gasps in oxygen and a shiver trembles through her.

Immediately, it's chaos. Vampires and humans collide, but with hugs and backslaps. Their yells and exclamations are of excitement and relief. Red eyes have faded, and a sea of color blinks in their place. Prejudices and fears are set aside as everyone stands on mutual ground.

Richard and Bianca remain at my side while Conrad disappears into the crowd, and together, we survey each and every face.

Among the humans, we find the President of France, of Germany, of the United States. We locate the Prime Ministers of England and Japan. We see battle weary expressions covered in dried blood. We see injury and regret. But we also see hope. And trust.

And it is *beautiful*.

Instead of dividing humans and vampires as Luca planned, he'd brought them together. They clasp hands with their undead brethren, share grins and don't cower from the fangs, and search through the deceased in a combined effort.

"This," Bianca says softly, "is exactly what Luca deserves."

***

Dusk paints the sky a beautiful red and orange. I gaze at it through the window of my hospital room, listening to the faint *beep* of the machine that monitors my heart rate, blood pressure, and oxygen levels. The tape holding the IV needle in place tugs at the hairs along my forearm, and I furrow my brow in discomfort.

This is such crap. I have to stay here for the next five days, until I'm well enough to fly, and then I'll be allowed to return to the orchard. I just want to go home. I want my mother, my room, Arizona sunsets, and Chancelot. I want the familiar.

Bianca comes in with a cup of ice water and a straw, and I turn my head to watch her cross the room. Her beautiful face is lined with fatigue, and the sorrow she's doing well at suppressing dulls her emerald eyes.

She needs the orchard just as much as I do. I'm convinced of it.

Holding out the cup, she slips the straw between my lips. "Drink slowly."

I roll my eyes and crack a half smile, revealing the silver wires locking my jaw together.

So yeah, great story. My cheekbone isn't broken—yay—but my jaw is—double yay (said with *much* sarcasm). Now it's four to six weeks of liquids, consumed through straws, and then I'll go in for another evaluation to determine if I'll need surgery to repair any damage.

"It shouldn't be much longer until your brother comes," she says, setting the cup onto the nightstand once I've finished drinking, "so I'm going to head to the hotel and get some rest. You'll be all right while I'm gone?"

I shrug. I'm a big girl.

She smooths the hair away from my face and gives me a sad smile. I return it, wincing at the pain it causes.

She shakes her head, sighing. "You're ridiculous." With a more amused smile, she leaves, closing the door quietly behind her.

Immediately, my grin falls away and I return my attention to the sky outside the window. My heart aches. For Father, for Bianca, for Conrad, for the Duchamp coven, for all those who fell last night. And for Alessandro, the man I can never have.

What I wouldn't give to see him one, more time.

The door opens, and I don't immediately turn my head. Most likely, it's Conrad or Richard with a nice, juicy steak pulverized into milkshake form. Bless their little ancient hearts.

When the arrival remains quiet, I roll my head on the pillow and look over.

My breathing stutters and tears spring to my eyes. Why? Why is he here? I shove back the covers as quickly as I can and stumble out of the bed. My legs collapse the moment I put weight on them.

And Alessandro is there, catching me, pulling me in to his chest, holding me close.

277

I shove against his chest while simultaneously twisting my hands into his shirt and tugging him closer. Anger and desperation battle one another for dominance. I don't want to be in his arms, but I can't seem to let go.

"I only have a minute," he whispers, cupping my face and lifting it toward him. His dark eyes scan mine. "Bianca said your brother just woke up, so I don't have much time. If he discovers me in here, he'll kill me."

I find myself drawing him even closer.

His eyes sweep over my injuries, noting the bruising and swelling in my jaw. He runs a gentle thumb over the area just below my lips, and then peels them down and narrows his eyes at the wires. "Who did this to you? Mr. Abrahms?"

At my nod, his expression turns murderous. I shake my head and attempt a smile. I'm all right, I try to say. He can't hurt me anymore.

He closes his eyes for a brief moment, drags in a deep breath, and then focuses the full force of his obsidian eyes on me. "I came to tell you something. You *must* listen." He glances quickly toward the door. "You are going to go after Luca, I know you are." When I frown in denial, he shakes his head. "No, you will. It's only a matter of time. But hear me on this. He cannot be killed that easily, Danika. He is ancient. Older than any other vampire I've ever met. Older, even, than the history books say."

What? I don't understand. My frown morphs into one of confusion.

"Did you ever wonder why I never fought back against him? Why I always went along with everything?" he continues, and I nod—I sure have. "Because I can't defeat him. It doesn't matter how strong I become, how strong Conrad becomes, or even how strong *you* become. He can't be killed by regular means."

Unease curls in my gut. I'm not liking where this is going.

"Luca isn't Luca Medici, born in the late 15th century." His gaze is piercing. "He's Viktor Carnigov."

Those words are like a sucker punch to the stomach, and I gasp. The first of his kind, father of vampires? The oldest of the oldest? No way! No freaking way! Conrad is going to flip when he finds out.

"Whatever happens, you *have* to stay out of this." He leans his forehead against mine, and his voice drops. "I know you. I know you won't. But please."

I can't do that.

Reaching up with a trembling hand, I smooth my fingers over his cheek. My decision must be visible in my eyes because he sags a little. I smile as best I can, hoping to soothe away his frown. He tilts my face and presses his lips against my scarred cheek, and my eyes close of their own accord. His warm breath feathers across my face, and I tighten my hands in his shirt.

I'll give myself this moment. I'm allowed to, right? When this is over, when he walks away, we'll be enemies. We'll never have this chance again.

Slowly, he pulls back.

I open my eyes, already swimming with tears, and nod toward the door.

It's time for him to leave. His five minutes are up.

He shoots a look out of the window and something close to pain flashes across his face. "I'll see you again." His eyes return to mine. "I promise."

Emotion swells and I shake my head, tears spilling over.

"We're not enemies, Danika."

I nod slowly, unable to look away.

"No."

I lower my hand to his heart and press, and he takes a step back, his hands falling away.

I feel his loss to the very depths of my soul, and even deeper still. It hurts to move away from him, to reject him, to know I'll never get the chance to love him as I've wanted.

But none of it hurts as much as it did seeing him drive a stake through my father's heart.

There is no going back for us, no second chances. All my walls come down, and the heartache, sorrow, bitterness, and grief I've been holding in rise up in freedom. My breath escapes on a sob, and his face twists with regret.

"I'm sorry," he whispers, reaching for me. I lean away from his touch and turn my head to the side. His hand drops, and he clenches it into a fist. "Fine. I understand." Crossing the room, he pauses at the door. "I *will* see you again, Halifax." He shoots me a genuine smile over his shoulder, one that lights up his eyes, and my heart skips a beat. "Whether it's next month or next year, I will find you."

And then he's gone.

Less than two minutes later, Conrad and Richard burst into the room. They take in my position out of bed, the tears in my eyes, and the flush to my cheeks, and Richard vanishes back into the hallway while my brother flies to my side.

"Are you all right?" Conrad does a quick inspection of me and the room. "Who was it? Alessandro?"

I look away, trying to reconstruct the walls before I have a complete breakdown in front of the most irritating, overprotective brother ever.

He growls, deep and feral. "We're leaving. Now."

I don't have the heart to tell him that Alessandro is truly gone this time. Now that my walls are down, I can't put them back up, and I'm breaking.

It isn't until three hours later, when I'm sitting on the private jet, preparing to depart for home, that I can suck in a real breath. I ignore the preflight procedures going on around me and stare out of the small window at the illuminated tarmac.

Alessandro's news that Luca Medici is, in fact, Viktor Carnigov has done little to stem the anger and bloodlust. If anything, it's made me even more determined to stake him. Instead of using his power as the father of their kind to build relations and educate, he's sought to destroy the world and divide it. He doesn't deserve the title he carries. He only deserves death.

And I'll give it to him.

Or die trying.

Finally, the plane takes off. The wheels leave the ground, and I shoot one, final look out of the window at a receding Paris. Somewhere, down there, I've left a piece of myself I'll never get back.

And I'm all right with that.

CONRAD

Yesterday, it poured. Big, fat raindrops that turned the dry ground to mud and Danika's horse corral to a lake. As lightening tore across the sky, and thunder echoed through the canyon, rivers ran throughout the orchard. The citrus trees bowed beneath the onslaught of water and wind.

The storm outside had raged just as furiously as the storm within the manor.

I gaze at the book in my lap, not truly seeing the words written in Father's elegant scrawl. My mind is a mess of hows and whys. How can I help my sister? How can I take my father's place and become Lord Halifax. How can I lead my coven? Why did he have to die? Why, why why...

The door opens, but I don't look up, assuming it's my father's secretary. "Scranton, where is Mother?"

"Hmmm, I'm not sure," comes the soft, feminine response.

My attention snaps up. "Laura!"

She smiles. "Hello, My Lord."

"Don't call me that." I rise. "Anything but *that*." Setting the book aside, I cross the room to her.

The smile dips, and her hazel eyes search mine with concern. "How are you? You look tired."

I laugh humorlessly. "Can vampires look tired?"

"Of course they can."

My hand finds hers, and she twines our fingers together. Slowly, I lift them to my mouth and press a kiss to her knuckles. "I'm fine. How are you? How is Lord Campbell?"

"I'm all right." She shrugs, but her eyes say anything but. "Lord Campbell is as difficult as ever. Especially after everything that's happened. It was twenty questions when I asked to come visit."

Anger throbs through me at her words. "He needs to release you."

"He won't." She raises an eyebrow. "I'm his Dilecta until after Dormiam, Conrad. That's like me telling you to release Danika."

"Never." Possessiveness swells and my fangs prick in my gums.

"Exactly." She smiles. "Anyway, how is she?"

Well, that line of the conversation is over. I try not to scowl. We never get anywhere with this argument. She knows how to counter it every time.

"It's been nearly two months since Paris, so her body is almost healed," I say, leading her over to the couch. We sit, and I wrap an arm around her, pulling her close. "But now it's as if her heart is weighted. And I can't break through whatever it is."

"It's going to take some time. Though her body is better, her heart hasn't healed yet."

"Father's death hit her hard." I drop my head back against the cushion and sigh. "She was forced to watch it happen." She nods, her eyes never leaving mine. "And then finding out that Luca Medici is Viktor Carnigov—she's driven in a way that scares me."

"You? Scared?"

"Very much, yes." My hand tightens on hers. "She spends every day in the training room. She barely eats, barely sleeps. She's killing herself trying to become stronger, and I don't know what to say to make her stop."

"Then don't. Let her train; let her fight. Her heart is broken, Conrad, and this is how she's dealing with it."

"But she's human, Laura. Her body can only take so much."

"Do you think it's possible that she *cared* for Alessandro Medici?"

Her question takes me by surprise, and annoyance flares at the possibility of my precious sister having feelings for the Medici scum. I finally release the building growl.

"I don't ask to make you angry," she says, giving me an exasperated look. "We both saw how they interacted in Romania. He spared your life because of her. You even said, afterward, that it wasn't normal for him to do so." She pats my chest. "Stop pouting. You look ridiculous."

Had I been pouting? I relax my face and flash her a tight smile.

"Have you found anything out about Viktor?" Her topic change is a relief.

"Not much." I pull away and snag up the book I'd been attempting to read before she'd arrived. "Father's records don't shed much light into him." I flip back a few pages and slide the book onto her lap. "According to this," I point at a paragraph near the top, "he disappeared around the late fourteenth century. No one knows where he went or what happened to him. But if this is accurate, then he must have resurfaced as Luca Medici when the Medici coven formed in the fifteenth century."

"How did nobody put the two of them together?"

"Would *you* have thought of it?"

She looks up from the text. "Of course not. Vampire history wasn't my strong suit."

I chuckle.

"Anyway," she sighs, handing the book back, "what do we do now?"

"Well, the Heads are meeting next month, and they'll discuss their next move."

"*We*, right? And *our*?" Her smile is strained. "You're a Head now, Conrad."

Those words hurt. "I wasn't ready for this. It wasn't time for me to take over."

"I know," she whispers, taking my hand, "but it happened. You have been preparing for this since your selection, and you can't let your father down. This coven is relying on you." Her fingers tighten. "Danika is relying on you."

That's right. I have to protect our Dilecta; I have to protect Dani. I have to keep this place safe and comfortable for her. This is her home.

"What's going to happen with Dormiam?"

Her question takes me by surprise. "What do you mean?"

"Does Viktor need to hibernate with everyone else?"

I hadn't considered that.

"If he does, then that makes more work for us Dilectas. We'll have to prepare for *his* awakening along with our covens." She shoots me a wry smile. "But if he doesn't," she swallows hard, "then he's going to turn this world to ash while you sleep."

I can sense her fear. Wrapping an arm around her, I pull her in close again. I want to assure her that everything will be all right, that we'll defeat him before that time comes. We still have nine months until we go beneath ground. But even *I'm* uneasy about the difficult task laid before us.

So I promise the only thing I can. "I'll keep you safe. Whatever comes, I'll do everything I can to protect you and Dani. We'll fight this together, Laura. Viktor doesn't know what he's started."

"I'll hold you to that."

I smile and press a kiss to her forehead. "And when this is all over, I'll make you my Lady."

ACKNOWLEDGEMENTS

I don't even know where to begin. So many people have pushed me and encouraged me along the way. I can't name them all.

First, I'll thank my husband for his love and support. He has encouraged me through every step of my writing journey, and I don't think I would be as motivated and proud of myself as I am without him. I'd also like to thank my three girls who are the light of my life and the reason I do what I do. They motivate me to do my best, and I am excited that I can share my imagination with them.

Second, I'd like to send a shout-out to my parents, Matthew and Barbara Kannegaard. My mom is my biggest critic, but also my biggest fan, and I can't imagine pushing myself this hard without her one step behind, urging me on. Also, I want to say a huge thanks to my sister-in-law, Holly, for her support and shared excitement for Confession's release.

Third, I want to thank my editor and all around lifesaver, Jaclyn Larmore. Without her, I doubt this book would be what it is. She has worked tireless hours to help me capture Danika's and Alessandro's characters, and her insight helped create the ending. I am so excited to continue this adventure with her and see where The Dilecta Confessions takes us.

Fourth, a big thank you to my brother-in-law, Rahlyn "Tate" Cleveland for his superb cover. You rocked it, man!

And finally, the biggest thank you to my Aunt Claudia. Last fall, she was taken from us by surprise, and her loss is felt very deeply. She was more than just family, she was the support, guidance, and editor for The Prophecy Trilogy, and I miss her daily.

Author's Biography

Joanna Ogan is a combat veteran with two tours in Iraq with the United States Army as an Interrogator and Source Handler. She has a Bachelor of Arts in English from the University of Phoenix. She enjoys cooking (a huge fan of Pinterest), spending time with her children outdoors, and reading just about anything she can get her hands on.

BOOK 2

SNEAK PEEK

I hunker into my coat, pulling it tighter around me to ward off the fall chill. My eyes scan the darkened street and alley, alert and wary, searching for the faintest movement. They should be here by now. Where are they? Why haven't they come?

I flick a look over my shoulder, up the alley I'm taking cover in, but nothing shifts there. Not even a whisper of movement. The shadows are heaviest here, obscuring my location from all mortal eyes. It's the perfect spot for spying.

The night's chill has sank beneath the layers of my black, leather jacket, and I suppress the shiver making its way up my spine. Just a little bit longer.

My sources said they'd be here tonight. I bite my lip, returning my roving eyes to the street in front of me. But why haven't they come? This warehouse is their meeting place, isn't it? I glance down at my watch. 01:00. Crap. By now, my absence will have been noted.

A chilly breeze sweeps up the street, causing dry leaves to dance along the pavement, and I lose my tight grip on the shiver. It hits like a convulsion, and I gasp in astonishment. Man, it's cold!

Fall in Phoenix, Arizona isn't what one would expect. It's not bitter, rainy, or filled with vibrant colors. It's dull, warm— with the occasional cold night, much like tonight—and just very *blah*.

But it's home, and it's beautiful.

Danika Halifax, here. Daughter of the Halifax vampire coven and precious Dilecta—*beloved*—and my newest job title: *vampire slayer*. Well…not *all* vampires. My family are undead, of course. No, just one.

Viktor Carnigov. The father of all vampires. The first of his kind. The oldest of the old. And the most powerful bloodsucker walking the earth. He's untouchable, unbeatable. And currently, undetectable.

About seven months ago, his coven resurfaced—the Medici Family—after two hundred years, and they began spreading chaos around the world. One hundred and fifty years of peace between humans and vampires was effectively destroyed overnight as nearly a thousand people were slaughtered by his coven.

For some *really* weird reason, I wound up in the middle of it. Not my fondest memory.

A bunch of stuff happened—a near kidnapping, assault by some radical humans, time spent in Romania and aboard a yacht in the Mediterranean Sea—leading up to the night that changed my life. The night my father was killed before my eyes. The night I nearly died.

I try not to think about it—who would, right?—but sometimes, the memories creep up on me. They clench my heart, seal off my airways, send me gasping for breath, hunched over in agony. I don't cry. I think I've forgotten how to. I haven't allowed myself to break since the wheels left the ground in Paris, taking me away from the one man I can never have. The one man who holds a piece of my heart—Alessandro Medici, Heir to the Medici coven.

My brother, Conrad, the current Head of the Halifax Family, says that I'm going to destroy myself trying to forget. But I like to say I'm *driven*, or *determined*. Those are better words than *desperate*.

And that's where I find myself tonight. Staked out in a dark alley, waiting for something I'm not sure is going to happen, all because I'm *driven* to end Viktor Carnigov.

Another shiver wracks my body when a second breeze sweeps through. How much longer?

"I *really* hope you have a good explanation for this, Dani."

Every ounce of alert tension escapes in rush, and I sag against the wall. *Conrad.* Of course.

"What are you doing out here?" He melts from the shadows, his silver eyes flashing momentarily with moonlight.

"Waiting."

"For?"

291

"How'd you find me?" I turn my head and meet his furious gaze.

"This is Phoenix. I can always find you."

I sigh and look away. Should have known. He rules the night, and these dark streets are his playground.

"Are you waiting for *him*?" His question, though softly spoken, oozes with contempt.

How I wish I could say yes. What I wouldn't give to see those obsidian eyes and that crooked grin, and hear my name upon his delectable lips.

"I haven't seen him in months." I reach up and adjust the hood of my sweatshirt. "You know that, Con." With one, last fleeting glance at the abandoned building in front of me, I turn and start up the alley. "Let's go. I'm cold."

He falls in beside me. "We need to talk when we get back to the orchard."

"Nah, I'm good."

"It's not an option." Steel creeps into his voice.

"Yeah…okay." I shrug, dismissing him and our conversation.

He leads me through a series of backstreets to a deserted road. A black car with heavily tinted windows and sleek body sits just on the fringes of a bright streetlight. He pulls the key fob from his pocket, unlocks the doors, and the headlights blink in response.

I stuff my hands into the jacket's pockets and head for the passenger side. He follows, opens the door before I can reach it, and then shifts off to the side, his hand resting on the top of the door.

"Get in." His silver eyes flash with warning, daring me to argue.

I don't. I slide into the red leather seat, jerk the door from his hands, and slam it in his face. He doesn't immediately move from beside the window, and I hunker deeper into my jacket, allowing the hood to slide lower and cover my eyes.

When he climbs in beside me, I turn toward the window, lean my head against the headrest, and stare stubbornly out at the sidewalk.

"Buckle up, Dani."

I ignore him.

"Now."

Heaving a sigh, I yank the belt down, jam the clip into its mechanism, and tug the strap back across my chest. And then I go back to glaring out of the window.

We don't speak for the duration of the drive to the orchard. With the freeway practically empty, he's able to get us home in half the time it took me to get there earlier this evening. As we pull into the driveway and he puts the car into Park, I'm unbuckled and out of the door before he realizes.

I don't make it far.

His hand closes around my upper arm, and he wrenches me to a stop. "I said that we're going to have a talk."

I meet his eyes, my expression cold. "I'm tired. And I want a shower."

"After." He drags me through the front doors, tosses his keys to a waiting newbie as we pass, and continues down the hallway toward Father's old study with a "call for Lady Halifax" hollered over his shoulder.

Great. Now Mother's involved.

A fire is burning in the massive hearth when we enter, and Conrad hauls me over to the couch and shoves me down onto it.

"Stay right there," he growls, and the anger in his eyes keeps me seated. I slouch in the corner, cross my arms, and glare back at him. "Don't look at me like that, Danika. I'm not the enemy here."

Mother sweeps in, her fiery hair disheveled and expression paler than normal. "What is it?" She glances between the two of us. "What's happened?"

"Danika snuck out tonight." He crosses his arms and raises his eyebrows in perfect imitation of a disapproving parent. "I found her near 32nd."

She gasps, and her eyes bug. "No! Danika!"

"Leave it alone, Mother." I heave a sigh. "Nothing happened."

"That's not the point," Conrad is quick to interject. "It's the fact that you disobeyed curfew and strayed from the orchard. I've been patient with you. I've put up with your attitude, your

293

anger, your self-imposed isolation. But this is too much. Have you forgotten what happened last time your whereabouts off the grounds were discovered?"

Anger boils over, and I shove back the hood. "Of course I haven't forgotten! It's *my* body that paid the price."

Scars. Both inside and out. Scars that line my cheekbone, cover my ribcage, travel from knee to upper thigh. A broken femur and a shattered jaw. A grief so deep, so painful, I can only ignore it because giving in will destroy me.

No…I haven't forgotten.

Blue eyes meet silver. "How can I, Conrad, when I see it every time I look in a mirror? In their eyes?" I gesture toward the door, toward the Halifaxs beyond. "Their pity and horror."

"Danika." Mother's voice is gentle. "Darling."

I look away from my brother and into the flames. "Don't ever ask me again if I've forgotten."

Silence elapses, broken only by the occasional pop of the fire. Neither Conrad nor Mother move from their places in front of me, and I keep my attention fixed elsewhere.

A niggle of remorse—fighting with them is my least favorite pastime. Where did the smiles and merriment go? The fun times? Why can't I look at them and feel the happiness I used to feel? In the last couple of months, the family dinners have ceased, rides with Chancelot have stopped, and instead of laughter, yells and fighting echo throughout the manor.

Nobody has time for me anymore. Surprising, since I'm their precious Dilecta.

Conrad is seldom home, off doing whatever it is the Halifax Head does. When he is home, he's locked in Father's study. Mother spends her nights either in her office in the sorting barn, or in the catacombs. She buries herself in work and ignores everyone else around her.

"Dani," he runs a hand through his hair, "listen—"

"It's never good when you start with that." I look at him coldly.

He drops his hand. "I'm not going to prevaricate. Who were you waiting for tonight?"

"Oh, big word for you! You sure you know what it means?" I raise an eyebrow, and he scowls. Heaving a sigh, I turn back to the fire. "It's none of your business."

"Anything you do is my business. I'm your brother, and your coven's Lord."

I snort. "Pretty sure your head," I motion toward his darkening visage, "just grew three sizes when you said that. Did it feel good? Have you been waiting for months to say it?"

"That's enough, young lady," Mother snaps. "You will show him proper respect."

"Or what?" I shoot her a glare. "You're going to keep on ignoring me? Return to the catacombs and hide out in your room?"

She rears back as if slapped, mouth gaping. I've never spoken to her this way, and I can see the hurt flash through her emerald eyes. But I keep going. The words spew forth like water from a broken faucet. Unstoppable once released.

"What have you done to help take down Viktor?" I glance between the two of them. "What have *either* of you done? What plans have you made?" I'm on my feet, pointing at her. "He killed your husband, your Lord, and you crumble. You don't seek revenge; you don't fight back. You curl into yourself and die. And you," I jab a finger toward Conrad, "keep me ignorant of everything. It was *my* life he almost stole." I stab my thumb in my chest. "*Mine*, Conrad. Not yours. I deserve the chance to fight back."

"Is that what this is about?" The anger in his eyes dulls. "Revenge? You're meeting someone in the middle of the night simply for *revenge*?"

"Not even close!" I counter, my voice rising. "I haven't been idle since returning from Paris. Plans are in motion."

"Is that what you think?" Mother growls, finally finding her voice, and my eyes snap to hers—that's new. "I'm not seeking revenge? That I've given up?" She advances toward me, and it takes every effort not to cower away from her. "I lived a hundred lifetimes at his side. I saw empires rise and fall, wars rip apart the world and good men heal it. I've fought and watched my friends and family die. Can I not mourn? Huh, Danika?" Her eyes flash dangerously. "Can I not grieve my husband? Am I not allowed to?"

My resentment deflates, and regret rises in its place.

Tears swim in her eyes, trickle down her cheeks. "I gave him an eternity of love. He was the other piece of me. If I decide to curl into myself and die, then *that* is *my* choice. You have no concept of what I am suffering, child. You cannot even begin to fathom my pain and sorrow. So do not sit there and cast judgement on me."

Words escape me. Seeing her anguish, so raw, twists my insides.

"Mother," Conrad wraps an arm around her trembling shoulders, "she didn't mean it. You know she didn't. We're all hurting."

She doesn't look away, giving me full access to the torment tearing her apart. I want to hold my ground, keep firm and unwavering beneath her glare, but I can't.

I bow my head and stuff my hands into the hoodie's pocket. "I'm sorry, Mother."

"You are grounded," she rasps. "Give Conrad your cell phone." I pull it from my back pocket and hand it over, tamping down on the refusal. "The training rooms are off limits." My head snaps up and I scowl. "Don't you dare look at me like that. Over the next month, you will be taught respect. I am finished with your attitude."

I clench my jaw and look away. Crap.

"You are the Halifax Dilecta." Her words whisper over me like a death sentence. "Your training will begin later this morning with Benice. You will present yourself promptly to the sorting barn at eight. If you are late, your punishment will increase. Do *not* test me. Now go."

Sucking in a sharp breath through my nose, I duck around them and storm from the room.

"Mother?" Conrad's voice chases me down the hallway.

"Leave it, son." Her retort comes a beat later. "It's time."

Made in the USA
Middletown, DE
21 August 2022